Saints and Martyrs

An Adepta Sororitas Omnibus

Further fiction from Black Library featuring the Adepta Sororitas

THE ROSE AT WAR
Includes the novellas *The Bloodied Rose*, *Wreck and Ruin* and *The Rose in Anger* plus several short stories
Danie Ware

MORVENN VAHL: SPEAR OF FAITH
Jude Reid

PILGRIMS OF FIRE
Justin D Hill

SISTERS OF BATTLE: THE OMNIBUS
Includes the novels *Faith & Fire* and *Hammer & Anvil* plus two short stories
James Swallow

THE BOOK OF MARTYRS
Alec Worley, Phil Kelly & Danie Ware

MARK OF FAITH
Rachel Harrison

THE ROSE IN DARKNESS
Danie Ware

DAEMONIFUGE
Jim Campbell & Kev Walker

REQUIEM INFERNAL
Peter Fehervari

Other stories from the Warhammer 40,000 universe

LEVIATHAN
Darius Hinks

• DAWN OF FIRE •
BOOK 1: AVENGING SON
Guy Haley

BOOK 2: THE GATE OF BONES
Andy Clark

BOOK 3: THE WOLFTIME
Gav Thorpe

BOOK 4: THRONE OF LIGHT
Guy Haley

BOOK 5: THE IRON KINGDOM
Nick Kyme

BOOK 6: THE MARTYR'S TOMB
Marc Collins

BOOK 7: SEA OF SOULS
Chris Wraight

SAINTS AND MARTYRS

— AN ADEPTA SORORITAS OMNIBUS —

ANDY CLARK | DAVID ANNANDALE | DANIE WARE

BLACK LIBRARY

A BLACK LIBRARY PUBLICATION

Celestine: The Living Saint first published in 2019.
'Celestine: Revelation' first published digitally in 2020.
Ephrael Stern: The Heretic Saint first published in 2020.
The Triumph of Saint Katherine first published in 2022.
This edition published in Great Britain in 2024 by
Black Library, Games Workshop Ltd., Willow Road,
Nottingham, NG7 2WS, UK.

Represented by: Games Workshop Limited – Irish branch,
Unit 3, Lower Liffey Street, Dublin 1,
D01 K199, Ireland.

10 9 8 7 6 5 4 3 2

Produced by Games Workshop in Nottingham.
Cover illustration by Paul Dainton.

A CIP record for this book is available from the British Library.

ISBN 13: 978-1-80407-536-4

Printed and bound in the UK.

For more than a hundred centuries the Emperor has sat immobile on the Golden Throne of Earth. He is the Master of Mankind. By the might of his inexhaustible armies a million worlds stand against the dark.

Yet, he is a rotting carcass, the Carrion Lord of the Imperium held in life by marvels from the Dark Age of Technology and the thousand souls sacrificed each day so his may continue to burn.

To be a man in such times is to be one amongst untold billions. It is to live in the cruelest and most bloody regime imaginable. It is to suffer an eternity of carnage and slaughter. It is to have cries of anguish and sorrow drowned by the thirsting laughter of dark gods.

This is a dark and terrible era where you will find little comfort or hope. Forget the power of technology and science. Forget the promise of progress and advancement. Forget any notion of common humanity or compassion.

There is no peace amongst the stars, for in the grim darkness of the far future, there is only war.

CONTENTS

CELESTINE: THE LIVING SAINT

ANDY CLARK

BEYOND

Consciousness, sudden and violent.

Her eyes snapped open and hellish light poured in. She sucked a breath down her red-raw throat, then coughed hard, doubled up, curling foetal on her side. Her eyelids flickered, and darkness threatened to swallow her again. Her mind kicked against it, fought back, surfaced. Another painful series of coughs wracked her, then subsided. She took a slow, shuddering breath, blinking quickly as her eyes adjusted to the glare.

Her surroundings resolved; her senses cleared, sight, sound, smell and touch coming slowly. She registered that she was lying on something hard and lumpy, an irregular surface that shifted beneath her as she moved. To her bleary gaze, it looked like a mound of pale stones and jagged debris, but no matter how much she blinked and frowned, she couldn't quite focus.

She could hear a low moan. The wind, she realised. It was warm, but not pleasantly so. Its touch was like the first bloom of fever-sweats that warned of illness to come. It bore a sharp tang. It took her long moments to place the stench. Sulphur, and something worse, some underlying stink of corruption that triggered primal revulsion within her. She pushed herself into a sitting position and redoubled her efforts to see straight.

What began as a fiery haze became a sky, though a more forbidding and ominous sight she could not have imagined. Blood-hued clouds roiled through a bruised void of purples and rotted greys. Vortices of black fumes whirled across the vista, ripping the bloody clouds to tatters and trailing crackling storms of lurid green lightning in their wake. Her gaze lowered, taking in the distant horizon with its jagged line of half-seen mountains. Fume-wreathed plains marched away from their feet.

She shifted again, fighting down feelings of dislocation. Her heart thumped as she realised that she had no idea where she was, or worse, even *who* she was. The questions almost escaped her lips aloud, before she realised there was no one there to answer. Something crunched beneath her palm, hard and splintering. She looked down with dawning horror.

Not stones.

Bone.

She snatched her hand back through the broken, brittle brow of an ancient skull. Bones ground beneath her as she moved, and this time she did let out an involuntary moan. She scrabbled backwards on hands and heels, as though to escape the carrion mound. Osseous matter cracked beneath her weight. Shards jabbed through the grey shift she wore, scraping her bare legs and arms. The macabre clatter of bone on bone grew, skulls and femurs and finger-bones grinding with her every movement.

She felt something cold and hard beneath her palms. She dragged herself backwards with a gasp of gratitude, until she sat on a slab of black-painted metal several feet across. It was part of something larger, she realised, buried in layers of bone, rusting and studded with rivets and old bullet-holes. Dimly, she perceived the faded remnants of an insignia still clinging to the metal, but she had no more attention to spare. The slopes of bone stretched away on all sides, spilling down and down, broken by jutting metal wreckage, tatters of coloured cloth and other, more organic looking remnants that she didn't care to identify. She couldn't tear her eyes away.

'Not a mound...' she said, her voice a dry croak. 'This is a mountain.'

Questions chased one another through her mind. She shut them into cages forged from her iron will, there to languish until she could address them rationally. Panic spread like hoarfrost in her gut, surged up through her chest. It met the fire of her determination and melted back as quickly as it had come. She took a deep, slow breath and closed her eyes, centring herself.

'Emperor, protect me and light my way,' she said, the words coming unbidden to her lips. They felt right there, natural, reassuring. She could not say for sure who the Emperor was, but she drew strength from His name. Feeling calmer, she opened her eyes and took mental inventory.

She could see no signs of movement beyond the occasional stirring of wind-tugged cloth. Whatever macabre carrion peak she found herself atop, wherever this wasteland was, she was alone here. She realised she had clenched her fists in readiness to defend herself.

'A fighter, then, perhaps,' she murmured, finding comfort in the sound of her own voice. It was deep and strong, a voice made for firm statements, stern prayers and binding oaths. But prayers to whom? Oaths of what? Seeing no immediate danger, she resolved to begin by answering as many questions as she could about herself.

She would open her mental cages one at a time and interrogate the thoughts within.

She took personal inventory. Her grey shift was unadorned, its material coarse against her skin. The body it clad was a powerful one; she could feel graceful strength in her every movement, and see wiry, chorded muscle shift beneath the skin of her arms and legs.

Her hair was shoulder length, and she could see from holding it out before her eyes that it was raven-dark. Beyond that, without a reflective surface she could tell little more about her age or appearance. What she had gathered for now would have to be enough.

She let her fingertips explore her facial features, moving down over her chin to her throat. She gasped and pulled her hands away as she felt a ragged ring of scar tissue there, bespeaking a catastrophic wound. Feeling nauseated, but needing to know, she gingerly felt around the circumference of her neck. Sure enough, the scar ran all the way around, and for a moment she felt an echo of something within her mind.

Screaming.

Flames reflected in churning waters.

Something towering and monstrous.

A light.

The strange sense was gone as suddenly as it appeared, moonlight glimpsed through tattered cloud. She frowned in puzzlement as she realised that the scar was gone too. She felt at the flesh of her neck with increasing agitation as she tried to find the horrible mark.

'How is that possible?' she asked the empty mountaintop. 'How is *any* of this possible?'

She had no possessions, that much was clear. No weapons or armour with which to protect herself, no food, drink, any other items of clothing or gear. Nothing to suggest who she was, or to help her survive.

'And no idea how I came here,' she said. 'But I have myself. That is enough.'

She knew she could not simply sit atop a mountain of bones forever. There was no telling what kinds of ferocious storms the brooding sky might disgorge, and she felt no desire to be plucked from this peak by a screaming gale or caught amidst ferocious lightning blasts. Though she felt neither hunger nor thirst, she doubted that would remain the case forever. Starving to death and adding her bones to the mountain held even less appeal.

Yet the thing that drove her to her feet was the desire for answers. Who was she? What was she doing in such a ghastly place? How had she come to be here? Who was the Emperor? She needed to know, and she would find no insights here.

She stood atop the mountain, shift and hair blowing in the hot winds. She stared down the steep slopes. They vanished ever downward on all sides into a thick crimson mist.

'Nothing to suggest a route,' she said. 'No hint as to where I must go.' Strangely, the notion held no terror for her. Instinctive as breathing, she closed her eyes and offered up a wordless prayer to the Emperor for guidance. To her surprise, she felt a faint warmth upon her cheek, as though a candle flame had been brought close to it for the briefest of moments. The sensation was there and gone, yet it was enough, its touch somehow pure, distinct from the clammy caress of the winds.

'Are you a god, then? My protector, perhaps?' Her questions fell dead and unanswered. Whatever the truth, she knew it would not be as easy as simply demanding answers.

She opened her eyes and turned in the direction from which she had felt the warmth. Steeling herself, she stepped carefully out, barefoot, onto the jagged carpet of bones. She began to make her slow and slithering way down the mountainside.

The going was treacherous. An ache built in her muscles until it became dull fire, and her chest tightened reflexively whenever she took in the nightmarish steepness of the slope. In places there was little more than a compacted cliff, and she was forced to spend long minutes scrambling crabwise across the slopes in search of a more forgiving descent. Splinters tore at her. Rusted jags of metal scraped her shins. When she was forced to put her hands down in a hurry, her forearms and palms were scratched and pierced until she left a trail of bright red blood drops behind her to mark her path.

Bone shifted underfoot with every movement, small avalanches of ghoulish matter clattering away down the steep incline to vanish into the mists below. She had to be constantly careful lest she twist an ankle or slip and fall; if she lost her footing, she might fall to an agonising death upon the jutting bone shards below.

Within minutes of beginning her descent, she found her heart thumping and her nerves singing from the constant exertion and peril. Briefly, as she clung by tenuous handholds to a protruding ribcage and felt for a foothold in the shattered arch of some ancient shrine, she contemplated turning back. Perhaps she could try another angle of descent? A glance upwards showed no obvious route of return, and she realised that – now that she had begun this perilous climb – her only option was to press on.

She gathered quickly that the mountain was not just made from the bones of the dead, but more specifically from those that had fallen in battle. It was apparent not only from the ways their limbs and skulls had been smashed, hewn and blasted, but also in the increasing quantities of rusted weaponry, armour and even vehicle hulls that peppered the mountainside.

Here, she picked her way carefully through a thicket of swords whose blades had been shattered and turned to rust. When there, she was forced to traverse the jutting prow of some manner of combat aircraft, its nose cone hanging downwards, its cockpit glass crazed with bullet-holes. Banners and pennants flapped in the wind, bearing myriad insignia that stirred feelings within her she could not identify. A portcullis gate flanked by eagles and lightning bolts here, a dark blood drop fringed by spreading wings there. Some seemed so familiar that she could almost taste their names on the tip of her tongue, yet she was left frustrated by each attempt to place them.

She had been scrambling downwards for perhaps an hour when a tangle of bones she was gripping cracked and gave way. She fell, her stomach lurching at the momentary weightlessness before she hit the slope feet first and spilled awkwardly sideways. Bones cascaded around her, clattering in a hollow storm of remains. She fell with them. She rolled and skidded.

Chest tight, she grunted with effort as she tried and failed to arrest her fall. Something gouged her arm. Something else crunched under her hip. A flare of pain shot up her leg and she cried out. She scrabbled for purchase as her speed increased, knowing with sick certainty that at any moment she would feel the slope vanish from beneath her as she sailed out into the void.

Her fingers found purchase at last, a solid chunk of metal that took her weight and arrested her plunge with a jolt. Her shoulder screamed in protest, but she hung on, heart thumping fast in her chest. She managed to get a grip on a femur with her other hand. She braced her feet against a jutting slab of stone and breathed out slowly. Fragments of bone continued to slither and roll past her, but the avalanche became a trickle, then stopped altogether. She realised that she had stopped just yards above a sheer drop.

'Thank you, Emperor,' she breathed.

As her pulse slowed, she looked to see what miraculous object had saved her life. Her eyes widened as she realised that it was a breastplate, moulded, lacquered black and edged with fine gilt filigree. Compelled by a feeling she could not name, she dug the fingers of one hand in around the segment of armour to work it loose, while clinging tightly to a rusty spar with the other. More bones scattered. For a moment she was gripped by vertigo as she wobbled on her perch, but at last she tugged the breastplate free and held it out before herself.

'It is not just the breastplate...' It was, in fact, torso armour both front and back, its clasps half-fastened, its plates dented and edged with verdigris. It was clearly meant to be powered in some fashion, for its interior boasted a webwork of fine circuitry, and she saw servo-actuator sockets ready to accept connecting components. A rent had been torn clean through both front and back. She let out a gasp as another sensory echo struck her. It was stronger this time, the sound of a blade rasping through metal, flesh and bone, accompanied by the acrid stink of smoke and burning flesh. She gritted her teeth as a tearing pain flared in her chest, there and gone in an instant.

She knew, then. This breastplate had been hers. It *was* hers. How that could be, she had not the faintest idea, but she knew it as surely as she still drew breath. As she turned the armour over in her hands, she saw a scrollwork plate set along its gorget. She ran her fingers over it, dusting away a patina of ancient grime.

'Celestine,' she read. The name was powerfully familiar. 'Is that... me? Am I Celestine?' The notion felt right, and she resolved that, until it was proved otherwise, she would claim this name for herself. It centred her somehow, made her feel less a wraith of this wasteland and more a being that ventured through it.

She considered throwing the armour aside, for it was battered and worn to the point of uselessness. Yet it was the first familiar thing she had seen in all this forsaken realm. She could not bear to part with it. She glanced down at her shift, ragged and torn where it had snagged bone and metal during her fall. She had been lucky not to suffer worse.

The armour would at least provide her some protection against another fall, and although she had no power pack for its systems, it didn't seem so heavy that it would encumber her overly. Awkwardly, mindful of the drop beneath her, Celestine manoeuvred the armour into place. She slid her arms through the holes, then sealed its clasps with an instinctive, practised ease.

'O divine machine-spirits, *demideus Omnissiah espiritum*, I beseech thee to shield my fragile flesh from harm.'

As the last clasp clicked into place, she blinked in bewilderment. Not only had the prayer of benediction sprung from her lips by some instinct, but the rent in her breastplate had vanished. The dents and grime faded as though they had never been. The armour she had donned had been a battered relic, but this was brand new, its lacquer shining in the bloody light, its scrollwork glinting. It took Celestine a moment to place the sudden hum that invaded her thoughts. She realised that an internal power source had activated within her backplate.

'Emperor, whatever miracle this is, I thank you for it,' said Celestine. The armour's restoration was inexplicable, but then, so was everything else about her situation. She chose to take it on faith that this development, at least, was in her favour.

Her spirits buoyed, she forged onwards. The descent was still challenging, but with her torso and back protected from harm it was at least somewhat less painful.

Sometime later, a glint of light on metal caught her eye. Sprawled in the tumbled wreck of a blackened landing craft were a great heap of skeletons, many crushed and mangled, some warped into unnatural shapes that she took care not to touch. There, amidst the mounds of remains, lay the armoured lower body of a warrior. Boots, greaves, leg and abdominal armour – it was all there, rusted into a single mass. Celestine felt intense discomfort at seeing that the body stopped at the waist, the ragged stub of a spine jutting out to vanish under a heavy slab of metal. Again, she somehow knew it to be hers.

Tentative, she reached out and touched one leg of the armour. She was rocked by the intensity of the echo that washed over her.

Screaming voices, frantic prayers, the sounds of engines labouring and terrible voices cackling and gibbering. The crackle of fire. The crash of guns in a confined space. Bullets and bolts flying in all directions. The howl of escaping air, and a moment of steely determination as she felt herself lunge for the rune that would drop the blast shutter and seal this entire section of the dropship off from the rest of the craft. The warp breach could not be allowed to infect the rest of the ship, not so close to their destination. She struck the rune, and the seventeen-ton blast door fell upon her like an executioner's blade.

Celestine came back to herself with a jolt. Had she died, she wondered? And if so, how was she alive now? How was such a thing possible? Was she remembering the lives of others, perhaps? Or was this all just some strange trick, part of a greater and crueller ruse that had brought her to this place and consigned her to a living purgatory?

Setting questions aside, Celestine braced herself upon a tilted drop-cradle and painstakingly dragged the armour into position, emptying it of its macabre contents before sliding and wriggling into it. She hissed with pain as rusted interior edges cut her flesh. She was forced to contort herself painfully to force her legs the last of the way down into the armour. Yet the moment she did, the same strange restoration occurred. System runes lit green upon locking clasps, rust flaked away and allowed joints to move whisper-smooth. Black armour plates gleamed. Celestine stood, armoured now from her feet up to her neck, and felt the strength humming through the suit she wore. The Emperor's warmth had set her on this path, she thought. That she had found these artefacts of her own, personal battle armour amongst the remains of the countless dead… it was no accident.

The notion gave her hope.

Her pauldrons she found upon a skeletal figure knelt as though in supplication amidst a forest of skulls impaled upon jutting bayonets. Somehow, again, she knew this body was also hers. The kneeling cadaver was watched over by the shattered statue of some ancient saint. Her arm segments and gauntlets she located a piece at a time, strewn down a long slope of bone scree below the teetering wreckage of a super-heavy tank, each with their own twisted skeletal arms and hands encased within them. How could her armour segments be strewn so far, she wondered, and seemingly belong to so many different corpses?

'Have I died more than once?' she whispered, shying away from the question when she heard how haunted her voice sounded.

By the time she found the last of her armour and slotted its components into place, she was well down amidst the drifting crimson mists, tasting their coppery tang in her mouth. She had hoped for a helm, to insulate her from the foulness on the air, but she had no recollection of ever wearing such a thing and none was forthcoming from the mountainside.

With each armour component Celestine located, there came another flash of sense-memory, each stronger than the last. She was immolated in a searing ball of plasma. She was struck down by an axe as large as a battle tank. She was riddled with explosive bolts until her body was sundered and her blood misted the air.

Each death-echo was horrifying and painful, yet each brought with it an increased sense of duty and determination, and the inexplicable knowledge that every life she had given, she had given for a righteous cause. Along with the horror and pain of each demise, Celestine saw also the hopeful faces that surrounded her, heard the prayers to the Emperor, and knew that by her own martyrdom she had secured victory or salvation for countless others. It was emotionally exhausting. With each fresh segment that she found, the temptation grew simply to cast it aside rather than shoulder the burden of the bloody memories that came with it. She rejected that notion each time. She was sure in the knowledge that each echo would pass, and leave her fortified and better equipped to find the answers she sought.

At last, fully armoured, Celestine strode down the shallower slopes of the mountain's foothills. Still she crunched over fields of skulls and ribs, femurs and spines, rusted blades and sundered guns and tattered flags. Yet her armour now shielded her from jabbing shards. With its servo-actuators aiding her balance and lending strength to her stride, Celestine made good time. She found herself picking her way between teetering heaps of remains that rose like cairns and carrion-piles. Many supported brass poles atop which she saw foul icons that caused her intense feelings of anger and revulsion. She saw an eight-pointed star and, as she wondered at the hatred that the crude shape awoke in her, a word rose unbidden to her lips. She spat it out like poison.

'Chaos.'

The memories were fleeting, her mind wanting to skate away from them. Instead she climbed a jagged mound and grasped the foul icon atop it with both hands. She wrenched the iron pole free with a snarl and cast it down. Then the monstrous images came in a blizzard that set her reeling, slithering down the slope of the cairn to fall to her knees at its base.

Yawning maws stuffed with fangs; armoured heretics with burning red eyes; mobs of screaming fools, deluded and enslaved by malevolent entities they could not comprehend. Looming terrors made of smoke and flame, sorcery and evil. These were the arch-enemies of her Emperor, and thus they were her foes also.

Celestine knew it to be true.

As the barrage of images passed, and she returned to herself, something shifted amidst the mists. A shadow crawled along the flank of a nearby ridge, a vague suggestion of long limbs and grasping talons. Red eyes flashed in the gloom, and a wave of hatred beat against Celestine like furnace heat.

'Warp spawn,' she snarled, meeting its fury with her own.

Celestine clenched her armoured gauntlets into fists, servos whining and powercells thrumming as they added their strength to hers. She snapped her head round as she heard bonemeal spill, knocked loose from another ossuary-heap by a second shadowy figure. There were more, she realised, slinking between the mounds and scrabbling closer like scavenging beasts around a carcass. Their eyes glowed like coals in the gloom, the only clearly visible part of them. Their voices came to her, low moans of hunger and hate with nothing human in them at all.

Celestine could fight, she was sure of that, but she could not defeat so many of these unknown fiends at once. Sensing that the boldest of them was about to pounce, she did the only other thing that she could.

She ran.

Aided by the servo-strength of her armour, Celestine broke into a sudden sprint and pounded away downhill. She felt the rush of hot air as several creatures leapt, their shadowy talons missing her by a hair's breadth. Howls of frustration chased her as she ran on, pulverised bone spraying up behind her heels.

Celestine careened downhill through thick red mists that reduced her visibility to a matter of yards. Bones and wreckage squirmed treacherously underfoot. Jagged mounds of detritus loomed suddenly from the fog, forcing her to dodge frantically around them at the last moment. Behind her, Celestine heard baying howls and the clamour of talons on bone as her pursuers gained on her.

'Emperor guide my footfalls,' she prayed as she ran. 'Lead me not unto disaster or mischance. Ward away the terrors that hunt me.'

Daemons.

The word came unbidden to her mind, along with the knowledge that if the abominations that snapped at her heels caught her then she would not just lose her life, but her eternal soul also. Celestine snapped a look back over her shoulder and saw dozens of glowing coals burning in the murk, drawing closer with every heartbeat. She ran faster.

The ground sloped steeply, and she almost fell, careening downhill amidst a shower of bones. Something dark shot overhead, and she had a split second to register that one of the daemons had leapt from the top of the rise to land in front of her. The monster spun towards her with a venomous hiss, lashing out with its claws. Rather than try to avoid it, Celestine clenched a fist and used her momentum to drive a thunderous blow into the creature's face.

She felt a raking pain in her side, followed by a vertiginous lurch as her fist passed straight through the daemon as though it were mist. Celestine cannoned forward and lost her balance, crashing down on the bone slope and rolling downhill. She skidded to a halt amidst a heap of skeletons still partially clad in armour not dissimilar to her own.

Celestine's head spun, and her chest heaved with the competing urges to suck in lungfuls of air or else vomit. There was no time to gather her wits. She could hear her attacker skidding down the slope above her, an alpha predator coming to claim its fallen prey. She glanced at her side and was surprised to see that her armour was wholly undamaged, though she could feel the hot pain across her ribs where the daemon had raked her.

'Incorporeal enough that I can't harm them, yet solid enough that they can butcher me,' she gasped, struggling to her feet and preparing to run again. She felt neither panic nor fear, for her iron will kept such sensations at bay, but Celestine knew that her situation was dire. Outrunning her pursuers seemed unlikely, yet to her immense frustration it seemed that she could not stand and fight. Celestine hated that notion of powerlessness more than anything, and resolved that, should the daemons catch her, she would contrive to end her own life rather than submit to their theft of it.

That was when the mist thinned for a moment and, in the hazy crimson light, she saw the blade. It jutted up from a bone cairn, just upslope from where she stood. It was long and straight, a bastard sword meant for single- or double-handed wielding. Its crossguard was fashioned into a winged skull of burnished gold. A garland of dead black roses hung from its hilt, which was gripped in a skeletal fist that thrust up from the heart of the cairn. Though the blade was tarnished and notched, bloody light still glinted on it in a way that nearly hypnotised Celestine.

This was her sword. She knew it as surely as she had known that each segment of armour she came across during the descent was hers. Perhaps, with this weapon in her hands, she could fight?

Her pursuers were almost on top of her; she could see the lead daemon slithering down the slope, more of its brood close behind. Celestine gauged the distance and made a snap decision. She could make it.

She lunged uphill, digging her toes into the uneven surface and pushing hard. She clawed at skeletal remains to propel herself upwards, giving a roar of pure effort as she raced the daemon to the mound. The beast was almost on top of her as she reached the blade, wrapping her hands around its hilt and giving a hard wrench. For a moment, the skeletal hand seemed reluctant to relinquish its grip, and she was forced to yank it a second time, even harder.

Bone disintegrated. The blade was made anew, gleaming in the bloodlight. Celestine drew it back as the daemon lunged. She swung, struck, and her attacker's head spun away into the murk trailing sprays of ichor. Celestine braced instinctively for the impact of its corpse, but the daemon's body passed through her like a cold wind and she turned, watching it discorporate into smoke as it tumbled to a stop.

Celestine flicked black ichor from her blade and stared at it for a moment, feeling the sense of utmost holiness that radiated from the weapon. She suffered no sense echoes this time, though she had braced herself for them. Instead there was simply an abiding sense of rightness, and of completion.

Now she had the weapon that the Emperor had bequeathed her.

Now she was a warrior again.

Now, she was Celestine.

Spills of bone and rusting metal skittered around her as the daemons surged down the slope. Raising her blade beside her head, Celestine braced her feet and made ready.

'Come, foul blasphemies, let me purge you in the Emperor's name,' she said with a tight smile.

The first creature flung itself at her, claws lashing wildly. She lopped off one arm and spun aside, allowing the pouncing daemon to tumble past her as the first one had. The next attacker came on more cautiously, feinting low then trying to rake its talons across her eyes. Celestine read its intentions easily and swayed back from the daemon's attack, before ramming her blade up through its jaw and out of the top of its head.

She ripped the weapon free as the daemon dissipated into smoke, in time to aim a disembowelling swing at the next fiend to attack. Another came at her out of the mist, and another. Then three attacked at once, one of the beasts managing to rip its claws through the meat of her thigh as she held off the other two. Celestine snarled with anger and despatched each assailant in turn, but she could hear a clattering commotion that suggested dozens more daemons were surging closer.

The fires of battle burned hot in Celestine's chest, but she knew that standing and dying upon this bleak hillside would not bring her the answers she sought.

'Golden Throne,' she spat, turning to run again, pouring all her strength and willpower into outdistancing the daemons.

Still they gained on her, and she cursed the futility of her plight as bone cairns and rusting wrecks flashed past.

'Does this damned mountain never end?' she gasped, legs and arms pumping as she ran.

As though she had summoned it, the ground levelled out with abrupt suddenness and then, to her surprise, began to slope upwards. Her pounding footfalls pulverised a last layer of bone, then fell upon hard black rock instead.

Celestine charged up the slope, through crimson mist so thick she could barely see a sword's length in front of her face. Howls and screams billowed around her, the pursuing daemons just yards behind. Surely the sudden change in landscape must indicate a chance of refuge? Surely she could not simply have passed from one interminable hell into another, there to be swiftly run to ground and torn apart by overwhelming enemy numbers.

Surely the Emperor meant more for her than this.

That was when the ground vanished, so abruptly that Celestine had no chance to react. One moment she was running full pelt up a rocky slope. The next she was sailing through thin air as the stone promontory ended in an abrupt ledge and hurled her out into the void.

Celestine fell, her hair whipping around her face, crimson mist billowing past on all sides. Behind her she heard the daemons' frustrated howls, receding swiftly as she plunged away from them into the endless red gulf.

The thought came to her that this was the end; not torn apart but condemned to a terrible plunge, perhaps to fall never-ending, perhaps to be dashed to red ruin on rocks far below. Then a strange sense swept through her, a miraculous unfurling of power that made her nerves sing and her soul tingle. Power surged through her body, and in a glorious moment of revelation a mighty pair of glowing gold and silver wings spread from between her shoulder blades. They snapped outwards, obeying her unconscious thought like muscle memory. They arrested her fall, caught the hot winds, transformed her plunge into a swooping glide. The mists swirled and parted before her and with a joyous shout she beat her mighty pinions and began to rise.

Celestine laughed as she soared upwards through the mists, beating her powerful wings as easily as she might command her legs to walk or her arms to swing a sword. Her hair billowed in the winds as she swept up and away from the bone mountain, bursting from amidst the crimson fog and into the desolate air above.

As the jagged horizon came into view, Celestine felt the candle-warmth of the Emperor's light upon her face. She felt, more than saw, the distant glow of its illumination, far, far away across the plains, among the fanged mountains.

There lay her destination. She knew it. She had faith in the Emperor's guidance. She had faith in her own strength.

Soaring on glowing wings of light, her silvered blade held firm against her chest, Celestine flew on over the blasted plains.

Towards the unseen light of the Emperor.

Towards answers.

404TH DAY OF THE WAR 0600 HOURS
IMPERIUM NIHILUS PLANET KOPHYN
CANYON-CITY TANYKHA ADUL LO:564-3/LA:675-9

Bells tolled over the Adul, calling the faithful to war. Their chimes echoed along the las-sculpted chasms and ravines into which the city was built. They rolled reverberant through shadowy cavern-habs and dusty subterranean manufactoria, candle-lit shrines and fortified cliff-side bunkers. They rang amid spills of rosy dawn light and the crash of booted, running feet. They mingled with the first volleys of gunfire.

Major Blaskaine was out of his bunk at the first sound of trouble. Nineteen years in the Emperor's service had honed his instincts to the point where Blaskaine's men joked – when they believed themselves safely out of earshot – that he had a touch of psyker prescience about him.

He allowed the men their grim jests.

Since Cadia's fall, any mirth was welcome, even at his expense.

This was not a day for jokes, however. As he marched down the shady corridor that linked his chambers to the Fourth Sector command bunker, Blaskaine reflected that precious few days on Kophyn had been.

'A pox on this worthless ball of rocks,' he muttered as he adjusted the collar of his uniform, double-checked the magazine in his laspistol and straightened out the medals pinned to his chest.

Still, it didn't do to look less than his best, even if there were no higher-ranking officers left to impress.

Blaskaine emerged into the command bunker to find it swirling with controlled pandemonium. The bunker was wide but low-ceilinged, its smooth stone walls typical of the las-carved chambers and corridors of the Adul. In places they were decorated by bas-relief Imperial angels and soldiery doing battle with mutants and traitors. In every carving, the forces of the Imperium reigned triumphant. If only that were true, thought Blaskaine.

Electro-lumen globes hung from the bunker's ceiling, casting cold light over the large strategium-table that dominated the centre of the room. Maps, charts, rolls of parchment and scattered data-slates covered the table from end to end.

One wall of the bunker was dominated by a huge bank of runic consoles, vox-units, long-range auspex receivers and other machineries of various opaque purpose. Cadian operators jostled elbows as they leant over them, working their controls and speaking in clipped tones into bulky headsets.

Those men and women looked tired but determined. It was an expression Blaskaine had become all too familiar with over the course of this campaign.

Junior officers, priests, servitors, signalmen, tech-magi, regimental life-guards, commissars and dozens of other assorted hangers-on bustled around the bunker. Conversations in High Gothic and Low Gothic mingled with binharic cant and plainsong to create a substantial din. Yet all fell silent as Blaskaine strode up to the strat-table. Salutes and genuflections were directed his way. As the last senior ranking officer of the Cadian 144th Heavy Infantry, such was his right.

'Situation report,' said Blaskaine, pleased to hear that he sounded calmer than he felt.

'Massive heretic assault incoming, major,' reported Lieutenant Kasyrgeldt, Blaskaine's adjutant. She plucked a data-slate from amidst the morass on the table and passed it to him. 'Armour and infantry elements moving up the wadi from the south-east and pushing on Hawk Gate. Scouts have detected a second force circling the mesa to assault Jackyl Gate from the west, and long-range auspex suggests aerial elements inbound on our position.'

'Clearly we merit substantial effort on the enemy's part, ladies and gentlemen,' barked Blaskaine. 'I believe we should be flattered.'

His words elicited a handful of mirthless smiles, here and there a couple of wry chuckles. These soldiers were under no illusions as to the dire situation, but they were Cadians. With their homes, their families and all they had known torn away from them, what cause had they to fear death?

'Enemy numbers?' asked Blaskaine as the hubbub of the bunker resumed.

'Substantial would be putting it mildly, sir,' said Kasyrgeldt. She showed him a parchment print-out, and Blaskaine quirked an eyebrow.

'Throne, Astryd... Tanks, artillery, cultists.' Blaskaine exhaled. 'Creed's ghost, where did they scrounge a Stormlord from? The War Engine is throwing everything at us, isn't he?'

'It appears so, sir. I think he means to have done with us today no matter what it costs him.'

'What's our state of play?' asked Blaskaine, plucking up a mug of recaff and pulling a face as he found it to be cold. Kasyrgeldt passed him a hot one.

'Generatorums two, three and four are still running,' she said. 'Sectors two and four still have void shield coverage. Both gates are fully garrisoned by soldiers of the Hundred and Forty-Fourth.. We have sixteen platoons still at fighting strength, if you include the Whiteshields.'

'No one is a Whiteshield anymore, Astryd,' said Blaskaine quietly, but she pressed on as though he hadn't spoken.

'Forty-two armoured personnel carriers, twenty-eight main line battle tanks, nineteen pieces of self-propelled field artillery including Manticores and Basilisks, and three scout tanks remain. Captain Maklen has, at last count, thirty-four per cent strength of the Cadian Two Hundred and Thirtieth mech-infantry remaining. They're ready to provide rapid response should a breakthrough occur. The Astorosian Ninth have mustered their engines in the runoff canyons near Jackyl Gate. We've substantial assets, sir.'

'But...?' prompted Blaskaine.

'Candidly, sir, we've no strategic options left to us beyond dig in and endure,' said Kasyrgeldt, keeping her voice low enough that only Blaskaine could hear. 'The enemy has a planetary population to utilise against us, and all of the materiel they've scavenged from a dozen battlefields... Not to mention a formidable manufacturing base to turn out fresh weapons and war machines. The odds are against us surviving the day, sir, but beyond that? They're even slimmer. And there's no hope of rescue or escape, not since the darkness fell. We're cut off, our astropaths are dead or mad, and we're likely the last Imperial holdout on a world that's already lost. No matter how determined they might be to die with honour, no matter how angry they might be at finding themselves fighting for another doomed planet, our soldiers know that it *is* doomed.'

'The commissars and the preachers are doing their part, yes?' asked Blaskaine.

'They are, sir, but they're fighting a rearguard action against their own sense of despair,' said Kasyrgeldt. 'There's a worrying streak of fanaticism supplanting good Cadian discipline. I think the soldiery are praying for some sort of miracle.'

'If it keeps our soldiers fighting, we'll take whatever we can get,' said Blaskaine, his mind racing. He knew his adjutant's dire summation was right, and try as he might, the major couldn't think of a way out of this rat-trap. 'Honestly, Astryd, it sounds like we could *use* a miracle right about now. Talking of which, where are the Sisters in all this? I'd expected to at least hear from Meritorius, what with violence in the offing.'

'The Sister Superior voxed word at first chimes, sir,' replied Kasyrgeldt, consulting another data-slate. 'They are already at the gates.'

'Of course they are,' said Blaskaine. 'Good martyrs all, eh?'

'The Battle Sisters are exceptional warriors, sir,' said Kasyrgeldt, a note of reproach in her voice. 'Their example is an inspiration to the soldiery, and frankly, I'll take the aid of half a hundred warrior women with power armour and bolters any day. Sir.'

Blaskaine raised a placating hand.

'There is no disagreement here, lieutenant,' he said. 'I've just never seen soldiers so eager to die in the Emperor's name. I don't see the sense in seeking out hopeless fights when one can live to fight another day, and I don't entirely trust the sanity of those who think differently.'

Blaskaine cursed himself as he saw Kasyrgeldt's expression set into a carefully neutral mask.

'Very good, sir,' she said, and Blaskaine wondered if he would ever entirely escape the ghosts of Cadia's fall.

Now was not the time to dwell.

'Carry on, lieutenant,' said Blaskaine. 'Have a voxman and a tech-priest attend me at console eleven. I've a war zone to coordinate.'

He turned away brusquely and marched across the command bunker, telling himself for the thousandth time that there was nothing he could have done that day, but that he could do something useful now.

Sister Superior Anekwa Meritorius stood atop the ramparts of Hawk Gate. Stocky and powerfully built, Meritorius was lent additional bulk by the ornate black and white power armour she wore. Her dark skin and bleached white hair contrasted sharply and, combined with the steely glint in her eye and the wide-bladed power sword sheathed at her hip, ensured she looked every part the stern Imperial warrior. Still, as she stared down at the horde of heretics sweeping towards the Adul, Meritorius felt little of the strength she displayed outwardly.

Hawk Gate was a towering armoured portal that sealed off one of only two main access points into the canyons of Tanykha Adul. Its hundred-foot-high durasteel gates were housed within an armoured arch, flanked by a pair of macro-bastion gun towers and overlooked by the rampart upon which Meritorius stood, amidst the Battle Sisters of her Celestian entourage.

Sister Maria Penitence shot her a zealous look.

'These gates would withstand bombardment by Titan-class weaponry,' said Sister Penitence, as though Meritorius had asked. 'Each gun tower is a fortress. Hundreds of Cadians garrison them, Sister Superior, and with our Sisters and the mission preachers spread through their ranks to bolster their faith, they shall not waver.'

'Sister Penitence speaks the Emperor's word,' said Sister Constance Indomita. 'The foe shall have little fortune throwing themselves at these gates, and even less should they attempt to scale the cliffs of the mesa. I believe I saw the Cadian engineers laying sufficient mines amongst those crags to blast an entire army of foes to pieces three times over.'

'Not to mention the automated turret networks that watch over the canyon edges,' added Sister Elena Absolom. 'Even with the enemy advancing in such numbers, I believe we shall best them with the Emperor's blessing.'

Meritorius found herself irritated by her Celestians' comments. It had been a hard campaign, and she made no secret of the pressure that had fallen upon her after Canoness Rokhsanja's demise, but she resented the notion that they might think her spirits needed bolstering. The alternative, that they truly believed what they were saying, seemed somehow worse. Thousands upon thousands of heretic warriors and war engines advanced under Kophyn's hard cobalt skies. Their ragged red banners filled the horizon, and the dust cloud that rose in their wake resembled an onrushing storm.

'The Emperor has no time for frivolous cheer, Sisters,' she snapped, fighting off the sense that they were all of a mind and she was excluded from it. 'Save your hopeful pronouncements for the Cadians.'

The Celestians exchanged glances that Meritorius chose to ignore, but they fell silent. Not so Preacher Unctorian Gofrey, a robed figure, dark of hair and steely of eye, who stood at Anekwa's left shoulder.

'Have a care, Sister Superior,' he said, his voice deep and hard as a ferrocrete slab. 'The Emperor may not put stock in baseless hope, but he frowns still more upon the craftsman that chips away his own foundations. So it is written in the Creed Imperius.'

'Thank you, Gofrey,' said Meritorius, voice tight, mouth a thin line. 'You ensure that we never go wanting for counsel.'

The preacher made the sign of the aquila, offering a hard smile that didn't reach his eyes. As was his habit, he touched his hand to his breastbone, where a lump indicated something hanging about his neck beneath his robe. Meritorius had never seen the priest's Imperial aquila, but she wouldn't have been surprised if it was scrimshawed from the bones of some luckless relative.

'The enemy will be upon us within the hour,' said Meritorius, turning away from Gofrey and addressing her Celestians. 'Go now, Sisters, and take your places amongst the Cadian ranks. I will converse with their senior officers and ensure that our defensive strategy is soundly implemented. Have faith, my Sisters, for whatever fate awaits us this day, we stand tall and strong in the Emperor's gaze, and we shall not be found wanting.'

'Deus Imperius Eterna,' they chorused, offering her the sign of the aquila.

'Stirring words, Sister Superior,' said Gofrey quietly as the three veteran Battle Sisters jogged away to their appointed posts. 'I hope for all our sakes that you mean them.'

'Don't you have soldiers to unnerve, Unctorian?' asked Meritorius without looking around.

'I have the Emperor's work to do, as do we all,' smiled the preacher. 'The fire must be lit.'

'Then go and light it, and leave me to do my duty,' said the Sister Superior.

'The Emperor watches us all, Anekwa,' replied Gofrey.

As she listened to him walking away, Meritorius silently hoped that his insinuations were unfounded. She cast her eyes to the heavens and offered up a prayer to the Emperor, hoping for the thousandth time to feel that spark of the divine that had once been her constant companion.

There was nothing. There had been nothing since the Great Rift tore its way across the galaxy, since the stars went out and His light was extinguished. Meritorius feared, in the darkest watches of the night, that her faith had been snuffed at the same time, just another candle flame drowned by the shadows. Did anything remain beyond the Rift? Was the Throneworld already gone?

Was she alone?

Such were the constant questions that she asked herself day in, day out. They were questions repeated over and again by the warriors she led and the soldiers they had found themselves fighting alongside. Cadia gone. The Rift devouring the heavens. The Astronomican vanished between one breath and the next. How could anyone maintain their faith in the Emperor and His Imperium in such a terrible time?

'And yet, that is what faith *is*,' she whispered to herself in a voice heavy with the frustration of having had this conversation with herself many times before. 'You have to believe *despite* it all. That's what gives faith its power, and the Emperor His. Just believe, and if you can't, then for Throne's sakes at least don't let them see you wavering. Not this close to the end.'

Meritorius heard a door bang open at one end of the rampart. A Cadian heavy weapons platoon spilled out, jogging along the fire-step to begin setting up their man-portable lascannons and heavy bolters. Meritorius returned their salutes, radiating steely composure as she activated the vox-link built into her armour's gorget.

'This is Sister Superior Meritorius of the Order of the Ebon Chalice, calling Major Blaskaine, Captain Maklen, Lieutenant Tasker and Sub-Duke Velle-Marchon. I bring you the Emperor's blessings and ask your counsel, my fellow war leaders, for the enemy is at our gates.'

Preacher Gofrey stalked the corridors of gun fortress Hawk-Alpha. He stared steadily at the Cadian soldiers he passed, enjoying how the men and women of the Imperial Guard averted their eyes and offered him the sign of the aquila. Almost, he thought, as though warding away his judgement, or more properly, that of the Emperor. They sensed his authority and they respected it, just as they should.

He passed squad after squad of warriors gathered before armoured firing slits. Cadians prayed over their lasguns. They clutched gun-metal aquilas as they beseeched the aid of the Emperor, and of the machine-spirits of their weapons. Some reached out to touch the hems of his robes as he passed.

As Gofrey walked, he preached.

'And yea, though the light of the Emperor may be occluded in this grim hour, His eye is never far!' cried Gofrey, his voice echoing along arched corridors and through bustling chambers. 'He expects of us, brothers and sisters. He expects of us and He judges most severely those who He finds wanting.'

He rounded upon a squad of troopers who were gathered around a battered vox-set and trying to coax the communications device back into life.

'Are you faithful?' asked Gofrey, his voice cold steel and fire.

'We are, preacher,' replied their corporal, a squat, pale man with tired eyes and too many scars. 'We are loyal servants of the Emperor all.'

'Is there taint amongst you?'

The man's expression hardened.

'There's no taint amongst the Cadian Hundred and Forty-Fourth,' said the corporal.

'Arrogance,' mused the priest. 'Is that why the void turned to madness? Is that why the Imperium burns? Is that why your world is no more? Are any of us truly free of taint?'

A thrill ran through his body as he saw the Cadians bristle with outrage. Gofrey's hand strayed towards the laspistol at his hip.

Do it, he thought.

React.

Betray himself for a heretic, so Gofrey may cut out another canker.

He centred his mind, focused the power of his will and risked the slightest mental nudge. If these men were impure, surely now they would reveal themselves. A muscle twitched under the corporal's eye. The man balled his fists, but to Gofrey's disappointment he held his place. The preacher knew he couldn't goad the man further; there might still be some amongst this dull flock who were truly faithful. For their sake, he must restrain himself.

'Cadia stands,' said the man through gritted teeth. 'And we are loyal.'

'Prove it to the Emperor, not to me,' said Gofrey almost conversationally, turning and walking away. The Cadians were forgotten already. There was no obvious taint there to excise. They weren't where his purpose lay. But it was here, somewhere in this den of corruption, and he would coax it loose. The Emperor would show it to him, before the end. He had given Gofrey his gifts for a reason.

His thoughts turned to Sister Superior Meritorius, as they had many times in recent days, and righteous anger filled him. Gofrey saw the cracks in the façade of her faith, saw the way they radiated outwards to corrupt all those she consorted with.

Another preacher, Munctian Dunst, met Gofrey on the stairs as he prowled down towards the next level of the tower. Dunst shied away, and Gofrey sneered as the portly old priest hurried past him without a word.

All of them were faithless, thought Gofrey. All of them were at fault. The mission had always been a poor jest, for how did you bring enlightenment to a galaxy of sinners? They had brought this ending upon the Imperium and now they lived in the ashes of the apocalypse they had wrought.

Yet there were men here still with the faith to serve the Emperor to the end. Unctorian Gofrey held his secret close to his chest, and the Emperor in his heart, and he would serve his final function before the end of all things. He was the arbiter of the Emperor's justice, and he would deliver it to all of the faithless, the moment their deeds betrayed them.

Starting, he sincerely hoped, with Sister Anekwa Meritorius. When the battle sirens started howling moments later, and the scream of incoming shells filled the air, Gofrey felt a smile stretch itself across his features and the anger burn hotter in his breast.

'The time of testing is here!' he cried, not caring to whom. 'Repent your sins, you faithless masses, for in the fires of battle we all shall be tried for our guilt.'

Sister Meritorius stood framed by the man-high crenellations of the battlements and watched the enemy begin their attack.

The vast majority of the foe advanced on foot, hordes of ragged ore-miners, smelt labourers and dust farmers armed with pilfered small arms and displaying the blood red bandannas and war paint of the War Engine's followers. They chanted and screamed as they dashed headlong towards Hawk Gate. Above them waved tattered crimson banners and brass icons, all depicting the same stylised skull sigil.

It was an unclean symbol of the Blood God, Meritorius knew. The rune of he to whom the desperate peoples of Kophyn gave their worship when the light of the Emperor went out. She hated them for that choice, with a vehemence that eclipsed all else.

'Enemy artillery drawing up on the ridge, ma'am,' said one of the nearby Cadians, peering through her magnoculars. 'I'd advise taking cover.'

'The Emperor protects,' said Meritorius as rippling muzzle flares lit the distant ridge.

'So does ferrocrete, ma'am,' muttered the Cadian as she ducked. A rain of shells tumbled down upon Hawk Gate, resolving from black dots against the cobalt sky to hurtling projectiles. Meritorius took a deep breath and willed herself to hold her ground. If it took the fires of the enemy's fury to burn away the numbing shroud that kept her from her faith, then so be it. Anything to feel the Emperor's love restored.

The shells hit and the world turned white. Thunderous detonations blanked out all other sound, and Meritorius felt the heat of the blasts as her hair and cloak billowed in the furnace winds. The battlements shuddered. Debris filled the air. Then it was over, and amidst the smoke and the first screams of the wounded, Meritorius found she was still alive. She raised a hand to a sharp sting at her cheek, her gauntleted fingers coming away spotted with blood.

'Shrapnel,' she said absently, then stared out through the smoke, trying to perceive the foe. She was dimly aware of the Cadians rising to their feet, looking at her with fresh wonder as they dragged their heavy weapons into firing positions.

'They will maintain their bombardment,' said Meritorius, her voice vox amplified through her gorget so that it boomed along the ramparts. 'The enemy seek to keep our heads down and our guns silenced while their infantry close. Remember the fate of Dasha Adul. Keep the foe from the gate at all costs, and remember, men and women of the Imperium, the Emperor is with you!'

The Cadians raised a cheer at her words and, as the smoke tatters and orders flickered through their vox receivers, they let fly into the onrushing cultist hordes. They were not the only ones. Every gun emplacement, artillery position and firing slit flared bright as the Cadian 144th vented their fury upon the charging foe. The front ranks of cultists were a few hundred yards from the gate when they erupted in fountains of blood, fire and tattered flesh. A hissing storm of lasgun fire fell like glowing rain to scythe down dozens upon dozens of howling heretics. Missiles whipped down on trails of smoke and detonated amidst tight-packed clusters of the foe. Heavy bolters and autocannons chugged, chewing red lines of ruin through the footsoldiers of the War Engine's hordes.

Hundreds died in minutes, yet thousands more poured in behind them. They scrambled and trampled over the bloody wreckage of their former comrades, wild eyed and bellowing. Hardly like humans at all, thought Meritorius. More like wild animals.

'Ma'am, incoming!' shouted the Cadian gunner as another volley of shells screamed down upon the ramparts.

'Cover!' roared Meritorius. 'Then up and resume firing! The Emperor is with you!'

Again, the fire and fury of the enemy's shelling shook the battlements. A hundred yards to her right a lucky shot passed between two crenellations and hit the firestep, blasting an avalanche of rubble and bodies down the backslope of the gate. Corpses and rockfall rained down on the Cadian Whiteshields waiting on the canyon floor. They screamed in agony, half buried beneath crushing rubble. As the field medicae dashed to reach them Meritorius saw one flattened suddenly beneath a late-falling chunk of masonry the size of a bunker door. Yet again, she herself was more or less untouched.

There was a day when such a thing would have made her faith burn hot. Now she found herself feeling little of anything at all.

The smoke cleared for a second time and Meritorius leaned out to add the thumping fire of her boltgun to the Imperial fusillade. Self-propelled shells whipped down into the enemy, every mass-reactive shot bursting another heretic as though they had swallowed a grenade.

As she fired, Meritorius activated her vox, speaking to her sisters and to the preachers of the Imperial mission that they had accompanied into the stars.

'The enemy press hard, but this is only the beginning and we must hold at all costs. Let your voices ring out, sisters and brothers. Let your prayers be heard by friend and foe alike.'

Confirmations flashed back to her, and amidst the din of battle she heard the beginnings of a battle hymn from the gun fortresses. Vox amplified by the Battle Sisters, the choral singing rose over the hammering of gunfire and the screams of the dying, haunting and beautiful and stern. Soon enough the Cadians joined their voices as best they could, a mighty hymn of defiance echoing from Hawk Gate to defy the hated foe.

Meanwhile, Meritorius switched channels.

'Major Blaskaine, this is Sister Meritorius,' she voxed.

'Receiving, Sister Superior,' came the Cadian's reply.

'Major, the enemy have drawn up prodigious artillery assets on the ridge north of the wadi. If they continue their bombardment of us unmolested, I fear they will compromise our defences quite rapidly.'

'Understood, Sister, we see them on auspex,' said Blaskaine, and Meritorius felt a moment's irritation at the man's relaxed tone.

'Then perhaps you would be good enough to intervene on our behalf, major?' she said.

'Wheels are already in motion, Sister Superior,' replied Blaskaine. *'I believe Captain Maklen is about to provide the enemy with a demonstration of what proper artillery looks like. I recommend you enjoy your vantage point and perhaps shield your eyes, Sister.'*

A basso roar rose from deeper within the canyon city, sounding for all the world like a catastrophic avalanche or ferocious earthquake. Meritorius looked back to see half a dozen bulky rockets thundering into the sky on thick pillars of fire and smoke. Manticore missiles, she realised, each one the size of an armoured personnel carrier, machine-spirit guided and packed with thousands of micro-bomblets.

'Throne alive,' breathed Meritorius as the enormous rockets lumbered overhead and spread out before beginning their death-dive towards the enemy. She saw the blasts a moment before she heard them, a flurry of apocalyptic light-flares that transformed the distant ridge into a roiling sea of fire. Mushroom clouds billowed into the air as the dragon's roar of multiple explosions reached her ears, and Meritorius watched the blast waves from the explosions hurl the rearmost ranks of heretics from their feet as they raced outwards.

'Emperor be praised,' said the Cadian gunner to Meritorius' right, looking again through her magnoculars. 'There's no enemy artillery left. There's nothing left...'

'Magnificent, major, the Emperor's wrath made manifest,' voxed Meritorius. 'Please relay my thanks to Captain Maklen and her gunners.'

'Will do, Sister Superior,' replied Blaskaine. *'Just don't ask for another demonstration. That was the last of the Manticore ordnance. The launchers are dry.'*

'Understood, Major Blaskaine,' said Meritorius, before breaking the vox-link. Such a display of Imperial might, she thought, and yet she felt nothing.

Meritorius sighed and looked down over the ramparts to see fresh waves of cultists pouring into the fight. So many heretics had been slain now that the living were using bulwarks of the dead for cover, digging in behind the bodies of their former comrades and raking the gate with fire. Bullets chewed along the ramparts, spitting fresh shards of shrapnel where they struck. Meritorius flinched despite herself, and a glance at the Cadian gunner showed that the woman had caught the moment of weakness. For an instant, the two of them locked eyes and Meritorius felt as though her failings were laid bare. She despaired as she saw the first stirrings of fear and doubt blossom behind the Cadian's eyes in response to her own. Then a round caught the gunner in the ear and blew out the side of her skull, throwing her body off the firestep like discarded waste.

The weapon's other gunner looked up at Meritorius, eyes hard and demanding.

Meritorius broke his gaze and turned back to the battle, firing another volley down into the massed foe. She had nothing to offer him.

Major Blaskaine ground his fists into his eyes, trying to rub the exhaustion from them and failing.

'How long have they been attacking now?' he asked, directing the question to no one in particular.

'Battle's been going for twelve hours and sixteen minutes, sir,' said Lieutenant Kasyrgeldt.

'It feels like days,' said Blaskaine. 'And we'll have nightfall soon. Won't that be a delight?'

The nights on Kophyn had been hellish for many weeks now. The natural stars of the void were no longer visible amidst the darkness. Instead, freakish auroras lit the night, lurid colours spilling and billowing through the stratosphere, twisting into the monstrous suggestions of leering faces and fanged maws. What celestial phenomena could be observed were wrong and unnatural, corresponding to no star-chart that Blaskaine had ever seen.

'If it's any consolation, sir, I doubt we'll have to last through the whole thing,' said Kasyrgeldt. 'I'm seeing fresh waves of heretic armour rolling up on Jackyl Gate. Looks like they've activated their Stormlord at last. The gate's defences are down to eighteen per cent effectiveness, and Captain Maklen already deployed most of her reserves to shore them up. There's no way we can stop that punch, and once the gate falls there'll be heretics swarming through the streets like vermin.'

The bunker shook, and the lights flickered. Dust trickled down from fresh cracks in the ceiling.

'Bloody enemy bombers,' spat Blaskaine. 'What I wouldn't give for a few squadrons of Lightnings to get up there amongst them.'

'If wishes were weapons, we'd have a Titan Legion on station,' replied Kasyrgeldt.

'Void shield generators failing above sector two,' called one of the console operators.

'Sister Meritorius reports another wave of enemy infantry approaching Hawk Gate, sir,' said another one. 'She's reporting weapon servitors and Dreadnought-sized mutants.'

Any last reserves of gallows humour Blaskaine might have used to deflect the severity of the situation drained from him along with the blood from his face.

'To openly invite the mutant into your ranks,' he breathed. 'It seems impossible for these people to have fallen so low.'

'In days as dark as these, anything is possible,' said Kasyrgeldt.

Blaskaine took a deep breath and stood from his own console. He placed one hand on the butt of his laspistol, and looked around the command bunker. Red runes flashed on every auspex screen. Operators talked rapidly into headsets, struggling to keep the strategic maps updated as wave upon wave of fresh enemies poured into the fight. The grim black signifier of the enemy's Stormlord flashed ever closer to Jackyl Gate, the super heavy tank grinding unstoppably towards the beleaguered bastion. It was no doubt packed with the axe-wielding Mas'drekkha soldiery of the War Engine's elite. Casualty reports spiralled by the moment.

'Ladies and gentlemen,' began Blaskaine, before the entire bunker shuddered again, more violently than before. Cracks shot through the bas-relief carvings, sundering Imperial angels and decapitating brave soldiers. The lumens went dark. Only half of them flickered back to life.

'Void shields gone,' came the report.

'Stormlord engaging at Jackyl Gate,' came another.

'Breach! Breach reported at Jackyl Gate,' barked another operator a moment later. 'Sub-Duke Velle-Marchon is committing the last of his tanks to seal the gap.'

Blaskaine shook his head. They all knew that a score of battle-damaged tanks wouldn't be enough to stop what was coming.

'Ladies and gentlemen,' he began again. 'It has been a damned honour to serve with you all, but I think we all know that the situation is irredeemable. I am giving the order for all remaining combat assets to fall back through the deep caves. Voxman, please pass my regards to Sister Superior Meritorius and ask her to hold Hawk Gate for as long as the Emperor permits.'

'Sir?' asked Kasyrgeldt as the Cadian operators exchanged glances. 'Should we not commit all reserves to holding Jackyl?'

'You and I both know that there's no victory to be had here, lieutenant,' said Blaskaine. 'Our duty now is to remove whatever assets we can from this combat zone. Whatever we salvage today can be used against the War Engine tomorrow.'

'Sir, we can't just let the gate fall,' blurted a junior lieutenant angrily. 'Throne knows we've done enough of that!'

Blaskaine pinned the lieutenant with the full intensity of his gaze.

'When Cadia fell we all lost something of ourselves, lieutenant,' he said. 'But we pulled out as strategy and sanity demanded, that the Imperium might use our remaining strength for something more than a pyrrhic gesture of defiance. So unless you want to march down to Jackyl Gate now and fight the enemy off with your bare hands, I suggest you shut up and follow orders, there's a good lad.'

Blaskaine stared hard around him, daring anyone else to challenge his orders. He could hear how it sounded, how laughable the notion was of staging any meaningful fight back if Tanykha Adul fell. And he knew the rumours, knew what they whispered about him ever since the fall of Cadia. But if there were more days yet to be lived, Blaskaine would just as soon live them, and he could salvage something in order to fight back on his own terms. He was duty bound to do so no matter what they thought of him for it.

Kasyrgeldt drew breath to speak, but at that moment a piercing shriek burst through every vox-set in the room. Operators yelled in surprise, ripping off headsets and reeling back from their consoles. The lumens glowed brighter, and a crystal-clear note sang in the air, growing louder by the moment.

'What in Throne's name?' gasped Blaskaine.

'Sir! The enemy aircraft. They're... they're just *gone,*' cried one of the operators, pointing at the runic display on his screen.

'Empyric augurs active, sir,' came another report. 'Some kind of phenomenon.'

'Define *some kind,*' barked Blaskaine. 'What is this, a weapon for the enemy to finish us with?'

'I don't...' The operator gaped in amazement at his conflicting readouts, two tech-priests chattering in binharic as they hunched over the console.

'Report from Sister Meritorius, sir,' shouted a voxman over the swelling note that filled the air. 'She says it's a miracle, sir. She asks you leave the bunker to look upon the skies.'

Blaskaine blinked, then turned and made for the exit, most of his command staff close on his heels. He followed the tunnels through the rock of the cliffside, making for the closest exterior balcony. As he went, he found himself advancing into a glimmering golden light that shone along the corridors like a false dawn. The high, singing note swelled and rose as he went.

Blinking in the glare, half-deafened, Blaskaine staggered out onto the viewing balcony and looked up. The deep shadows of the canyon city were thrown into stark relief by a spill of what looked like golden starlight, falling from on high.

'What is that?' shouted Kasyrgeldt, shielding her eyes and squinting upwards into the golden glare that filled the skies.

'Are those enemy planes?' asked a sub-lieutenant, pointing to flaming trails of wreckage tumbling from on high.

'Three points north-north-west,' barked an operator, staring through heavy ocular augmetics into the very heart of the blaze. The light began to dim, the note to fade, and as they did Blaskaine saw what the man was referring to. The glow had come from something. No, some*one* now drifting down through the night skies and descending towards Jackyl Gate.

A metal-winged figure, armoured, holding a glimmering blade, her hair flowing in a dark mane around her head.

'Vox-set,' he demanded, clicking his fingers at an operator who dutifully hurried forward with the man-portable set he wore on his back. Blaskaine grabbed the handset and flicked to Sister Meritorius' frequency.

'Sister, care to explain to me who in the Emperor's name that is?' he barked. 'And perhaps you could enlighten me as to what in the name of the Golden Throne she just did to the enemy aircraft?'

Meritorius' voice, when it came back to him, was so full of hushed awe that it gave even Blaskaine pause.

'Major, I think… I believe that it is the Living Saint.'

'Living Saint?' gaped Blaskaine.

'Yes, major,' said Meritorius, sounding every bit as bewildered as he. *'I believe she has come to us in our hour of need. It is Saint Celestine.'*

BEYOND

Celestine flew through an ever-changing realm. The skies roiled overhead, turbulent strata of colour intermingling with streamers of glaring light and racing masses of cloud. At times there were faces amidst the thunderheads, vast and hideous things with rolling eyes and leering maws. Suggestions of avian abominations screamed through fanged beaks. Terrible yet beautiful visages stared down before breaking apart into flickers of energy like writhing worms. Winds blew hot and cold, carrying smells as variegated as sulphur and camphor, fresh bread and rotting flesh, warm skin and ancient ice and burning parchment and vomit.

Below Celestine, the lands rolled past in an ever-shifting morass. Some were so otherworldly and ethereal that her senses could barely perceive them. Others were all too tangible. She soared over a glimmering shore whose sands were formed from minute gemstones. Ragged things staggered through the glittering beauty, humanoid figures that sifted listlessly through an impossible fortune with callused hands and cried up to her.

'A bite of food, my lady, just a bite!' wailed one.

'Water, please, water,' gasped another, yet soon enough their desperate avarice dragged their eyes back to the riches at their feet. Celestine felt sorrow and pity mingle with disgust and flew on, for she knew she could not help these wretches.

Beyond the gemstone shores came an ocean not of water but of flowing energy that shimmered and pulsed through kaleidoscopic colours beyond her ability to name. The longer that she flew above that hypnotic ocean, the more its colours captivated her. There seemed some deeper meaning to the patterns of light and shadow that she could discern if she could only just...

Celestine realised with a start that she had flown so low she was almost touching the ocean's surface. She banked up and away with a cry of alarm, in time to see something huge shifting below the waves. An eye the size of a building glared up at her then was gone, but its look of frustrated hunger stayed with Celestine long after the monster itself had vanished.

Next came a shattered land of deep canyons and craggy islands that floated around one another like untethered clouds. Chains hung from beneath those rootless isles, ending in cages that each contained a slumped and hopeless figure. The moans of the legion of wretches rose to Celestine's ears, but she looked away, for she knew somehow that these souls were far beyond her aid. Atop each island rose a tower of black marble and pale bone, each supporting crackling orbs of fire that leapt and spat furiously as terrible creatures capered around them and waved long, black blades.

So it went on. She passed over a revolting swamp of bubbling fluids and effluvia in which writhed maggots the size of tanks. She flew high above a castle of crystal and vellum that sprawled for miles upon miles and teemed with garishly coloured creatures that leapt and screamed. A plain of swivelling eyes, a torrential river of screaming souls, a great empty blackness that radiated the most dreadful sense of sorrow, all passed below her.

Always, Celestine felt the candle's warmth upon her cheek. Always she sensed more than saw the light glimmering just beyond the horizon, and as she pressed on she steeled herself to the terrible sights. None of it would distract her from her purpose. None of it would prevent her from finding the answers she sought.

'How long have I flown?' Celestine wondered aloud. Time felt fluid and strange, and she realised that she could not say whether she had been airborne for hours, days, perhaps even weeks.

Still she felt no hunger or thirst, and that thought disturbed her in and of itself. At least, she realised, she was beginning to feel the drag of tiredness upon her limbs. Yet though the sensation was somehow reassuring in its physicality, it was also problematic.

'I cannot imagine finding refuge in this terrible place,' she murmured to herself. Since the mountain's slopes, Celestine had not run afoul of any of the denizens of this realm, but she doubted that such good fortune would last forever. Still, knowing that sooner or later she would have to rest, she cast a dubious eye below her for some safe eyrie or sheltered nook within which she might take rest.

She soared over a region of infernal volcanic chasms, hellfires burning in their depths and black ash carpeting the lands about them. Yet as Celestine looked down upon the merciless realm it transformed before her eyes. As though her scrutiny had summoned it, Celestine found herself flying above a city.

Streets and buildings marched away in all directions as far as the eye could see. The buildings were looming, their architecture gothic, encrusted with grim statuary. Bleak factories and towering spires pressed close against mouldering tenement stacks and forbidding fortresses and sprawling industrial plants. Streets and roadways wound through the sprawl, so deep and shadowed that they resembled ravines between forbidding mountain crags.

The place was deserted, as far as Celestine could see, and looked as though it had been for many long years. The buildings leant against one another like drunkards, their glassaic windows hollow and shattered, their fascias crumbling in disrepair. A howling wind blew through empty doorways and sent dust storms dancing along empty streets. Somewhere a bell tolled, mournful and sporadic as though caught by the callous breeze.

Celestine realised that night-black clouds boiled overhead, thick and viscous as oil. From them fell flurries of what she first took to be snow, until the flakes touched her skin and stung her with their heat. Celestine hissed through her teeth and wiped one finger against her cheek. It came away smeared with darkness.

'Ashes,' she said. 'Or something worse. And hot enough to burn.'

The clouds were settling lower now, and the rain of hot ash fell thicker from them. Celestine realised that to remain aloft amidst such conditions would be dangerous. The hollow buildings below represented the best chance for shelter that she was likely to see.

As she flew lower, a sense of brooding malevolence reached up to caress her nerves and cause the hairs to rise on the back of her neck. Celestine felt a dreadful malice radiating up from the dark streets, a watchfulness and threat that belied their empty appearance.

'No, not down there,' she said, mindful of the swirling ashes now filling the skies. 'I will seek shelter amongst the higher places.'

Soon enough she saw a tall tower block that loomed into the sky, its flanks shattered by cracks. Tilting her wings, she swept lower, soaring in even as the first stinging flakes of ash kissed her flesh. The holes in the building's sides looked ancient, and the darkness inside it was sepulchral.

'But it's shelter,' she said. Celestine swooped in through the nearest rent and alighted amidst the shadows.

She prowled through the darkness with her sword held double-handed in front of her. Old boards creaked beneath her tread, and the hum of her armour's power pack sounded loud amidst the silence. Insectile things squirmed through dark corners, and though she was far from squeamish something about their half-seen shapes made Celestine's flesh crawl. As her eyes adjusted to the darkness, she realised she was in some sort of dwelling, but one that had not seen occupancy in a long, long time. Items of meagre furniture were scattered about, old chairs whose stuffing was escaping, and tables canted at strange angles on warped legs. Everything had a patina of grime and a feeling of decay and, the harder she stared, the more wrong it looked. Chair legs blended into floorboards like melting tallow. The room seemed to shift and settle subtly just beyond her peripheral vision, as though it were trying to close in around Celestine whenever her back was turned. A lopsided shelf bore pict frames, but every one was cracked and blackened as though by fire; whatever images they had once displayed were lost, and Celestine dragged her gaze away as the dark smudges that remained swam before her eyes.

On one wall was hung an eagle symbol, two headed and spread-winged. In such a small room, the large decoration seemed dominant to the point of incongruity, but Celestine sensed that there was something subtly wrong with it too. The shape of the symbol looked off to her, too jagged and twisted, its eyes cruel and its beaks open in idiocy or hunger. Perhaps both. Disquiet swelled in her heart at the sight of this bastardised symbol, and she sensed a cruel malice lurking behind the entire scene.

Celestine shook her head and moved on, keen to be out of the suddenly claustrophobic room, with its yellow-stained walls and its deep shadows. To remain felt like leaving her head poised between the yawning jaws of some monstrous thing and trusting they would not snap suddenly shut. She walked on into a hallway that tilted at a drunken angle, its floorboards split and ruptured upwards. Celestine picked her way down the hallway and into another room, this time some sort of communal washroom. She stopped at the sight of old blood smearing the tiles of the walls and floor, its source concealed within one of the wash-stalls towards the darkened rear of the room. Something dripped, slow and irregular, and as her eyes adjusted to the darkness she saw tendrils of some organic matter spread across the tiles. Their pale tips quested like blind worms, turning mindlessly in her direction and swaying as though scenting the air. Revolted, Celestine backed out and left the secrets of that noisome place undisturbed. Still she cast glances behind her until its door was out of sight, in case something should emerge from the unseen darkness.

She hastened on, the floor creaking beneath her, and passed swiftly through a succession of rooms each more oppressive and mournful than the last. Small family shrines lay toppled and abandoned or smeared with foul substances long dried to a black crust. The echoes of lives lay overturned and rotting, many broken as though hurled about and trampled. Somehow, the rooms where everything was almost intact, almost in place, were worse. They made Celestine feel unutterably sad, and her disquiet grew with each chamber, as though danger grew nearer by the moment.

She stopped in another shadowy corridor, listening carefully for any signs of movement. By this time, Celestine's heart was thudding, and her senses were screaming of something predatory and terrible stalking her through the ruins. Though the city had looked empty, Celestine's instincts were ever more insistent that it wasn't so.

'I'll find no rest here,' she murmured. 'Only death.' She cocked her head, frowning, listening hard. A sound came to her, a distant fragment too vague to place yet somehow familiar. Celestine considered dismissing it as just another artefact of this strange place, but then it came to her again, a little more distinct. A voice, warped by echoes and muffled by distance, but unmistakably a human voice. Female. Shouting.

'No, not just shouting,' she breathed. 'Praying.' Moved by a sudden sense of urgency, Celestine set off through the ruined building to seek the source of the sound.

* * *

A few minutes of hurried passage through the ruin brought her to another ragged wound in its flank. She edged carefully into the room, half of which had simply torn away from the building's core like a rotten tooth parting company with a gum. Buckled floorboards jutted out over a drop filled with tangled rebar and mouldering rubble. Beyond, the gloomy cityscape was revealed again, now blanketed by a steady fall of hot ashes.

Celestine stopped, balanced upon a jutting outcrop of boards and peering at the buildings half-visible through the ash fall. She barely dared breathe as she listened hard for the sound to recur.

There. Her head snapped round and she peered down from her vantage point at the street below. Light flared suddenly, hot and fiery amidst the drab greys of the city. It was there and gone in a heartbeat, but it left an impression seared into Celestine's vision. She was sure she had seen something moving in the firelight, a figure darting from one building to the next at ground level.

A voice floated up to her. Its words were echoes, but its tone was unmistakable. Celestine heard anger there, and fervour, and hate. It was a tone of righteous revulsion for something unclean, and it struck a sympathetic chord in her.

Celestine launched herself out into the ash fall, glad of the armour that protected most of her body from its searing heat. She looped down, a quick dive that she ended by tucking in her wings, shielding her face with her arms, and smashing through the remains of a broken window. Celestine rolled to a stop, finding herself crouched on a rusting gantry several levels above a derelict factory floor. Machinery, pipes and conveyors were everywhere, all of them thick with rust and verdigris. They possessed an uncomfortably biological aspect, the pipes sheathed in thin skeins of veined flesh while infernal lights flickered in the bowels of the largest machines.

As she looked over the railing, Celestine saw again that flare of fiery light. This time the voice rose clear and strident, echoing up through the shadowy factory and rebounding from ancient mechanisms.

'In the Emperor's name I abjure thee, warp spawn. I banish thee with the holy fires of the Master of Mankind,' it cried.

Flames flared again and, as Celestine watched, a figure dashed across the factory floor, entering from one side of the building and sprinting hard for the other. It was a woman, clad in threadbare robes. Her dark hair flowed behind her as she ran, and she held a pair of burning brands, one in each fist. Upon her back, Celestine saw a sword was sheathed, half-concealed by the woman's flowing robes.

Celestine drew breath to call out, but then the woman's pursuers smashed through the doors and windows and the front of the factory and spilled across the floor. There were dozens of them, hunched and gaunt with tattered bat's wings sprouting from their shoulders. Their snouts were long and fang-filled, and as they yawned wide they let out terrible keening cries. The creatures scrambled along on gangling limbs that ended in hook-like talons, and their dark flesh was tufted with matted fur. They were singularly hideous, and Celestine knew that they meant to chase the fleeing woman down and devour her.

The woman spun, stopping between two rusting hunks of machinery. She swept her burning brands up to point at her pursuers and bellowed.

'Emperor's light consume you!'

Roaring tongues of flame leapt out from each brand, hungry fireballs of golden light that shot through the gloom to explode amidst the monsters. They screeched and writhed as they burned, and those not caught by the twin blasts recoiled, wings flapping frantically.

The woman turned and ran again, and almost at once the things were after her, fresh beasts spilling through the shattered factory frontage to join the pack.

Celestine set off along the overhead gantries at a run. She ignored the cables that writhed like worms as she passed, the doors yawning like toothless maws in walls that could not be reached, and leading to rooms that appeared curiously inverted and unsettling. Her footfalls clanged on old metal. Wires sang and bolts groaned at her armoured weight, and the catwalks shuddered and swayed.

Below, Celestine saw the woman running as fast as she could. The monsters were catching up to her, though, spilling over one another and uttering their keening cries as they ran their prey to ground.

Up ahead, Celestine saw a break in the walkway. She gripped the haft of her blade tight and leapt through the hole. She spun in the air as she fell, glowing wings unfurled as best she could amidst the tangled confines in an effort to slow her descent. Celestine came down like a comet, slamming into the ground between hunters and prey with enough force to crack the ferrocrete. She rose from her crouch, blade held ready, and eyed the oncoming monsters. They had barely slowed at her sudden appearance, and Celestine saw their gaze was fixed solely on the fleeing woman at her back.

'You shall not have her, daemons,' she spat, and as she said it the word sounded right. Daemons of the Chaos Gods. Her age-old foes. Celestine felt righteous hatred surge within her. She leapt to meet the shrieking daemonspawn with a defiant roar.

Celestine swept her blade in long arcs, hacking at the horrible things as they came at her. Her first blow opened the skull of one daemon and took the forelimbs from another. Her return swing opened another creature's throat, then lopped the head from a fourth. Each wound vomited black ichor, stinking filth like old sump oil that sizzled as it spattered the floor.

The daemons clawed at her with their hooked talons and

snapped with their fanged maws. Yet she realised, as their blows clanged from her armour and rang off her blade, that the creatures weren't trying to kill her. They were frantic to get *past* her, to continue their pursuit. It was as though, in their idiot hunger, they barely registered Celestine's presence at all.

The thought sent fresh anger and disgust surging through her, and she used it to lend greater strength to her swings. Celestine spun, hacking her blade through several daemons then using her wings to smash another into a machine with bone-crushing force. The last beast dropped, broken but still trying to drag itself after its prey.

For all her efforts, Celestine realised that as many daemons were spilling past her as were falling to her blade. A lucky claw-swing rang against her shoulder and buffeted her sideways. A scrambling daemon raked its claws at her face, forcing her to leap backwards with a curse.

'Fight me, you vermin!' she shouted. 'Are you truly so mindless?'

It seemed the creatures were, as they flowed on after their original quarry with hungry shrieks. From somewhere far back amidst the shadows, Celestine heard the fiery brands roar again.

'If I want to save you, I'm going to have to fight at your side,' she said, and launched herself skywards. Celestine beat her wings and shot through the air, weaving a perilous path between jutting chunks of machinery, dangling wires and sagging conveyor belts.

Sweeping over the hunting daemons, Celestine smashed through another stained-glass window that depicted the death of a world at the hands of a blazing orb from the skies. She shot out into a shadowed street, and amidst swirling clouds of ash she saw the woman sprinting up a winding metal stair at the street's far end.

'Wait! I will aid you,' shouted Celestine. The woman didn't even glance back, instead darting around a corner at the head of the stair. The daemons flowed after her.

Celestine beat her wings and gave chase, shielding her eyes from squalls of hot ash that danced like dust-devils down the darkened street. Rounding the corner at the head of the stair, she saw the trailing tails of the woman's robes vanishing into a tumbledown structure at the other end of an alleyway. Daemons plunged into the building's cavernous doorway, and fire flared within it.

With a snarl, Celestine kicked off the wall and powered herself along the alleyway in three swift wingbeats. Raising her blade, she dropped from the sky and slammed down amidst the daemons that were clambering over one another to get through the doorway.

Three swift, hacking blows saw unnatural flesh part and ichor spray. Celestine lunged through the mangled corpses of her foes and into the gloom of the building beyond.

Celestine found herself in a single room perhaps twenty feet wide and double that in length. Four columns had singularly failed in their task of holding the place's roof aloft; it sagged in several places, drab daylight and skirls of ash spilling through. Mouldering pews sat in rows, all facing a low mezzanine at the room's far end. Upon that platform stood a toppled altar, the rubble of what might once have been an eagle statue, and the woman she had been pursuing. She had set her burning brands in sconces at either side of the mezzanine, and they threw flickering light across the old shrine.

'The door, there isn't much time!' shouted the woman. Celestine spun at her urging and saw there was indeed a door on the inside of the archway, hanging open. She grabbed it and, her strength easily overcoming the groaning protest of rusted hinges, swung it shut against the onrushing mass of daemons. The woman was next to her in a heartbeat, sliding a heavy key into the door's lock and turning it with a satisfying clunk.

Immediately the door shook as something struck it from

outside. It juddered in its frame as more impacts came thick and fast. Mindless shrieks rose from without.

'My thanks, angel,' said the woman. She did not seem in any way out of breath from her exertions, standing tall and noble despite her threadbare attire. In the half-light, Celestine could see that her features were graven and proud, with a stern cast to her brow and an intensity in her dark eyes that was unsettling to behold.

'Who are you?' demanded Celestine. 'What are you doing in this place? For that matter, *where* is this place? And why are the daemons so intent upon you?'

The woman smiled, and the expression illuminated her face with beatific beauty.

'I am Pilgrim,' she said. 'I am here because this is where I must be. As to why the daemons seek me so? They detest my strength, my purity. It burns them worse than the ashes that fall from the skies for it has the power to bring hope where none exists, and so they will not suffer me to live.'

'I hate them,' said Celestine simply, and realised with a calm righteousness that it was as true as anything she had ever said.

'Such is only just and proper, for you are an angel of the Emperor, and thus are you righteous,' said Pilgrim. The door shuddered and banged, and she led Celestine away from it, down the dusty aisle of the shrine towards its narthex. Celestine glanced about the structure, noting more daylight filtering through grubby leaded crystal.

'Where are we?' asked Celestine again. 'I have been following a light, was that... you? Do you know of it?'

Pilgrim glanced back at her and smiled, but she did not answer.

'This place is not secure, they will soon break in,' Celestine said. 'How do I help you escape?'

Pilgrim shook her head. 'No, Celestine. Ask that which you really wish to know,' she said.

Celestine frowned, one question falling over another in her

mind. This was the first living being she had met since waking and suddenly she found she had too much to ask and precious little time to ask it in. Could she even trust this woman, she wondered? Her heart said yes, but everything in this realm was shifting and illusory. How could she place her faith in anything at all?

With that thought, she knew what she must ask.

'Who is the Emperor?' she said. 'Why do I know of him, and why do you call me his angel?'

Pilgrim's smile deepened. From the roof-spaces, Celestine heard the scrabbling claws. The door banged in its frame, splinters spitting from the wood. Dark shapes moved outside the windows.

'The answers that you seek are already within your heart,' said Pilgrim. 'The Emperor has been your companion and your guide for a long, long time Celestine. As have I.'

At that moment there came a splintering crash as the door was hammered from its hinges. Daemons spilled through it like a flood-tide of dark flesh, blood-red eyes and flashing claws.

'Get behind me!' barked Celestine. 'Up onto the mezzanine and take up your weapons.'

Pilgrim fled up the aisle, yet to Celestine's annoyance she made no move to recover her brands. Instead she dropped to her knees before the toppled alter, bent her head, and began to pray.

Celestine swept her blade through the first surge of daemons that came at her. Foul flesh parted and she leapt back, beating her wings once and coming down with a thump before the steps up to the mezzanine.

'You will not touch her, filth,' said Celestine. 'In the Emperor's name, I swear it.'

The daemons surged again, and Celestine hacked her blade in a figure of eight, driving them back and slaying several. As the daemons fell, lights flared in the corners of her vision. A glance showed her candles, sitting in sconces around the chamber's edge.

Why several of them had suddenly lit she didn't know, but as she ran another daemon through then lopped the head from the next, more of them blossomed into flickering flame.

There came a sound like the rushing of a gale-force wind, and the tide of attackers redoubled. They poured into the shrine, smashing through the windows in razor sprays of crystal and squirming like maggots through the rents in the ceiling. All Celestine saw was a heaving mass of daemonic flesh, scrabbling limbs, beating wings, yawning jaws, and jagged fangs and talons. Yet she felt no fear at the impossible odds she faced, just a furious desire to fight until not another breath remained within her body.

Celestine swung and hacked, stabbed and parried. She kicked out to shattered daemonic limbs. She drove her blade pommel into open maws and smashed fangs to flinders. The horde mounted like a wave before her, filling the shrine in a grotesque horde of the living and the dead, yet still she fought. Talons raked her armour and slashed the skin of her cheeks. She was driven back step by step, up the mezzanine stairs, yet not a single slavering daemon passed her guard to reach Pilgrim.

With every abomination that Celestine slew, more candles flared to life. They glowed along the flanks of the shrine. They burned bright in dangling iron chandeliers. Their flames leapt in alcoves and drove back the darkness. And now Celestine realised that a furious white light was building behind her. Celestine could hear Pilgrim still praying fervently to the Emperor, and without conscious thought she joined her voice to the chant.

'And lo, though the daemons of the Dark Gods gather around and about, and though all the tribulations of the darksome realm press close upon my soul, still shall I walk in His light, still shall He show me the way and drive back the noisome and the unclean! I am His blade and His righteous angel, as He is my saviour and my lord, for His is the power, and His is humanity to shepherd and protect just as I too shall

shepherd and protect them as His faithful servant! And in His light the heretical and the abomination shall be purged with righteous fire, with flashing blade and holy admonition! Lo, and the darkness cannot touch upon me, for the Emperor protects!'

With those last bellowed words, the light at Celestine's back swelled to a supernova that blazed across the chapel and filled it up with holy light. Daemons screamed and flailed as their flesh tattered like clouds in a gale. They bleached burning white and evaporated, pulsing shockwaves of energy hurling them away and banishing them from existence.

As suddenly as it had begun, the banishment ended, and the light faded away. Yet Celestine saw that the candles still burned, and their warm light filled up the shrine and banished the shadows to the spaces beyond.

She turned, her armour running with daemonic ichor, her skin cut and torn.

'Who are you?' she asked again. Pilgrim rose and turned. Placing one hand upon Celestine's shoulder, she led her around the tumbled idol to a stone font that stood forgotten at its rear. Firelight danced on the clear water that still filled it, and as Celestine and Pilgrim leaned over the reflection, the truth was revealed.

'We look the same,' said Celestine.

'You know that is not true,' said Pilgrim.

'We *are* the same,' amended Celestine, her tone wondering. She looked away from the reflection and into Pilgrim's eyes. She saw her own revelation reflected in the other woman's pupils.

'I am your faith in the Emperor,' said Pilgrim. 'In this place I am given corporeal form. I am the strength you derive from the God Emperor of Mankind, the purpose with which His service fills you, and the righteous strength that is yours alone to wield.'

So saying, she drew the sword from her back and dropped to one knee before Celestine, bowing her head and offering the blade.

'I am glad to be yours,' she said. 'I am glad to be your companion, and I will do what I can to guide you through the wilderness, Saint Celestine.'

Celestine felt shock at the title. Saint? How could she be a saint? Were they not those who had died in the cause of holiness? And yet, Celestine realised, she had seen her own mortal remains dotting the flanks of the bone mountain like morbid shrines. The thought that she might be a being possessed of some form of divinity stunned her. It was too immense a notion to accept, and for an instant Celestine's mind reeled. Then, just as suddenly, she was filled with a sense of rightness as she levelled her own blade and laid it flat against the one that Pilgrim proffered. Celestine was suddenly calm, accepting. There was a flash of light, a keening note, and the two swords became one.

Celestine stepped back, jaw clenching as knowledge and memory flooded through her. Battles uncounted, prayers spoken, speeches delivered in the darkest of hours. She saw the flames of hope and faith that she had lit, and she felt the full and true love for the Emperor of Mankind flow through her.

'Pilgrim, I thank you for this gift, and for these answers,' she said.

'The gift you give yourself. The answers you fought for and earned,' said Pilgrim. 'Call me now by my true name, for I am Faith, she that is embodied within one of the Geminae Superia. I am at your command.'

Celestine smiled.

'Faith, then,' she said, and found that even the word gave her strength. There was much still that eluded her, much she didn't remember, but this was a beginning. Now that the Emperor was with her, in her heart, she felt she could achieve anything.

'Rest now, Saint Celestine,' said Faith, taking up her brands. 'Sleep, and I will watch over you until it is time to set forth once more.'

Celestine nodded, retiring to one of the mouldering pews and making herself comfortable as best she could. She felt safety and contentment for the first time since waking, and as the candle-light bathed her face, her eyelids grew heavy. The last thing Celestine saw before sleep took her was Faith, standing silent sentry beside her, her burning brands ready in her hands.

'The Emperor protects,' whispered Celestine again, and then darkness fell.

405TH DAY OF THE WAR 0730 HOURS
IMPERIUM NIHILUS PLANET KOPHYN
CANYON-CITY TANYKHA ADUL LO:564-3/LA:675-9

Sister Superior Meritorius walked down the Emeritus Canyon, into a sunrise she hadn't thought to see. The Emeritus was one of three primary canyonways within the city, over three thousand yards deep, its walls thick with cavern habs, gantry-ways and protruding structures. Many showed battle-damage from the fighting, but the simple fact that they stood at all amazed her.

She led her Sisters along the ferrocrete highway at the canyon's base, ignoring their muttered prayers and the excited whispers that threaded between them. They passed the burned-out hulks of Leman Russ battle tanks, and dodged around others that were still hale, hearty and rumbling along the roadway. Exhausted Cadian and Astorosian soldiers sprawled by the roadside, some offering weary signs of the aquila to the Battle Sisters as they passed.

'It is a miracle, is it not, Sister Superior?' said Sister Penitence as they walked, her voice tight with restrained excitement. 'The Living Saint walks amongst us, and we are saved.'

'We saved ourselves,' corrected Meritorius. 'The Emperor aids those who fight for themselves, Penitence. Do not forget it.'

'No, Sister Superior,' said Sister Penitence, sounding in no way chastised. Yet Meritorius couldn't deny that their survival was nothing short of miraculous. As she watched rose-and-gold illumination spilling over the lip of the canyon, she supposed that she should feel relief, perhaps even joy. Certainly her Sisters did; she could sense the electric undercurrent running through them at the thought of standing in the presence of the Living Saint.

Instead, Sister Meritorius felt hollow, crushed on some level by the simple realisation that even the coming of Saint Celestine herself did not appear to have rekindled her faith. She saw the rapture and amazement on the faces of the women she led, heard the excited chatter of the more zealous Cadians, and then looked inside herself and saw nothing but the same bleak ashes she had known these past weeks.

Meritorius hated them all for their easy raptures. She couldn't help it, and she hated herself all the more because of it.

Rounding a long bend in the canyonway, Meritorius and her warriors emerged into the full spill of dawn light where it fell through the ruptured remains of Jackyl Gate. Sister Absolom sucked in a breath at the sagging ruin of the gate's fortifications, and the mounds of blackened corpses still burning in the morning sun. Black smoke boiled upwards in greasy columns. The bodies of the dead had been bulldozed aside as best the Cadian tanks could manage, to make the approach to the gate navigable. The loyalists were cast onto burning pyres, over which Imperial preachers spoke rites of devotion. The heretics went into excavated pits that more than one Cadian soldier had used that morning as a latrine.

'There she is, in the gateway,' said Penitence with awe. Meritorius saw, and wished that she shared in the glories that her comrades so keenly felt. Celestine stood atop the wrecked hull of the traitor Stormlord, its shattered carcass jutting half-way through the gates where it had finally been laid low. She was framed against the sunrise, her silhouette rendered angelic by the metal wings of her ornate jump pack and the golden halo of sunlight that played about her head. Hundreds of Imperial Guard soldiery and Kophyni civilians had massed around the tank. Many were knelt in worship. Others cried out in religious ecstasy, or simply stared in adoration.

'And there are Sisters Constance Indomita and Imani Intolerus at her side,' said Meritorius. 'An honour indeed, to be selected as the Geminae Superia.' One I will never be worthy of, hollow remnant that I am, she thought miserably.

Saint Celestine had appeared many times throughout the history of the Imperium, always when the darkness seemed absolute and the servants of the Emperor needed aid most desperately. At such times, it was customary for her to select two Battle Sisters, should any be present, to serve as her Geminae Superia, bodyguards and advisors both. It was said that the act of choosing imbued those Sisters with powers bordering upon the supernatural, though another, darker tale told how they rarely lived to see victory, for the mantle of self-sacrifice in their mistress' name settled heavy about their shoulders.

This had never stopped a single Adepta Sororitas warrior from answering Celestine's call, of course.

Indomita and Intolerus now wore the jump packs and carried the twinned pistols that went with the rank of Seraphim. Even from a distance, Meritorius could see that they carried themselves differently, standing tall and proud beside the Living Saint.

'Come then, Sisters, let us hear what she has to say to the faithful,' said Meritorius. 'I see the Astra Militarum top brass have already answered the Saint's summons. Let us not keep them waiting.'

Major Blaskaine stood near the rear of the crowd with his command staff around him. Captain Maklen of the 230th had joined him, as had Lieutenant Tasker of the 88th. The Astorosian sub-duke could be seen some way deeper into the crowd, surrounded by his strategic court, who all stared with rapturous awe at the Living Saint.

'I'll admit, she's an inspiring sight,' said Blaskaine.

Captain Maklen shot him a sidelong look. She was old for an officer, her features lined and her hair steel grey. Her advanced years had done nothing to undermine Petronella Maklen's strength of personality, however. Now she snorted at Blaskaine's words.

'I'll be sure to send a runner up front at once to let the Saint know you approve of her appearance, Charn.' Maklen's every word was bitten out and crisp, her diction faultless. It was no wonder, Blaskaine thought wryly, that the soldiers of her regiment referred to Captain Maklen as 'Her Ladyship'. Though he had noted it was said with a fierce loyalty.

'You know what I mean, Petronella,' he said with an easy smile. 'Emperor knows the woman turned the entire fight around last night, and I doubt we'd be still living if it hadn't been for her. But still...'

'Still *what?*' asked Maklen, arching an eyebrow.

'Faith has its place within the Imperial war machine, but in my eyes, it should always take a firm second place to solid discipline and rational conduct.'

Maklen snorted again and shook her head.

'Upon her arrival, Saint Celestine descended upon Jackyl Gate and rallied the defenders as they were about to break and run. She killed eighteen Mas'drekkha single-handed then crippled the engines of that ruddy Stormlord and used it to block the breach. Word of her arrival bolstered courage throughout every battle-front on which we fought, and Throne alone knows what she did to the enemy bombers when she arrived. You know that's not even half of it, Charn, and yet you can still stand there giving her that look.'

'What look?' asked Blaskaine, trying to rally.

'*That* look, disdain and cynicism,' said Maklen, turning back to regard the Saint where she held her hands out in benediction to the praying masses. 'It's unbecoming and bad for morale. Besides,' added Maklen quietly, 'while the Saint was doing all that, what were your orders again, Charn? I forget...'

Blaskaine bit his tongue and looked away, feigning interest in the crowd. Retreat had been the soundest strategic option at the time, he told himself. They'd retreated from Cadia, hadn't they? That had been on the orders of old Creed himself, the great and famous general. How could he possibly have factored divine intervention into his strategies at a moment like that? Only a fool looked to their faith to save them at such times; it was a motivational tool, nothing more.

Yet as he looked up at the stern visage of the Living Saint and saw the love and intensity in her gaze as she looked upon the faithful, some small part of Blaskaine wondered whether he had been wrong to think so.

'She's going to address the crowd,' said Lieutenant Tasker, awe and excitement clear in the younger officer's voice. Blaskaine saw that Celestine had indeed stepped forward and held out a hand for silence. Slowly the throng around her quieted, eyeing her with expectant adoration. She was their saviour, that look said, and they would do anything she commanded. Blaskaine shook his head quietly, and made a mental note to keep his head no matter what occurred. Someone had to.

'Faithful of the Emperor, I wish to commend you,' said Celestine, her voice deep and powerful, utterly filled with conviction. 'In the dark of the night you fought like lions. You stood your ground against the heretic, the degenerate and the unbeliever, and you did not falter.'

As she said this, Blaskaine felt as though Celestine's eyes found his for a moment. He looked away hurriedly, frowning.

'The Emperor saw your bravery!' cried Celestine, and the crowd around her cheered. 'He saw your faith, and He heard your prayers,' she said, her voice carrying over the din like a gunshot.

More rapturous cheering erupted. 'He recognised your sacrifices, and He sent you His Living Saint to lead you to victory!' She brandished her silver sword above her head. The dawn sun shone from its blade as the faithful howled their devotion and uttered fervent prayers.

'But our work is not yet done,' said Celestine, motioning again for quiet. It fell swiftly, the crowd utterly in the Saint's thrall, desperate to do anything that would please her. Blaskaine felt her power, the magnetic pull of her, the heat and power of her faith stoking his own. He found he was clutching the aquila that he wore about his neck and couldn't quite convince himself to let it go, for all his reservations.

'The darkness above has fallen across fully half of the Emperor's realm,' said Celestine, her sombre words eliciting cries of denial and moans of sorrow. 'This world of Kophyn is but one of hundreds cut off from the Emperor's light! But all is not lost, faithful! In adversity so we show our true strength, and though His light may not reach us here, now, know that the Emperor still sees our courage and He hears our prayers. Now is the time we must prove our faith by fighting harder than ever to dispel the darkness and drive back the servants of the Dark Gods! Now is the time we must snatch victory from the jaws of defeat! We must raise aloft our shining blades and drive them into the heart of every traitor and heretic until they drown in an ocean of their own tainted blood. Can you do this, faithful?'

Screams.

Cheers.

'Tell us how, Saint!' cried others.

'The Emperor protects!' came shouts and sobs and rapturous screams. Blaskaine shook his head again, this time in amazement. He liked to pride himself on a rousing speech every now and again, but this was something entirely other.

'For now, look to your wargear, gather your rations, and arm those who carry no weapon,' said Celestine. 'Offer prayers to the Emperor and make ready for battle, for there can be no rest for us until this world is returned to the embrace of the Master of Mankind. Emperor go with you, faithful. Be ready to muster when you hear the bells chime.'

With that, it was clear that the audience was over. Blaskaine expected the crowd to linger, and for many to try to reach the Living Saint or beg her personal benediction. Instead they turned, all the rank and file soldiery and the citizens alike, and flowed away into the Adul to do as they were bidden. Many made the sign of the aquila or shot last, adoring glances at the Saint as they departed.

'Throne alive, absolute obedience,' said Blaskaine.

'That's the power of faith at a time like this,' said Lieutenant Kasyrgeldt from her position at his right hand.

'Well, time to discover what the Saint wants of us,' said Captain Maklen as the last of the crowds dispersed, leaving only the command groups of the Astra Militarum and the Battle Sisters standing in the shadow of the gate. Celestine stepped down from the hull of the ruined tank, flanked by her Geminae Superia, and strode to meet them.

'This should be interesting,' said Blaskaine.

'Thank you for attending my summons,' said Celestine, favouring them all with a pragmatist's smile. This close, Meritorius could feel the Living Saint radiating power. Even weighed down by the cold ashes of her own faith, the Sister Superior felt the heat of the Saint's beating upon her. As one, the surviving Sisters of the Ebon Chalice dropped to their knees and bowed their heads, raising the sign of the aquila to Celestine. She motioned for them to rise.

'I don't see we could very well refuse it,' said Major Blaskaine.

'You came to us in our hour of need, after all.' He gestured towards Celestine with a self-effacing smile. Meritorius thought the man was working rather harder than normal to affect his normal insouciance, and felt irritation that he would attempt to diminish the Saint so.

'What would you have of us, my lady?' asked Sub Duke Velle-Marchon, bowing deeply. His strategic court stood around him in their armoured finery, staring with undisguised awe.

'I would have your strength, and your faith, and your aid, Gastar Velle-Marchon,' said Celestine.

'You know my name?' asked the sub-duke, blinking at her through his monocular. He removed his crested helm and ran a hand through his short-cropped hair, bowing again.

'I know the names of all faithful servants of the Emperor, sub-duke,' said Celestine warmly.

'You have the Astorosian Ninth, or what is left of us,' said Velle-Marchon.

'And I am sure that I speak for all my comrades in arms when I say that the might of the Cadian regiments of Tanykha Adul is also at your disposal,' said Captain Maklen. 'But my lady Saint, to what end?'

'Victory, Petronella Maklen,' said Celestine.

'On Kophyn?' blurted Blaskaine. The Saint turned her gaze upon him, and Meritorius saw him quail.

'Yes, Major Blaskaine, victory in the Emperor's name,' said Celestine. 'You harbour doubts?'

Blaskaine looked around and saw the gaze of the other officers upon him, many of them disapproving. The glares from several of Meritorius' own Battle Sisters were downright poisonous. She, for her part, merely watched to see if he would be cowed by the aura of power crackling around Celestine, or if he would fight his corner. Why did she not feel as her sisters did? Where was her awe at this magnificent woman? Why did she alone seem to feel doubt as Blaskaine did, even as she felt anger at his questioning? Meritorius felt such frustration in that moment that she would have done anything to climb outside herself, to be anyone else at all, any one of her sisters whose faith still burned hot and uncomplicated in their breast. Who even was she without her faith? What was her purpose here?

'Yes, my lady, I've a few, as should any officer here who considers themselves worth their commission,' said Blaskaine. 'I know that you've only just arrived here from… wherever you were… but I can only assume that no one has appraised you of the situation. If that is the case then I can only apologise for laxity on our part, but you must understand, lady Saint, that conventional strategic victory is not a possibility on Kophyn.'

Celestine looked serious.

'You believe this world to be already lost, major?' she asked.

Meritorius was surprised to hear Maklen speak up in Blaskaine's defence.

'My lady, with the greatest respect, the major is correct. We've barely six thousand able soldiers surviving between all our regiments, and far too few armoured units to properly transport or support them. What few aircraft we had left were lost last night, as were the majority of our abhuman reserves. We've near as many wounded as ambulatory, and enough supplies and materiel for a few weeks' survival at most.'

'And what of the enemy, and how he came to command such power here?' asked Celestine. 'Sister Superior Anekwa Meritorius, tell me of the War Engine.'

Meritorius' tongue clove to the roof of her mouth as the Saint turned her full regard upon her. She took a deep breath and cleared her throat.

'The War Engine is a renegade warlord, Saint. None have laid eyes upon him and lived, for he coordinates his campaigns from a hidden location that we have been unable to find,' said Meritorius. 'Our mission had barely reached Kophyn when the darkness fell, and the world was cut off. We tried to shepherd the people, my lady, but...' Meritorius found she couldn't look Celestine in the eye. The weight of the Sisters' failure settled between her shoulders and forced her to bow her head.

'But there is much ignorance in this galaxy, and you could not stem its tide at such a dark and terrible hour,' said Celestine. 'Do not shy from failure, Sister Meritorius. Embrace it. Understand what it can teach you. And do not shoulder blame that is not yours to carry. Continue, please.'

Meritorius looked up, but her voice remained low and sombre as she recounted the rest of the harrowing tale.

'When the people of Kophyn could not reach their Emperor, when the astropaths found themselves cut off from the light of the Astronomican, many feared that the end had come. They resorted to local folklore. Grim superstitions that had never been fully uprooted amongst the mountain miner-clans. They directed their prayers to a darker being, and so the War Engine came. A madness spread amongst the people. Sedition. Heresy. The Cadian regiments arrived early in the war, their ships spat from the void storms by pure chance. They joined the fighting, but it was already too late. With the planetary defence force turned, much of the civilian populace mobilised against us, and the War Engine's formidable strategic leadership...' Her voice faltered again.

'Defeat followed defeat, though it was through no fault of Sister Superior Meritorius,' said Blaskaine grimly, and she shot him a grateful look. 'The situation was always untenable. We were on the defensive from the start, dashing from one fire to the next, never able to establish where our enemy's stronghold lay or muster a proper counter-offensive. Not that we didn't give it a bloody good try a few times.'

'What if I were to tell you that I know precisely where the seat of the War Engine's power lies, the source of the madness that has claimed the people of this world, and that it is but four hundred miles from this very spot?'

'I would say that I sincerely wish you had come to us six weeks sooner, when such intelligence could have made a difference,' said Major Blaskaine bitterly, eliciting several hushed gasps from Velle-Marchon's advisors.

'My lady, what are you saying?' asked Captain Maklen carefully, ignoring her superior officer's words.

'I am saying that I know where and how we must strike at our enemy to defeat him and break his grip upon this world,' said Celestine. 'The Emperor did not send me here by chance. I am to lead the faithful in a crusade. A crusade to liberate Kophyn from its Chaos oppressors and return this world to the Imperial fold.'

'My lady Saint, you ask us to martyr ourselves,' said Meritorius, shocked at her own utterance. Celestine turned to look at her again, a strange expression upon her face, but Meritorius pressed on. 'The enemy have millions of warriors and countless armoured assets to hurl at us. Last night we witnessed but a portion of their true power. We will fight for you, Saint, but what you ask of us is suicide.'

'Have faith, Sister Superior,' said Celestine. The thought rose unbidden in Meritorius' mind that she would give anything, anything at all to feel faith again. She knew a moment's panic at the thought her emotions might show on her face, but Celestine carried on without comment.

'What I ask will not be easy. Few of us will live to see its end, for truly it is a martyr's road. But at its end lies the salvation of this world, and the Emperor's blessings for all of those who fought to secure it, the living and the dead alike.'

'You're suggesting we go on the offensive, with a force that can barely make better than foot-marching speed, across the dust plains of Kophyn against a world's worth of enemies?' asked Major Blaskaine. 'With the utmost respect, we stand in the best remaining defensive position we're going to see–'

'A position that you were all too ready to abandon last night, major,' said Celestine.

'Be that as it may, this is madness,' said Blaskaine, looking around for support from his comrades. 'We're all ready to die for the Emperor, my lady, but why throw our lives away so fruitlessly?'

'The foe scattered to the winds after their defeat,' said Celestine. 'But they will return. You all know this. And when they come against you, you will find that this is not a fortress, but a cage within which you will be trammelled and slaughtered. *That* is a fruitless waste, for it serves no purpose but that of the Dark Gods.'

She looked around at each of them in turn, challenging any to dispute her logic. Meritorius could not.

'Well then,' said Captain Maklen after the silence had grown thick and awkward. 'I say bugger it! Why ever not? One last glorious crusade in the Emperor's name, surely better than dying like rats in a hole.'

Meritorius saw stirrings of agreement amongst the assembled officers. Her own sisters murmured loudly in support, several offering up prayers. Still nothing sparked inside Anekwa, though she willed it to with all her might. But she could see the sense of marching out over digging in, at least.

'What of the wounded?' she asked.

'Those that can travel will be armed and returned to ranks,' said Celestine. 'Those who cannot should take to the caves of the Adul and barricade themselves in. With the Emperor's grace, by marching out to war we will draw the gaze of the enemy away from our fallen, for the heretics upon this world serve a bloody god who seeks war above all things.'

'And you say you know where we would go, where we should

strike to potentially end this war?' asked Major Blaskaine. To Meritorius' surprise, the man sounded half-way convinced. She saw cogs turning behind his eyes.

'That is correct, major. If we are strong and true, if we show faith and do not falter, then the Emperor has shown me that we can achieve victory upon this world, and that the truly worthy may even live to revel in it. And even for those who do not, there may be other opportunities along the hard and bloody road. Revenge. Catharsis. Redemption.'

Meritorius saw a muscle twitch under Blaskaine's eye, but the major's jaw set hard.

'Then I'm with Petronella,' he said.

'We can hardly watch others commit to the word of Celestine, and not do so ourselves,' said Meritorius. 'The Order of the Ebon Chalice are yours to command in this, Saint.'

Affirmations came swiftly after that, the last of the officers pledging their strength to the endeavour.

'My thanks, friends,' said Celestine when they had finished. 'We do the Emperor's work. Now, gather about and please, those with maps and data-slates provide them. We must plan our crusade and gather our strength, and time is against us.'

Hidden amidst the smoke-wreathed shadows of the funeral pyres, Unctorian Gofrey had watched the Saint persuade the Imperial leaders to commit to her plan. Now, as their council of war broke up and they went their separate ways, anger burned within him, hotter than the corpse-fire behind which he hid. What kind of fools were these, to be taken in so easily by her honeyed words? No wonder the Imperium had fallen, thought Gofrey, if heretics such as these led its armies.

No, this supposed Saint was nothing of the sort. He knew. He saw with the Emperor's eyes, saw clear and true.

Gofrey had witnessed many terrible things in his life, and he knew a daemon when he saw one at work. Her sudden manifestation, her aura of power, the way she had beguiled all around her with displays of strength and compassion.

So holy.

So convenient.

So false.

The Emperor had already sent a servant to this world, and Gofrey was he. And now, with the arrival of this silver-tongued harridan, he knew at last what task the Emperor had for him. The damned fools before him were already lost to her wiles, but there was one man left upon Kophyn with the faith to stand up to the winged temptress. Before this war was done, Unctorian Gofrey would see the Emperor's justice meted out to she who epitomised all that had brought the Imperium to ruin.

He would banish the so-called Saint and display her true and twisted nature for all to see.

As he turned and paced back into the Adul's depths, Gofrey clasped the thing that hung on a leather thong about his neck. Yes, he thought, he had secrets, and power, and he saw the truth.

'Praise the Emperor,' whispered Gofrey as he vanished into the shadows. 'Praise the Emperor...'

BEYOND

Consciousness – welcome, filled with a dawning sense of purpose. Celestine opened her eyes onto candlelight and took a slow breath. She saw that Faith stood near the shrine's arched entrance, beside the splintered remains of the door.

'You are ready to depart, Saint?' asked Faith.

'I am, but if you will permit me, I have many more questions,' said Celestine. She yawned, stretched, noted that she still felt neither hunger nor thirst.

'I will answer what I can, but I know little more than you do yourself,' said Faith. 'My power lies in belief more than in wisdom.'

Celestine walked to join Faith, her armoured feet ringing against cold stone. She stopped and looked out of the shrine's doorway onto ashen desolation.

'Where is the city?' she asked. Through the arch lay nothing but drifts and dunes of ash, a blackened desert where once had stood the mouldering ruins of civilisation.

'Buried. Burned away,' replied Faith. 'Or else slipped elsewhere through this dreamer's silent maelstrom.'

'What is this place?' asked Celestine. 'Faith, I asked you before but you would not answer me then. Will you answer me now? Where are we? Why have I awoken here? What am I supposed to do?'

'You know where you are, Saint,' said Faith. 'Just as you know that, at this moment, both you and I are of this realm, yet not of it. As to what you must do, I believe that you already know that also.'

'The light,' breathed Celestine.

'For now, you feel it only, but soon I believe it will be revealed to you,' said Faith.

'It is the light of the Emperor, is it not?' asked Celestine.

'The very same,' said Faith, smiling.

'Will I find my answers there, Faith?' asked Celestine. Faith did not reply, but her smile did not leave her face, either.

'How will you travel with me, then?' asked Celestine. 'I won't leave you here, not now that I've found you.'

'I am a part of you, one of the trinity,' said Faith. 'I may fly as you do, if you but believe it so.'

She stepped out through the empty archway into the ashen wastes, Celestine following. A clearing of bare stone spread around the shrine for a distance of perhaps twenty feet in all directions. A perfect circle into which the ash had not settled or slid.

Celestine's attention was drawn back to Faith. She arched her back as though stretching out the kinks from a long night's sleep. As she did so, wings spread from her shoulders beneath her robes. They glowed like Celestine's own, but where the Saint's were formed from the golden light of the noonday sun, Faith's were moonlight-silver, shot through with glimmering streamers of amethyst.

'They are beautiful,' said Celestine.

'They are as much yours as they are mine,' said Faith. 'Now, Saint, lead as you always have.'

Celestine closed her eyes and shut out the hiss and shift of ashes in the cold desert air, the rumble of the fiery clouds above, the distant howling of unnameable things. She sought for the light of the Emperor, and after a moment of silent prayer, she found it.

Warmth blossomed upon her face like a sudden sunbeam falling through a window, and she could not quite suppress a smile.

'This way,' she said, leaping skywards. Faith followed her, burning brands in hand, and their wingbeats whirled the ash into a storm in their wake.

An immeasurable span of time passed as two angels flew on through twisted skies. Celestine attempted to question Faith further, but always the answers were the same; either Faith would assert that Celestine already knew, or she would simply smile her warm and enigmatic smile and fly on without a word.

The lands had become less formless and shifting, the ashen deserts instead remaining a fixture that rolled on beneath Celestine and Faith for miles beyond measure. Eventually they began to see shards of glimmering crystal bursting up through the dead ground. First came isolated outcroppings, then what Celestine thought of as crystal copses. Those soon became a forest until they overwhelmed the ash altogether and melded into undulating crags and hills of jagged crystal through which deep ravines and tunnelled passages ran. The crystal itself described many strange and wondrous shapes and ranged through vivid blues and lurid purples to acid greens and garish, almost sulphurous yellows.

Fires danced here and there upon, or even within, the crystal crags. Some were small and isolated flickers, others sweeping conflagrations that sprawled for miles.

'What fuels those fires?' wondered Celestine. 'There is nothing down there to burn.'

'Sorcery,' said Faith, and now her smile was gone.

As they flew on, Celestine saw that the land ahead was rising. A veil of shimmering silver mists rose before them, then parted like rippling quicksilver to reveal monolithic mountains rising upon the horizon and drawing swiftly closer. Celestine's eyes widened as she took them in, for they resembled tongues of flame hewn from the same crystalline substance over which she now flew. They were beyond immense, soaring up and up and ever up into the roiling void so that their peaks were lost eventually to sight amidst clouds of foul-hued energies.

Somewhere up there, amidst the jagged crags, Celestine saw a faint glimmer of something pure.

'There, the Emperor's light, I see it!'

'Shall we test these wings of ours and fly towards it?' asked Faith.

'I am not sure that even the power of flight could carry us so high,' said Celestine. 'Nor would I brave that swirling maelstrom unless I had no other choice. Besides, Faith, look.'

She pointed with her blade towards the base of the crystal peaks. Down there amidst the desolation rose a crystalline dais the size of a fortress, whose top pressed flush against the lowest slopes. Upon that wide span of shimmering blue-and-mauve crystal could dimly be seen a seat or throne, and upon it sat a humanoid figure. As they watched, Celestine and Faith saw the figure gesture. In response, braziers to either side of the throne burst alight.

'Something awaits,' said Celestine.

'I believe you are correct, Saint,' said Faith.

'Let us not keep this stranger waiting,' said Celestine, tilting her wings and swooping down towards the dais far below.

Celestine's feet touched the crystal dais, and she folded her wings in behind her back. Close to, she saw that the figure sat upon a throne of shattered rock. It was swathed in heavy black robes, and what little of its face was visible was concealed behind a bone mask. It hunched forward intently, and Celestine saw the glint of a sword's pommel rising between the figure's shoulders. It resembled that carried by Faith. Firelight from the burning braziers danced upon it.

'She is not dissimilar from myself, Saint,' said Faith, making to approach. Celestine held up a hand. She felt the intensity of the figure's gaze without needing to see it.

'Caution, Faith, all may not be as it seems,' she said.

'Caution,' spat the figure. Its voice was hoarse and croaking, but recognisably female. 'What time is there for caution, anymore? Approach my throne or begone.'

Celestine exchanged a glance with Faith then stepped forward, blade held ready.

'Who are you?' asked Celestine. 'How do you come to wait for us in this place?'

'Questions and uncertainty,' snarled the figure, and its robes stirred as it shook its head. 'You are not what you should be. You are lessened, a vessel half-empty and not worth the filling.'

Celestine frowned and stopped a dozen paces from the figure's throne. Her hand strayed to the hilt of her blade and stayed there. The crystal mountains towered over the dais, dizzying in their immensity. Grinding thunder rumbled overhead.

'Name yourself, creature,' said Celestine. 'I command you in the Emperor's name.'

A retching noise split the silence. It took a moment for Celestine to realise that the sound coming from behind the thing's mask was laughter, cold and cruel.

'You think you are worthy to evoke the Emperor's name, do you?' asked the figure. 'Very well, Saint Celestine. I am Purpose, and I wait for you here in the hopes that you may yet prove me wrong.'

'She *is* worthy of the Emperor's name, and of His love and protection,' barked Faith. 'She is the Living Saint, the beacon of the Emperor's light and the deliverer of His true servants.'

'You, fasten your lips and know your place,' spat Purpose. 'Faith and entitlement make for poor companions, and many suffer beneath the lash of their good intentions.'

Faith recoiled with an expression of dismay, that turned swiftly to anger. She lifted her burning brands, and Celestine again gestured to her to hold back.

'What have I done, Purpose, that has angered you so?' she asked. 'Who are you to me, that I should care to prove you right or wrong?'

'It is what you have not done, Celestine,' said Purpose, leaning further forwards in her throne. She laid her hands upon its arms, and Celestine saw flashes of pale skin spotted with age, long nails lacquered mourning black. Aquila tattoos ran across both sets of Purpose's knuckles.

'And what is that?' asked Celestine, wary now.

'The war still rages.' Purpose bit out the words, injecting each syllable with venom. 'The Primordial Annihilator continues its rampage at the expense of the Emperor's realm. And here you stand before my throne again, with the temerity to ask what is yet to be done.'

Celestine's mind raced as she tried to make sense of Purpose's words. Though the sense of them was clear, still her memories were full of holes, half-formed and too far occluded to help.

'I do not know of which war you speak, though clearly it is one between the Emperor and the Chaos Gods,' she said. 'You sound as though you would hold me solely accountable for its continuation.'

'Should I not, then?' asked Purpose, and Celestine heard the sneer clear in her voice. 'Yet what was the bargain you struck, so long ago? What was the quest to which you swore your soul, and the reward you were promised for your sacrifices? What was your promise, before you were Celestine?'

'I do not remember,' said Celestine. 'But if this war rages between gods then you cannot–'

'I can, and I must!' snarled Purpose, surging up out of her

throne. Faith swung her burning brands to bear, but at a gesture from Purpose they were extinguished. Another flick of her wrist and the surface of the crystal dais convulsed. Jagged shards whizzed through the air as the dais burst open in a dozen places, and rattling chains of black iron surged upwards like serpents.

Faith cried out as chain links wound around her again and again, binding her in place. Meanwhile, Purpose advanced inexorably upon Celestine, who stood her ground with her sword-point levelled.

'The war still rages, and you come before me asking who, and why, and how,' spat Purpose. 'You should be in battle. You should be spreading the light of hope to those who have none. You should be striking down the unrighteous with the Emperor's own fury. You should already have triumphed, and in your triumph have led all others at last to theirs!'

Chains clattered towards Celestine, coiling in the air then lunging towards her. She struck one nest of links away with her blade, but three more slithered around her arms and dragged them down with strength that even she could not resist. Celestine snarled as she was dragged to her knees, more chains bursting up to coil around her neck and drag her head forwards until she knelt before Purpose as though in supplication.

Celestine heard the slither of metal against cloth, heard Faith give a strangled cry of alarm. She understood that Purpose had drawn her blade.

'If you mean to strike my head from my shoulders then do so, but know that every time I fall in battle the Emperor brings me back,' Celestine snarled. 'I have seen it.'

'It is a privilege hard-earned, not a right freely given,' said Purpose. 'And it is not for you, but for all those whom you serve.'

With that, Celestine heard the sharp swish of the blade through the air and felt searing pain. Yet Purpose struck not at her neck, but at the places where her wings emerged ethereally from her armoured shoulders. Pain exploded through Celestine and she gritted her teeth, determined she would not cry out. Blood sluiced down her armoured limbs, slicking the ground around her. Another swish, another hacking blow, and an awful sense of severing. It was agonising, but Celestine refused to make a sound. She clung to her blade one-handed and strained against her chains.

A third blow came, then a fourth, and suddenly the chains around her limbs relaxed. Light-headed with pain, Celestine nonetheless wrenched against her bonds with all her might. This time they gave, shattering before her furious strength. She surged to her feet, swinging her blade up, dimly registering the twin fires of agony between her shoulder blades and the tattered remnants of her fine gold wings strewn on the ground.

Celestine stopped mid swing, staggering with arrested momentum. Purpose stood before her, hood thrown back and skull mask revealed. Her eyes stared through its sockets, wild and red-veined. Her hair spilled in a grey mane around it.

Before Purpose stood a young girl in a simple white shift, a child no more than eight years of age. Celestine had not seen her approach; she seemed simply to have appeared. Purpose had a fistful of the girl's black hair, and had laid the blade of her sword across the child's throat. The girl stared imploringly at Celestine. Her eyes were dry, and her expression composed despite the blade that glinted before her.

'What is this?' asked Celestine.

'An innocent, one of those you swore to protect,' said Purpose. 'Just one life amongst countless billions. Yet how much can she mean to you, this child, when you stand there with your oath unfulfilled? Kinder, is it not, for me to kill her now and spare her the slow horror of your betrayal? Your failure?'

Celestine's mind raced. She forced aside her pain and confusion, the vast and horrible implications of Purpose's words. She ignored the bone-masked woman altogether as she locked eyes with the child instead.

Carefully, Celestine lowered her blade.

'It is alright, child,' she said gently. 'I won't let her hurt you. What is your name?'

'Don't you know?' said Purpose with a derisive snort. 'Have you lost even that amidst your slow dissolution?' The girl just stared at Celestine, a tiny tremor of her lip the only clue to the terror she was holding in check.

'Just stay still, child, and do not fear,' said Celestine. 'I'll save you from this.'

'You can't save her, any more than you can save anyone else,' said Purpose. Celestine's eyes snapped up and she locked her gaze with that of the woman in the bone mask. The Saint's voice, when she spoke, was hard as clashing steel.

'If you do the slightest harm to that child, then I swear by the Emperor's name that I will take my sword and drive it through your heart. Do you doubt me?'

'I do not,' said Purpose, and Celestine frowned as she heard a slight note of approval in the woman's voice. 'Perhaps there is hope for you yet, Celestine. Perhaps you may still prove yourself.'

'If I do, will you let her go unharmed?' asked Celestine. She had no idea how she might protect this child amidst such a hellish realm, or how she would bring her to the Emperor's light without placing her in even more danger. Even how the child had come to stand before her at all. She just knew, with absolute certainty, that she must defend her.

'I swear it,' said Purpose.

'Then what must I do?' asked Celestine, though in her heart she thought she already knew what she would hear next.

'Climb,' said Purpose, and Celestine closed her eyes, exhaling slowly. She opened them again and looked past Purpose, at the jagged immensity of the mountainside rising into the haze high above.

'How far?' asked Celestine. 'To where?'

'It is not for you to ask such questions,' replied Purpose. 'Is your faith not sufficient, Celestine?'

Celestine shook her head. She slid her blade into the sheath on her back.

'Very well,' she said. 'But if you harm that child, I will hunt you to the ends of this infernal realm, and no amount of trickery or manipulation will be enough to save you from my wrath. I care not which gods rule here, nor how far from the Emperor's light we stray, I will do this thing.'

'Just climb,' said Purpose. 'We will remain behind, for this you must do alone.'

Casting another reassuring look at the child, and what she hoped was a meaningful glance at Faith, Celestine strode past Purpose and approached the crystalline rockface. Close to, it was jagged and riddled with cracks, its surface glinting with shattered reflections. Somewhere beneath the surface, flickering fires danced as though trapped in a glacier or a deep, frozen pool.

Finding handholds would not be an issue, thought Celestine. She stared upwards, and vertigo tried to set her staggering. No, she thought, the danger here was not the nature of the climb, but its hideous duration.

'Emperor, lend me strength that I may save this innocent soul,' said Celestine, and with those words she gripped her first handholds and pulled herself upwards.

At first, the climb was a straightforward affair. Between her own strength and that of her servo-assisted armour, it was a simple enough matter for Celestine to drive metal-clad fingers and toes into cracks and haul herself steadily upwards. The pain between her shoulder blades had not lessened, but she was able to push the sensation to the back of her mind and seal it behind a wall of iron.

The memory of the child's frightened face helped her to do so.

Celestine's thoughts whirled, Purpose's words reverberating through them. What was this war that the Emperor fought against the Dark Gods? Was she truly burdened with its ending, and if that were so, had she truly failed in her duty to end it? How many innocents were suffering for her failures? And why did the thought of that child's peril disturb her so much more deeply than the notion of others' suffering?

'Because it does, and you know it,' she said, addressing her blurred reflection in the crystalline rockface. 'Is it just because she was right there in front of you? Or...' Celestine wasn't sure how to finish that thought, but she knew that she felt a connection to the girl and that it was enough to propel her, hand over hand, up the cliff face.

A glance upwards made Celestine wish that she hadn't looked. The climb stretched endlessly into a kaleidoscopic haze, and the shimmer of the crystal surface made her vision swim with hazy half-images as though the cliff itself were rippling and pulsating.

Jaw set, Celestine looked down instead and was surprised to see that the same many-hued clouds had closed in below her. She had been climbing for a matter of minutes, yet already the crystal dais had vanished into the haze, taking Faith, Purpose and the girl with it.

The climb now appeared endless. Celestine clung to the jagged crystal cliff and took several slow breaths, fighting the irrational panic that seized her at this thought. She had come to take her wings for granted, she realised. Now, with the drop vanishing away below her, she felt their absence keenly. Logically, the ground must still be down there below her. But what if it wasn't? whispered a treacherous part of her mind. This place was as inconstant as the ocean waves, and a million times more mutable. She had no guarantee that, the moment the ground was lost to her sight, it had not been lost to her altogether.

'Faith, if we have become separated, you must look after that child,' muttered Celestine into the vox-bead in her armour's gorget. She had no reason to think that her fellow angel would hear her, but somehow the action felt right. Like maintaining a connection. 'If you can hear me, Faith, you do whatever you have to. Just keep her safe, and I will find you again.'

Celestine took another slow breath then forced her limbs into motion. Whether the ground was there or not was immaterial. Her task was to climb, and so climb she would. She had to trust that she would reach the top of this nightmarish ascent. She had to hope that the Emperor still watched over her.

As Celestine continued to climb, a wind blew around her. It was puckish and gusting, trying to prise her from the rockface. Grim-faced, Celestine resisted its efforts and forged on.

The minutes crawled by and she fell into a rhythm. Seek the next handhold or foothold. Move a limb to it and secure her grip, by force if necessary. Test that her new anchoring point could take her armoured weight. Haul herself upwards. Repeat. Her heart thumped steadily with the exertion, and a slow warmth suffused her limbs. She sought a ledge or deeper crevice where she might secure herself for a few moments' rest, but nothing was forthcoming.

The climb wore on and Celestine lost track of time. The wind moaned and shrilled through the crystal crags. Tatters of purple and blue cloud scudded past her. Occasionally Celestine thought she saw shapes moving in the haze above, dark suggestions of huge, winged things whose attention she dared not attract. At such times she froze, hugging the cliff face and pressing her cheek against the crystal, praying to the Emperor that the mysterious creatures would pass her by. It was not that Celestine feared battle, but in such a place, without even the facility to draw her blade and make a stand, she had no illusions as to her hopes of surviving.

Celestine's limbs began to burn. Her joints ached with the effort of constantly hauling herself upwards. Her fingers and feet grew sore from driving into the cliff face again and again. Though her armour was perfectly fitted and padded, still her skin began to chafe against its inner surfaces through the constant toil. Sweat prickled Celestine's skin, and stuck her hair to her forehead and neck. Her blood thumped steadily in her ears. With so many other sources of pain dragging at her, the fire from her severed wings threatened to break through again and steal her strength with its intensity.

Still she climbed, though she could no longer say how long she had been doing so. Perhaps it had been hours, now? Perhaps it had been days? A small part of Celestine wondered if she had ever done anything else but climb, whether all that came before had simply been an illusion, and whatever hopes she had for reaching the summit were just a mirage. She knew the dangers of such thoughts. She crushed them ruthlessly, yet her doubts could not be entirely driven away.

'Emperor, lend me strength,' she prayed, but if her deity answered or offered her his protection she didn't feel its benefit. Perhaps he could not reach her in this place, thought Celestine with alarm.

'Perhaps it is worse than that. Perhaps he hears you and he doesn't care,' said a voice she recognised as her own, yet she knew she had uttered no words. It took Celestine's tired mind a moment to register that the voice belonged to her blurred reflection, still staring back at her from the crystal depths.

It smiled, though she did not.

She stopped climbing and screwed her eyes shut, keeping them that way for a long moment before opening them again.

Her reflection remained, staring at her with eyes that were little more than warped smudges. Behind it, through it, she saw many-coloured fires flickering.

'I am still here,' it said. *'You cannot escape me, Celestine, any more than you can escape the purgatorial task to which you swore yourself. Your Emperor doesn't care about your suffering. Those you suffer for do not care either. You toil, and you sweat, and you bleed, and none of them care at all.'*

'Base trickery,' said Celestine, beginning to climb again. Her limbs had settled into a position of comparative rest, and now she felt fresh pain throbbing through them as she forced them into motion again.

'Do you even know why you fight?' asked her reflection.

'I fight… for my Emperor,' Celestine said through gritted teeth.

'A god should be able to fight his own battles, do you not think?' asked her reflection. *'And besides, Celestine my dear, you can't lie to me. I'm you. So. Why do you fight?'*

'I fight to protect those who cannot protect themselves,' said Celestine. 'I fight to bring light and hope to the Emperor's flock.'

'Do you indeed?' asked her reflection, and its laughter was the bright crackle of fresh kindling. *'So, you are a martyr, are you? A selfless soul, dragging herself through the purgatorial wastes for the sakes of countless billions who neither know nor care about her sacrifices in their name? That has a rather pathetic sound to it, does it not, my dear?'*

'For the strong to sacrifice themselves to protect those with less strength than they, this is the mark of faith and goodness,' quoted Celestine, drawing the words from her patchy memory of the Imperial Creed. 'For though the almighty flock of mankind may bear little worth individually, as one they serve the Emperor's will, and a single man or woman may magnify their worth to the Emperor a thousandfold through the offering of their blood.'

'Your scripture is a little dated, my dear,' said her reflection with a blurred grin that looked too wide for its face. *'They quote a rather darker version of that creed in this desperate age.'*

Celestine blinked as her reflection shimmered and vanished, replaced within the crystal surface by a hazy image of a battle-field. Skies burned dark over an ashen wasteland of trenches and razorwire. Wrecked tanks burned like will-o'-the-wisps amidst the gloom, and vaguely Celestine saw hordes of soldiers advancing between them across this hellish no-man's-land. In the distance, she saw the icons of the Chaos Gods rising above further trenches and bunkers, while Imperial aquilas waved above the advancing army before her.

The vision shifted, drawing closer, moving with Celestine even as she doggedly continued to climb. She tried to look away, but she could not do so and also search for handholds. Nor could she risk climbing with closed eyes. And so she was forced to watch as the vision showed her the pale, hollow-eyed masses advancing beneath Imperial banners. She saw their cruel faces and pinched features, deep-sunken eyes dulled by stupidity and pain. Priests of the Imperial faith strode amongst them in bloodied robes, and plied gold-handled lashes across their ragged backs.

'Let all sacrifice themselves to protect the Golden Throne, for this is the mark of faith and obedience,' bellowed the nearest priest. 'For the flock of mankind is worthless as all but grist for the mill of battle, and war is the Emperor's will, and lo. The only worth of man or woman is as blood to be spilled upon His golden altar.'

Around him, the soldiers raised a sorrowful cry and pressed forwards into the guns of the foe. Celestine looked away as the slaughter grew bloody, and the image faded, became her reflec-tion again.

'Are these the people you die for, my dear?' it asked, sounding almost sympathetic. *'Surely they too are martyrs to the bloody*

creed of the Emperor you cling to? What difference can you make as just one more wasted life?'

'I do not have to answer you,' said Celestine. 'You are *not* me, and your lies will find no purchase upon my soul.'

'I am nothing more than an expression of your own doubts,' taunted her reflection.

'I do not doubt, for I have the Emperor to watch over me,' said Celestine.

'The cripple, the cadaver locked forever in gilded repose, the careless would-be-god for whose obscene ambitions all of mankind has suffered for ten thousand years,' hissed her reflection. ***'That Emperor? He doesn't watch over you, Celestine my dear. He is little more than a ravenous corpse.'***

With each utterance, Celestine's reflection filled the gaps in her memories. Yet what returned was horrifying, soul destroying. Celestine remembered the Imperium, remembered how, with each new incarnation of herself she had seen it darken and decay. The Emperor was trapped forever within His Golden Throne, the Chaos Gods sent fresh legions to assail mankind's domain with every passing day, and as the millennia ground past so hope and courage were replaced by ignorance, fear and oppression. Each recollection was like a physical blow, making her ears ring and spots dance before her eyes. She felt sick to her stomach, and for a moment it felt as though she might simply relinquish her grip upon the rockface and let herself drop.

Her reflection's grin widened further, nearly splitting its head in two.

'You remember, do you not? You remember the Imperium you fight for, how worthless it all is, how pointless.'

'It is *not* pointless,' spat Celestine. 'There is strength yet in humanity. There is good. There are those worth saving.' As she said this, the image of the child flashed through her mind again, lost now, so far behind. Her reflection wavered, and Celestine saw a suggestion of ghostly images flicker in its place, of loyal warriors fighting on against the odds, of herself standing in their midst with the Emperor's light singing about her and her blade flashing in her hand. The harder she focused, the more the images resolved themselves and the more of her memories slotted back into place. Celestine realised that, for every grim recollection that weighed her down, there was another memory of heroism and victory against the darkness that buoyed her up.

The fires deep within the cliff face pulsed, and her reflection swam back to the fore. Its smile was gone, though its face was still subtly deformed.

'Do you remember how it all began for you?' asked her reflection, brows drawing down into a scowl. ***'Would you like to remember? Allow me to help.'***

Its image wavered away again and now Celestine saw a corridor within a fortress. It was tilted, and part ruptured, mortar spilling in where one wall had collapsed. Flames danced, smoke billowed, and wounded men and women screamed for aid. Celestine saw herself amidst it all. No warrior, this woman. She wore a robe of brown and grey, imprinted with Imperial aquilas in black and gold. She was crouched in the ruins, face bloodstained from a scalp wound, clothes and skin smeared with ash. She looked angry and fearful in equal measure, and Celestine felt again a ghost of the emotions she had felt that day.

'The last battle,' she breathed. 'The Emperor's palace.'

'Yes,' whispered her reflection. ***'The bombardment. The evacuation that came far too late. You were less than a footnote that day, cast aside...'***

'No, I was chosen,' snarled Celestine, and the image before her rippled like a pool into which a stone has been hurled. A huge figure stood over Celestine, light shimmering from his magnificent armour to suffuse the corridor. Her crouch of fear became a protective stance, and for an instant she saw the suggestion of something beneath her, shielded by her body. Golden light reflected in her wide eyes.

The image rippled again, and the figure was gone. The scream of falling munitions filled the air, mingling with the despairing wails of human voices to create a cacophony of the damned. Explosions blossomed and all-consuming flames roared along the passage. Celestine saw herself stare into the onrushing firestorm with a look of utter despair, her hair and robes flapping in the furnace wind, her skin blistering before the intense heat.

'He left you to die,' hissed the voice of her reflection. Yet in that instant, Celestine knew her tormentor had slipped.

'No, he gave me a task,' she said. 'He gave me a choice. A duty. A purpose.'

In the moment before the firestorm struck, the image shuddered again. Celestine's expression of terror shimmered away like the illusion it was, and she saw upon her face a look of such absolute determination that it made her heart swell with pride. Again, there came the momentary suggestion of a shape beneath her, afforded the meagre shield of her body. Then flames consumed everything, and the vision faded.

'Your purpose is to suffer endlessly for the undeserving and the ungrateful,' spat the voice of her tormentor, whose image had now become a formless blur centred around a leering maw. ***'You die, and die, and die again. You will die over and over until the ending of the universe and the final damnation of all. You will watch the stars perish in the blazing heavens, Celestine, and you will know that it was all for nothing.'***

Another image shimmered before her, Celestine clad in the tattered garb of the Repentia, a roaring eviscerator in her hands. Celestine falling amidst her failed sisters, her corpse lying amidst theirs, another wasted death. Celestine focused her mind and the image rippled, revealing her chest still rising and falling as she clung instead to life until her sisters found her and declared her survival miraculous.

'I will be slain, and slain again,' agreed Celestine. 'But each time I die, I will also live, and each time I live I will fight, for that is my duty. That is my side of the bargain that was struck that day. And with each life I will know satisfaction in service, and with each death I will know contentment in acceptance, for with every battle fought and life given I do my duty to the Emperor and His endless flock. And so do I come ever closer to *my* reward.'

With that, Celestine felt fresh strength fill her limbs. At the same time, her tormentor spat a frustrated curse and faded from view, smoke and fire vanishing deep into the cliffs and out of sight.

Celestine looked up and there, above her, she saw a ledge. In the same instant she found herself staring into the large, dark eyes of the child she had left far below. The girl looked over the ledge for a bare instant then ducked back, vanishing from Celestine's sight.

The Saint gritted her teeth and dragged herself upwards with limbs that burned and shuddered. She dug her gauntlets into the cliff face and hauled her armoured weight upwards in a series of lurching movements. She ignored the drop below her, the shapes moving in the murk, the rumble of thunder and flame amidst the clouds.

She reached up again and suddenly she was grasping the lip of the ledge. She hauled, panting with effort, and pulled herself up and over. She rolled away from the drop and onto her back where she lay, heart pounding, limbs burning, breath rushing in and out like a bellows.

'Celestine!' The shout brought her up into a fighting crouch, her sword held ready despite the aching exhaustion of her limbs. She realised that the ledge was sizeable, a crystal platform fifty feet across, and at its rear was a dark fissure. A cave mouth, she realised, leading into the cliff face.

Between her and that dark rent knelt Purpose, her body leant forward and her head lying on a block of gore-stained brass. Faith stood off to one side, burning brands in hand, staring at Celestine for guidance. Over Purpose loomed a huge figure, massively muscled and easily twelve feet in height. The being was part-armoured in dark red plates that were held to its otherwise naked form with brass chains. Its face was hidden behind a blank red helm that mounted curling ram's horns of huge size and bore a stylised skull rune upon its eyeless faceplate. Its skin was marred with scarification, repeating the skull rune over and over again, and in its hands it held a massive headsman's axe.

'Order the blow, Celestine.' The axeman's voice rumbled out from behind its helm in an inhumanly deep snarl.

This blade hung poised, ready to swing down and lop Purpose's head from her shoulders with a single blow. It took Celestine's tired mind a moment to realise that the figure was waiting on her word.

Purpose looked up at her with red-rimmed eyes. Her bone mask was gone, lying shattered to one side. Revealed was the face of a tired old woman, weathered with sorrows and cares unnumbered. Tears tracked across her face.

'I am sorry, Saint,' said Purpose. 'I am sorry for all that I have put you through. I will not ask your forgiveness. I do not deserve it.'

'Where is the child?' panted Celestine, recovering her breath by degrees.

'Gone,' said Faith.

'Gone where?' she asked. Before Faith could answer, the hulking figure growled behind its helm and brandished its axe.

'Order it...'

'It awaits your decision, but its patience is thin,' said Purpose.

Celestine eyed the monstrous figure and felt nothing but revulsion. This was a creature of Chaos, monstrous and tainted. Celestine felt anger at all that Purpose had put her through, the pain and danger she had subjected her to. The image rose again in her mind of Purpose with her blade to the girl's throat, and a wave of hate and fury rose up within her. For the barest of instants, Celestine wanted to command the monstrous figure to strike.

Yet in that same instant, Celestine realised that the anger she felt was not her own.

'Purpose, I know your true name, and it is Duty,' said Celestine. 'And if the Dark Gods think for an instant that I would allow such a tainted abomination as this to act as the arbiter of my will, then they prove only that they cannot possibly understand the depths of my faith, or my conviction, or my strength.'

With that she sprang. The monstrous executioner swung its blade down with all its might and Duty screamed. There was a resounding clang as Celestine's blade stopped the executioner's axe bare inches above the nape of Duty's neck.

'I defy you, as I defy all the works of the Dark Gods,' snarled Celestine, arms shuddering with the effort of holding back the executioner's blade. 'I accept my duty for it is every bit as much a part of who I am as is my faith, and I spit upon you and all your filthy kind!'

Servos whined in her armour as she pivoted, forcing her blade upwards and driving the executioner's weapon back. The monstrous warrior roared, the sound muffled by the faceplate of its helm, and swung its weapon back for another blow. Celestine grabbed Duty by one shoulder and hurled her unceremoniously aside before diving the other way. The monster's axe fell and struck the brass block. Sparks spat from the impact, but both Celestine and Duty were unharmed.

With a rumbling growl, the executioner wrenched its weapon

out of the block and lumbered towards Celestine. Wingless, her back to the empty void, she took up a fighting stance. She was exhausted from the climb and this hulking monster shuddered with unnatural might. Yet perhaps if she could goad it into a reckless charge she might lunge aside and send it pitching off the ledge to its doom.

The executioner staggered as a raging blast of fire struck it from the side. Celestine saw Faith advancing on the monster, burning brands raised and a look of murderous determination on her face. The executioner spun her way, then staggered as another pyrotechnic blast hit it from the other direction. It spun again, flesh blackened, and Celestine saw that Duty was on her feet and wielding burning brands of her own. Wings had burst from the woman's back, shimmering in the colours of ruby and obsidian.

Celestine didn't waste her chance. She charged, ramming her blade through the executioner's back, its tip aimed for the heart. The monster bellowed in pain, stiffening as though electrocuted as her sword point exploded from its chest in a shower of blood.

Muscles rippled under worm-pale skin as the executioner tried to turn. Celestine cried out as her blade was wrenched from her hands. She threw herself flat as the enormous axe thrummed over her head, then rolled away as the executioner's foot slammed down where her head had been.

Flames billowed again as both Faith and Duty hammered the monster with their burning brands, and it staggered with another muffled roar. Blood showered from around both point and hilt of Celestine's sword and the executioner stumbled.

Surging to her feet, Celestine dodged another almighty axe-swing and grabbed the hilt of her sword. With a grunt of exertion, she dragged the blade free.

'Emperor, guide my blade!' she cried, then spun on her heel and whipped her sword in a hissing arc. It struck low and hacked through the executioner's right knee, severing the leg entirely. The creature gave another roar of mindless fury, but it was powerless to stop itself toppling sideways and crashing to the ground. Blood jetted from the stump of its severed leg and poured from the holes in its back and chest. Still it tried to drag itself towards Celestine, axe clutched in one massive fist, eyeless face locked upon her.

Faith and Duty strode closer and bathed the monster in flame until its flesh crackled and body fat spat and sizzled.

Still it crawled, emitting grunting snarls. Celestine eyed the ruined creature with disgust.

'Such are the wages of heresy,' she intoned, raising her blade high. 'Such is the fate of all who defy the will of the Emperor.'

With that, Celestine's blade whistled down and struck the monster's head from its shoulders. Molten gore jetted, spattering Celestine's greaves, and the axeman's remaining limbs drummed against the rock as though its body still fought against death. Only when she was quite sure that it had stopped moving, and was finally, irrevocably slain, did Celestine allow herself to drop to her knees in exhaustion.

412TH DAY OF THE WAR 1300 HOURS
IMPERIUM NIHILUS PLANET KOPHYN
MANSEYT CRATER FIELDS LO:722-6/LA:633-4

Major Blaskaine rode in a borrowed Taurox armoured personnel carrier named *Endurance*. For the past seven days, the vehicle had acted as his mobile command base and Blaskaine had to admit that, for a cramped and often sweaty metal box on tracks, he had become quite fond of the old girl.

At night, when temperatures plunged, he had been glad of the vehicle's ability to pressurise and seal off the interior atmosphere. Now, though, with the midday suns beating down, he rode high in the vehicle's cupola with the hatch open and his cap off. Blaskaine luxuriated in the simple pleasure of the wind blowing through his greasy hair as the Taurox rumbled along. If he was honest with himself, it was a rather pleasant surprise simply still being alive; Blaskaine found his spirits disproportionately lifted by the act of still breathing.

The view wasn't much to speak of, of course. It rarely was on Kophyn. The planet was hard and scarred, a ball of rock and dust that had been deemed worthy of habitation only because of the rich mineral deposits running through its geological strata. Currently, the crusade was advancing across a dusty plain under a hard blue sky, with not so much as a scad of underbrush or a jutting rock formation to break up the lifeless monotony.

Endurance travelled near the head of the straggling column of tanks and soldiery that made up Saint Celestine's crusade. The vehicles were forced to move at marching pace, for there had not been enough armour to mobilise everyone, and so progress had been steady at best. Still, reflected Blaskaine, they had been phenomenally fortunate thus far. Aside from a few scattered cult warbands and a single column of rusted renegade tanks, the crusade had met no serious resistance in an entire week trekking through hostile territory.

'Nothing short of miraculous, really,' he muttered to himself, and was surprised to find he meant it less acerbically than he had thought. Still, it unsettled him; in Blaskaine's experience, an unseen foe was more dangerous than one stood proud before you. He had thought about convening quietly with the other Cadian officers to discuss their absent enemy, perhaps to arrange additional scouting parties, but he had put the decision off. Blaskaine told himself this was because they couldn't spare the scouts. The truth was he couldn't bear the thought that his doubts might be answered by warriors he had long respected now spouting zealotry and talk of unquestioning faith.

He could see her up there, at the very front of the marching column. The Saint, flanked by her Geminae Superia, striding along amidst the Adepta Sororitas. She walked like everyone else, even though he had seen her fly with ease. The message wasn't lost on Blaskaine. He felt a momentary twinge of guilt as he glanced back at the Cadian soldiers marching stolidly through the dust trail kicked up by his armoured personnel carrier.

His reverie was broken by movement below him. Blaskaine scooted back to make space as Kasyrgeldt passed a vox handset up to him.

'Captain Maklen for you, sir,' said Kasyrgeldt. 'Sounds like trouble.'

Maklen's Leman Russ Executioner, *Sunderer*, was half-way back down the column. The potent plasma-tank was barely visible through his magnoculars amongst the dust clouds kicked up by the vehicles surrounding it.

'Thanks, Astryd,' said Blaskaine, taking the bulky handset and hitting the 'receive' rune as his adjutant ducked back into the troop bay of the Taurox. 'Captain Maklen, this is Major Blaskaine receiving.'

'Charn, my scouts are reporting possible trouble up ahead,' said Captain Maklen.

'What nature of peril comes our way?' asked Blaskaine, wondering to himself whether now, as he had suspected, the other boot was about to come crashing down.

'We're approaching the Manseyt Crater Fields,' said Maklen. *'Prime ambush territory. And we're only a hundred miles shy of the Khatmadh'Nul mountains now.'*

'Closing in on Shambach against all odds,' said Blaskaine.

Shambach, the City of Ingots, was the ancient prayer city of Kophyn, and served as both the planet's spiritual and mining capital. It resided in a rocky valley at the feet of holy Mount Imperator. Its blessed mines had been the richest on Kophyn for over a thousand years.

It was also, according to the Saint, the enemy's primary stronghold and the source of the corruption that had beset the planet. She wouldn't say how she knew this, of course, or what precisely the nature of that corruption was, and Blaskaine had become increasingly infuriated over the previous seven days with her firm insistence that he 'have faith and trust in the Emperor'.

Still, he reflected sourly, such blandishments seemed enough for everyone else and he wasn't one to fight losing battles. Privately, Blaskaine figured that dying beneath the guns of one traitor stronghold was much the same as dying beneath the guns of any other, and all would offer an equal chance to salvage some manpower and escape when matters inevitably went south.

'Yes, but we'll never make the City of Ingots if we run and get slaughtered by enemy ambushers out here,' said Maklen, her regal tones snapping Blaskaine back to the present. *'The Salamander crews are reporting huge renegade icons jutting from some of the craters.'*

'Seems a bit blatant,' said Blaskaine. 'Could just be scare tactics, heads on pikes, that sort of thing?'

'Perhaps,' said Maklen, sounding singularly unconvinced. *'It could also portend some dark sorcery or other. Throne knows they've demonstrated ample aptitude for the conjuring of nightmares since this all began.'*

'Well, thank the Emperor we've a Saint on our side then, eh?' said Blaskaine before he could stop himself. He winced at the cold silence that hissed back to him over the vox.

'For a man with the nous to rise to the rank of major within the Cadian military, you really can be a spectacular arse sometimes, Charn,' said Maklen eventually.

'That, Petronella, is beyond question,' said Blaskaine. He knew Captain Maklen well enough to know that, so long as she subjected you to the odd biting insult, you were still on her right side.

'Well, just see to it that such blasphemous twaddle doesn't reach the ears of the soldiery,' she snapped. *'Or, Emperor forbid, the missionaries. If they were zealous before the Saint's arrival, they're positively fanatical now. It's a powerful weapon, might even give us a fighting chance in this madness, but I believe it's made some of them dangerous.'*

Blaskaine's thoughts jumped to one priest in particular, the rangy one with the wild eyebrows and the penchant for baiting the soldiery. He'd had to discipline the man three nights ago at camp when he heard him preaching fire and damnation for all. Since then he'd caught the priest's wild-eyed gaze fixed upon him more than once. It made him deeply uncomfortable.

'You will find no argument here,' said Blaskaine. 'So, what is the best course of action, in your opinion? Circumnavigate the crater field or push on? What sort of delay are we talking about if we go around?'

'Substantial,' replied Maklen. *'But Charn, it isn't our decision, is it?'*

Blaskaine sighed heavily before keying the 'send' rune again. 'No, captain, it is not. Have you advised the Saint?'

'I wanted to warn you first,' she said. *'But you know what she's going to say, don't you?'*

'Press on, and let the Emperor guide our path,' he said heavily.

'Precisely, and that tone of voice is why I wanted to give you a moment to adjust to the notion before I spread the word to Celestine, Tasker and Velle-Marchon.'

'Thank you, Petronella,' said Blaskaine.

'You're a damn good officer, Major Blaskaine. I'm proud to serve under you and I consider you a friend. But really, would a little more faith kill you?' asked Maklen brusquely. *'He's sent us His Living Saint, for Throne's sakes. What more indication do you need that the Master of Mankind still watches over us?'*

Blaskaine scowled, then shook his head and laughed mirthlessly.

'Between you and I,' he said, keeping his voice low, 'I'm amazed there's a single Cadian left with any faith in the Emperor after the death of our world. She was there, too, don't forget. She fought the Despoiler himself alongside Creed, and yet the Cadian Gate still fell after ten thousand years of resistance. It fell during *our* watch. With Celestine present at the death, might I add. There was no divine intervention that day was there? No last-gasp route to salvation for the loyal folk of Cadia. Doesn't it make you feel angry, Petronella? Ashamed? Betrayed? How do you do it?'

'Major Blaskaine, I would have thought it obvious,' replied Maklen, the crackle of the vox making her tone hard for him to read. *'It is only because of our faith in the Emperor that there* are *any Cadians left.'*

With that, she cut the vox-link, leaving Major Blaskaine to

brood. He looked to the eastern horizon and saw that dark clouds were gathering in their path, wisps of vapour coagulating unnaturally quickly into thunderheads that swallowed up the sky. The occluded light of the suns turned watery and grey.

Blaskaine pulled his cap back onto his head and set his jaw.

'Very well,' he said grimly, and found himself hoping that there *were* enemies waiting for them up ahead. He had a sudden, powerful need to shoot something.

Sister Superior Meritorius checked the clip on her bolter for a third time. Still full, she thought. Still clear, well oiled, all in good order. Even now, with all that beset her mind, she found her equipment drills came automatically. They were a touchstone, she supposed.

Warriors stirred around her, and a string of pips shot through the vox network.

'The Cadians and Astorosians have closed up their formation and unshrouded their weapons,' observed Sister Penitence. 'They are ready to advance into the crater fields. At last.'

'That was impressively swift for so large a formation of soldiery, Sister,' said Sister Absolom. Penitence grunted in reply, clearly unimpressed.

The crater fields lay dead ahead, the flat regularity of the plains broken and torn where ancient asteroid impacts had ruptured the bedrock. Some of the craters had lips that rose several hundred feet into the air like the severed slopes of dispossessed mountains. Others simply plunged away into dark pits. From the lips of many craters rose huge icons of Chaos, towering iron shafts wrought on an industrial scale, supporting dark skull sigils the size of landing pads. Their lowering presence was beyond ominous, thought Meritorius.

'The skies darken,' she said, casting her eyes towards the heavens. Overhead, black clouds had gathered until the crusade found themselves mired in twilit gloom. Some of the Imperial tank crews had chosen to activate the stablights mounted on their turrets, and Meritorius found herself glad of their stark illumination.

'Faithful warriors of the Emperor,' cried Saint Celestine from nearby, her voice vox amplified so that it rolled across the Imperial lines. 'We press on with prayers upon our lips and gladness in our hearts. Fear not the shadow on high, nor the symbols of the Dark Gods, nor any threat of foes ahead. The Emperor will test us in whatever way He sees fit, but I know that we shall all prevail, for we have true faith and its light can illuminate any darkness.'

Around Meritorius, her Sisters raised a mighty cheer. She saw the faith shining in their eyes, the ferocity of their determination, and felt the gulf of loneliness widen around her. Self-loathing warred with anger and recrimination in Sister Meritorius' heart. How could she stand before a Living Saint of the Emperor and yet feel nothing? Why had this curse fallen upon her?

Hard-eyed, she raised her voice to cheer as loud as any of them. She had a duty to lead these women into battle, and she would not be found wanting, no matter how clogged with ash her soul had become.

Saint Celestine turned and advanced, her Geminae Superia close at her side. At the same time, the Imperial crusade force surged forwards amidst prayers and hymns, the snorting of tank exhausts and the massed tramp of boots.

'Ten miles of this terrain, give or take,' said Sister Absolom as they strode out at the army's head. The Sisters of Battle formed a black-and-white-armoured spearhead that would lead the push through to the other side of the crater fields. 'Perhaps three hours' loaded march through rough terrain.'

'Do you think the enemy are out here, or have the icons simply made the Cadians paranoid?' asked Sister Penitence.

'We've seen scarce sign of resistance so far,' said Sister Absolom.

'Perhaps their forces are far afield, fighting other Imperial hold-outs of which we've no knowledge?'

'Or perhaps they fell upon Tanykha Adul and are even now closing on our trail,' said Sister Penitence, darkly. 'The Saint soars aloft, surely she can just tell us if the enemy are lurking ahead?'

'She is not a literal angel,' said Sister Meritorius, her voice harder than she intended. 'Even with that artificer pack upon her back, the Saint would have to put herself dangerously out of position to scout the highest craters. Besides which, I would not wish to stray too close to those clouds, would you?'

The first sparks of lightning were now crackling through the clouds overhead. A dry heaviness settled in the air, making everything feel close and charged. Corposant flickered across the towering Chaos icons, making them appear unnaturally energised.

Despite her words, Meritorius couldn't shake the traitorous feeling that the Saint *did* know whether there were enemies out here and had simply pushed on regardless. Thus, it came as no shock to her when, an hour into their march, the groan of vast horns echoed out over the crater fields and masses of silhouettes appeared upon the lips of the highest craters.

'The foe is here,' shouted Meritorius, pressing the arming stud on her boltgun. 'Look to your faith and your firearms, Sisters! For the Emperor, get ready to fight!'

Alarm signals shot back along the tightly ranked column of the Imperial advance. They crackled through vox-channels. They flashed from tank to tank by means of raised hazard pennants. They echoed in the tight, disciplined barking of orders from Cadian sergeants. Blaskaine heard most of themas he sat within the belly of his Taurox with a headset clamped to his ear.

'I need numbers, enemy positioning,' he said. 'Are there any of them behind us?'

'Negative, sir,' said Kasyrgeldt as information flowed in to the vehicle's command console. 'Looks like two sizeable forces, emerging from craters here and here.' She jabbed at the console's rudimentary auspex screen with her finger. 'No word from the rearguard of anyone moving behind us.'

'Split the platoons and push them out to flanks,' said Blaskaine. 'Staggered firing lines with sight-line priority to the heavy weapon squads. They've got bare slopes of rock to charge down, let's punish them every step of the way.'

'Yes, sir,' said Kasyrgeldt, and began disseminating his orders via vox. Meanwhile, Blaskaine switched channels.

'Lieutenant Tasker, do you receive?'

'Receiving, major,' came Tasker's voice.

'Your lot are in reserve,' said Blaskaine. 'Hold the centre, watch our rear, and if the lines look like they're about to break, reinforce immediately.'

'Yes, major,' said Tasker, sounding irritatingly upbeat as always. The lieutenant didn't help his case as he signed off with a heartfelt *'The Emperor protects!'*

Blaskaine scowled as another booming horn blast echoed across the crater fields. He could hear the muffled sounds of tanks and infantry redeploying beyond the hull of his transport and took a moment to feel thankful for good Cadian efficiency.

'Captain Maklen, Sub-Duke Velle-Marchon, Sister Superior Meritorius, do you read?' he asked, keying into the group command channel. Voices came back to him, and he heard battle hymnals being sung in the background.

'Major, the enemy are upon us,' announced Velle-Marchon, with altogether too much relish for Blaskaine's tastes.

'I had noticed, thank you,' replied Blaskaine. 'Maklen, Velle-Marchon, I'm spreading my soldiers out into firing lines. Deploy your armour squadrons along their back lines and lend supporting bombardment. We'll pound them to dust before they get anywhere near us.'

'Major, respectfully, a solid armour charge to either flank could shatter them before they even get into small arms range,' said Velle-Marchon. *'The men are reporting mobs of miner-cultists and turncoat planetary militia, and not a great deal of anything else.'*

'Doesn't that strike anyone as strange?' asked Maklen. *'I know the ways of heretics are obscure at best, but they've had time to prepare for our arrival and* this *is all they offer us?'*

She fed the vid-feed from her tank's turret optics through to their command screens. Blaskaine watched the grainy image of several thousand screaming figures running pell-mell down the slope of a crater to the northern flank of the Imperial force. They were dashing headlong, miner's garb and defence trooper body armour daubed with bloody marks and ashen skull runes. Yet it was true, he thought. This was hardly a masterful ambush.

'There is more to this,' came the voice of Sister Meritorius. She sounded grim, thought Blaskaine, but that was nothing out of character. *'Look to the storm, the icons.'*

The image in Blaskaine's monitor blurred and swung wildly as Maklen ordered her vox-thief redirected. It settled again with one of the obscene icons slightly out of focus at its centre and the black stormclouds heavy behind it.

'Throne...' breathed Kasyrgeldt as she peered over Blaskaine's shoulder. The icon was flickering with streamers of unnatural light, and smoke was boiling up from somewhere near its base, out of sight behind the crater's mountainous lip. Meanwhile, the clouds themselves roiled unnaturally. Lightning flashed through them, and Blaskaine's frown deepened as he realised it was crimson, the colour of spilt blood.

'The enemy prepare to strike at us with deviltry from beyond the void.' The Saint's voice came suddenly through the command channel,

and Blaskaine realised she had been listening in the entire time. The thought made him feel obscurely guilty, though he hadn't been consciously excluding her from command decisions. At least, so he told himself.

'What should we do, Saint?' asked Velle-Marchon.

'Follow your major's orders and pray to the Emperor,' said Celestine. *'They have burned offerings and given sacrifice to the Blood God, and that which they have set in motion cannot now be prevented. We can only endure, with faith in our hearts. Remember, the Emperor's eye is upon us and His protection is upon our souls.'* With that, Celestine cut the link.

Blaskaine blinked. 'Well... you heard the Saint,' he said after a moment's pause. 'Still, if the Emperor protects then He does it with good Cadian steel and massed las-fire, so let's be about it. Captain, sub-duke, you have your orders. Sister Superior, I assume your warriors will bolster our lines?'

'We shall, major,' said Meritorius. *'For the Emperor.'*

'For the Emperor,' chorused the officers, before setting to their duties with a will.

Meritorius jogged into position, her remaining Celestians flanking her. One of her Battle Sisters raised a reliquary on a banner pole at their backs, leading the Cadian soldiery around them in a bellicose battle prayer.

Cadian squads ranged away to either side of the Sisters' position, their lasguns sending hissing volleys up the crater slopes. More Sororitas could be seen peppered along their lines, bolters roaring as they added their fire to the fusillade. The Cadian tanks loomed at their backs, and the dusty soil seemed to jump with the shockwaves as their cannons boomed again and again.

Cultists charged towards them in a screaming mass and died with hideous rapidity. Explosions blossomed amongst their lines, hurling tumbling corpses through the air. Las-blasts and bolt shells snatched more men and women from their feet by the second.

'Their charge won't even reach our lines,' said Penitence. 'The heretics submit themselves to senseless slaughter.'

'The Saint says otherwise,' said Meritorius, casting a glance back to where Celestine stood atop a Taurox transport, her Geminae Superia flanking her. 'There is some heretic sorcery at work here, can you not feel it?'

She certainly could. Even as she raised her bolter and fired into the howling foe, the hairs were standing up on the back of her neck. Lightning cracked dry as firewood overhead, and lurid red. Thunder rumbled like an angry god. The energies gathering around the icons danced faster. They made her feel nauseous to look upon.

'Mist,' shouted a Cadian in surprise. 'Mist rising from the dead!'

Meritorius saw he was right. The ragged remains of the enemy force were still pelting closer, snapping shots off from autoguns and laspistols as they charged. She had no doubt a similar spectacle was playing out on the southern flank. Yet her attention was captured not by the charging foe, but by the seething crimson vapours that rose from the dead behind them.

The miasma grew thicker by the second, and as their guns continued to hammer and the cultists continued to fall, so it swirled and gathered.

'Sacrifices,' she breathed. 'They were ritual sacrifices, all of them!'

The sky suddenly lit with a ferocious webwork of blood red lightning blasts, and amidst a crash of furious thunder a blood-red rain began to fall. At the same instant, searing bolts of energy leapt from the huge icons that loomed over the battlefield. They struck the mist like sparks struck amidst promethium fumes, and a raging firestorm erupted upon the crater's slopes.

Meritorius' eyes widened as she saw dark figures swim into view through the smoke and the fire. Horned heads rose. Bestial roars clamoured above the hammering of gunfire. A sulphurous wind howled down to batter the Imperial lines.

'Gird your souls and stand your ground, servants of the Emperor,' Meritorius cried. 'For they have conjured daemons!'

Major Blaskaine spun the hatch release and leapt from the side of his Taurox, laspistol already in hand. He had heard the terror in the voices spilling through the vox, then everything had been drowned out by a cacophony of howling, shrieking voices that had caused him to tear the vox-set from his head with a snarl of pain.

He had exchanged a look of horror with Kasyrgeldt, then they had drawn their weapons. Blaskaine's boots hit the dirt and, braving the hot red downpour that immediately drenched him, he raised his magnoculars to peer upslope into the infernos that raged to the north and south.

Just as quickly, he dropped the magnoculars with a spasm of horror, recoiling and managing only through sheer force of will not to vomit.

'Throne almighty,' he gasped. 'What in the Emperor's name are those things? Monsters? Mutants?'

'Oh Emperor, sir, this isn't rain, it's blood,' said Kasyrgeldt in horror.

Blaskaine tasted copper. He grubbed blood from his eyes in revulsion, felt it coursing hot and wet over his skin, saturating his uniform. He looked upslope again and saw the enemy – the true enemy – were now charging towards the Imperial lines. Loping, long-legged creatures with red-scaled skin and horned heads brandished black blades as tall as a grown man. Monstrous hounds the size of horses raised baying howls as they barrelled down the slopes. Massive brass monsters burst from the flames and surged forwards on clattering mechanical legs, their flesh-metal forms twisting and writhing as they sprouted cannons and piston-driven claws. And there, amongst the masses, spreading vast, bat-like wings as it loomed to its full height, was a nightmare given living form. Thirty feet tall or more, the daemon lord had a nightmare approximation of a hound's visage and wore a brass helm crowned with jagged horns. In one huge fist it held a black-bladed battle axe, in the other a coiling brass whip. Its body was all dark red muscle and brazen armour plates, and it stood upon gigantic hooves.

Blaskaine's thoughts leapt to the Imperial scriptures that he had read in his youth, to their talk of warp spawn that bedevilled the Imperial saints and devoured the souls of heretics. His mind rebelled at the notion that what they faced here might be no natural enemy at all, but rather some malefic manifestation from the beyond. It was impossible, surely. The worshippers of the Dark Gods were simply deluded, were they not? But then, he thought, an Imperial angel led his forces to battle this day. And if he accepted that, *truly* accepted it, then could the daemons of Chaos not also be real, literal creatures also? He quailed at the thought.

The wicked creature threw back its head and gave a bellow of pure fury that swelled louder and louder by the moment. Cadians fell to their knees amidst the bloody downpour and screamed their terror. The Imperial fusillade became ragged, some soldiers firing wild, others dropping their weapons from nerveless hands.

Blaskaine's vision swam as the roar filled his mind, and suddenly he was somewhere else.

He stood by the runic panel that would close the lander's loading ramp. Flames filled the skies and the ground shook. Behind him, wounded soldiers moaned and prayed, but so few. So few. Out there amidst the apocalyptic ruins of the burning cityscape, he could see the people of Kasyr Haslen striving desperately to reach their evacuation point. They reeled through the smoke, clutching bundles to their chests that he told himself were personal belongings and nothing more. Please, Emperor, they were nothing more. Flames roared. The flight crew screamed at him that they had to leave now before tectonic destabilisation pitched the lander over and escape became impossible.

Blaskaine stopped listening. He watched the people struggle and falter as the ground shook and molten rock burst up amongst them. He looked back at the soldiers in his charge and for one, shocking, shameful moment he thought of his own life, his own desire for escape. In that instant, he made his choice. It was his hand that pressed the runic panel. His voice he heard telling the flight crew to dust off at once and make for low orbit. His ears that heard the despairing screams of Cadian soldiers and citizens who were just yards from safety when he made his choice.

His shame, that would stay with him for the rest of his days.

Daemons surged down the crater slopes beneath a blackened sky. They screamed and howled as they fell upon the hapless Imperial soldiers. Blood sprayed, and heads tumbled from shoulders as the daemonic fiends plied their blades.

Preacher Gofrey bellowed prayers to the Emperor as he fired his pistol full into the face of a needle-fanged monster. His shots blew craters in its foul visage, but it was the vehemence of his faith that truly sent it reeling. Gofrey fired again and again, sending the unclean being howling back into the void whence it came.

'Fight, you cowardly dogs, fight!' he roared. Some of the soldiers around him complied, but they were spraying fire in blind panic. Most could not even manage that, stumbling or collapsing amidst the bloody rain, helpless against the onrushing foe. It had happened the moment the daemon lord roared, thought Gofrey. Some fell curse was upon the Cadians and the Battle Sisters both, and he thought he knew its source.

Unctorian Gofrey turned back to stare venomously at the true agent of the enemy. There she stood, atop an Imperial tank, her wings spread behind her and her blade in her hand. Her chosen Sisters were on their knees, struggling with the same terrors that beset their comrades. Yet Celestine stood tall, her visage set as though carved from stone. Her eyes burned and Gofrey saw tremors running through her limbs, even from this distance, sweat beading at her temples and running down her face. The blood rain hissed off the tank's hull, yet not a drop touched Saint Celestine. No vitae soiled her perfect form, thought Gofrey in disgust.

Fools might take that for a miracle, for the Emperor's power shielding His Living Saint from the corruption of Chaos. They might believe that she was doing battle with the onrushing daemons on some level beyond the physical, in a form that could only be perceived through the senses of the Emperor's angels.

Gofrey knew better. He saw the way reality shimmered like a haze around the Saint. He witnessed, in fleeting after-images, the way the air boiled to flame around her and the ground seemed for a moment to fall away so that she stood atop a mountain of splintered bone and broken skulls. She was a thing of the empyrean, a being spat from the maw of the warp time and time again. What was that but a daemon, thought Gofrey, feeling his Emperor-given senses sing with the truth. Unnatural energies boiled from the Saint just as they boiled from the daemons of Khorne. Gofrey knew what she was, and with the absolute certainty of religious hatred, he reached for that which hung beneath his shirt.

It was time. The Emperor had spoken.

Then, the Saint leapt into motion, and Gofrey's moment was gone.

The daemon's roar filled Sister Meritorius' world.

Sister Meritorius saw not a rain of blood, but of ashes. She felt agony within her chest and looked down to see the chestplate of her armour glowing with fiery heat. Meritorius tried to scream, instead coughing up a blackened cloud of smoke that plumed before her. She couldn't breathe, could barely see. She clawed at her chest and ripped away molten clots of armour that burned into the flesh of her fingers.

Meritorius thumped to her knees, tortured chest heaving as her armour's breastplate burned away from beneath. She looked down at the scorched hole where her chest should have been, felt her sanity teeter at the sight of a blackened flesh crater full of embers that were already dying out. No heart, just a charred ribcage full of ashes. Meritorius looked up, oily tears streaking her face, to see a vast hole burned in the skies high above. That was where the ashes fell from, she realised. Terra, burning, and her faith, burning her alive from the inside out along with it.

All was ashes, thought Anekwa Meritorius. All was lost.

A sudden flare of golden light broke through the suffocating vision. It bathed her like sunlight parting clouds, and as it did the ashes billowed away and her chest became whole once more. She sucked in a screaming gasp of air, and the tears that tracked down her cheeks were once again just tears.

A figure slammed down beside her, and she looked up into the eyes of an angel.

'Saint,' she gasped.

A horned thing lunged, howling, and the Saint sliced it in half at the waist. She spun and stabbed, laying another fiend low before her Geminae Superia thumped down beside her on trails of flame and let fly. Their bolt pistols thundered and more daemons came apart in sprays of gore and ichor.

'Sister Superior Meritorius,' said Celestine as her hair danced in the furnace winds and a golden halo blazed at her temples. 'The Emperor's work remains before us. Will you fight beside me?'

Meritorius opened her mouth to reply, but no words would come. The light, she thought. That golden light, that spilled from the Saint like the rays of a blazing star. How could she have ever thought that light had gone out? Had she truly been so blind?

Strength surging through her limbs, Sister Meritorius rose to her feet.

Embers became sparks. Sparks became flames. Anekwa Meritorius gave herself gladly to the fire as she felt it flow through her.

'I will,' she said and, raising her bolter, she let fly.

Major Blaskaine thought he saw a wall of fire sweeping across Cadia's ravaged surface. He had waited too long, and now they would all be killed. But then he saw it as the dawn, a golden sunrise that filled his senses and warmed him to his very core.

As suddenly as it had gripped him the vision was gone. Blaskaine realised he was knelt in a bloody morass, Kasyrgeldt slumped next to him, as their soldiers fought and died before them.

'Throne above!' he cursed, surging to his feet.

Blaskaine snatched up his laspistol and stared hard-eyed at the horrific melee. He grasped the situation in moments, the same sharpness of strategic thought that had served him so well these last years resurfacing amidst that golden glow.

Though the Imperial soldiery outnumbered them dozens to one, the monsters' trickery had robbed the Cadians of their advantage and allowed them to crash headlong into close combat. Huge, scale-fleshed hounds with brazen collars about their necks clamped their jaws around screaming soldiers and shook them like bloody rags. Hellish warriors leapt and spun amidst the Cadian ranks, lopping off heads with every sword blow. Grotesque flesh-engines the size of tanks trampled through the Imperial lines, raking them with cannon fire, while barely a hundred yards away the daemons' lord stomped and bellowed. Blaskaine clamped down on the bowel-loosening terror that the monster evoked, wincing as he saw it swing its mighty axe and smash an Astorosian battle tank onto its side with a single blow.

'Sir?' Kasyrgeldt's voice was uncertain as she staggered to her feet. 'Sir, what was… I saw…'

Blaskaine nodded, knowing that he must look as haunted as she. He had seen Cadia fall in flame and blood for a second time, and he had thought that was the worst manifestation of the Great Enemy's malice he would ever witness. But now this, now these abominations for which he could produce no rational explanation. Blaskaine found himself hurled into a war between angels and daemons. Adrift upon such maddened tides, he realised that clinging to his trust in strategy and tactics, firearms and ordnance simply would not be enough to keep him afloat. Understanding dawned in Blaskaine's mind, ushered in by his veteran's sense of expediency; he must stay sane and find a workable solution to an impossible situation, one that all the practical teachings of the Tactica Imperialis were singularly insufficient to provide. Thus, as so many had before him, though perhaps not in such stark and pragmatic terms, Major Charn Blaskaine embraced the hope of salvation through faith.

'It doesn't matter, Astryd,' said Blaskaine. 'There's only one word for what we fight here. Daemons. Look to the Saint's light for guidance, for it is a battle beyond mortal comprehension.'

Blaskaine shook his head in mute amazement. Saint Celestine stood amidst the Cadian lines, towering over Sister Meritorius with golden light radiating from her in waves. The Saint swung her sword and a daemon fell away, bifurcated. Another lunged at her and she drove her sword point through its skull, before spinning and hurling its corpse away from her. Her Geminae Superia kept firing, their every shot rupturing another empyric entity and sending it screaming back into the void.

As the golden light spilled from the Living Saint, so it dispelled whatever foul glamour had beset the Cadians. Soldiers staggered to their feet, blinking or praying or scrabbling for their guns. Stalled

Leman Russ tanks shuddered as their crews restarted their engines and tracked their turrets to new firing solutions.

'Charn,' came Captain Maklen's voice over the vox, woozy as though she'd just awoken. *'What in the Emperor's name was that?'*

'Deviltry, I believe the Saint called it,' said Blaskaine, feeling his anger surge. 'Cruel visions meant to render us victims.'

'Cadians will never be victims.' He heard steel returning to her voice, her indignant anger matching his own.

'Cadia stands,' snapped Blaskaine, checking the load on his las-pistol and wiping blood from his eyes.

'And so it shall forever unto the ending of the Emperor's light,' agreed Maklen. *'Now, if you'll excuse me, major, I've got crews to shake into action.'*

'By all means,' said Blaskaine, feeling more himself by the moment. And furious. He felt absolutely furious. The worst and most difficult moment of his life had been turned into a weapon to undermine his steely Cadian discipline, to accuse him of unworthy cowardice; it was a violation of his mind and soul. Worse, it had cost the lives of dozens of his men as he lolled in the dirt.

'No more,' he snarled, grabbing a vox handset from inside the Taurox and pulling it out on its unravelling cord. Fear still threatened to turn his legs to jelly and crush the breath in his chest, but Major Blaskaine's anger and his newfound spark of faith were enough to drive the feelings back. No matter his personal terror, the major thought, his soldiers must see only Cadian courage.

'Blaskaine to all Cadian soldiery,' he barked. 'Get your sorry selves up out of the mud and open fire at once. Feel the Saint's light on your souls. Flamer squads, move up and purge line breakers. Heavy weapons, target those combat walker... beasts... the six-legged things with all the guns. Pray to the Emperor and push these monsters back. Cadia stands! The Emperor protects.'

He saw his warriors rallying as the Saint's light bathed them and his words cut through their terror and madness. Lasguns and plasma guns flashed. Grenades thumped. To his rear, tanks jumped as their cannons discharged, shells streaking through the bloody air to blow daemon engines to pieces.

Then the daemon lord turned towards him, and Blaskaine's blood ran cold. It trampled corpses into the mud as it strode towards him. Its whip lashed out and snatched a Battle Sister from her feet, hurling her through the air to crunch into the side of a tank with bone-breaking force. Its axe swung, and a tank was cloven almost in two, flames and smoke exploding from within.

Without hope or reason, Blaskaine raised his laspistol and fired, again and again. The beams of energy flashed from the daemon's breastplate, leaving no discernible mark. Kasyrgeldt raised her shotgun and added her own fire to his. It made no difference.

The daemon lord stormed towards them, fire licking from its nostrils, vast bat wings spreading behind it.

'It has been a pleasure, sir,' said Kasyrgeldt. 'No matter what happened on Cadia, it's been a damned honour.'

Blaskaine felt a wash of gratitude towards his adjutant, then the daemon's shadow engulfed them and brought cold terror with it.

There came a flash of light, a flare of fire, and something streaked like lightning across Blaskaine's field of vision. Something wet and scalding splashed him, and he fell back with a yell of pain. Blaskaine hit the ground and his gun spilled from his hand. He looked up and there she was, standing over him, wings spread and Geminae Superia stood at her side. The daemon loomed above them, but something was wrong with it. *More* wrong, Blaskaine corrected himself, feeling faintly unhinged.

Its head looked strange. Deformed. And then a great chunk of the daemon's helm simply fell away, taking a chunk of its skull with it. The daemon staggered, half blinded and with boiling ichor spilling from its grievous wound. Celestine flicked bubbling gore from her blade and looked defiantly up at the monster.

'Come then, daemon. Do your master's bidding, and I shall do mine.'

The daemon bellowed and swept its axe in a scything arc, moving far faster than anything so massive had any business doing. Celestine parried, but the force of the blow was enough to throw her sideways into Blaskaine's Taurox. The vehicle rocked on its tracks with the force of the impact and Blaskaine cried out in horror.

The Geminae Superia leapt skywards on trails of fire, unloading their bolt pistols again and again into the daemon. It bellowed and swatted at them as shells punched into its flesh and detonated to leave gory craters. It lashed out with its whip and struck one of the Geminae from the air. She slammed into the ground near Blaskaine, and groaned in pain as she rolled over, stunned and bleeding.

The daemon turned towards Celestine, stomped towards her, raised its axe.

Blaskaine didn't think. He surged to his feet, snatching one of the Sister's bolt pistols, and placed himself between the monster and the fallen Saint. Blaskaine squeezed the trigger and sent one, two, three self-propelled shells slamming into the daemon's ravaged face. They detonated in quick succession and wrenched the daemon's head sideways, ichor spraying from the wound.

For a scant second, Blaskaine allowed himself to believe that he had slain the monstrous thing. Then it turned the ravaged remains of its face back towards him, and he saw nothing but psychotic murderlust burning in its remaining eye. The daemon swung its axe back and then swept it towards him. Blaskaine felt a thunderous impact, then everything went black.

BEYOND

Consciousness, a return to pain, to a quest unfulfilled. Celestine opened her eyes and saw Faith and Duty standing over her, their wings furled about their shoulders, their burning brands in hand. They looked down at her expectantly, and for a moment she felt nothing but exhaustion.

She knew now who and what she was and understood something of the eternal task she was sworn to. Yet still she didn't know precisely *where* she was, why or how she found herself in this place. Her only certainties were that she had to follow the Emperor's light onwards, and that whatever forces were arrayed against her in this place, they surely weren't done testing her. The thought of struggling on just made her feel so tired that for a moment she almost let her eyes close again. Then she thought of how far she had come already, the dangers she had overcome, and the face of a little girl who was lost somewhere in this hellish realm.

It was that last thought that drove Celestine to her feet.

'How long?' she asked Faith and Duty.

'Time has little meaning here,' said Faith.

'Long enough to recover some strength, at least,' added Duty.

Celestine nodded. She gathered her blade up from where it lay near the Executioner's mangled remains. Part of her had hoped that her wings might have been restored through rest, but a flex of her shoulders told her this was not the case. There was nothing there but a deep ache, the sharp soreness of wounds freshly closed. Every joint in her body ached, every tendon and muscle felt stretched past its tolerances, and she could feel every bruise and abrasion from her battles with the daemonic entities of this realm.

Celestine squared her shoulders and shut it all away, deep in her mind. She inspected her blade, as much to give herself a moment to find her centre as to ensure the weapon was in good condition. She'd already known it would be clean, shining, without nick or notch. She knew that the weapon was a gift from the Emperor and that meant it was impervious to the corruption of this place. She hoped that the same was true of her.

'The cave, then?' It wasn't really a question. She could see the glimmer of the Emperor's light, impossibly high above, but without wings there was no way that she could continue the ascent up the mountain's face. Her limbs hurt at the mere thought.

'It seems the only route forward,' said Faith. 'And where there is a path to follow, you can be sure that the Emperor has placed it before your feet.'

'Before we move, Duty, the girl...' Duty shook her head. Celestine noticed she looked younger now, her hair darker, her features a harder facsimile of Faith's.

'I am sorry, Saint, but I know no more of the child than you do yourself,' Duty said. 'If you do not yet remember who or what she is, or why you care for her so, then I can no more tell you than you can tell yourself.'

'And neither of you knows where she went? I saw her, looking over the ledge shortly before I reached it.'

Faith and Duty exchanged a glance, shook their heads apologetically.

'I did not see her, Saint,' said Faith.

'Nor I,' said Duty. 'But I can offer you this gift. My service, Saint, always, and my blade.'

With that, Duty knelt and presented the blade she had borne upon her back. As before, Celestine laid her own sword against it, and in a flash of light the two blades became one. Duty rose, burning brands in hand, and nodded once to Celestine with an unreadable look upon her face.

Celestine took a last look back the way she had come, the warm wind tousling her hair as she gazed from the cliff face out over the formless, hazy wastes at her back. Then she turned towards the jagged cleft in the rockface to her fore and, feeling the faint candle's warmth flicker upon her face, she walked into the darkness.

The cave, it transpired, was more of a fissure. It was jagged and narrow. Celestine, Faith and Duty were forced to pick their way carefully into the gloom, avoiding wickedly sharp shards of crystal that jutted from all around. Strange fires shimmered deep within the walls, clashing with the illumination from Faith and Duty's brands and causing weird shadows to dance and jerk around them.

'At least we don't walk in darkness,' said Duty.

'Rather darkness than the illumination of the unclean,' replied Faith, picking her way around a vicious nest of crystal blades.

'It is the Emperor who provides our illumination,' said Celestine.

She pressed on, her sisters advancing in her wake. As she did, a strange scent assailed her nostrils. It began as a curdled taint to the air, a slight tang of something sulphurous and sweet. The subtle scent became a rotten stench as they pressed on, and soon all three were breathing through their mouths and recoiling from the reek of putrefaction that swirled around them.

'Something unutterably foul lies ahead,' said Duty. 'Yet that is our path.'

A grey-green mist was drifting around their feet now, and Celestine noticed that the crystal walls were streaked with veins of something black and slimy. It spread like capillaries beneath the glinting surface, pulsating slightly and resembling nothing so much as rot or mould.

The fissure ended abruptly, emptying out into a huge cavern. No, Celestine realised, it was not a cavern.

'A tunnel,' she said aloud. Roughly circular in shape, the tunnel's floor and ceiling were hundreds of feet apart, its walls equally far-spaced. It stretched away to right and left, with numerous fissures like the one they had crept through radiating out from it.

It was also noxious. The black fingers of rot became radiating root systems here, burrowing through the surface of the broken crystal on every side. A slick of thick, dripping slime coated the walls and ceiling, and pooled in a stagnant mire upon the tunnel's floor. It was the colour of rancid pus, shot through with vivid streaks of what looked like diseased blood.

'Emperor protect us from the corruption of Chaos,' said Faith, choking on the revolting fumes that rose from the mire.

'Where now, Saint?' asked Duty. 'Do we follow this noisome tunnel or try to find a route onwards through another fissure?'

'This tunnel was not manufactured, but rather burrowed. These side-passages are nothing but cracks, where the over-stressed crystal has fractured due to the passing of something huge,' said Celestine. 'I don't believe they will lead us to anything but a dead end. Besides which, I feel the Emperor's light blooming against my left cheek. I believe that is our path.'

'The sinister side,' breathed Duty. 'Perhaps we will be fortunate, and whatever abomination created this passage has moved away to our right.'

'Do you truly believe it would prove so easy?' asked Faith. Duty snorted and shook her head. Celestine offered them both a grim smile.

'We will be tested, and we will prevail. It is the way of this place and the will of the Emperor that it be so. Come, sisters. Let us not keep our destiny waiting.'

The passage snaked through the crystalline bedrock with a slow, undulating motion. It wound on and on, thick with billowing gases and a heavy stench of rot. The slurry that coated the floor varied in depth, so that one moment they might be trudging through ankle-deep filth, only to find that the next it reached up to their knees or even, for one intolerably revolting stretch, their waists. Celestine was thankful for the sealed armour that covered her body and kept the slime from touching her skin. She felt for her sisters, whose robes provided no such protection. Soon enough they were utterly caked in gangrenous liquid, their faces pale with nausea.

Unnameable things floated amidst the slime, clots of matter and rotted bone that Celestine felt no desire to investigate. The mucal effluent that coated the walls became thicker the further they pressed on, dripping in heavy glops to land with noisome plops in the sludge of the tunnel floor.

Again, Celestine found her sense of time fluctuating. It was hard to say how long they pushed on through the river of filth, the tunnel snaking lazily through leftward and rightward bends, passing through crystalline grottos where stalagmites had been bulldozed aside and left to jut up from the slime in shattered pieces. The journey felt as interminable as the climb before it, an endless wading trudge with no end in sight.

As they picked their way out of another deeper mire and saw the tunnel arc once again to the right, Faith stumbled. Celestine caught her and pulled her upright again, but she saw to her alarm that Faith's skin was sheened with sweat and her eyes were red-rimmed and feverish. Her hair was plastered to her cheeks and neck, and she was shivering as though palsied. The fires of Faith's brands had died, leaving her clutching a pair of blackened sticks.

'Saint, I am sorry, this place...' gasped Faith. 'I ail.'

Celestine looked at Duty, who stood pale and grim-faced but otherwise untouched.

'We will support you, sister,' said Celestine, ignoring the aches and pains that howled from every inch of her body. She swung one of Faith's arms around her shoulders and Duty did the same on the other side. So they pressed on again, slow ripples spreading away from them as they ploughed through the nightmarish river of filth.

From around the next bend, Celestine heard a low murmur of sound, growing steadily in volume as she drew closer.

'Voices?' asked Duty.

'The moans of the damned,' croaked Faith. Celestine felt herself grow cold at the awful sound, felt the hairs rise on the nape of her neck.

Faith's prophecy was borne out as they rounded the slow bend to a ghastly sight. The tunnel bored away from them, arrow straight and disappearing into a haze of brownish-green gases and whirling motes that Celestine realised were flies. The walls and ceiling of the tunnel writhed with movement, and it took her a moment to make sense of it. When she did, Celestine's mouth drew down in horror and revulsion.

'People,' said Duty, sounding equally aghast.

'There must be thousands of them,' said Faith dully, head lolling as she stared through the lank hair of her fringe.

Human shapes carpeted the walls and ceiling of the tunnel, apparently stuck fast in layers of thickened slime. Looking at those closest to her, Celestine saw that they all exhibited signs of decay and disease. Flesh crawled with fat buboes and dripping lesions. Parasites swarmed through lank hair that came away in clumps.

Eyes stared blindly, yellowed with cataracts, while mouths full of rotted teeth and blackened gums opened to emit piteous moans of despair.

'What new horror is this?' asked Celestine. Duty only shook her head, while Faith gave a low moan alarmingly close to the sounds coming from the damned souls trapped in the tunnel.

'Is that something moving down there?' asked Duty, pointing with one of her brands. As she did, Celestine noted its fire was guttering, but her attention was caught by the suggestion of something stirring at the corridor's far end.

Something truly immense.

'Whatever hewed this tunnel and created this hellish place draws near,' Celestine said. 'Here, then, is our test.'

'Do you still feel the Emperor's light, Saint?' asked Duty, stifling a cough. Celestine glanced at her and saw that her sister was beginning to flag, much like Faith before her.

'I do,' she said. The sensation of candle-warmth still caressed her skin, feeling as though it shone down upon her brow like the fleeting warmth of a winter's sun.

'That is... that is good,' said Duty, before her knees gave way and she pitched forwards. Celestine cursed as Duty slumped on hands and knees into the diseased sludge of the tunnel floor, carrying Faith down with her.

Sheathing her blade, trying to ignore the huge form surging gradually closer along the tunnel, Celestine grabbed both of her sisters by their robes and dragged them to where the floor curved up into the nearest wall.

Damned figures turned their blight-raddled faces towards her and gave pleading moans. Several raised shaking hands to grasp at her. Others waved rotted stumps in desperation. Celestine ignored them, though it pained her to do so. She had no desire to lean her sisters up against the slime-slick wall, but it was that or let them slip into the sludge and drown. She propped Faith and Duty beside one another, making sure they still had a grip upon their brands. They looked at her gratefully, doing what little they could to help.

'Saint...' tried Duty. 'I... sorry...'

'Hush, just do not let yourselves become like them,' said Celestine. 'I need you, both of you, if any of us is ever to escape this nether-hell alive. For now, I will stand in your defence.'

So saying, Celestine took several paces back into the slime, looking for more level ground. She braced her feet and brandished her blade, trying to penetrate the murk to make out precisely what was flowing down the tunnel to meet her.

It didn't take long to resolve, and when it did, Celestine wished the creature had stayed hidden. What approached was an immense maggot, its pallid flesh bulging taut and undulating. Thousands of chitinous legs jutted from its mass and dragged it along the tunnel, sending bow waves of filth rolling before it and heedlessly crushing those damned souls unlucky enough to be ground over by its immense bulk. Cyst-like openings squirted sprays of slime with every motion, coating the walls and drizzling down to the floor below. A wave of indescribable stench flowed before the creature, so utterly foul that it made Celestine light-headed.

Worst, though, was the thing's face. At its front, the vast daemon maggot tapered, segments of chitinous armour gathering in overlapping waves around an immense maw. Several circular rows of fangs the size of battle tanks gnashed at her as the maggot got closer. Within, protruding from amidst a mass of pulsating red flesh like some obscene tongue, was a distinctly humanoid head the size of a boulder.

Three eyes stared at her, bulging black orbs ringed red and dripping tears of pus. Cracked and rotted antlers protruded above them, while below was a leering mouth several feet wide, lined with razor fangs and set amidst quivering white jowls and chins.

With a sound like a thousand sacks of offal being shaken together, the daemon maggot drew to a halt, looming over Celestine. She held her blade high, and it glinted in the half-light. Flies and stinking gases billowed around her, and the monster's smile widened. Though it could have crushed her in an instant, Celestine was surprised as the maggot showed no signs of attacking.

'Whatever you are, creature, you stand between me and the Emperor's light,' said Celestine.

'Oh, little Saint,' rumbled the maggot, bilious slime drizzling from its mouth as it spoke. *'I am far too swollen to stand at all. Do you not clearly see my munificent magnificence?'*

'I see an abomination,' said Celestine. 'I see a foul daemon of the Chaos Gods, that I shall smite down with the Emperor's wrath.'

Even as she said it, Celestine knew how ridiculous a threat it was. The creature was several hundred feet in height and she had no way of telling how far back its revolting body stretched. Miles did not seem an unreasonable guess.

'And how would you do that?' asked the daemon in an affable tone, as though discussing an amusing hypothetical with a fractious child. *'I mean you no disrespect, morsel, but you are so very tiny and, well…'* The maggot shook its huge body, causing the entire tunnel to shudder in sympathy. The groans of the damned grew to terrified wails. *'I will devour you in a single bite,'* the monster roared, before breaking into a booming salvo of laughter that caused Celestine to stagger.

'The Emperor will guide my blade,' she said, desperately seeking any place that she could strike at this monster. Its face seemed an obvious target, yet even that was more than a hundred feet above her, beyond rings of cracked fangs and dripping, acidic slime.

'If you only had your wings, eh, morsel?' said the daemon as though reading her thoughts. It pouted its lips in a revolting moue

of mock sadness. ***'But you don't. Your sickly little sister cut them off, didn't she? Oh the irony!'***

As the echoes of the daemon's cheerful bellow rolled away, Celestine stared up at it. Perhaps if she could goad it closer...

'If you are so powerful and I so weak, why do you hesitate?' she asked. 'Come and devour me, if I am but a morsel to you.'

The daemon laughed again, sending ripples rolling down its slime-slick body.

'I do not need to devour such a fragment as you. I wish only to enjoy discourse. You are going nowhere, little Saint.'

Celestine stared defiantly up at the daemon. She stole a glance at her sisters and saw to her horror that blotches and rashes were creeping over their skin as the slime of the tunnel walls slowly sealed itself around their forms. Duty stirred weakly. Faith just lay, catatonic, as the slime lay claim upon her. Celestine looked back at the daemon, despising its knowing, somehow sympathetic smile.

'Whatever you're going to do, you need to do it quickly,' chuckled the daemon. ***'Yet what is there to do, little morsel? You cannot go back. Your Emperor expects you to go only forwards, always forwards. Yet here I am, the immovable obstacle that puts the lie to your irresistible force. You cannot help them. You can only watch them sicken into damnation. Entropy is a beautiful gift.'***

'I do not accept that,' snarled Celestine. She took three running steps and launched herself at the daemon. She leapt high and brought her blade down in a whistling arc, slashing easily through pale maggot-flesh. She was immediately driven back as rancid fat and slime jetted out from the wound and splattered her from head to toe.

She staggered, retching and spitting, coated in stinking filth. As she ground the slime from her eyes she heard the daemon laughing and saw the wound she had inflicted sucking slowly shut.

'I felt not a thing, little morsel,' mused the daemon. ***'But by all***

means keep hacking away. That is, if you don't mind drowning yourself. Grandfather Nurgle has been most generous to me. I am full to the brim with his magnanimity.'

Celestine spat, a small part of her mind screaming in horror as she felt *things* wriggling through the slime that had coated her.

'What do you want?' she shouted, frustrated and furious.

'I just wish for you to realise how damnably powerless you are,' said the daemon, and to her horror Celestine was sure this time that it sounded truly sympathetic. *'You follow your Emperor's light, and a little faith, a little duty, these things are supposed to be enough to propel you along the path? The obstacles He expects you to overcome. The horrors you must face, the hardships you must endure, and for what?'*

Again, the image of the girl's face flashed into Celestine's mind, but as she looked up at the immovable cliff of diseased flesh looming over her she felt despair threaten.

'Oh, I know, how can you ever reach her with me in the way?' asked the maggot. *'Poor little child, lost and alone in the realm of the gods, and you powerless to help her. I don't suppose she'll last long, if she's even made it this far.'* The daemon shook its head sorrowfully.

Celestine's mind raced, but she could not see any way out.

'Your sisters sicken. There are minutes, at most, until they are beyond your aid,' said the daemon. *'You are thinking that you could perhaps flee, drag them with you and find another route. But you know that wouldn't work. You are tired, Celestine. Even your despotic Emperor knows you'll never make it.'*

Celestine felt the truth of the daemon's words as every ache and pain that she had shut away surged back to the surface. Her knees wobbled for a moment. Her grip almost faltered upon her blade.

'I do not wish to eat you, little morsel, but...' The daemon seemed to consider for a moment. *'Perhaps it would be kindest?*

You have failed them, after all.' In that moment Celestine knew that the daemon meant not only her sisters, not only the mysterious girl to whom she felt such a strange, wordless bond. Not even the Emperor. She stared along the corridor at the countless human souls, trapped in despair. Had they all died because of her?

'If only you had ended the war as you said you would,' sighed the daemon. ***'But I understand. You are one woman and it is such a vast galaxy. You have more chance of heaving my bulk aside single-handed than you have of extinguishing the fires of war that swallow the stars.'***

Celestine felt doubt gnawing its way into her heart. Mucal filth had all but claimed her sisters now; they had begun to resemble the other damned souls trapped in this terrible place. What *could* one person do against such overwhelming horror, she thought. Her faith in the Emperor had brought no aid that she could see. Her duty was clear to her, but it was too big for her alone, surely.

'I cannot…' she whispered as a moment of weakness shook her and her exhaustion returned a thousandfold. 'I just… cannot…'

Then she looked up into the daemon's eyes and saw the hunger there, the avaricious leer of a miser about to gather up another armload of coin. She thought about the girl, lost and alone in a land of monsters such as these. She felt a moment's self-loathing at her own weakness but saw that in turn for the trap it was. No, she didn't hate herself for all of this. She hated the daemons that tormented her, and her sisters, and all the other humans that they treated as little more than playthings, soul-currency to be gathered up as a dragon hoards gold.

'You desire me to surrender. To relent,' spat Celestine, standing straighter. 'You want me to give up because you know that the only way you will ever stop me fighting is if I lay down my blade of my own volition,' she said, raising her sword before her again. She felt righteous anger well within her, white hot fury that this revolting mound of offal had so nearly manipulated her into giving in.

'What is there to fight for?' asked the daemon, its tone mocking. *'An Emperor that doesn't care about you? A species of pitiful, selfish beings who know little of your sacrifices for them and care even less? They have all given up already, Celestine, and that makes them wiser than you!'*

Revolting spittle sprayed Celestine as the daemon bellowed, and its rotten stench redoubled in foulness. She ignored both.

'And whose word do I have for that, daemon?' spat Celestine, standing firm against its ground-quaking bellow. 'Ever since I awoke in this place, filth like you have been trying to convince me that my task is thankless, endless, *doomed*. But that begs the question, why would the daemons of this realm keep trying to convince me of such a thing, unless it were a lie designed to rob my strength and steal my will? Unless, in fact, I stand tall in the love and light of the Emperor, a blade in the hand of the entire human race?'

Celestine's voice rose to a shout, and as it did a golden halo leapt into being at her brow. She felt a magnificent unfurling between her shoulders as golden wings grew once more from her shoulder blades and stretched out behind her.

'You are nothing!' roared the daemon, all hint of its former, solicitous tone drowned in a tide of anger and contempt. *'Who are you to stand against the storm of the primordial annihilator?'*

'I am Saint Celestine of Terra, you sack of rancid filth, and until my last breath I will defy you and the vermin-gods you serve!'

Celestine leapt, her wings beating powerfully and carrying her towards the daemon maggot's head. At the same time, golden radiance surged from her like a newborn star, flooding the tunnel and causing the daemon to recoil with a roar of pain.

'I name you the Worm of Doubt,' cried Celestine, weaving

around the thing's huge fangs and lashing out with her blade. 'And I strike you down for all of humanity!'

Her blade bit home, lopping the daemon's head from its fleshy neck in a single, clean cut. The head splashed into the slime, still bellowing in fury, and the monster's body surged forwards, attempting to crush or devour Celestine. Yet where her radiance shone along the passageway the worm's thousands of victims were stirring and gasping, their ailments sloughing away and their strength returning. Thousands of faces twisted in sudden anger as they realised that the worm had fed upon their despair and trapped them within its foul larder. Thousands of hands reached out to snatch at the daemon's rancid flanks, to punch and tear. Warriors drew blades no longer crumbling to rust. Soldiers swung firearms to bear that until moments earlier had been nothing but ancient junk.

The Worm of Doubt writhed as its viscous hide was punctured from thousands of points at once. Celestine felt the blazing heat of flames at her back as Faith and Duty soared up to join her and pour their fire into the ragged stump of the daemon's neck.

'My thanks, Saint,' said Duty.

'I am sorry that we failed you,' said Faith.

'You have never failed me,' replied Celestine. 'Let us finish this together.'

With that, they lunged at the daemon as its victims tore at it from every side. Half drowned in its own filth, the worm's head continued to rant and rave, but its howls became piteous wails of agony as more and more of its fleshy body was torn and blasted. The immense maggot writhed, its limbs lashing out to tear its victims apart by the dozen. It crushed more into paste against the tunnel walls, and snapped at Celestine, Faith and Duty with its huge maw.

They wove easily aside from its clumsy attacks, three angels striking again and again with fire and blade. The light of the Emperor shone from them all, with the radiance of a furious star that burned deep into the daemon's flesh and reduced swathes of its flesh to cracked black ash.

Wailing in agony, the daemon jack-knifed its huge body. Its immense forequarters slammed against the tunnel roof once, twice, thrice. On the fourth impact the crystal cracked and shattered. By the sixth, jagged cracks raced along the tunnel and shards of crystal rained down to puncture the vast, revolting maggot. At the eighth thunderous blow, the tunnel's ceiling sundered altogether, and the entire space caved in with a shattering roar like a billion mirrors breaking.

Daylight showed through the shattered mass.

'Now!' shouted Faith as crystal shards rained around them. 'Before we are crushed!'

'What of the daemon's victims?' cried Duty.

'They have already earned their freedom from this damnation,' said Celestine with warm certainty. 'They are victims of despair no longer, and in death their souls will fly free to join with the Emperor's light. We must follow them.'

Her sisters needed no further urging. The three angels beat their wings and surged upwards through the jagged rain of crystal shards, leaving the Worm of Doubt to be crushed by the devastation of its own death throes.

Above, golden light blossomed, and warmth bathed Celestine's face.

'The light of the Emperor!' she cried, and drove upwards through the last of the crystal rain into the golden skies beyond.

415TH DAY OF THE WAR 1840 HOURS
IMPERIUM NIHILUS PLANET KOPHYN
TWO MILES FROM THE WALLS OF SHAMBACH
LO:801-1/LA:631-3

Blaskaine woke to the sway of the Taurox crossing rough ground. The familiar smell of unwashed bodies in a close metal box invaded his nostrils. The sounds of the engine rumbling and his command staff talking into vox headsets reached his ears. It was comforting, somehow.

'Wa–' Blaskaine croaked, before a coughing fit seized him and doubled him over. At least, it tried to, but he found his movements restricted. He opened his eyes to see Lieutenant Kasyrgeldt and a regimental medicae leaning over him, looking both pleased and concerned.

'Thank the Emperor!' said Kasyrgeldt, hastening to undo the straps that Blaskaine realised were binding him to one of the Taurox's bench seats.

'Careful when you sit up, major,' said the gruff medicae. 'You're still on the mend. Sir.'

Blaskaine waved them away, coughing again as he rolled into a sitting position and immediately regretted it. Pain stabbed at him from what felt like every part of his body. His head felt light and woozy, his limbs weirdly numb.

'W-water,' he managed to croak, and a metal flask was pressed carefully but insistently into his palm. He looked up gratefully at Kasyrgeldt, whose face wore a professional veneer of concern, then put the canteen to his lips and drank.

It was glorious.

'Not too much, sir, you've been unconscious for a couple of days,' said the medicae. 'You've been on thrice blessed intravenous fluids, so your body will need to adjust to the introduction of more mundane humours.'

'Blessed?' asked Blaskaine, wincing up at the man. His head felt muzzy, and something was off about the balance of his body.

'The Saint herself,' said Kasyrgeldt, a hint of awe in her voice. 'You saved her life, she said, and so...'

Blaskaine blinked. The Saint had blessed the medicae fluids that had been pumped into him? Hazy memories pieced themselves back together and he flinched at the thought of the daemonic horror he had stood against. He couldn't picture it now, he found; only a roaring darkness, a blood-fire haze. His mind was protecting itself, he supposed. His sanity might not long survive that sort of memory.

'Sir, your wounds were substantial,' said the medicae. 'Compression breaks, crush injuries, impact trauma. I have done everything I can, but you will need to see an augmeticist as soon as possible. Third grade or above, I would say.'

'Wait, what?' Blaskaine's thoughts snapped into sharper focus at the word augmeticist.

Those who fitted bionic augmetics.

Augmetics to replace parts of the human body too broken to be saved.

He gritted his teeth and looked down.

Blaskaine stared at his broken body for a moment, the foreshortened stump of his left arm, the bulky compression harness whose pipes vanished into his chest and abdomen. The heavy bionic splint-cage that encased his left leg, joints like rivets punching through stitch-puckered flesh.

'Oh,' said Blaskaine in a small voice, then promptly vomited his first drink in three days all over his lap.

Half an hour later, the major had dressed as best he could in a spare uniform. The medicae had, with profuse apologies, been forced to cut holes in the garments to allow for the ugly surgical enhancements. Blaskaine bore the man's attentions with what shaky dignity he could muster. Now he sat on the same bench that he had apparently bled upon, and been operated upon, and then lain upon as he teetered slowly back from the mortal brink. He held a foil ration pack in one hand, in his *only* hand, sucking its paste-like contents through a straw as Kasyrgeldt spoke.

Something in the back of his head wanted to start screaming. Blaskaine instead took refuge in the emotional numbness that had settled in his mind like a blanket of snow. He would bury himself under that blanket for as long as he could. Hopefully he wouldn't have to really face any of this, not really, before their desperate mission saw them all dead.

He realised his thoughts had wandered.

'I'm sorry, Astryd, could you repeat that?' he asked, his words still a touch slower than he was used to. After-effects of the anaesthetic philtres, according to the medicae. Blaskaine wondered if it had more to do with being smashed three hundred yards through the air by... no, he wouldn't think about that. He forced himself to focus on his adjutant, to make sense of her words.

Kasyrgeldt glanced down at the data-slate in her hand, then back to Blaskaine. Masking a flash of sympathy, he wondered, or maybe disquiet? After all, was he really in any fit state to act as senior officer?

'Of course, sir,' she said. 'As I was saying, since the crater fields we have remained undetected by enemy forces during our advance through the agriponic hydroplexes outside the city. In the days since you lost consciousness, we have seen no further sign of the enemy.'

'None?' asked Blaskaine, a sudden surge of suspicion dispelling the fug around his mind like cold water dashed in his face. 'Isn't this meant to be their heartland? Their seat of power? They should be on us like bloodmites.'

'There are several theories,' said Kasyrgeldt, clearing her throat. 'Captain Maklen maintains this must be evidence of further Imperial holdouts still besieged elsewhere on the planet, and that the War Engine emptied his territories of followers in a bid to crush us all. That does seem viable.'

'You said several theories?' asked Blaskaine.

'Yes, sir,' said Kasyrgeldt. 'Velle-Marchon is adamant that the enemy believed their ambush would crush us, that they have arrogantly left themselves no second line of defence.'

'In a hundred-mile radius?' asked Blaskaine. 'No, he's wrong.'

'I thought so too, sir. The other prevailing theory, which I should say stems from the Battle Sisters, is that it is a miracle. They say the Emperor has favoured us and hidden us from the enemy's sight that we might do His work.'

There was a moment's silence between the Cadians, before Blaskaine nodded.

'That also sounds plausible,' he said.

'Er… I suppose… yes, sir, given everything else we've seen.'

'It's alright, Astryd,' he said wearily. 'I know what you're thinking. But why not? We've fought daemons from scripture. We've seen an angel of the Emperor banish them. Throne, when that… *thing* came for her, I didn't hesitate.'

'You were incredibly brave, sir,' said Kasyrgeldt, but he waved her away.

'You never know,' he said, his mind wandering back to his last sight of Cadia. 'Perhaps I've reset the scales a little in my favour. Anyway, what do the other officers think? Meritorius? Tasker?'

Kasyrgeldt cleared her throat.

'As I said, sir, Lieutenant Tasker was killed during the ambush, along with the great majority of his soldiers.'

'Ah. Yes. You did,' said Blaskaine, trying and failing to recall her words. 'And our other casualties?'

'Again, as I said, sir, they were substantial. The full breakdown is here for you to see if you wish, but in essence we have perhaps half our starting infantry strength remaining, a little over a third of our tanks, and a handful of self-propelled artillery pieces. Oh, and the surviving Battle Sisters and priests, of course.'

'So, barely enough to stage a stand-up fight,' said Blaskaine.

'We also have the Living Saint on our side,' replied Kasyrgeldt.

'That we do, Astryd, and she may yet see some of us through this,' said Blaskaine. 'What remains of us, anyway.' He managed not to glance down at his ruined body.

'We can hope and pray, sir,' said Kasyrgeldt. 'We'll know one way or another soon enough. The crusade left the agriponics behind several hours ago and entered the spoil-zone around the city. We've a few last ridges to crest, and then we'll be in sight of the walls.'

'And then, I would imagine, even our luck, blessings, whatever they are, will run dry,' said Blaskaine. 'Still, no sense delaying things. Hand me that data-slate.'

Kasyrgeldt hesitated. Blaskaine realised that the hand he'd tried to reach out with was no longer there. He cleared his throat and set aside his ration pack before reaching out to take the slate.

Unctorian Gofrey lurked in the shadow of Blaskaine's Taurox. The vehicle had stopped on the leeward slope of the last ridge before Shambach, using the high crest of the spoil to shield it partly from enemy eyes. Dozens of armoured vehicles and thousands of soldiers waited around it. They had drawn up into attack formations but halted here to await the final plunge.

Gofrey had chanced a quick look over the ridge, had seen the ancient stone city that rose up in tangled tiers to meet the feet of Mount Imperator. The mine workings could be seen up there amidst the streets of the Orc District, their cavernous entrances glowing with unholy red light.

Spike-lined ditches had been dug outside the city limits, to foul an attacker's approach. High ferrocrete walls had been raised around the City of Ingots, incongruous in their ugly functionality. Their ramparts were lined with various heavy cannons and artillery emplacements and thronged with cultists. Red banners rose above them, while emblazoned upon the ugly walls were runes to both the Blood God and the War Engine. The latter sigil depicted a crude, humanoid figure formed from interlocking gears. It had a horned helm, an axe for one hand and a cannon for the other. Some claimed it depicted the War Engine himself, though Gofrey was confident that was an exaggeration spread around by the renegade warlord to appear more fearsome.

The enemies of the Emperor were given to falsehoods, he had thought, casting a venomous glance towards the Battle Sisters and their so-called Saint.

Gofrey had then drifted down to his current position of concealment, most Cadians giving him a wide berth. A couple of sentries had tried to move Gofrey along but he transfixed them with his wild-eyed stare and nudged hard. They had been a hundred paces away, walking downhill and entirely unsure of their purpose, before they had regained the capacity for independent thought. By then, Gofrey was out of sight and out of mind.

Now, he listened with self-righteous anger as Major Blaskaine held a vox-conference with Celestine and the other crusade leaders. The soldiers around Blaskaine's transport had cheered the man when he had emerged, awkwardly, from its top hatch to survey the scene. Cheered was perhaps too restrained a word. They had all but praised the major as though he himself were another risen Saint.

It had been his self-sacrificing act that had done it, of course, stepping in the way of the rampaging warp entity long enough for Celestine to find her feet, and for the Cadian tank captain to draw a firing solution. The next instant, the daemon had vanished under a hail of artillery fire and sword blows, and the battle had turned from there. Blaskaine had paid for that victory with his own blood. His mangled body would never fully recover.

And the men knew it, Gofrey thought sourly. Oh, didn't they know it. At least Blaskaine had had the good grace to appear bewildered. But that was not enough, for it was all too clear that even the major had now been taken in by the so-called Saint's lies. Gofrey had thought to perhaps take the man into his confidence, but now, as the wounded martyr and talisman of the crusade? Not a chance. Gofrey clutched the thing beneath his shirt and muttered a prayer of thanks to the Emperor for his clarity of sight.

'Yes, Saint, I understand,' Blaskaine was saying. 'So, the Basilisks concentrate all fire upon sector nine of the outer walls, and we rush the breach. That is your plan?'

'Even if the artillery does bring down a section of wall, by the time we cross the open ground to exploit it our enemies will have moved their reserves into position to block us,' came the tinny voice of Captain Maklen through the voxponder. *'I'm sorry, Saint, I'm not sure I see this working.'*

'We will not wait for the breach to be opened,' replied the Saint, her transmitted voice redolent with serenity and conviction. *'I trust in the Emperor. A way shall open for us, and we shall pass through it, then on into the streets and towards the mines before the foe can react. The Emperor has shown me that the source of this world's corruption lies deep within those mines. We will fight our way through to it, and we will defeat it.'*

'You are suggesting that we charge the wall *before* the breach is made?' asked Blaskaine. 'What if our artillery cannot get the job done in time, or at all? We'd be left sat before fifty-foot-high ferrocrete ramparts with no way forward or back, at the mercy of their guns.'

'If the Saint says that the breach will be made, then it will,' came Anekwa Meritorius' voice. *'Have faith, major.'*

'Oh, I do,' said Blaskaine, and Gofrey skinned back his lips at the solicitousness he heard in the man's voice. 'But I must think of the lives of my soldiers.'

'Of course, such is only right and proper, for the good shepherd thinks first of his flock,' said Celestine. *'I will lead my Geminae up onto the walls and we will do what we can to combat the gun crews from there. And my Sisters will lend their prayers to this endeavour, the better to shield our attack beneath the glory of the Emperor's light.'*

There was a moment of profound silence over the vox, during which Gofrey hoped that one or other of the Imperial officers might see sense. Surely the daemon Celestine could not have bewitched them all?

'So be it, I'll disseminate the orders now,' said Blaskaine. 'We move in fifteen minutes.'

'Emperor have mercy on us all,' said Captain Maklen.

'He will,' said Sister Meritorius, and Gofrey was surprised to hear the conviction in her tone.

'He will not,' hissed Gofrey under his breath. They were all damned, then. They would be led to the slaughter like the faithless cattle they were. Well, he would move amongst them like the proverbial wolf, ready to do his last duty for the Emperor.

Gofrey had already nudged a handful of particularly suggestible Cadians. The broken, the resentful, the dismayed – they would follow his commands when the time came. He had a few more candidates in mind, and, by the sound of things, scant time to act.

'Emperor, fear not, there is still one faithful man alive upon this world,' said Gofrey, setting off down the ridge towards the massing Cadian soldiery. 'And he has the strength to do Your will.'

Engines revved and banners unfurled as the order to attack rang out along the Imperial lines. The Cadian regimental standard, with its portcullis gate and eagle-clutched lightning bolts, fluttered proud in the breeze. There was no speech given, no stirring words for a suicidal assault such as this. There was only the presence of the Saint, shining like a guiding star. That, thought Sister Meritorius, was enough. When Saint Celestine had stood over her in the crater fields, when she had banished Meritorius' doubts and raised her up to fight anew, it had changed everything. Meritorius still felt shame, but now it was not at a paucity of faith within her; rather, she felt shame that it had taken her so long to recognise that the light of the Emperor did not shine down from the heavens, but rather it burned bright from within every one of His faithful servants.

She set off at a jog, wielding her bolter by its pistol grip in one hand and her crackling power sword in the other. Her Sisters advanced around her, Imagifiers raising their icons high as the few dozen Battle Sisters raised their voices in the Prayer of Faithful Lambastation. They led the way over the ridge, spoil-grit grinding under Meritorius' boots before the ground dropped away and she found herself accelerating into a run as the slope took her. Imperial Guard tanks and transports roared as their track units rose proud of the ridge then dropped, slamming down as the vehicles accelerated. Massed men and women of Cadia poured in alongside them, hundreds upon hundreds of the desperate faithful charging into battle upon the promise of a miracle.

As she hit the flat ground at the bottom of the slope, Meritorius knew it was a miracle they hadn't already been blasted into oblivion. There was no way the enemy could have failed to detect such a sizeable force outside their walls, and she was just thankful that gunships and rocket strikes hadn't already put paid to their assault.

For all that, she found that she was in good spirits. As the rippling roar of Basilisk fire echoed from behind the ridge, Meritorius realised she truly believed they would open a path. Their shells whipped away towards the city, still a good half mile ahead, and hammered the designated wall section. Fiery explosions blossomed, and she felt their heat within her heart. Meritorius had seen the light, she supposed. Or rather, she had seen what the light of the Saint laid bare. The Emperor was not gone, the Throneworld had not burned. Meritorius knew this now, with a certainty that could only be faith. She recognised that, if there had been a darkness upon her soul these past weeks, it had lain within her, not without. The canoness' death, the coming of the storms, the fall of this planet's faithful; to endure such a string of punishing blows, one coming upon another, and then to find herself solely responsible for the wellbeing of her Sisters in a war that seemed wholly impossible to win?

It was no wonder the galaxy felt darker.

She enjoyed the simple sensations of her footfalls pounding bedrock and her weapon grips in her hands. There had been no miraculous transformation within her, just a gathering of perspective. The realisation had come upon her, as she watched the Saint defeat the daemons of Chaos, that the end had not come yet. Meritorius might not feel her faith as keenly as she once had, but she knew it lay within her still, regathering its strength. For now, she fought for a holy cause in the light of Saint Celestine, alongside faithful and determined Battle Sisters of her Order, for an Emperor who she now knew still watched over her even in her darkest times.

For Anekwa Meritorius, that was enough.

A terrible droning roar began to rise from deep within Shambach. It was an industrial siren whose note had been corrupted into something dark and unnatural. Meritorius realised that the sound was not continuous; it was a voice, forming dark words, bellowing them forth with such a force of hatred that they struck like physical blows.

'The voice of the War Engine,' she cried. 'Shun its words, faithful. They are naught but the bellowing cries of a mindless beast!'

Around her, Meritorius' Sisters chanted louder, more fervently, matching their battle prayers against the War Engine's call.

Behind them, the Basilisks spoke again, sending another hail of shells whipping overhead. Yet now the guns of Shambach answered, and in that moment Meritorius realised just how desperate their odds were. If the barrage-fire of the Basilisks was a roll of thunder, the cacophony of the city's guns was the full-blown fury of the storm. Dozens of wall-guns lit with fire. Emplacement weaponry opened up, heavy bolters and stubbers chugging mercilessly as they spat shells at the charging Imperial army. Deeper booms rolled from within the city bounds, explosives sailing up from hidden artillery positions to plunge down upon the Imperial lines.

'The Emperor protects!' cried Saint Celestine, who soared at the front of the army with her jump-pack wings spread and her sword raised.

The next instant fire and thunder transformed the world. The ground shook beneath Meritorius' feet, almost throwing her onto her face. Her armour's inertial dampeners kicked in, compensating for buffeting shockwaves of overpressure. Explosions blinded and deafened her, and as they cleared she saw sundered bedrock and bloody bodies raining from the skies.

Imperial tanks burned, their gutted carcasses rolling to a stop.

Wounded soldiers lay and screamed in horror, in agony, in fury.

Yet the Saint's light was still there, untouched at the forefront of the assault, shining bright as the Emperor's own Astronomican to guide their way.

'Do not slow your pace!' ordered Meritorius, her voice vox amplified to carry over the terrible roar of battle. 'Sisters, commence the prayer of Holy Abjuration!' The Sororitas raised their voices in plainsong again, and as they did so a shimmering haze grew in the air around them.

Artillery boomed. Shells filled the air, whipping both ways.

More explosions.

More death.

'Beware the ditches,' came Captain Blaskaine's voice over the general command channel. Yet it was not so easy, amidst the smoke and mayhem. Meritorius herself almost pitched forwards into a yawning trench. The metal spikes that lined it made it look like some monster's starving maw. She leapt the gap, thumping down on the other side. Several of her Sisters were less fortunate, and cries of pain rose behind her as they fell.

A trio of Leman Russ battle tanks thundered past on Meritorius' right, cannon barrels elevated. The trio fired, shots whipping away to slam into the ramparts with explosive force. Enemy field guns disintegrated, their ammunition touching off and raising a rippling firestorm that reduced screaming heretics to windblown ash.

Meritorius bellowed an inarticulate sound of triumph at the sight, that was choked off as a massive shell whistled down and landed upon the central tank. She shielded her eyes before the blast blinded her, but this time she was thrown from her feet. As Sister Penitence hauled her upright, Meritorius saw that two of the Leman Russes were nothing but wreckage while the third was still forging on towards the walls with one track unit half torn away and its hull aflame.

'Keep moving!' cried Meritorius to whoever could still hear her. 'Sisters, raise your prayers to the Emperor in this dark hour!'

She ran again, heading for the walls, following the light of the Saint as it shot away towards the ramparts. Around her, her Sisters' voices soared and this time the hazy illumination blazed.

'Whatever that is,' came Captain Maklen's voice over the vox, *'keep it up! Look at the enemy gun crews, they're blinded!'*

Without the benefit of multi-spectral augurs and targetter arrays, Meritorius could see nothing of the foe, but she had faith, and sure enough the enemy's bombardment slackened as the Sisters continued to sing.

Meritorius surged through the smoke, still leading more than twenty Sisters of Battle, who in turn led hundreds of screaming Cadian soldiers. Explosions blossomed ahead, showing where the Basilisks' shells struck the wall yet again.

They were so close now. This must be it.

She burst through the last whipping trails of smoke and staggered to a halt.

Wall section nine still stood.

Battered. Blasted. Riven with gaping cracks, and ablaze from one end of its battlements to the other.

But still very much intact.

Shots rained down from neighbouring wall sections, punching two of Meritorius' Sisters from their feet. Cadians staggered in behind them, their massed ranks easy targets gathering barely a hundred feet from the foot of the wall. The ravaged remains of the War Engine's glyph leered down at them. To Anekwa's eye it looked triumphant.

'Find cover!' she barked. 'Suppressing fire against the walltop. Heavy weapons, hit the breach with everything you have. Flamers, burn those heretics you can reach. Faith and determination, sisters and brothers. The Emperor will not forsake us!' She raised her bolter and sprayed shots up at the walls, hoping against hope that her words rang true.

Within his Taurox, Blaskaine swore quietly and vociferously. The runic display on his auspex was crude, but it showed him enough. He saw the Saint atop the walls, wreaking a platoon's worth of butchery amongst the enemy gun crews. He saw the Basilisks continuing their bombardment of section nine. But he also saw the Imperial advance stymied as it reached a breach that did not yet exist. The attack was piling up, spreading out like liquid pooling against a flat surface.

'Spread them out,' Blaskaine ordered over the vox. 'Use the shell holes and wrecks for cover. Maintain fire.'

It was all he could do. His Taurox was halfway across no-man's-land, picking its way between the ditches, following a pair of Leman Russ Punishers towards the walls. They were amongst the rear lines of the attack, but they would be at the walls soon enough.

'And what then?' he asked himself.

'Sir?' queried Kasyrgeldt, lifting one earphone of her headset.

'What then, Astryd? Do we just mass at the walls and wait? We'll be butchered in a matter of minutes.'

'The Saint said we must have faith, sir,' said Kasyrgeldt, and Blaskaine nodded in frustration. The churn of emotions in his chest was too complex to convey: that he *did* feel faith in a way he hadn't ever, even before Cadia's fall; that he had to preserve the lives of his soldiers if he could; that every line of strategic scripture he had ever learned was screaming at him to order a retreat and rethink this suicidal assault; that he desperately didn't want to admit defeat and pull back those assets that could yet be saved, lest he see again those he left behind on Cadia reflected in every soldier who fell during the subsequent rout.

Instead, Blaskaine settled for a surly grunt. His eyes flicked to the vid-feed from one of Maklen's tanks near the wall. It showed the Saint, glowing like a star as she leapt and spun along the rampart with her blade lashing and stabbing. Heretics flung themselves at her and were smashed away, sent flailing over the ramparts or hacked into bloody rags. The Geminae Superia fought at their mistress' side, pistols blazing as they gunned down artillery crews and heretic militia. It was a stirring sight, but alone, Blaskaine knew it still wasn't enough. Then, over the vox, came a desperate voice that filled his veins with ice.

'Mayday, mayday, this is Gunnery Sergeant Hokwis to any available Imperial forces! Basilisk battery under attack! Repeat, we are under attack by massed cultist forces! Origin of assault unknown, numbers overwhelming! Creed's ghost, they've got Mas'drekkha leading them! Repe–'

Hokwis' voice cut out amidst a squeal of static. Blaskaine looked at Kasyrgeldt, her horrified expression echoing his own.

'No artillery, no breach,' she breathed.

'Throne *damn* it,' snarled Blaskaine, trying to thump the console with a fist he no longer possessed. This was not how the attack was meant to go. He had seen the glory of the Saint. He had *saved* her, for Terra's sakes! How could things turn out this way? Was this his punishment for Cadia, he wondered? Was it a punishment upon all of them for letting the Gate fall?

No. This wasn't the work of the Emperor. That still lay before them, he realised, no matter the odds, no matter the cost.

'This is Blaskaine to all forces,' he barked over the vox. 'All small arms, concentrate upon the walltop. Everything heavier than a damn lasgun, fire on the breach. We'll make a gap even if we have to tear the walls down with our bare hands! The Emperor expects of us, ladies and gentlemen, and we shall not disappoint Him!'

'Noble sentiment, major, but let the armour handle this, eh?' Captain

Maklen was addressing him on a private channel. He frowned, glancing at the auspex to see her designator rune moving towards the front lines. Several of her most veteran engines formed a spearhead in front of her Executioner, and infantry scattered from their path.

'Captain, even your guns aren't going to bring that wall down without an awful lot of supporting fire and a Throne-sent miracle,' said Blaskaine.

'I am well aware of the tolerances and capabilities of my engines, major,' replied Maklen, her tone haughty.

'Then what… Wait, Petronella, what are you doing?' He gripped the console with his remaining hand as he realised her spearhead wasn't slowing. One Russ' signifier blinked out, then a second. Maklen and the two remaining tanks forged on, almost at the front lines now.

'There can be no greater demonstration of one's faith in the Emperor than to offer up that which one holds most dear upon the altar of His greatness,' said Maklen.

'Don't quote scripture at me now, captain!' snapped Blaskaine. 'This is not the time!'

'I would say it is precisely the time, since I shan't be getting another chance,' replied Maklen, and Blaskaine heard an undercurrent of sorrow and acceptance beneath her dignified tone.

'Captain! Your experience and skill are required if we are to carry this attack home. Whatever you are planning, I order you to halt your advance and fire upon the breach immediately!' barked Blaskaine.

'I'm sorry, major, but you know there's only one way that wall is coming down now. Thing about running helm on an Executioner, you accept early on that you're essentially in charge of a damn great bomb on tracks. I've had a better run than most, and it's been an honour to serve alongside you.'

'Petronella, there's another way!' he said as he saw her tank's rune break the front line and race for the breach, the two remaining Russ designators peeling off to let her go. 'There has to be!'

'Faith, duty and sacrifice,' came Petronella Maklen's last words over the vox.

Sister Meritorius saw the plasma tank surge out of the Imperial lines, rolling over the bodies of the dead, ploughing through flames and wreckage. A storm of fire hissed from the machine's hull, yet miraculously it kept going, shells and rockets ricocheting from its heavy armour. Meritorius knew precious little of the sacred mysteries of the Omnissiah, yet even she could see the way the tank's plasma coils were glowing alarmingly bright and steam was gouting from its exchanger vents.

'They're going to overload in the breach,' she breathed, then shouted, 'Down. Down and cover, now, now, now!'

Around her, Sisters and Guardsmen alike shielded their eyes and ducked down as best they could. The tank slammed at full speed into the shuddering wall section, and then the world turned white. The explosion was so ferocious that it extinguished Meritorius' hearing completely. Everything seemed to stop for an instant, replaced by the purity of holy bright light.

Then sound rushed back in, the sounds of flaming rubble crashing down, the screaming of wounded soldiers, and the avalanche rumble of wall section nine caving in upon itself.

Meritorius was up in a heartbeat, blade raised and crackling. She looked upon the remains of Captain Maklen's sacrifice and felt righteous fury building within her. Meritorius was glad for Maklen, in that moment, for the captain was with the Emperor now, but at the same time she felt nothing but hatred for the heretics who had driven Petronella Maklen to give her life.

'We have our breach!' she bellowed, her vox-amplified voice

rolling like thunder. 'Praise the Throne, we have our breach! Advance, in the Emperor's name!'

Warriors rose, bewilderment turning to fury as they saw the gaping hole where Captain Maklen's martyrdom had opened the way. As one, the beleaguered Imperial war machine surged into motion and charged for the breach. Meritorius led the way, and as she pounded through the still-glowing rent in the ferrocrete wall she saw the light of the Saint descending from above to lead them onwards.

'To victory,' bellowed Anekwa Meritorius. 'To victory!'

BEYOND

Celestine soared upwards into golden light that shone as bright as the heart of a star. She heard a singing note growing all around her, and her soul sang in chorus with it, for surely here was the divine light of the Emperor.

'We have found that which we sought, sisters!' she cried, but there was no reply from Faith or from Duty. Celestine realised that the light about her had become so fulminating that she could no longer see the mountain from within which she had flown, nor the churning skies that had loomed above her for so long, nor even her two sisters who just moments before had flown at her side.

'Faith? Duty? Where are you?' shouted Celestine. Her only answer was that singular note, the ring of cut crystal swelling by the moment into a deafening chime that vibrated through Celestine's body and seemed to shiver her bones.

There was no up or down, nothing around her by which to navigate or orient herself. There was only the light, so blinding she could barely keep her eyes open, and the sound, so deafening now that it was all Celestine could do to endure it.

'It is the unfettered might of the Emperor, a last test against which I must prove my worth,' she told herself, yet so loud had the ringing around Celestine become that she might as well not have spoken. She felt a wetness upon the sides of her face that might have been blood trickling from her ears. She closed her eyes against the glare yet still she could see it even through her eyelids.

Celestine was blasted by light and sound, saturated with it until she felt as though everything that made her what she was might dissolve and be scattered as motes upon the air. Still she beat her golden wings, striving to climb higher and higher into the light.

To turn back is to fail in the sight of the Emperor, to be sealed outside the final gate, she thought. To turn back is to be consigned to that purgatorial wasteland forever, or until my soul curdles and rots away amidst the corruption of Chaos. She knew she must press on. She must…

Yet every wingbeat brought pain more severe. Celestine burned in the heart of a divine furnace. She was battered by tidal waves of sound, pierced by blades of searing illumination and razor-sharp symphony. All coherent thought was driven from her mind, all but that one idea.

Do not turn back…

Do not turn back…

Do not…

Do not.

Light and sound vanished so suddenly that it was as though a bomb had gone off inside Celestine's mind. The cessation of stimuli was shocking, and only after a moment did she realise that she had been, and still was, screaming.

She closed her mouth and opened her eyes, fighting a heartbeat's fear that she must surely have been rendered deaf and blind.

Instead, Celestine found herself sprawled upon soft grass beside a fast-flowing stream of crystal clear water. The scent of flowers reached her nostrils, and as her ears stopped ringing at last she caught the sigh of a gentle breeze through leaves, and the lazy drone of insects.

Celestine sat up, bleary, bewildered. She felt the gentle warmth of the sun upon her skin, its dappled light falling through the stirring branches of trees that stretched out their limbs to form a dome canopy above the clearing.

'What is this?' asked Celestine, feeling mistrust rise in her chest. She received no answer, save the gentle chuckling of the brook and the soft soughing of the trees as they danced lazily in the breeze.

Frowning, Celestine rose to her feet. She was thirsty, she realised, for the first time since she had awoken atop the mountain of bone. She was hungry, too. She glanced at the ice-clear waters that flowed past, and at the fruit bushes that grew here and there amidst the treeline. Celestine shook her head and set her jaw.

'I will not trust anything of this realm, no matter how fair it might seem,' she said. Yet she could not help but feel out of place, the bloodied warrior in her filth-stained armour, too harrowed in mind and soul to accept the natural bounty that surrounded her. It was as though everything else were a gentle symphony, and she the only jarring note.

Celestine sensed nothing of the Chaotic corruption that had surrounded her in the lair of the worm, or in the ashen city, or upon the mountain of bone. That said, she felt nothing of the Emperor's divinity in this place, either. Celestine decided that she would not relax her guard. Instead, eyes flicking around for possible threats, she drew her blade and prepared herself for some monstrous thing to come crashing through the trees.

'Faith, Duty, please respond,' she said into her gorget vox. Static hissed back at her. 'Sisters, are you out there?' Celestine tried again, but still received no answer.

Minutes passed. The breeze shifted the trees with a gentle hiss. The waters of the stream flowed on. The sunlight danced through the branches, spreading a delicate play of light and shadow across the lush grass of the clearing. Celestine felt her eyes drawn to its shifting shapes despite herself, and something tickled at the back of her mind as she watched the soft play of light and shade. A memory, perhaps, moving just below the surface of her conscious mind.

She wasn't sure how long she stood like that, alive for threats, before a plump and fuzzy airborne insect bumbled through the air and settled upon her right pauldron. Celestine snapped her eyes towards it, ready to slap the creature away at the first sign of a threat. It ignored her entirely, fastidiously cleaning its limbs, turning in a slow and inadvertent circle as it struggled to reach its own hindquarters. It was, Celestine reflected, as absurd a spectacle as she herself must currently make.

'Oh, for goodness sake,' she said, shaking her head and dropping her guard. She brushed the insect away and it set up an indignant drone as it wobbled away through the air. 'I cannot stand here forever, blade raised against non-existent threats,' Celestine told herself. 'If my sisters are lost then I must find them, and whether this is some paradise of the Emperor's making or just another veil of mists, I will not discover the truth stood here.'

Celestine closed her eyes and felt for the Emperor's light. After a moment she realised that all she could feel was the warm sunlight as it caressed her skin. The sensation was good, pure somehow, but different to the ephemeral candle flame that had guided her path thus far. Celestine opened her eyes, surprised and disquieted.

'And yet, what if they are one and the same?' she asked herself. Realising that she had no other form of guidance for the moment, and unwilling to simply guess at a random direction in which to travel, Celestine resolved that she would follow the light of the sun. A glance at the canopy told her that, for the moment, taking to the air was not an option. Instead, Celestine folded her wings close in to her back and, taking a moment to fix the position of the sun in the sky, she strode off towards it with a look of determination upon her face.

Perhaps an hour passed as Celestine marched through the idyllic woodland. There was underbrush enough to add to the forest's beauty, but not so much that it impeded Celestine's progress. The trees grew tall and proud. She found that the longer she looked at their gnarled bark and spreading boughs, the more familiar they seemed.

'Where *is* this place?' Celestine asked herself, yet no answer was forthcoming. Whatever memories moved in the deeper currents of her mind, they refused to surface.

She slowly became aware of another sound upon the air, a roar both breathy and distant that set her to scanning for threats again. Passing through a thicket of spry saplings, Celestine heard the sound a little clearer and felt an involuntary smile quirk the corners of her mouth.

'The ocean,' she breathed. 'That is the sound of waves breaking upon a shore.'

Celestine felt a simple happiness in her heart, a sense of peacefulness that she could not quite account for. She wondered why this was so familiar.

'Faith, Duty, if you can hear me I am approaching a stretch of coastline,' voxed Celestine. 'Sisters, make for the sound of the waves or, if you can get airborne, move towards the coast and look for me there. I am proceeding and will take the lie of the land.'

She pressed on, out from under the eaves of the forest. Scattered fruit trees formed a natural orchard around her, their boughs heavy with ripe crimson orbs, but they were no longer dense enough to be called woodland. Celestine ignored them and marched on across the loamy soil under a clear blue sky. Tatters of white cloud rode the winds high above, and winged shapes wheeled, causing her to raise her blade again. Yet Celestine soon identified the creatures as nothing more than some species of coastal avian, and she dismissed them as irrelevant.

Ahead, the land rose into a steep bluff with tough grass tufts clinging to its leeward side. Celestine knew, though she didn't know how, that this ridge was the trailing edge of a huge sand dune. Beyond its crest, the soughing of the waves promised a beautiful ocean view.

Celestine felt happiness growing within her. She knew a wash of contentment that she could do nothing to dispel, a sense of familiarity that she could neither place, nor shake off. It was maddening and pleasant in equal measure.

As she dug her armoured feet into the slope of the dune and began to climb, Celestine glanced up towards the crest.

She froze.

Up there, jarring and incongruous in this beautiful but empty place, she saw the silhouette of a human head and shoulders just visible above the ridgeline, looking away from her towards the ocean. They were small, rendered in silhouette by the sun, which spilled over the dune and limned the figure's dark hair with gold.

She knew them.

She began to climb again, suddenly as nervous and eager as one who has long been away from the love of their life, and now hurries impatiently towards reunion. Celestine's heart thumped in a chest tightened by nerves and anticipation. Thoughts of potential dangers, of her lost sisters or her current location, were driven from her mind by the singular thought that she would at last...

Celestine stopped herself, halfway up the dune. She would at last what? Be reunited with a child that she had met only hours or days ago? She would at last catch up to this silent figure who had come and gone like a mirage, remaining just out of reach?

Did she know her, truly? Her caution returned, and one hand tightened on the hilt of her blade. What, if anything, did she know in this place, except that nothing was what it first seemed?

The child had not moved. She had not responded to the whine

of Celestine's armour servos or the crunch and skitter of sandy soil shifting beneath power-armoured boots, though she must surely have heard both. She merely sat, still as stone but for the slight stirring of her hair in the sea breeze.

Cautious now, Celestine altered the angle of her climb, circling out around to the right of the child as she ascended towards the top of the dune. Her blade glinted in the sunlight, its killing edge keen, the silver catching the light in tight ripples. She imagined what she might see as she finally set eyes on the child's face, dreading some ghastly apparition sent to lure her in then set upon her, the poisoned barb at the heart of some paradisiacal death trap.

'Just a child,' she said aloud as she finally set eyes on the girl. She was as Celestine remembered, a slight little thing with dark hair and dark eyes who looked up at her curiously. The girl scrunched her face up in a squint, shielding her eyes with one hand.

'Hello,' she said.

'Hello,' replied Celestine, uncertain what else to do.

The two of them remained that way for several heartbeats. Celestine saw their shadows form a frozen tableau down the dune's flank, the tall warrior with a blade in hand and wings folded tight to her back, the wisp of a child staring up with innocent curiosity.

Celestine realised with a start that she still had her sword raised. Hurriedly, she sheathed it.

Of the two of them here, it was she that must appear the monster.

'Who are you?' asked Celestine, trying to keep her voice gentle. The girl looked in no danger of startling or fleeing, but Celestine had little enough experience with anyone that wasn't a warrior or a foe. Little girls were wholly unfamiliar territory. She would take no chances.

'I'm Hope,' replied the girl.

Celestine blinked as the name sparked something inside her, a jolt that ran through her whole body.

'What are you doing here, Hope?' asked Celestine.

'I'm watching the waves,' said Hope. 'Would you like to join me?' she added shyly after a moment's pause.

'I… thank you, Hope, I shall,' replied Celestine, unsure how else to respond. As gently as one could in full power armour, she settled herself near the girl. Celestine left a clear three feet of sand and air between them. She told herself it was to avoid making Hope nervous, but she wondered if it would be truer to say it was for her own benefit.

'The view is beautiful,' said Celestine after the silence had stretched long between them. She found she meant it. The dune's windward slope swept away before her, golden sand dotted for the first dozen yards with tufts of grass. Further away, the sun-warmed sands of the beach sloped down to the tide line, where they became slick, several shades darker where the waters had retreated. The ocean itself was a magnificent immensity beyond, its waves questing in and out amidst dancing sprays of foam near the shoreline. They rippled slow and stately atop the depths further out, crowned with gold by the sun's rays. Eventually, the vista faded until sea and sky became one upon a distant and hazy horizon.

Celestine waited for the child to speak, but Hope had returned to staring at the view, her short legs stretched out in front of her, a stalk of grass idly twisting in her fingers.

'Hope, where is this place?' asked Celestine.

'The beach beyond the woods,' said the child, sounding distracted.

'That much I can see,' said Celestine gently. 'But *where* is this? Are we… is this a world in real space? Or somewhere else?'

Hope didn't reply, just kept twisting her grass. Celestine decided to try something else.

'I've seen you before, haven't I?' she asked. 'You were there at the bottom of the cliff, then again at the top of the ascent. And I'm sure I've seen you again since, running ahead of me through the shadows. How did you come to be here, Hope? How did you survive?'

Hope glanced at her.

'That lady wasn't nice,' she said. 'She hurt my arm.'

'I know, Hope, and I'm sorry that she did that, but she was not herself,' said Celestine, trying to sound as kindly as she could. 'Have you seen her? Or the other woman that I was with?'

Hope shook her head. She frowned with childlike severity at the grass that was twisting apart in her fingers.

Celestine sighed. She returned her gaze to the horizon.

'Why don't you know where you are?' asked Hope, after a pause. 'Are you lost?'

'Yes, Hope, I think I am,' said Celestine. 'I was following a light, and it led me here, but now I do not know where *here* is, and I do not know what to do next.'

Hope's frown deepened, and Celestine had the distinct impression that the child was giving her words serious consideration.

'What if here is where you were going?' she asked. 'What if you've arrived?'

Celestine laughed ruefully.

'It's a lovely notion, child, but I have a duty. There is a great task I must complete before I can rest.'

'Oh,' said Hope. Then, after a pause, she asked: 'What is it? Your task?'

'You helped to remind me of it, Hope. Do you not recall?'

The girl shook her head.

'Do you know what monsters are, Hope?' asked Celestine gently. Hope nodded quickly. 'Well, there are monsters out there, in the galaxy. They come from somewhere else, somewhere wicked, and it is my job to send them back.'

'Are there lots of monsters?' asked Hope in a small voice.

'There are, but you must not fear. I am equal to my duty,'

Celestine said, her voice hardening with determination on the last few words.

'Do you have to fight them alone?' asked Hope.

'No, I have my sisters, wherever they have gone,' said Celestine. 'And there are others. So many others, all sworn to fight the monsters too.'

Hope frowned. 'But… if there are so many people who can fight the monsters, why is it *your* duty? Couldn't you stop, and let them do it instead? You could stay here. It's nice here.'

Celestine paused, a reply half-formed in her open mouth. She was rocked by the sudden certainty that she could do what Hope suggested. She realised that she could divest herself of her armour, lay down her blade to be buried by the shifting sands, and simply stop fighting.

Yet as she looked at the little girl she felt a sudden stab of recognition, a stiletto of emotion that slid between her ribs.

'Who *are* you?' asked Celestine again. Hope merely looked confused, her expression turning down at the edges as the sharpness of Celestine's tone threatened to upset her.

'I'm sorry, child,' said Celestine. 'I just… I am not sure if you can understand this, but when I look at you I feel such a keen sense of familiarity. It is as though, were I to do as you suggested, to remain here with you, I would come to know at last who you are, and what you are to me.'

Hope blinked, and Celestine realised the girl was fighting tears.

'Stay?' Hope asked suddenly. 'Stay this time?' Celestine felt her breath catch at the aching need she felt to sweep the child up in her arms and comfort her. There was such aching sorrow in Hope's small voice, so much more sorrow than any little girl should ever have to feel.

'Oh, child,' she breathed, and realised that she was fighting back tears of her own. 'What do you mean, this time?'

'Don't you know?' asked Hope, and now the tears did come, squeezing from the corners of her eyes and tracking down her cheeks. Her narrow chest hitched, and a sob escaped her.

'Hope, I...'

'You always leave!' shouted the little girl, suddenly furious. She pushed herself to her feet and ran off down the dune, puffs of sand kicking up behind her heels. The shredded twist of grass drifted to the ground in her wake.

'Hope!' called Celestine, starting to her feet. The girl didn't reply, dashing pell-mell down the slope of the dune and onto the flatter sands at its base. She was running towards the tideline, and suddenly the roar of the waves was loud in Celestine's ears as they rolled hungrily in. What had seemed peaceful and picturesque now became greedy, the waves a rapacious presence that boiled forwards to grasp at the sand. She felt a surge of fear for Hope, who was sobbing disconsolately as she ran towards the waters.

Celestine launched herself into the air, sand swirling away from her wingbeats. She arced up into a sky that darkened with racing storm clouds and arrowed down over the beach. A few swift sweeps of her wings carried her over Hope and saw her thump down in the wet sand before the girl, Celestine placing herself protectively between child and ocean.

Hope kept running and thumped into Celestine with what little force she had, throwing her arms around the Saint's waist. Celestine heard the gravel-throated roar of incoming waves and dropped into a crouch, encircling Hope with arms and wings both. The cold, dark waters hit Celestine from behind and rocked her forwards. Icy foam boiled around her legs and Hope screamed amidst her sobs as the water drenched her. The waters all but engulfed Celestine for a moment, and she held tight to the tiny life within her arms.

Then the waves receded, and Celestine rose with Hope cradled in her arms. She strode back up the beach, a sad certainty dawning within her. Hope clung to her, wet and cold, her tears slowly subsiding as she pressed her cheek to the hard surface of Celestine's breastplate. As they walked back up the beach the sun split the clouds again. Columns of golden light swept the beach like searchlights, widening as the clouds tattered away into nothingness.

Celestine stopped at the foot of the dune and knelt, placing Hope gently on the ground. The girl's shift was soaked, but the warm sun was already making inroads into drying it. The tears that tracked her face would take longer to dispel, thought Celestine.

'Stay,' said Hope again in a tiny, plaintive voice, but Celestine shook her head.

'I am so sorry, child, but I cannot,' she said. 'That was not the deal. I know now that if I were to stay I would know you, and you and I would have the peace of that knowing. We would dwell in this beautiful place and it would feel like all the reward that I could possibly expect for the lives beyond count that I have given. But Hope, if I stayed, it would destroy us both as surely as if I had let you be swept away by the ocean waves. To surrender to temptation would let the monsters in. Do not ask me how I know this, child, for I cannot tell you. I just know.'

'But I'm lonely,' said Hope. 'And you never stay. It's never done.'

'One day, Hope,' said Celestine. 'Have faith, my girl, one day it will be.'

'Promise?' asked Hope, and the desperate trust Celestine heard in the girl's voice made her soul hurt.

'I promise, Hope. No matter what I must do, what I must give, I will not fail in my duty. And one day, when I come to you here, I will stay. We will know each other, and we will understand, and that will be enough.'

And then she stood and turned away, and told herself as she did so that she didn't feel the suffocating pain of her heart breaking within her breast. Traitorous thoughts whirled through her mind as she took first one pace away, and then another, and another, as she tried not to hear the little girl that she left crying in her wake.

Had she once been hers, Celestine wondered. Or was she in some way her? Her innocence? Her chance at life? Celestine didn't know, but her blade felt suddenly heavier than it ever had, the cling of her armour claustrophobic and hateful, and the little girl's soft sobbing made her want to hurl it all aside, to gather her up and hold her close until her crying stopped.

'Emperor, I swear to You that neither daemon nor heretic shall stand between me and that which You have promised, and that I will fight for You until the fires of war are quenched in the blood of Your butchered foes,' said Celestine as she walked towards the ocean. Her voice was razor-sharp steel, tempered by pain and fury. 'But though I am Your faithful servant, and though I have only love for You in my heart, I say this now. You keep her safe until my task is done. You fill her days with simple happiness and You keep her mind from thoughts of loneliness or loss. The Emperor protects, that is what I have always told those who look to me for guidance. So, protect her, and honour her, or I swear that the last heart I plunge my blade into will be my own, as many times as I must, for I shall do no further duty for You.'

Celestine waited for some bolt of divine wrath to strike her down for her blasphemous words, but none came. Instead she walked on towards the hungry waves and did not once look back.

As she reached the tide line, the waters shuddered and swept aside. They parted for her and where her armoured feet fell Celestine found the sea bed hard and firm, cracked dry earth where there should have been wet sand.

With every pace she drove the ocean back. With every moment the golden light of the sun turned a bloodier hue, until it became sullen firelight dancing amidst drifting clouds of thick black smoke. The ground shuddered as though to the beat of some vast heart, and as it shook, so it heaved and cracked. The waters of the ocean roared down into those fissures, vanishing amidst gouts of steam even as coils of rusted wire grew from the desiccated soil like razor-weed. Celestine felt her heart harden with every step she took through what was rapidly becoming an arid and broken no-man's-land, where bloodied corpses burned in ragged shell holes and the sky was lost amidst the fume of battle.

Still, she did not dare look back.

'Halt. I sense her,' came a voice, crackling from Celestine's gorget vox.

'Faith?' asked Celestine. 'Is that you?'

'Saint, it is I,' came the reply. *'Emperor be praised! We thought you lost for sure.'*

With a few swift adjustments, Celestine routed Faith's transmission into her armour's basic auspex unit and triangulated her location – perhaps a mile ahead, through the wastes.

'Stay where you are,' said Celestine. 'I will come to you. Is Duty with you?'

'I am, Saint,' came Duty's reply. *'We have searched for you for many days amidst this grim place. Where have you been?'*

'For me it has been but a matter of hours,' said Celestine, picking her way through the desiccated ruins of a battle long since fought. She skirted a rusted tank, something hulking and Imperial whose blasted remains were lodged amidst a mound of rubble. 'As to where I was…' She found she could not bring herself to speak of it. She didn't want to. The forest and the beach were hers.

Hope was hers.

Within minutes Celestine and her comrades were reunited. Faith laughed in unalloyed joy when she saw Celestine through the smoke, while Duty's frown gave way to a wolfish grin.

'My sisters,' said Celestine, observing that neither of the angelic women showed any sign of the hardships they had endured. They were unmarked by the foulness of the worm's lair, and their robes and armour were unsullied by dirt or blood. Their brands burned bright, as did their eyes.

'Saint,' said Faith. 'You are here at last.'

'But where is here?' asked Celestine.

'Why, it is the end,' said Duty. 'And it is the beginning. It is that which we have sought together, which you have sought for yourself. Whatever your last trial was, you have passed through it.'

With that, the smoke began to roll back, billowing away from them as though driven by a wild gale and revealing a cracked plain that sprawled away for mile upon mile. At the same instant Celestine felt again the candle's warmth upon her skin, but this time it swelled to a simmering heat and then to a roaring fire, a searing star, and its light and heat bathed her in a way that the saturating glare from before had not. This felt right, it felt wrathful, and she felt her heart beat faster as the call to war filled her.

'The Emperor's light,' she said as golden rays fell upon them from on high. She looked to her sisters. She thought, briefly, of Hope where she sat atop her dune, waiting. Then Celestine locked Hope away, deep in her heart where nothing could touch her, and drew her blade.

'Do you know who you are?' asked Duty.

'I am the Emperor's blade, and His guiding light,' said Celestine. 'I am the candle flame in the darkness when all other light has failed His faithful servants. I am Faith, and Duty, and Hope.'

'We're ready, Saint,' said Faith approvingly.

'We are as ready as you,' said Duty.

'Then let us do the Emperor's will,' said Celestine, launching herself skywards. As she beat her wings powerfully and soared upwards into the light with her sisters at her side, she wondered whether this time would be her last.

The light of the Emperor swelled.

Golden and pure, it filled Celestine's world.

Celestine soared upwards, into the Emperor's light. Faith and Duty spiralled ever closer to her until the three of them swept upwards as one, their eyes alight with the magnificent radiance of the Master of Mankind. For an instant, Celestine felt the feather touch of small fingers upon her cheek and saw again a small figure sat atop a dune as the waves rolled in and out below.

'We will see one another again,' she said, and to her ears it sounded like a promise.

Celestine felt etheric winds lifting her higher and higher, speeding her ever faster towards the light. The light from Faith's and Duty's wings swelled and engulfed them in fiery haloes of ruby and amethyst. As one, their ethereal forms shimmered and folded into Celestine's own. She felt their strength flow into her and whispered silent thanks as she hurtled towards the light of a searing star that grew closer with every passing breath.

The veil shimmered around her. She both was, and was not. She both knew, and did not know. She died. She was reborn. And for one glorious moment she perceived all that she had done, and all that she had fought for, and saw all the millions of candles that she had lit across the galaxy as their light burned ever brighter against the encroaching night.

Then the veil parted before her, and the winds of eternity swept her on towards rebirth, towards her destiny.

She flew.

She fell.

She was Celestine.

415TH DAY OF THE WAR 2240 HOURS
IMPERIUM NIHILUS PLANET KOPHYN
SHAMBACH ORE DISTRICT LO:800-8/LA:631-2

The Taurox juddered to a halt. Blaskaine could hear small arms fire ringing from the hull. Something exploded nearby, rocking the vehicle on its tracks and almost throwing him from his feet as he put out a hand he no longer owned to steady himself. Kasyrgeldt caught him. He shot her a grateful look.

'Ladies, gentlemen, now we come to it,' said Blaskaine. One-handed, he awkwardly checked the load on his laspistol. Three-quarter charge remained. That would be enough. He looked around at the soldiers crammed into the bay. Kasyrgeldt, holding the shotgun that she had sworn by for as long as he'd known her. Two comms officers who had set aside their headsets for bulky portable vox-packs, the medicae – even the vehicle's two drivers, who stood with lasguns humming. In the mines, there would be no room for armoured vehicles, or for non-combatants.

'We stand ready, sir,' said Kasyrgeldt.

'Damned right we do,' said one of the drivers. Jans, Blaskaine thought. The man's name was Jans. It was better to know the names of those he would die beside.

'The Saint has led us this far, and now we must follow her again,' said Blaskaine. 'She is spearheading attack force alpha, going in through the Holy Lode workings. Sister Meritorius has force beta and the Sainted Seam workings. That leaves us with force charon and the Gilded Depths. Anyone that penetrates the enemy sanctum at the mines' heart…' He paused.

What *would* they do if they got that far? What would they find? Saint Celestine had been vague on that point. 'We are Cadians. We will know what to do when we get there,' he finished.

'Kill every heretic in sight, sir?' ventured Kasyrgeldt, racking the slide of her shotgun.

'That would be a damned good start,' agreed Blaskaine. 'And we'll work from there. Cadia stands!'

'Cadia stands,' they barked back at him. Then Blaskaine hit the release rune. The Taurox's back hatch swung open to admit the din of battle, and he led the way out into the streets beyond.

In a nearby courtyard, Anekwa Meritorius stood and stared into the mouth of damnation. Her twelve remaining Battle Sisters stood at her side, and behind them several hundred battle-weary Cadians knelt in prayer on the worn flagstones. She had commanded them to make their obeisance to the Emperor, and they had gladly obliged.

Before them, the mountainside rose monolithic into the night sky. Las-cut into its flank was the cavernous entrance to Sainted Seam working, a huge rocky tunnel-mouth ringed by industrial machinery. Servitor-cart tracks ran from massive ore-hoppers dotted around the courtyard and vanished into the unnatural crimson glow that pulsed from the mine's maw. A droning note echoed from within, an unnatural sound that set Meritorius' teeth on edge.

From behind her came the thump of cannon fire as the Astorosian Leman Russ transports of the rearguard engaged again. The tanks were parked in the street beyond the courtyard, forming a bulwark of plasteel and iron that the enemy militia would not quickly breach. Back there, through the gloom, Meritorius could see smoke rising from the fires that spread through the city streets. Fires they had lit as they fought their way through. Cleansing fires.

'It is not an inviting sight, is it?' said Sister Absolom, indicating the mine entrance.

'When has the Emperor ever asked us to walk into paradise to do His will?' replied Sister Meritorius with a humourless chuckle.

'There is no worth without suffering,' said Sister Penitence. 'But today, it will be the heretics that suffer.'

'Truly,' said Sister Meritorius, slamming a fresh clip into her boltgun. She turned to the Cadians, who were even now rising to their feet and readying their weaponry. They looked battle-weary, she thought, but their eyes shone with zeal. Few of them had truly believed that they would make it this far, and that they had done so only stoked the fires of their faith.

Faith, Meritorius could use.

'Brothers and sisters, loyal servants of the Emperor! The Saint has led us to the very gates of victory,' she began, her gorget amplifying her voice to a magnificent boom. 'Do you have the strength to pass through them and into the everlasting light of the Master of Mankind?'

They cried their assent.

'For the Emperor!'

'The Emperor protects!'

'Cadia stands!'

'Beyond this threshold the full might of the heretic, the daemon and the abomination shall be set against us,' shouted Meritorius. 'Do you have the faith and the courage to face them? Do you have the fortitude to prevail?'

More cries and shouts, louder and more vehement than before. Meritorius felt the hot winds of their conviction fanning the embers of her faith into flames. Energy coursed through her, a sense of purpose purer and more ferocious than any she could remember.

'Here, on this day, in this place, we have our chance to strike a blow against the Dark Gods themselves!' she roared. 'Here, by the grace of the Emperor, we shall raise our blades and our guns and we shall tell the daemon "no more!" Here, now, we will cleanse the taint of Chaos from this world with our blood so that when the new day dawns over Kophyn, it shall dawn upon a world that is loyal and pure!'

Frenzied cheers met her words. The Leman Russ gunners let fly again and explosions billowed beyond the buildings that ringed the courtyard. Sister Superior Meritorius turned to face the hellish maw and levelled her crackling blade at it.

'Forward, in the name of the Emperor and Saint Celestine!' she cried, and as one they advanced.

Unctorian Gofrey hastened down a red-lit tunnel with his laspistol glowing hot in his hand. Around him advanced the sons and daughters of murdered Cadia. The tunnels had narrowed as they pushed into the mines, funnelling the soldiery until only a handful of warriors could fight abreast. They moved up with well-drilled efficiency, dashing between the cover of side passages and burned out generators, overturned servitor-carts and makeshift sandbag barricades. Their lasguns and support weaponry howled as they sprayed fire at the cultists moving through the crimson glow. Dead from both sides layered the stone floor, Cadians in blackened flak armour and fatigues, cultists in cannibalised mining garb, crude face masks and foul robes of flayed skin.

Gofrey bellowed his hate as he marched through the press. He shoved Cadians aside where they impeded his progress and fired his laspistol as though hurling the bolts of energy by hand. Each shot found another cultist, punching through faces and chests and leaving them sprawled in the dirt. Return fire whined around him, bullets finding homes in Cadian bodies or blasting stone shrapnel from the walls. Gofrey was plying his mindcraft to its fullest, a raging headache building behind his eyes as he nudged the enemy into changing their aim or panicking just as they pulled the trigger.

He didn't care. The spectacle of a priest walking miraculously untouched through a hail of fire was worth the pain for it would inspire and terrify in equal measure, and thus ease his passage. He would burn out his own mind if he had to, just so long as he did his duty first.

'And lo, though the hordes of the unclean and the unworthy did stand before them, and though the hordes were many and the faithful men were few, still did the Emperor's servants prevail, for their hearts were pure!' he bellowed, his deep voice booming over the howl of gunfire and the sawing warp-note on the air. The Cadians who heard it rallied and fought all the harder, while their heretical enemies quailed in fear.

Another heretic burst from behind a barricade and charged at Gofrey, screaming and brandishing a revving rock-cutter. Gofrey adjusted his aim without breaking stride and shot the man through the knee. The cultist fell with a cry and his rock-cutter landed on top of him in a snarling spray of blood and bone chips.

Gofrey barked a cruel laugh and marched on.

'To me!' he shouted and sent a nudge to those Cadians whose wills he had suborned. A handful of soldiers broke from their positions and hastened to his side, ignoring the shouts of surprise and anger that came from their sergeants.

One such officer tried to stop two of her soldiers from breaking ranks, grabbing one of them by the arm. Gofrey shot the sergeant in the face, throwing her body back against the stone wall.

'Do not impede the Emperor's work, *witch!*' he hissed. Gofrey ducked down a side passage before the startled Cadians could react, and his thralls – a dozen in all – followed. Their expressions were blank and slack, but their lasguns kept firing just as well, scything down the handful of cultists that dashed up the passage to meet them.

Something exploded close by and a rush of smoke billowed. Gofrey's robes danced in the furnace winds. The lumen globes strung by wires along the ceiling clinked together and flickered on and off. Gofrey didn't care; even should the lumens go out, the diffuse crimson glare that suffused the passages would be enough to navigate by. Even if he lost that light, he had the burning beacon of his faith to guide him.

She was up ahead somewhere. Somewhere close. He could sense the false star of her soul amidst the gloom.

'I am coming for you, deceiver,' he muttered, and clutched that which hung about his neck, that which lay always close against his skin.

His secret, hidden for so long, soon to be revealed.

'Major Blaskaine, how far has your assault group progressed?' The Saint's voice came through on one of the voxmen's backpack sets. Just hearing it filled Blaskaine with new strength.

That was fortunate, he reflected, because his original store was fading fast.

Blaskaine was still technically convalescent, sorely wounded and hobbling into battle on a leg full of pins while fluids gurgled through the pipes of his compression harness. It was painful and exhausting, but now here came the voice of the Saint, as soothing as any healing balm.

'Saint Celestine, we have progressed–' He paused to check the auspex that Kasyrgeldt held out for him. 'Just over half a mile from the entrance of Gilded Depths workings. Cultist resistance is stiffening rapidly, my lady. Our advance has slowed to a crawl.'

But they were still advancing, dammit.

Blaskaine and his command squad ducked into a side-chamber, a claustrophobic rest space for miners with a few rusty metal benches, some bare lumen globes and a rack of hooks protruding from the wall for respirator masks to hang on. Outside, the fury of gunfire echoed amidst battle cries and the screams of the wounded and dying.

'Keep pushing forward, major,' replied Celestine. *'My group has progressed almost a mile into the workings, as have Sister Meritorius' warriors. I believe that we are nearing the enemy's inner sanctum. The Emperor requires heroism of us all in this darkest hour.'*

Blaskaine should have felt anger or perhaps resentment at the implication that his forces were lagging. Instead he felt only an intense desire to do better, not to let the Saint down.

'We shall redouble our efforts,' he voxed.

'The Emperor guides your path this day. You will make him proud,' said Celestine before cutting the vox-link.

'You heard the Saint,' said Blaskaine, looking around at his command staff. 'It's time we broke this damn deadlock. Kasyrgeldt, appraisal.'

The lieutenant set her auspex on one of the metal benches with its screen visible to them all. She laid a data-slate next to it, on which updating estimates of their and the enemy's strengths scrolled constantly in runic script.

'As you can see, this section of the workings has a single primary tunnel that runs south-west to north-east, away from the entrance and towards where the Saint believes our destination to be. We've the strength in numbers to force our way up the tunnel, but only slowly. Worse, the enemy are using side-tunnels here, here and here,' she pointed to skull runes flashing on the auspex, 'to move flanking forces in from the levels below us each time we threaten a meaningful breakthrough.'

'Can we outmanoeuvre them, or block those tunnels?' asked driver Jans, leaning intently over the auspex with his knuckles on the table.

'Our enemy has a greater native knowledge of these workings than we do,' said Kasyrgeldt. 'Our chances of catching them out through manoeuvre are slim. As for blocking the tunnels, that would require careful application of explosives. Our sappers would have to–'

'We're not blocking the tunnels,' said Blaskaine. A strange calm had settled on him, an acceptance.

'Sir? You have a plan?' asked Kasyrgeldt.

'Simpler than that, Astryd. I have faith,' said Blaskaine.

'Sir?'

'Our enemy are fanatical, and what they lack in concentration of force, they make up for in delaying tactics and a steady stream of reinforcements,' said Blaskaine. 'Our numbers, meanwhile, are finite, our time even more so. The Saint requires every warrior that can do so to break through to the heart of this complex, for that is where the only battle of any import will take place. We are not going to make it in time if we continue to fight this battle of attrition, and if we fail her now then it won't matter what else we do. Lieutenant, what is this tunnel here?'

'That's a crawlway, sir,' said Kasyrgeldt. 'A conduit for cabling and gas-transference when the servitors are at the rockfaces.'

'If I'm reading this right, it runs from one hundred yards behind our current position to this location, half a mile deeper into the mines at the exchanger hub, yes?'

'That is correct, sir,' said Kasyrgeldt, her eyes lighting with excitement. 'And with the mines inactive, there's no gas down there. Soldiers could make their way along the crawlway at a crouch. We'd cover a half mile in a matter of minutes and appear substantially behind the enemy's current front lines. Throne, that's brilliant, why didn't I see it?'

'When you've served as long as I have–' began Blaskaine with a ghost of his former smirk, but Kasyrgeldt was waving a hand, her face falling.

'No, wait, sir, I *did* see it, but I discounted it. If we fell back on that position it would be a slow manoeuvre with this many soldiers. As soon as the enemy grasped what we were doing they could simply activate the compressor pumps and flood gas through the crawlway, or else just follow us down or collapse the passage.'

'Not if they're busy engaging a rearguard,' said Blaskaine. 'One-fifth of our remaining force will hold position while we quietly filter squads back and through the tunnel. When our numbers thin, the rearguard launch a full frontal assault up the main tunnel, draw the enemy's fire and hold their attention long enough for the remainder of our soldiery to fall back on the crawlway, enter it and proceed to the exchanger hub. With the Emperor's grace, that is.'

'It is a desperate decision but it would have a high chance of success,' said Kasyrgeldt. Blaskaine felt pride as he watched his adjutant and protégé working the numbers. As he had known she would, Kasyrgeldt set her jaw and looked him in the eye.

'Sir, permission to lead the diversionary attack,' she said.

'Refused,' said Blaskaine. 'I will have that dubious honour, lieutenant.'

She looked confused, then horrified.

'Major, you can't. You are the senior officer in charge of this entire operation.'

'I can, Astryd, precisely because I am the senior officer and as such you are all required to follow my orders and allow me to get myself killed in whatever damn fool fashion I so choose,' said Blaskaine. 'Look at me. One arm, one and half legs at a push, worn down and wounded so badly I might as well be dead. What use will I be to the Saint if I come hobbling into the heart of the enemy sanctum? I could, perhaps, die on the War Engine's blade in a particularly distracting fashion?'

'Sir, I know that your wounds are shocking, but with the proper medical attention–' began the medicae, but Blaskaine cut him off with a sharp look.

'Do not mistake this for maudlin self-pity,' he said. 'I am not some dewy-eyed martyr. I am not committing suicide by combat, and I'll shoot the first soldier to suggest it. I have led a long life in the Emperor's service and during that time I have sacrificed many, many lives, some of them in exceptionally difficult circumstances. I have always told myself that those sacrifices were necessary for the furtherance of a greater Imperial good, and I stand by that to this day.'

He heard again the sound of desperate cries, saw the fires of Cadia's death throes cut off by the closing ramp of his drop craft. He knew that he had done the right thing, the difficult thing, no matter what anyone else said.

Sometimes just because one did the right thing, that did not stop one being damned for it.

'If fighting in the light of the Saint has taught me one thing,' Blaskaine continued, 'it is that sometimes, to do our duty to the Emperor, we must be willing to sacrifice more – all, in fact – with nothing more than faith that our ending will prove worthwhile. I have finally come to a pass where the most strategically viable sacrifice I can make is that of my own life, not those of others. I will not have that decision diminished by questions about my reasoning. Do I make myself inescapably clear?'

The Cadians around him saluted, their faces grim.

'Astryd, I'm placing you in operational command of assault force charon,' said Blaskaine. To her credit, his adjutant didn't protest any pretence at unworthiness, only nodded, her face pale but resolute. 'Furthermore, I would have it recorded by all present that I am at this time enacting my right as a senior officer of the Departmento Munitorum to make a field promotion.' Blaskaine fumbled awkwardly with one of his uniform pockets and produced a small metal pin, a skull with eagle's wings stretching from it, chased in gold.

'Astryd Kasyrgeldt, I hereby promote you to the rank of captain of the Cadian One Hundred and Forty-Fourth Heavy Infantry. May you serve the Emperor with honour, pride and heroism.'

Kasyrgeldt's expression was unreadable as he pinned the captain's badge to her tunic and stepped back with a wan smile.

'It looks right on you, captain,' said Blaskaine.

'Thank you, sir,' she said.

'Don't thank me, just earn it,' said Blaskaine, wincing at a pain in the stump of his arm. 'Now, I'm sorry to say that second and fourth platoons will be remaining with me as rearguard. They look to be the worst torn up, according to your slate. Don't worry, captain, I'll give them the good news. Just leave me one of the vox-packs and I'll coordinate the muster from here. Meanwhile, you pull everyone else off the line bit by bit and get them moving through the crawlway. Keep it subtle. We'll hold out for as long as possible before we launch our push.'

'Yes, sir,' said Kasyrgeldt. She paused, as did the rest of the command squad, then as one they saluted him again.

'Enough. Get moving before my self-preservation instincts kick in and I volunteer one of you in my stead,' said Blaskaine, keeping his tone bluff to mask the tangle of emotions tightening his chest. His soldiers hurried out of the chamber, ducking back into the screaming maelstrom of battle and thence to their appointed places.

Kasyrgeldt was the last to leave. She looked back at Blaskaine, and he saw fierce loyalty in her eyes, along with something else that it took him a moment to place. Approval, perhaps? Or was it pride?

'I won't let you down, sir,' she said.

'You never have, Astryd, even when I didn't return the courtesy,' said Blaskaine, then cleared his throat. 'Go. Make the Emperor proud.'

'I will sir, I just hope I can impress him as much as you have,' she said, and with that she was gone.

Blaskaine took a deep breath and looked briefly at the stone ceiling. He listened to the gurgle of fluids through his surgical brace, felt the ache of his whole body, and worse, the pulsing darkness in his mind where he had forced the memories down.

He offered a silent prayer to the Emperor and hoped that his reasons truly were as dutiful and selfless as he had said. He thought of the Saint, of her golden light and her holy magnificence, of how his sacrifice would aid her in winning a great victory against the forces of Chaos. That was enough.

Blaskaine picked up the vox handset and keyed in a channel, linking to the vox-units of second and fourth platoons where they fought upon the firing line.

'Ladies and gentlemen, this is Major Blaskaine,' he said. 'I have new orders for you.' He drew a deep, shaking breath. 'You are not going to like them, but you must trust me when I tell you there is no other way...'

Sister Meritorius ducked, allowing her enemy's axe blade to whistle over her head. She surged back up, lunging with the point of her power sword. It plunged through the ornate breastplate of the Mas'drekkha warrior, its molecular disruption field parting metal, flesh and bone. The man's eyes bulged behind the eye holes of his leering daemon mask. She ripped her blade free and kicked his legs out from under him.

The Mas'drekkha fell and Meritorius stamped hard on the back of his head with one servo-assisted boot for good measure. Bone crunched and blood squirted, and her enemy convulsed in his death throes.

'Fight, fight for the Emperor!' she roared, swinging her bolter up and firing down a side-tunnel. Another Mas'drekkha jerked as her bolt-shells punched through his torso, then detonated in a spray of viscera as they exploded inside him.

Assault force beta had advanced at a relentless pace, the Cadians struggling to keep up with the power armoured Battle Sisters. Meritorius and her Sisters sang as they fought, proud hymns echoing down the tunnels. Still, the droning note that filled the air had grown louder with every step they took deeper into the mines, and now it all but swallowed their plainsong whole.

A squad of Cadians dashed past her, pelting up the steep slope of the tunnel with their bayonets fixed and lasguns spitting fire. Three of them fell to autogun rounds before their charge slammed home against the mob of cultists at the top of the stone ramp. Another two went down with Mas'drekkha axes embedded in their bodies. Blood flew as the two forces engaged, and Meritorius dashed in to help.

Her bullish assault slammed one cultist from his feet with a crunch of bone. The sweep of her power sword saw another collapse without a head, blood fountaining from the stump of his neck. A third warrior came at her brandishing a miner's pick.

'Blood for the Blood God!' he screamed.

Meritorius caught the downswing of his weapon on the flat of her sword, then twisted it and disarmed the cultist with a flick of her wrist. She smashed the pommel of her sword into his eye, hard enough to cave in the front of his skull.

'You were not even worth my blade, heretic,' she spat.

'Sister Superior, auspex suggests a massive space beyond the next bulkhead door,' voxed Sister Absolom. *'The Saint's signifier rune is closing. We are converging upon the same point.'*

'The enemy's sanctum, no doubt,' replied Meritorius. 'That would explain the sudden onslaught of Mas'drekkha.'

They had so far used meltaguns to cut through two huge armoured bulkheads that had been raised to cut off inner tunnels within the mines. They would handle this one in the same fashion. Meritorius switched vox-channels.

'Assault force beta, all warriors, rally to these coordinates,' she commanded, uploading the location of the bulkhead. 'Gird your courage, sons and daughters of the Emperor, for we come at last to the heart of heresy.'

She switched vox-channels again as warriors streamed past her and along the high-ceilinged tunnel that led towards the bulkhead.

'Saint Celestine, are you receiving me?'

'I hear you, Sister Meritorius,' came the Saint's voice, strong as steel and musical as a choir.

'Your forces and ours are about to converge,' said Meritorius. 'I believe we are at the threshold of the enemy's inner sanctum. What of assault force charon?'

'They are overcoming delays. Sacrifices must be made, Sister, but they will join us when the Emperor appoints it their hour to do so.'

'Will you lead us in this final battle?' asked Sister Meritorius.

'I will fight at your side,' replied Celestine.

'I am not... That is, I have not...' said Meritorius, her voice trailing off.

'You are, you shall, you always have and will,' replied the Saint without hesitation, and the firm warmth in her voice left Meritorius in no doubt that Celestine had seen the ashes and the fire both within her heart. *'The void is dark, Anekwa Meritorius, and all stars wax and wane within it. But they rarely stop burning, and the darkness cannot diminish them.'*

With that, Celestine cut the vox-link. Sister Meritorius felt an incredible sense of release, a lightness in her chest and in her mind. The Saint knew, and far from passing judgement she offered only acceptance, and strength.

'Emperor be praised,' said Sister Meritorius and set off along the tunnel at a run.

She emerged through an arched entrance onto a metal gantry that ran above a wide staging chamber. Its floor had been levelled with ferrocrete and stencilled with bays and numbers for the dozens of mining machines and prefabricated labour units it played host to. These had been dragged out of position and heaped up to form barricades. Several side-chambers led off from it, perhaps administration offices or rest areas during more peaceful times. The chamber's ceiling was strung with hundreds of lumen globes, whose light flickered fitfully amidst the hellish red glow. Most of the chamber's north wall was taken up by a heavyset metal blast shutter designed to slide open from the centre. It was daubed with the runes of the War Engine, repeating over and over in hideous proliferation, and looked far newer than the rest of the room.

Gunfire and screams echoed madly around the chamber. Meritorius saw that a hard core of Mas'drekkha and flesh-robed cultists were holed up here, dug into the side-chambers and hunched behind the barricades of machinery. They had crew-served heavy stubbers that raked back and forth across the chamber, streams of bullets whining from metal and stone, and punching through Cadians in puffs of blood. Dotted amongst the Mas'drekkha, she saw several especially huge and overmuscled warriors with black hoods, billowing skin-cloaks and ornate axes. She presumed these must be their champions – the cult leaders who had led their people astray, who had manipulated simple superstition into something darker. Meritorius could see the foul blessings the arch heretics had received for their works, shallow augmentations of strength and physical presence.

'Scant enough rewards for the souls of an entire world,' she muttered in disgust. 'Such are the wages of heresy.'

The Imperial forces had pressed up behind several barricades, but were otherwise confined to the chamber's southern entrances. Sprawled Cadian bodies showed where abortive attempts had been made to charge the stubber-nests.

'Sisters, the enemy are dug in here and seek to prevent us from reaching their sanctum. Shall we relent?' Her vox message was met by a suitably strident chorus of denial from the nine Battle Sisters that still lived.

'Sister Superior, if the Cadians launch a two-pronged push up the flanks, it should afford us the chance to move on the central barricades,' voxed Sister Penitence. *'Once there we could hurl frag grenades into the closest gun-nests, and–'*

Meritorius didn't hear the end of Sister Penitence's plan, for at that moment Saint Celestine swept into the chamber from its south-eastern entrance, her Geminae Superia close behind. The Saint launched herself through the enemy's fire, bullets ricocheting from her armour. One Geminae landed atop a toppled hauler and unloaded her pistols into a stubber crew, blasting them apart. Celestine herself fell upon the Mas'drekkha with a cry of holy rage, her blade slicing through their bodies.

Behind Celestine, a second Imperial force flowed into the chamber with their guns blazing and Meritorius saw the balance of the battle shift. The stubber gunners tried frantically to draw a bead on the Living Saint, and their reserves burst from cover with howls of battle-lust.

'The enemy have thrown away their advantage in their eagerness to spill blood for their foul god,' cried Meritorius, her eyes shining at the magnificent sight of the Saint in battle. 'So do all the slaves of the Dark Gods fail and falter. Forward, faithful, and slay them all.'

Gofrey was livid. He had intended to catch the false Saint while she battled through the confined tunnels. He had planned to set upon her from all sides, to spend his attendants' lives in an ambush that would have brought him close enough to strike the killing blow. Instead, he had been forced to fight his way through wave after wave of cultists. Each conflict had slowed him and, though he had seen the glow of Celestine's radiance ahead through the murk more than once, ever the agents of the enemy had impeded his holy work.

'Just further proof of the daemon-witch's heretical nature,' he muttered to himself.

Ahead he heard the din of battle as the so-called Saint led the charge. Gofrey had half-expected her to abandon the army before the walls, and then had waited for Celestine to turn upon her followers during the assault up through the city's winding streets and into the tunnels beyond.

Now, though, he knew her game. The Dark Gods do battle with one another and use mortals as their playthings and tools, he thought as he stalked along a sloping tunnel. Surely, then, this false-Saint was a servant of a rival deity and would use them to strike down the War Engine before turning upon those who remained. Worse, perhaps she would lead them on into damnation unutterable, then those in turn would fight for the Gods of Chaos!

No. He would not suffer this witch to live another minute. This ended now. He saw an archway ahead, saw Cadian squads dashing through it and into a storm of criss-crossing gunfire. He would find the false Saint here and expose her for all to see, for Gofrey's faith was pure, and witches must be burned.

He nudged his thralls and sent them jogging ahead, slack faced with their lasguns ready. One, though, he kept with him. A gunner in whose hands thrummed a plasma gun primed and ready. A weapon enough to kill even the risen Saint.

He smiled.

Gofrey broke into a run, and as he did so, at last he drew out the mark of his order upon its heavy chain and let it hang proud upon his chest.

The rosette of the Holy Ordo Hereticus. The witch hunters of the Inquisition.

Inquisitor Gofrey charged into the swirling melee in the chamber, the fires of his faith burning inferno-hot in his breast. The witch Celestine would die, and all would see in the moment of her fall that she was but a daemon temptress sent to lead them from the Emperor's light.

Gofrey beheld her winged shape ahead and snarled a command at his thralls. As one, they advanced with their guns raised.

In a smoke-filled corridor, strewn with bodies, Major Blaskaine crouched behind a pile of sandbags. He bled from several bullet wounds, and could barely feel his pinned leg any more. The flesh had torn around several of his crude medical sutures, and more blood soaked his uniform. It hardly mattered now, he thought. He must have bought Kasyrgeldt long enough. The Emperor could grant him that much, couldn't He?

Bullets thumped into his barricade. A few Cadians still remained, firing their lasguns back at the enemy from positions of cover nearby. But they were a spent force, and the enemy was massing for a last push.

Blaskaine checked the charge on his laspistol again. Flashing close to spent. Still a few rounds left, he thought. Perhaps the last was for himself. But no, he couldn't waste them. Each shot was for another heretic his soldiers – his warriors – wouldn't have to fight.

'Let this be enough,' he said as he heard the enemy's chanting reach fever pitch. 'Emperor, I pray, let this be enough to settle my debts. Let this be my atonement. Let me be forgiven. And save me a seat next to Captain Maklen at Your table, hmm?'

He thought again of the Saint, leading the faithful survivors to victory on Kophyn despite all the odds stacked against them.

It was enough. Blaskaine hauled himself to his feet. He levelled his pistol shakily into the red haze and sighted through one eye at the milling figures half-seen through the murk. He snapped off a shot, then another, then one more. At least one of them connected, and he was sure he saw another cultist go down. One final heretic sent to damnation before his end. Suddenly, a hail of return fire shredded the barricade and his body into bloody tatters.

Charn Blaskaine's body hit the ground, but he felt no pain. He felt only the calm smile of acceptance that spread across his features as the world vanished down a dark tunnel and the light of the Emperor blossomed before him.

'Emperor... be praised...' he whispered, and then knew no more.

Sister Meritorius sprinted across the open ferrocrete, enemy fire whipping around her. She fired back, pumping shell after shell into the heretics behind the barricade, blasting them apart. Her faith was a blazing fire. The Saint was leading them to victory. Even as she watched, Celestine swept her blade down and took the head from another of the hulking enemy leaders.

That was the last of them.

The enemy were slain.

Only the War Engine remained.

'Sisters, meltaguns,' ordered Meritorius over the vox. 'Blast us a path. Surely the enemy's foul master lies beyond this portal.'

Several Battle Sisters moved up, accompanied by a handful of Cadian weapons specialists with melta weaponry of their own. They poured microwave fire into the bulkhead until it glowed and shuddered. The bulkhead began to sag as their fire chewed through it, and Meritorius brandished her blade as she prepared to face whatever lay beyond. The sawing warp-note in the air rose in pitch and vehemence, becoming a scrapcode roar. She looked to the Saint, who stood ready atop a barricade with her Geminae Superia flanking her. Celestine's face was composed, her calm absolute. Meritorius drew strength from it.

From behind her, Meritorius heard a commotion. She looked around with a sudden premonition of dread. A squad of Cadians was loping forwards with weirdly blank expressions on their faces, and her eyes narrowed as she saw Unctorian Gofrey accompanied them. Meritorius' frown deepened as her gaze alighted on the talisman slung around Gofrey's neck. She felt a moment of puzzlement as she absorbed the import of the Inquisitorial rosette. Then she took in the angle at which the Cadians were holding their guns, the thrumming plasma gun at the rear of the squad, and Gofrey's mask of wild-eyed hate.

Perhaps, if there had been any psykers surviving within the Imperial force, they might have sensed the stirrings of empyric powers being used amongst the Cadian ranks, and alerted their superiors.

Perhaps those psykers would have warned their masters of the raw power they sensed, lurking somewhere within the Imperial ranks. The potent blend of psychic might and utter conviction hanging like a thundercloud over them all. The danger that the energies of the Great Rift might have tainted that power.

But the force had no psykers. None except for Inquisitor Unctorian Gofrey, a witch sent in secret to find witches, an extremist of the most unmerciful and single-minded sort. A man for whom that which did not originate in flesh and blood and iron was by its very nature unholy and suspicious. A man who saw witches at every turn and had but one solution for dealing with them.

'Saint!' yelled Meritorius, trying to throw herself between the Cadians and the Saint. Celestine's Geminae were quicker, and as the lasguns flashed the two armoured Seraphim bounded into the path of the bolts. Sister Intolerus was blasted from the air, half of her face shot away. Sister Indomita weathered the storm of las-shots and returned fire, blowing two Cadians off their feet.

Gofrey howled, and Meritorius saw his eyes blaze with otherworldly power. Sister Indomita was hurled sideways by an unseen force, smashed through the air as though by the hand of a petulant god. She hit the far wall of the chamber with bone-breaking force and fell, limp as a rag doll.

Meritorious opened fire on Gofrey as, around her, the Imperial forces turned in amazed confusion to see the conflict at the heart of their advance. Meritorius' bolts were intercepted by the bodies of Cadian thralls, who flung themselves into the path of her fire without a moment's hesitation.

In return, their fellows opened fire on Meritorius and drove her into cover.

The Saint turned with a look of utmost sorrow upon her face.

'Unctorian Gofrey, you need not do this,' she said, and though she did not raise her voice, still it carried over the sounds of gunfire, the droning warp dirge, the hiss of melting metal and the crackle of fires. 'Your fanaticism has blinded you and made you an unwitting tool of the foe, and in your zealotry and your fear you turn your hate upon that which you do not understand, even though it be the Emperor's own gift to you.'

'A witch's lies,' spat Gofrey, and his eyes flashed again. Meritorius watched aghast as a tracked cargo hauler the size of a small tank was hurled across the chamber. Celestine dived aside, evading the sailing mass which instead slammed into the weakened bulkhead and tore through the softened metal to crash on, into the chamber beyond.

The warp dirge redoubled in volume. Meritorius saw into the space beyond the bulkhead, saw a nightmarish mass of brass gears and pistons and roaring furnaces, bloody muscle and stitched flesh and staring eyes, rune-scrolling cogitator screens and flaring lenses, all stamped again and again with the skull rune of the Blood God Khorne.

The Cadians nearest the collapsing bulkhead cried out in terror as segmented metal tendrils and coiling cables slithered from the darkness. They tore off limbs and punched through bodies to shed sprays of blood. They coiled around necks and ripped heads from shoulders, dragging the severed skulls back into the mass of the daemonic abomination.

'Is that the War Engine?' croaked Meritorius in horror. Her sanity threatened to crack under the strain of the sight, and only her newly restored faith kept it bolstered. Then she heard a fresh eruption of gunfire and spun back in time to see Saint Celestine sweep down upon Gofrey's Cadians. The Saint fought with the flat of her blade, clubbing one man senseless then spinning and backhanding a woman to knock her unconscious to the floor. In return, las-fire rang from the Saint's armour and a frag grenade clattered down at her feet. Celestine kicked the explosive away and then drove her fist into another Cadian's face, flattening him.

Recovering their wits and seeing the Saint in danger, a handful of Cadians from assault group beta raised their lasguns and advanced on Gofrey, yelling at him to cease his assault. Brave, thought Meritorius, to challenge the Inquisitorial seal. Their bravery earned them death, for Gofrey had none of Celestine's restraint and crushed the Cadians' skulls with a flick of his mind.

'She is no Saint!' bellowed Gofrey. 'She is a daemon witch, sent to lead you into damnation! Turn your guns upon her in the name of the Holy Inquisition!'

Some of the Cadians stood and gaped in confusion, as did most of the Imperial preachers. Yet Cadians are amongst the most highly trained and disciplined soldiers in the entire Astra Militarum, and, in the absence of a commanding officer from whom to derive their orders, most made snap decisions as to their loyalties. Maybe thirty per cent of them obeyed Gofrey's command. The rest chose their faith in the Saint, and as Meritorius watched in horror the chamber descended into civil war, Cadian squads turning their gun butts and fists upon one another. It would be scant moments, she saw, before these exhausted, highly strung warriors lost the last of their hesitation and began shooting.

And still the War Engine's tentacles slithered further into the chamber, and its roar increased in volume.

It was then that Meritorius knew what she must do.

'Sisters,' she barked through her vox. 'This discord serves only our foe. Have faith that the Saint will defeat this false Inquisitor. We must banish that which we came here to banish. We must slay the War Engine.'

With that she turned her back on Celestine, who fought now in the midst of a mass of brawling Cadians, and advanced upon the tentacled horror beyond the bulkhead. Meritorius raised her boltgun and began to pray, uttering the booming High Gothic words of the Rite of Banishment. Her weapon thumped, sending shell after shell whipping through the bulkhead to punch into the daemon's flesh and blow sprays of gore from its mass.

The fusillade thickened as Meritorius' Sisters joined her, bolt shells and meltagun blasts ripping at the convulsing daemon. Its roar grew louder, more furious as its cogs were smashed and its flesh ruptured, as cogitator screens shattered, and eyes burst, and furnaces spilled their glut of flaming skulls.

Cadians had joined her, Meritorius realised, their faces grim as they fought to complete the task the Emperor had set before them. Not all of them, though, she saw; the sight of this daemonic horror had been too much for some of the brave soldiers, and they ran mad with terror or fell to their knees, clawing their own faces bloody.

Tendrils lashed out, punching through a man to her right and tearing him in two. A segmented metal tentacle lined with blades whipped around Sister Penitence's waist and hauled her forwards. Penitence was still screaming her hate and firing her bolter into the monster's mass as she was stuffed whole into a blazing furnace maw.

Yet the daemon was quivering and shuddering, its flesh becoming translucent as its grip upon reality faltered.

'Pray, Sisters!' cried Meritorius. 'Keep firing!'

It was then that she heard the distinctive whine and scream of a plasma gun firing behind her, and a sudden chorus of horrified cries.

'The Saint!'

'Emperor, no!'

'Burn the witch!' came Gofrey's furious shout.

'Heresy!' howled another voice, full of outrage and fury.

'Hold position, eyes forward, do not relent!' bellowed Meritorius, internally screaming in frustration. She had to know what was happening at her back, but to relent for even an instant would be to let the beast rally and consume them all.

'Grenades!' barked Meritorius, palming a handful of krak charges and hurling them into the shuddering mass of the daemon that had turned Kophyn into its own private slaughterhouse. More charges followed, sailing through the air in a cloud and clattering into the daemon's chamber to implode with ferocious force.

The War Engine heaved and shuddered hugely. Its digitised roar reached a deafening crescendo and its flesh-metal tentacles lashed out again and again, yet now its body was burning and torn. Its ichor spewed in gouts across the chamber floor, and in places it began to turn transparent then vanish altogether. Chunks of machinery clattered to the floor, no longer held within the corrupted mass of daemon flesh. Wires sparked. Cogitator engines clattered down to silence.

'Flamers!' ordered Meritorius, and brave soldiers advanced through the nest of flailing limbs to ply jets of fire across the disintegrating abomination. Several paid the ultimate price for their courage.

Meritorius fired again and again until her clip ran dry and she slammed a new one into place. She ignored the sounds of gunfire and screaming and clashing blades behind her, shut out the boom of Gofrey's voice and the cries of the wounded, and kept firing.

Anekwa Meritorius did her duty.

At last, the War Engine blew apart with an explosive blast of furnace-hot winds and atomised gore, and a death scream so deafening that it caused lenses to crack and ears to bleed.

At last, with the abomination before her slain, Meritorius was free to turn and look upon the horror that had been wrought behind her back.

Inquisitor Gofrey could feel blood streaming from his nose, weeping down his cheeks from eyes that must by now be red with burst vessels. He had nudged dozens of Cadian soldiers to his cause, pushing so hard that he had killed almost as many as he had successfully enthralled. He didn't care. It was a faithless man who balked at the cost of doing the Emperor's will.

It wasn't done yet, though. The Saint's armour was cracked and blackened where las-bolts had pierced her body. She had torn free of her encumbering jump pack after Gofrey had crushed one of its finely crafted wings with his mind. Her face was a mask of blood where a Cadian sergeant's sword had opened her scalp, yet still her eyes remained locked on Gofrey with furious intensity.

Other Cadians, those too far lost to heresy to hear Gofrey's warning, had rallied to her. Now she came at him with her blade raised, and the once proud soldiers of the Astra Militarum flayed each other with point-blank gunfire.

'This heresy ends now!' roared Gofrey, and nudged his plasma gunner hard. The man's first shot had been stopped by a Cadian selflessly hurling herself into the path of the blast. Determined to avoid the same thing happening again, Gofrey focused his will and, with a scream of pain, bludgeoned aside those soldiers between himself and the false Saint. Bodies tumbled, bones broke, and something in the Inquisitor's mind tore.

'Now,' he growled, through the white-hot wash of agony. 'Overcharge and fire!'

His thrall obeyed, the coils of the man's plasma gun glowing, its capacitors screaming as they gathered their ferocity. The false Saint saw the danger and lunged, but too late. There came a blinding flash, a howl of energetic discharge, and Celestine was struck full in the chest by a ravening ball of sun-hot plasma.

The shot lifted her from her feet and threw her backwards to crash against the mangled metal of a barricade. She gasped in agony, and well she might, for Gofrey saw with vicious satisfaction that her chest was a molten ruin of fused armour and blackened flesh and bone. How the damned woman was even still breathing with such a crater in her was beyond him, but Gofrey knew now was his moment. As the faithless cried out in dismay at their Saint's fall, Unctorian Gofrey strode towards her, his vision shimmering crimson at its edges.

'Now, witch! Now, daemon! Now comes the judgement of the Holy Inquisition! Now I shall do the Emperor's work and strike you down, that the scales may fall from the eyes of all who have followed you unto damnation!'

It was then, as he stood over the bloodied, gasping false Saint, that something roared and struck Gofrey in the back with sledgehammer force. The world jolted, and it took him a moment to realise that he had been driven to his knees, his entire back reduced to a blazing mass of agony. Gofrey fumbled behind himself and his palm came away dripping and red.

'What…?' he croaked.

* * *

Captain Kasyrgeldt pumped her shotgun and advanced towards the fallen preacher. Somehow, he was still upright, despite the full-bore blast she had unloaded into him. She resolutely ignored the wounded form of Saint Celestine beyond him, lest the sight undo her entirely. What in Terra's name had happened here, she wondered.

'All Cadian soldiery, stand down and ship arms with immediate effect!' she barked, her voice carrying more authority than she felt. Around her she saw soldiers stepping back with relief, others shaking their heads and dabbing at bleeding noses as though emerging from some sort of trance. One man swung his gun to bear upon her but was instantly clubbed down by the soldiers to either side of him. No one else reacted.

Impossibly, the Saint was pushing herself to her feet, blood sluicing down her legs from the catastrophic wound in her torso.

'Saint Celestine, please don't try to move,' urged Kasyrgeldt, then yelled for a medicae. Celestine shook her head and took careful, steady paces towards Gofrey, her blade held in one shaking hand.

'Unctorian Gofrey, your zealotry and fear have blinded you and made you a tool of the enemy,' rasped the Saint, blood trickling from the corner of her mouth.

'Lies,' Gofrey hissed, still trying to fight his way to his feet despite the wads of buckshot that had severed his spine. Kasyrgeldt frowned as she felt waves of force emanating from the fallen priest, then gasped in shock as she saw those same forces stir his robes and lift him to his feet.

'In the very lair of the abomination that enslaved this world to the will of the Dark Gods, you turned the Emperor's noble warriors against one another at the moment of their triumph,' said Celestine, her voice grating and raw. 'You are no better than Horus the betrayer. Heretic I name thee, *traitoris extremis*.'

'Do not listen to her lies,' Gofrey screamed, apoplectic with rage,

and Kasyrgeldt heard clearly the madness in the man's voice. Exhausted Cadians stared from every side, unsure whether to intercede, whether to aid the Saint or restrain her bloodied assailant, wary still of the Inquisitorial rosette that hung from his neck.

'You have profaned the Emperor's faith and made of it a lash with which to goad your fellow man,' spat Celestine, raising her blade double-handed. 'You do not believe in the will of the Emperor, but instead invoke His name to excuse your own monstrous deeds. I have love and sympathy in my heart for every loyal soul, no matter how wayward or lost they might be. But you, Unctorian Gofrey, your very fanaticism has transformed you into that which you hated most, and the darkness will be lessened by your passing.'

Kasyrgeldt felt unnatural forces whirl into being around Gofrey and cried out a warning to the Saint. Celestine's blade swung through the air, a streak of silver amidst the gloom, and the Inquisitor's head tumbled to the bloody ground. His body followed it, the thrumming pressure leaving the air as Gofrey's powers died along with his mind. The next instant, the Saint fell in turn, her sword slipping from her grip and her eyes rolling up into her skull.

1ST DAY OF PEACE 0616 HOURS
IMPERIUM NIHILUS PLANET KOPHYN
SHAMBACH ORE DISTRICT LO:800-8/LA:631-2

They bore Saint Celestine out through the mines and into the cold night air. Meritorius allowed Captain Kasyrgeldt to assist her and her Sisters in bearing the Saint out of the daemon's lair. Tears ran down their faces as they walked, stately and sombre, bearing Celestine upon a makeshift bier.

The crimson glare was gone from the tunnels, so that only bare lumen globes lit their path. The awful droning dirge had halted in the instant of the War Engine's demise. Now silence reigned, and in it the clink of wargear and the whine of armour servos was as loud as Celestine's ragged breathing. The Cadians were too exhausted, or else too stoic, to set up any sort of mourning cry for the fallen Saint, and when the priests had attempted to exhort them to it, Meritorius had silenced them with a cold glare.

This would not be a grotesque spectacle of zealotry. She had witnessed where such perversions of the Imperial faith led a man, and his body burned at her back, consigned to the same fires as the daemon. Meritorius knew it would be dignified, for it was what she deserved.

They laid the Saint upon the stone flags of the courtyard through which they had entered the mines. They set her broken Geminae Sisters beside her, offered the same honour in death as their mistress.

The Cadian medicaes did what they could, applying gels and dressings, but they expressed their doubts that Celestine would even regain consciousness, let alone live through her terrible wounds.

And so Meritorius and Kasyrgeldt stood, attending the Saint as her breath rattled in and out, unsure what else to do. Aides came and went, providing the Cadian captain with data-slate reports that she looked over swiftly before muttering orders and sending her subordinates hurrying away. Meritorius nodded in approval. Major Blaskaine was right to promote that one. Command came naturally to her.

'Listen, the fighting has stopped,' said Kasyrgeldt.

Meritorius realised the Cadian was right. She could hear fires burning, voices crying out in loss or bewilderment or pain, but no gunfire.

'The city languishes beneath a pall,' she said. 'Do you suppose that, with the daemon's banishment, its influence over the populace was broken?'

'I fear the truth is rather grimmer,' said Kasyrgeldt as she scanned a data-slate handed to her by one of her aides. 'We're receiving reports of mass suicides amongst the cult forces. They correspond with the daemon's demise.'

'All of them?' asked Meritorius, aghast. Thousands upon thousands, taking their own lives in unison, she thought. And all of them once loyal servants of the Emperor.

'All of them,' confirmed Kasyrgeldt.

'Perhaps it is better,' said Meritorius. 'They were irrevocably tainted. There would have been no forgiveness for them this side of the grave.'

'I'm just glad they aren't still in the field and seeking revenge,' said Kasyrgeldt. 'I feared this would prove a pyrrhic victory at best and yet, here we stand. Thanks to her.' She looked down at the prone form of the Saint. 'Should we offer up prayers?'

'My Sisters already do so, but if any of your soldiers wish to join them it would seem appropriate,' said Meritorius. 'The Emperor should know the victory that the Saint led us to this day, and of our gratitude to her.'

'He does...' came Celestine's rasping voice as her eyes opened. They knelt at her side.

'Rest, my lady, don't exert yourself,' said Kasyrgeldt. 'You've been sorely wounded.'

Celestine offered the Cadian a wry ghost of a smile.

'The Cadian talent for understatement... still survives, I see,' she whispered, and a cloud passed across her features. 'I am... sorry, captain. I fought at the fall of your world, and... I could not save it.'

Kasyrgeldt appeared lost for words, and so Meritorius spoke for her.

'Saint, you have led us to a great victory upon Kophyn with the light of your faith.' More soldiers were gathering now, Cadians and Battle Sisters and even a few surviving Astorosian tankers forming a sombre crowd around the fallen Saint. Many bore hastily dressed wounds, while others leant on lasguns as makeshift crutches. Still they only had eyes for Celestine, and Meritorius thought briefly that they must resemble some scene from scripture. Perhaps, if she ever escaped this world, she would see to it that the moment was recreated in glassaic or tapestry.

'I fought alongside you, and...' she paused, choking. 'I offered the Emperor's counsel, nothing more. It was your faith, your strength and courage, your determination... that brought us victory this day.' Around the circle, the wounded soldiers stood a little taller, fires kindling in their eyes at the Saint's words. Meritorius felt a surge of tremendous love for Saint Celestine in that moment, for she had helped her to stoke the fires of her own faith again and now they burned hotter than ever before.

'The daemon is banished, yes?' asked Celestine, coughing painfully. Her balled fist came away from her lips arterial red.

'It is, Saint,' answered Meritorius. 'We slew it by bolt, and by blast, and by flame.'

'An initial inspection suggests that the War Engine was as much machine as daemon,' said Kasyrgeldt. 'Our engineers are working on the hypothesis that the locals had some sort of Dark Age thinking machine hidden away up here, and that for whatever reason they activated it when the Rift came. We can only guess at their motivations, or how the machine-intelligence came to be corrupted by a daemonic entity, but...' Kasyrgeldt tailed off as she felt everyone's eyes upon her.

This is an officer who boils everything down to data to cope with loss, Meritorius realised.

The Saint placed her hand upon Kasyrgeldt's and nodded slightly.

'My thanks, captain. It is good to... to know the nature of the corruption that we have put a stop to here today. But there is such a thing as blessed ignorance, for the daemon corrupts those who seek to understand rather than abhor. Burn... everything that remains, and have your priests purge their...' The Saint broke off as another coughing fit wracked her.

'Of course, my lady,' said Kasyrgeldt.

Meritorius felt a slight warmth upon the nape of her neck. She looked up, and saw the first light of the dawn sun was creeping around the mountain peak.

'What do we do now, Saint?' she asked, looking back down.

'You have served,' said Celestine, her voice wavering down to a whisper. 'You have found faith and duty within yourselves... you must strive every day to keep them in your heart. You are the soldiers of the Emperor, and you will carry your light forwards into... the darkest of places without... without fear or doubt.'

'My lady, we will do as you ask,' said Kasyrgeldt. 'But I fear we will never do so beyond the bounds of this world, for we have no way to escape it.'

'The Emperor… provides,' whispered Celestine with a smile.

The Saint's breath rattled painfully in her ruined chest. Surely, thought Meritorius, she did not have long. The sun's rays limned the mountain peak as the sky flushed pastel blue and russet above them. A spear of sunlight fell upon the courtyard, and the assembled soldiery gasped in awe as it crowned Celestine with a flickering halo. Meritorius thought she saw peace in the Saint's eyes in that moment, but something else as well, a sense of foreboding perhaps.

'Sir!' came a shout as a vox-officer pushed through the circle to reach Kasyrgeldt's side. 'Sir, it's a damned miracle!'

Kasyrgeldt shot the man a sharp glare. 'Strevsky, show some damned respect,' she snapped in a low voice. 'Now, what is it? What's a miracle?'

'Ships, sir,' said Strevsky, suitably chastened but still burning with excitement. 'Imperial Navy ships in orbit and requesting to speak to our senior officer.'

'How can that be?' asked Kasyrgeldt in wonderment. 'We were cut off. No one even knew we were here.'

'Astropathic vision, sir,' said Strevsky. 'The captain wasn't too clear, but it sounds as though someone saw something divine, a golden figure that led them through the storms and got them here, now…'

'The Emperor provides,' breathed Meritorius. She looked down at Celestine, but her words of thanks died on her lips. The Saint's eyes had turned glassy and unblinking. Her body had become utterly still.

Saint Celestine had passed beyond the veil.

BEYOND

Consciousness, sudden and violent.

Her eyes snapped open and hellish red light poured in. She gasped and sat up, one hand going to her ruined chest. She found it whole beneath her palm, the material of her shift undamaged, the flesh beneath it unsullied.

She blinked as her vision slowly returned, as she perceived the osseous mountain upon which she had awoken. She did not know her name, nor where she was, nor how she had got here. As panic threatened, she felt a slight warmth upon her cheek, like the light of a candle or the brush of small, warm fingers.

In that moment she knew she must follow it, and that if she did, all would eventually be well.

CELESTINE: REVELATION

ANDY CLARK

Machoria burned. The heat of its flames beat against her back. Blood-stink was in her nostrils, the cries of the fearful and wounded in her ears. Ash skirled around her on furnace winds. Celestine flexed her knuckles about the grip of the Ardent Blade. She planted her feet more firmly upon the roadway that led from the city gates and willed away the pain of her wounds.

'Emperor, give me strength,' she murmured, drawing comfort from the familiar words. The God-Emperor was always with her. In every war cry, every swing of her blade and every step she took. They had a pact, she and He.

While it endured, so too did that bond.

Still, His presence was hard to feel in this place. Warp fires swallowed the sky all the way to where the Khori Mountains rose like jagged horns on the horizon. Closer to hand, what had once been hydroponic fields had been reduced to blackened bedrock. The crops had been annihilated by the enemy's bombardment, the waters turned to a steam that mingled with the blood-haze in the air. Corpses rose in tangled mounds before the walls. Some were the bodies of agri-labourers unfortunate enough to be caught outside the gates before they shut. Those were many days old now, barely more than bone. Others, fresher, had been soldiers of the Astra Militarum, brave men and women of the Coskan Minotaurs and the Sarmathian 86th.

All martyrs to the Emperor's glory, she thought. *All alike in death.*

Their living comrades occupied trench lines that stretched along the foot of the walls to Celestine's right and left. Others manned the Machorian battlements, doing their best to keep the city's guns firing, even as flames licked up from the buildings below. They traded fire with the enemy's artillery, hurling ordnance towards the foothills of the Khori range. Relentless volleys screamed back at them.

Horns brayed from within the mists. The sound was brazen, a ferocious roar that swelled until Celestine swore her bones vibrated. It droned on and on until she feared it must drive the Imperial soldiery mad.

At last, the horns faded. As they did, the panicked voices of Coskans and Sarmathians became audible from the trenches.

'Steady, sons and daughters of Sarmathia, steady!'

'They come again!'

'No, please, no. Emperor preserve us.'

Gunshots rang out as regimental commissars did their duty.

Celestine wished her Sisters still stood by her side. All had fallen, every one of the Mission whose presence had anchored the Machorian garrison's faith. Even her Geminae Superia were lost, their deaths more painful to Celestine than any physical wound. The enemy had come again and again, had focused their hate upon the Battle Sisters and spent countless lives to see them fall. Now Celestine was alone amidst the masses, a figurehead to those who remained but as separate from them as a lonely mountaintop was from the ocean floor. In divinity lay isolation.

The beasts come to finish me, and if I fall then all is lost.

She could see them now, insubstantial figures charging through the mists. Their war cries echoed as though across an impossible gulf. Yet their eyes shone fire-bright, hundreds of coals burning through the veil as the foe drew closer.

Daemons.

Celestine saw many-legged fleshmetal monsters lumbering through the enemy ranks, things whose maws blazed like furnaces. Cavalry came on like an avalanche of brass while there, in the centre of the line, strode a towering abomination clad in spiked brass armour. It bore an axe taller than Celestine in each fist. Eight horns crowned the monster's helm. Braziers blazed atop its shoulders, skulls blackening amidst their flames.

'Arnokh,' Celestine growled. Then, in a calculated gesture of contempt, she turned her back upon the advancing horrors. She swept her gaze instead across the soldiers cowering in their trenches and raised her voice to a shout.

'Soldiers of the Imperium. Men and women of the Emperor's realm. Our enemies come to test us yet again.'

Servo-skulls hovered low, recording her address with auto-receptors and transmitting it to the thousands of Imperial soldiers still clinging to this city by their fingernails. Celestine felt their desperate need as a weight upon her soul, trying to drag her to her knees.

'They have assailed us time and again. They have thrown at us all their hate! All their rage! But have we buckled before them? No!'

She could sense the foe getting nearer with every heartbeat, their menace swelling at her back, the ground vibrating beneath her feet.

'We will never give way to these abominations. Why? Because they are filth, dredged from the darkness to test our faith, and that faith is *strong!*'

Celestine brandished the Ardent Blade high so that it gleamed like a star in the firelight. Soldiers gripped their lasguns tighter at that sight, stood taller, or so she hoped.

'The God-Emperor is with us this day! His will is wrought in me, and I shall lead you to victory! Now *fight*, sons and daughters of the Imperium! Fight with me, and win!'

Celestine spun to face the foe's onslaught. As she did so, she tried to believe her own words. Yet even as the guns of the Imperial Guard sang their hymn of death, even as daemons were struck down to tatter away in bursts of embers, she could not help but doubt.

The abominations are legion, and our soldiers so weary, she thought. *Emperor, I am so weary.*

Then the enemy were upon her and there was no more time for thought.

Blood-skinned daemons hissed, hacking at her in a frenzy. Celestine met their wild onslaught with controlled wrath. A parry, warp-forged darkness ringing against adamantium then a sweep that took her assailant's head. A sidestep, a swing and a second attacker lunged past her with a howl of rage. She cut downward. Slicing the daemon in two, the Ardent Blade passed through the beast's spine and out through its chest as easily as though Celestine had cut smoke. A third daemon fell to her blade. A fourth. With a thought, she triggered her jump pack, its outstretched wings carrying her clear of the foe.

'For the God-Emperor!' she yelled, surging back into the daemons and banishing two more with a mighty swing of her blade. Gore flecked their lips as they battered at her guard. Celestine's sword sank into the eye socket of another daemon and blew it apart in a cloud of embers.

Keep fighting, she told herself. *The Emperor is with you.*

Celestine readied herself for a fresh onslaught.

It didn't come.

The abominations melted back into the mists like wraiths, giving her a glimpse of las-fire blistering the air, of shells raining down upon the daemonic hordes. Wild with terror, soldiers ran from the monsters that hacked their way into the Imperial lines.

A new presence loomed before her. Arnokh the Bloodlord,

master of this infernal host. Once he had been a Space Marine of the Emperor's own Legions. What stood before her now was a charnel horror whose perfidy had burned worlds.

How far they fall...

'The Emperor's angel,' he hissed.

'The Blood God's puppet,' she replied, dropping into a guard stance. Arnokh was thrice her height and many times her stature, an armoured mountain driven by hate. She drowned in the stinking gloom of his shadow.

'You have fought well for a corpse-worshipper,' said Arnokh with a mocking chuckle. ***'I will honour your efforts by taking your head myself.'***

'Mightier than you have tried and failed,' she spat.

'There are none mightier than Arnokh the Bloodlord,' he roared, hefting his axes and storming forward.

'There is the Emperor,' she replied with a grim smile. 'There is *me*.'

Arnokh's first swing came down like a thunderbolt. Celestine triggered her jump pack and sprang aside, leaving the axe to crater the roadway. One foot touched the ground before she fired her jump pack's thrusters again and jetted forward, blade levelled at her enemy's throat. Arnokh swayed aside but his sheer bulk counted against him. The Ardent Blade stabbed deep into his collarbone, giving a hiss like quenched steel as it met his blood. Celestine slammed one foot into Arnokh's chest, ripping her blade free and firing her jump pack a third time. She twisted in the air, metal wings whirling as she spun away from his return blow. An axe passed so close to Celestine's face that she could hear the damned souls screaming within the blade.

She landed in a fighting crouch.

Molten gore spilled from the wound in Arnokh's shoulder. Celestine smiled without mirth, inclining her head.

'You fight well, for daemon spawn.'

Arnokh bellowed. Celestine's smile vanished as she felt empyric energies whirling towards her foe. The braziers on Arnokh's shoulders flared as though someone had flung promethium on their flames. The blood-mist poured into him and his flesh glowed crimson, black veins standing out across his body as it swelled with might. His eyes blazed behind his visor, and suddenly, the blood-mist was thick enough to choke.

'Blood for the Blood God!' Arnokh howled. He attacked with redoubled speed, a rushing avalanche of blades. Celestine ducked his first blow, leapt aside from his second and tried to strike out at one of Arnokh's wrists. If she could sever a hand, lessen the onslaught...

His next swing was aimed not at Celestine's body, but instead at the right wing of her jump pack. Already committed to her own swing, she could not twist away. Arnokh's axe carved through the wing and caused the jump pack's machine-spirit to vomit sparks. Even as shorn metal pinions hit the ground he struck again. Dragged off balance, Celestine could not avoid his axe and was instead forced to parry. It was like trying to stop a speeding tank. The shock of the impact raced up Celestine's arms, jarred her shoulders. The shockwave jarred her thoughts and as it did, something blossomed behind her eyes.

Pain. A surge of white-hot pain unlike anything Celestine has ever felt. Is she still alive? How can she be? Something has happened to her, hasn't it? She doesn't know; it feels as though she is falling faster and faster.

She recalls shells raining down.

Explosions.

Screams.

She recalls the eviscerator's grip beneath her palms, the roar of its chain teeth as they split flesh and bone. A word comes to her then: Repentia. Celestine feels a surge of shame, a desperate need to atone, and yet also the incredible release of that same weight lifting from her. The pain is a key that unlocks the shackles of her soul.

Searing light blazes, washes through her. Something is changing, something fundamental. She cannot grasp it as it slithers quicksilver through her thoughts.

Celestine feels desperate frustration, the powerlessness of mortality, of work left undone. Atonement is not the same as fulfilment. She registers disbelief as the pain grows worse still, threatening to burn her away like scourging flame, threatening to erase all that she is or has ever been. Yet what is she? What could she be? The light wheels about her then focuses before her, a star, a light leading her onward.

The pain abates.

Reborn.

She is reborn, and this light... can it be? Is this the first time she has endured this? Somehow, she knows it will not be the last. Not until her purpose is done.

Celestine reeled back from Arnokh's blow. She tried to reconcile the flurry of images dancing behind her eyes with the desperate battle before her.

What was that? A vision? A memory?

It had been so vivid, so tangible.

What do you seek to tell me, God-Emperor?

Had she received such visions before? Celestine thought perhaps she had, but it was hard to know. The mark of divinity was upon her, the Hieromartyr of countless Imperial crusades through Throne alone knew how many lives. Yet at her core she was still mortal. She was both blessed and cursed with a mortal's mind. Such a vessel was not meant to traverse death's threshold as many times as she had. Celestine had to fight for every part of herself that endured the crossing, every time.

Things get lost...

All this raced through Celestine's mind in a heartbeat, yet still the distraction was almost enough to kill her. Arnokh's axes licked out again. Dragged off balance by her foreshortened jump pack, she smashed them away with increasingly desperate parries.

Her broken wings hung crackling from her shoulders, dead weight. Celestine reached with a shaking hand and hit the uncoupling rune, shedding her jump pack and stepping clear of its mangled remains.

An angel without her wings is an angel still, she thought, but her defiance was tinged with doubt.

No time for this, she thought as Arnokh loomed over her, sought to smash her into the ground with his sheer mass. Freed from the broken jump pack, Celestine weaved aside from his trampling hooves at the last instant. She felt the daemon prince's axes cut the air above her as he passed.

Her blade sliced a line of white fire across his hip.

Celestine wheeled to face Arnokh again, but he was on her more swiftly than she could have believed. If the wounds she had dealt the daemon prince affected him, he didn't show it. Axe blows fell like artillery shells. Celestine weaved, cut, stabbed and hacked. Her breath caught upon hooks. The servos of her armour howled as they sought to lend her speed to match that of her foe.

Celestine's foot slipped in blood. She recovered her balance with preternatural speed. Still too slow. Arnokh's axe missed her neck but hit her collarbone instead. Bone snapped. Pain rocketed through her mind again and with it came a fresh vision.

Celestine walks alone down stone steps. None may accompany her. This is the Emperor's will. She knows it as surely as she knows her own name. Statues glower from shadowed alcoves as she passes. A soft play of coloured light falls about her shoulders, starlight filtered through stained glass. She smells incense on the air, feels the rasp of her robe against her skin. Gooseflesh prickles at the subterranean chill of the crypt. The ground is hard, furred with dust beneath every bare footfall.

She is deep within the crypt now. Sanctus Lys carries on somewhere above her, but she is not part of that backwater world. Not here. Celestine is one instead with something sacred, something ancient that exists in a space all its own. The weight of centuries presses down, stilling the air, causing sound to fall dead upon the worn flagstones. She reaches out with a trembling hand and brushes away the dust of ages.

She reads the name chiselled into marble.

Saint Katherine.

Celestine is in the presence of true divinity, and it fills her with such a complex rush of excitement, trepidation and hope that no room remains for the fear. Self-doubt accuses her of presumption. A shrill inner voice bids her flee whatever punishment the Emperor reserves for unworthy pretenders such as she. The awe is stronger, though.

Her eyes meet the stone gaze of the figure carved into the sarcophagus' lid. Something passes between them in that instant, a feather-touch upon her senses. It feels like permission. She reaches out towards the sarcophagus.

It is the following dawn when Celestine walks the stone steps again. Yet this time she ascends from darkness into light, and she does so clad in the holiest of armoured raiment. Ancient servo-motors purr as though newly installed. Moulded armour plates sit like a second skin against her own, as though the suit had been fashioned for her alone. The Emperor has led her to this gift, and while she wears it, she knows that the spirit of Saint Katherine walks alongside her. The light from the shrine's stained-glass windows embraces her and she feels the warmth of daylight on her skin. Its radiance haloes her brow.

One second she is ascending the steps, the next her feet leave the ground as the light swells about her. Celestine's heart thunders. She is borne aloft within a column of radiance and in that instant, she feels the Emperor's hand upon her soul like never before. Dimly she registers figures within the shrine turning to stare at her, falling to their knees in supplication. They are beyond the light and so in this moment they do not bear upon her reality at all. Celestine rises level with the shrine's stained armourglass and hears the voices of an invisible choir swelling in praise. Neither means any more to her than the small figures who gaze up from below. Celestine is one with the Emperor. She is one with Saint Katherine, and in sacred trinity they spread their arms wide and throw back their head as the light pours through her.

In that moment, Celestine knows with the absolute certainty of faith that she is the Emperor's vessel.

She is His blade.

She will *be worthy.*

Celestine staggered back. Sparks drizzled from the Armour of Saint Katherine where it had known the bite of the daemon prince's blade. She couldn't see the wound Arnokh had dealt her for it was too close to her neck, but she could feel blood welling from it like water bubbling up from a blessed spring. Her strength went with it, pattering onto the desecrated ground. She could barely move her sword arm and had to banish a mental image of it hanging from her body by strings of gristle.

Another vision, she thought, desperate to regain focus. *Or another memory. Something of His, or something my own? Emperor, help me to find clarity.*

Arnokh fell upon her like a storm. Celestine deflected one blow with a scream of effort, sidestepped a second. Perhaps, if she could just–

The daemon prince's clenched fist, still wrapped around the haft of one axe, hit Celestine in the chest with bone-shattering force. Armour crumpled. Her ribs broke like a bundle of dry twigs trodden underfoot. She hit the ground on her back and her eyes filled with the fires that danced where clouds should be.

Celestine stands in the shadow of the Cathedrum Miraculous on Aspiria and knows she has come too late. Part of her knows also that she has been here before, that this haunted place is one she swore never to set foot inside again. That part can only watch helpless as the Celestine who is here in this moment raises her blade to signal the Battle Sisters at her back.

They have fought for three days and three nights to reach this place. Aspiria's ruddy sun is even now seeping over the horizon, spreading into the polluted sky like spilled blood staining dirty cloth. Shafts of radiance fall through the cathedrum's shattered windows and between its cracked arches. They drape Celestine and her Sisters in a molten glow, but they bear little warmth.

Even before she climbs the steps to the cathedrum's doorway she suspects she knows what she will find. The worst of it is that she and her warriors could have done no more. They could have fought no harder, done no better. Celestine harbours no illusions. They cut a red path of ruin through the heretics, fit to fill the planet's folklore for centuries to come.

They have brought hope. Her latter self knows they have brought victory, also, for the Word Bearers cast so much strength into her path that Celestine has torn the heart from their invasion.

Still they are too late to bring salvation. At least for those within.

Celestine knows this and yet she climbs the steps anyway. She must see. She must know, remember, for how else will she atone for those who died with prayers for salvation spilling unanswered over blistering lips?

The stench hits her first. There is the reek of promethium, the clag in her throat that speaks to vast quantities of ashes. There is another smell, fainter but inescapable. Burned flesh.

Celestine stands upon the lintel and looks upon the remains of a pyre that must have reached all the way to the cathedrum's ceiling. She sees gibbets jutting thick as the stumps of a felled forest. They, and the remains lashed to them, are all burned black.

Thousands of Imperial faithful have died here. Priests of the Ecclesiarchy. Sisters Famulous, Dialogous, Hospitaller.

Celestine feels sorrow. She feels guilt. Yet more than either, raging as the fire must have raged, she feels hatred for all those who serve the Dark Gods.

Here beneath the blood-hue of Aspiria's dawn, Celestine hates the servants of Chaos with a fervour she never knew she possessed. She swears to the Emperor that she will purge every last heretic from His realm if it takes her a thousand lifetimes.

Celestine tried to force her broken body to move. Shells streaked the skies above her. She heard the voice within that told her to move, to crawl if she must, to get away from the monster that was killing her and back to the soldiers in their trenches. Celestine yearned for the tribal companionship that had been a balm to her species since they had huddled together in caves and levelled spears at the darkness without.

She could not go to them. She knew that, really. To see her as human would break their belief in her as the divine avatar of the Emperor's will. Worse, it might even break their faith in the God-Emperor Himself.

Besides, they cannot help you, not against this foe. All they could do is die.

But still she longed to be safe.

Safe from pain.

Safe from duty.

She felt the agony awaiting her within the broken remains of her mortal shell. Instinctively she shied away. Then, out of nowhere, Celestine felt a hand take hers. Its touch was faint as gossamer.

'Stay,' said a small voice, little more than an exhalation of breath against her ear. *'Don't go back. They'll hurt you. Stay. Please.'*

'They need me,' said Celestine. Distantly she heard the screams of dying soldiers, the gibbering of daemons, the brazen laughter of Arnokh. His shadow loomed above her, one axe raised for the decapitating strike.

'It will be over quickly,' said the voice. The touch upon her hand became a tug. *'Stay.'*

Celestine knew that she had met this manifestation many times. She knew also that it was some part of herself. It was the part that wanted to stop fighting, to cast aside the bargain that she had struck with the Emperor, the part desperate to at last be free of the impossible weight of others' need for her divinity even if it meant giving in.

Giving up.

Yet there was no salvation either in flight or capitulation. She would not fail the men and women of the Imperium who looked to her to be their beacon. She would not fail the Emperor. Not while there was breath left in her body.

'My purpose,' said Celestine, as much to herself as to the other presence that haunted the void. 'My gifts. My hate. My duty. Only I can do this. You know that. They all need me.'

'I need you.'

Celestine felt something within her break as it had a thousand times before. Into how many shards could someone's heart shatter before it could never be pieced back together?

And it was *their* fault, she realised with growing fury. The traitors. The heretics. *Their* weakness, *their* cowardice that had set the galaxy aflame and forced her to forever fight the fires they lit. This war would rage until the stars burned out unless the Emperor's servants found the strength to end it.

Only she could give them that strength.

The touch upon her hand was gone. Celestine surged up through the darkness like a blazing comet and back into her body. The light of the Emperor mingled with her own righteous wrath and seared away the agony of her mortal form. It poured out of her, a starburst that sent Arnokh reeling back with a howl of shock, one arm thrown across his eyes. The daemon prince's skin blistered black at the touch of the light. Sulphurous smoke rose from his boiling flesh.

Celestine felt herself borne aloft upon the light as she had been on that day so long ago. She looked down in judgement upon her foe. The light pulsed from her and drove the blood-mists away. Daemons went with it, their cries of hatred fading to nothingness. Celestine felt the eyes of the beleaguered defenders upon her and this time she knew with certainty that their hearts soared at the sight of her.

The light pulsed from Celestine a third time, a golden shockwave that sent Arnokh staggering back and hurled more of his daemons into the abyss. In her peripheral vision Celestine caught the shimmer of angelic pinions spreading from her shoulders, framed against the burning skies. She felt strength surge through her limbs, felt herself renewed.

She felt faith, duty, hate.

Celestine's feet touched the ground and then she was running, the Ardent Blade held low to one side in a double-handed grip. As she pounded across the earth beneath a fiery sky, she screamed a war cry that rang like thunder.

'For the God-Emperor!'

Blistered, half-blinded, Arnokh swept his axes towards her but Celestine was ready. She leapt. Her blade sliced up and across the daemon prince's chest, cutting deep before ripping out through his jaw. He staggered and Celestine landed, launching into an immediate flurry of blows. Holy light shone from her, so bright Arnokh could barely look. Gore sluiced from the wounds she dealt him. The braziers upon his shoulders guttered, pouring smoke. He swung for her neck but Celestine evaded the blow and cut another deep slice through the daemon's midriff. Arnokh bellowed and chopped downwards, seeking to bisect Celestine. She dodged with ease. Her sword licked out and took his hand off at the wrist. More blood fountained.

'Blood for the Blood God!' Arnokh swung his axe at her head. Blazing like a star, Celestine brought the Ardent Blade up. This time when the weapons met, they did so in an explosion of sparks. She felt her feet skid across the ground, but both Celestine and her blade held firm.

'I don't shed your blood for him,' she snarled. Servo-motors screaming in her armour, Saint Celestine thrust with all her might and drove Arnokh's axe aside. Two hands firm upon her weapon's grip, she thrust the point of the Ardent Blade deep into the daemon prince's chest.

Arnokh stiffened. His maw yawned in a silent howl, light spilling from it. Radiance burst from his helm and erupted through every chink in his armour. The braziers on his shoulders leapt with golden flames then exploded. His axe hit the ground and shattered.

Arnokh the Bloodlord vanished within the Emperor's light.

When it faded, all that remained of him was ashes on the wind.

At the daemon prince's demise, the fires above died. As they flickered out, they gave way to blue skies. As the sun's light spilled down so Celestine's own faded, yet even as it did, she heard voices raised in battle hymns. Cheers rang from the trenches. Banners waving, priests at the fore, the Coskan and Sarmathian soldiers ploughed into what remained of the daemon horde.

The city still burns, and many more good souls will be slain before this fight is over, thought Celestine as the weight settled upon her shoulders again. *Another enemy waits for me beyond the veil, and my duty is far from done.*

But as she watched the cheering Imperial soldiery drive their enemies back, Celestine knew that they would be victorious, and that she had done her part in that. For today, that was enough.

Ardent Blade flashing, Saint Celestine charged in to join the last battle for Machoria.

EPHRAEL STERN: THE HERETIC SAINT

DAVID ANNANDALE

PART ONE
IMPERIUM NIHILUS

Prologue

MONSTER

'We must be getting closer,' Lord Inquisitor Otto Dagover said to the dead man. 'I think we *are* getting closer.'

'Why do you think we are getting closer?' the dead man asked. He spoke without inflection or understanding. His eyes were blank, unfocused. He was upright, his spine held vertical by the iron armature connected to the clumsy wheeled chassis that enclosed his legs. His arms hung limp, and a gnarled mass of networked electrodes covered his shaven skull like a nest of spiders.

'The stories are multiplying,' Dagover said. 'We heard so many on the last two worlds. And they were more detailed than the myths we have become accustomed to.'

'Why do you think they were more detailed than the myths?' the dead man asked. The corpse's name had been Kayon Velthaus. He had been an inquisitor, younger and less influential than Dagover, but an intelligent operative, and Dagover had enjoyed speaking with him. He missed their conversations. Sadly, Velthaus had not survived the century and more since the Astronomican had vanished. He had succumbed, despair for the future overwhelming his ability to withstand the wounds he had suffered after yet another skirmish with the abominations of the Ruinous Powers. How long ago had that been? Twenty years now? Perhaps thirty? Dagover could not remember, and had no desire to check. It was not a point of pride to have been conducting ersatz conversations with a servitor.

He needed someone to talk to, though. There was no one in the crew he could confide in. Velthaus had been his sole confidant. And so, when the other inquisitor had been on the point of breathing his last, Dagover had commanded that he be made into a servitor. The mindless being's task was a simple one. Whenever Dagover paused, the servitor's voice box repeated his last words in the form of a question. Velthaus was mobile, and Dagover sometimes had the servitor follow him through his rounds on the battle cruiser *Iudex Ferox*. Such processions attracted the fearful gaze of the crew. Dagover knew what the two of them looked like. Velthaus was dead by almost every measure except for the machinic impulses that forced blood through his veins and movement in his body, and yet he seemed closer to life than Dagover. Velthaus' torso was still human. His face was slack, but held traces of youth. Dagover was a monstrous scarab in power armour. He had lost his real arms hundreds of years ago. In their place, he had long, adamantine prosthetics with multiple joints. They were more arachnid than human. The body contained by his power armour was a vestigial thing, barely impinging on his awareness any longer. It lived, and that was enough. His face was a horror of crevasses, hanging flaps of skin and sharpened teeth, framed by a few strands of lank, grey hair. Hooks held the ends of his lips up, minute galvanic shocks giving him the means to move his mouth. His eyes were lenses now, and he was glad of this, because they were less prone to illusion than organs of the flesh. The only flesh he had pride in was the patchwork of leathered xenos hide that formed his cloak.

To the observer, he was a thing that refused to die, controlling a puppet that could not die. Dagover was not displeased by the impression he created. Fear was useful, especially in these dark times. He did not know if the Imperium still existed. He had only the faith that it must. He could not rely on the faith of the crew being strong enough. Not when even Velthaus had despaired. Fear, though, was much easier to renew than faith. So he used the grotesque display of this particular servitor when it suited him.

Most of the time, though, he kept Velthaus here, in his study. Xenos skulls hung on the walls between shelves that groaned with texts forbidden to all but a select few inquisitors. His desk was a black monolith, large enough to be a funereal monument. Most of the volumes stacked on it were analyses of the worlds and the systems that marked out the course of the *Iudex Ferox*'s journeys. They formed a map for Dagover. Less a physical one, more a historical record. They were one of the means by which he tracked his quarry. And he was growing close. He had to believe that he was.

He was not on the verge of despair. But he would welcome tangible hope.

'The stories are more detailed than myths because they are told by eye-witnesses,' he said to the servitor. 'Even though it was from a great distance, they saw something important. Something that changed them. They beheld the proof that the Emperor still protects. The Imperium exists. It has not fallen. Because someone is still fighting for it.'

'Why do you think–'

'Silence.' The servitor's robotic question was going to feel too much like an actual interrogation.

Velthaus was quiet, yet the unfinished sentence lingered in the air.

Dagover believed because he must. And because he knew he was not pursuing a phantom. The damage visited upon the Ruinous Powers was real. Dagover was seeing more and more of it, and the battles in which it had been inflicted were becoming increasingly recent.

Recent enough that the *Iudex Ferox* had something close to a full crew complement again. During the worst days after the coming of the darkness, his encounters with the abominations had brought the battle cruiser to the brink. The damage could no longer be repaired, and a few more losses would have robbed it of the ability to travel at all. It had come close to becoming a hulk, Dagover's giant tomb in the void. And then he had come across the first world that the sacred terror had visited. The daemons had been purged from Evensong. Hope, tentative though it was, had returned to the planet. And with it the will to fight. Dagover discovered that his recruits were of finer quality if, instead of ordering a forced harvest of bodies, he called for volunteers and told them the truth – that he was looking for the being who had brought terrifying salvation to Evensong.

'My lord inquisitor.'

The words brought him out of his reverie. The *Iudex Ferox*'s auspex officer, Bathia Granz, was in the doorway to Dagover's study. Her stance was diffident, cautious, as was the case with every officer that addressed Dagover, especially when they had to do so alone. But there was also an aura around her of barely suppressed excitement.

'We are entering orbit over Parastas,' Granz continued.

Dagover nodded and rose. He and Granz walked down the great corridor towards the bridge. The vaulted ceiling was sixty feet high, and a row of columns to the left and right sectioned off each side into cloisters. Before the darkness came to the Imperium, there would have been hooded figures at prayer in the shadows of the cloisters. They were gone now, more casualties of the *Iudex Ferox*'s long night. The renewal of its crew was still partial, and fairly recent.

On the capital of each column was what, to a stranger's eye, might at first appear to be a coat of arms. They were Dagover's trophies, gathered over his centuries of service in the Ordo Xenos. Mounted on shields were the preserved heads of the Imperium's alien foes. They were frozen in the moment of their deaths, images of hatred and pain amber-locked in time. There were orks, tyranids, kroot, vespid, barghesi and more. Beneath each head were crossed swords, guns or bladed limbs – the weapons of the fallen foe. There was something of both the respect for a valiant warrior and the relish of desecration about the exhibits. It reflected Dagover's feelings. He had not added many trophies of late. The abominations he had had to fight during the last century should have been the province of a different ordo. But where were the forces of the Ordo Malleus, now that they were needed more than ever? Vanished, gone. Swallowed by the night along with the rest of the Imperium.

At first, Dagover said nothing in response to Granz's news. He felt just enough of the same excitement that he had to be certain his voice was its usual dead calm before he spoke again. He had hope for Parastas. Expressing it prematurely, though, would be a mistake.

'Our search will end here, lord inquisitor,' said Granz. For an officer to voluntarily speak to Dagover, their excitement had to be intense.

'You are very confident, Granz.'

'The preliminary scans have shown signs of battle.'

'Recent, you think?'

'Very, my lord. Possibly ongoing.'

'Those are good signs. But even if there is combat occurring, that is not conclusive. What we seek is not the only explanation for a war.'

'But the pattern is correct, my lord,' said Granz.

'That is true.' The trail the *Iudex Ferox* had been following did not appear random. The battle cruiser had moved from one world to another where the Ruinous Powers had been dealt a heavy blow, the battle a little more recent each time, and the systems formed a rough line close to the edges of the monstrous warp storm that had opened more than a century ago – the storm whose coming had marked the disappearance of the Astronomican and with it, as far as Dagover could tell, the collapse of the Imperium. He refused to believe the collapse was total. If it were, he did not know how long he could hold off the despair that had doomed Velthaus. For Dagover, the end of the Imperium would be the end of all hope, but it would also be a cruel, mocking fulfilment of his life's work. The line of worlds where salvation was not a forlorn hope gave him strength. They had found the first few such planets too late for Velthaus, but not for him. The pattern was too pronounced to ignore. It was almost as if someone were seeking to create a barrier that might contain the warp storm.

'Parastas is part of the pattern,' Granz insisted. 'We have found *her*, my lord. *She* is here.' Granz's voice trembled with joyful awe. She was one of the most recent additions to the crew, and one of the few aboard who was a first-hand witness. She had seen the sacred terror from a great distance, but she *had* seen her, and been marked forever by her witnessing.

'Be confident we *will* find her, but be wary of the certainty we *have*,' Dagover cautioned.

'Yes, lord inquisitor.'

'You acquiesce, yet something tells me you aren't really listening.'

'Forgive me, my lord,' Granz said quickly, turning pale. 'I hear and obey. I do not mean…'

'I understand,' said Dagover. They reached the doors to the bridge. 'I understand that Parastas looks promising. Show me, then, what has you so convinced.'

The massive bronze doors parted before them and they entered the bridge. Dagover nodded to Shipmaster Reya Avaxan's greeting. The servo-motors of his armour humming at the edge of hearing, he mounted the steps to the raised strategium in the centre of the bridge. Granz activated the hololith table. It lit up with the latest results from the auspex array. Granz's smile when she saw them was radiant. 'Look!' she cried. 'This is the area we thought was most promising during our approach. We were right! We were right! Praise to the Emperor! His dread-servant walks upon Parastas!' In her religious ecstasy, she seemed to have completely forgotten her fear of Dagover.

The inquisitor leaned over the hololiths, studying the region. Granz amplified the magnification, and the results that had her so excited became clearer.

'Here,' she pointed. 'Heat blooms from recent combat.'

Dagover nodded. 'The intensity of the battle must have been high.'

'And there is distortion in the feed. There is a lot of residual warp energy.'

'So it would seem. This is promising, Granz, but not definitive. This is also a wide area.'

'It is, lord inquisitor. It looks like there have been, and are, numerous battle fronts.'

'And not along a coherent line.'

'Not a line, my lord. A ring. See? The damage we are seeing on the scans appears to have taken place at various times, but if we consider the locations of the front lines…'

'Yes,' said Dagover. 'I see.' He stretched out a limb. His iron-clawed finger traced the lines of combat. Less than two thousand miles across, Parastas was a shrine world, its entire rocky surface covered by necropoleis, monuments, vaults and chapels. It was easy to see patterns of battle from orbit. The shrines had afforded its geography a blocky artificiality, and now it looked as if huge claws had been dragged through the architecture. And the lines had a centre.

There was extensive damage on the other side of the fronts. Fires raged in regions that Dagover took to be occupied by the enemy, and chains of volcanoes were in constant eruption. But Granz was right to be excited. There was a concentration of activity around the front lines, with signs of counter-attacks radiating out from a single location.

'What do we have at the centre?' Dagover asked.

'The latest scans are just coming through, my lord.' Below the strategium, cogitators chattered and mono-tasked servitors moved back and forth between them, carrying strips of data-scrolls to feed back into the machines. The hololiths became progressively more detailed, and Granz was able to increase the magnification still further. 'There is some kind of structure there,' she said. 'A tower, I believe.'

'Then we will begin there,' said Dagover.

His voice was still calm. He felt the hope, though. Despite himself, despite the fear that it might prove to be false yet again, he felt the hope.

I

WOUNDS

Ephrael Stern soared over a breaking landscape. Tremors shattered the crust, gathering strength as if in anger at her arrival. The abominations knew she was coming for them, and at their command the volcanic chain had erupted. Crevasses opened, swallowing vaults and mausoleums; a wall of lava raced outward, transforming the surface of Parastas, creating a plateau miles high, burying all trace of the monuments that had been there. It pained her to think of the destruction this struggle was bringing to the sacred memorials of the Imperium. It was only small consolation that they had been tainted by the worldwide sweep of corruption she had found on her arrival.

Even amongst this destruction, she had faith the shrine of Saint Aphrania would still be standing. It was deep behind the enemy lines, deep within the heart of the Parastas incursion. But it was on the highest peak. It was the holiest site on the desecrated shrine world. It would have resisted.

She had faith.

She had faith.

The heat from below grew, spiking until the auto-senses of her armour strobed with warning runes. Stern shaped psychic lightning into a protective shell around her, and she flew on, closer and closer to the blinding fire and the colossal roaring where once there had been mountains. She passed into the heart of the destruction. The land beneath her screamed. It was a roiling cauldron of eruptions. Enormous columns split away from the mountainsides and tumbled, turning molten, into the magma. The roar of the destruction was a fury that came in waves, yet never seemed to subside. The blood of the world boiled.

As she reached the furnace, the daemons came for her. Through burning air, they streaked her way, screaming their fury, their material forms torn and ragged. The abominations of different aspects of the Dark Gods charged together. The injuries to the materium had been so large on Parastas that daemons of every description had poured over the world like disparate swarms of insects. A plague united in their hatred of a single enemy.

A cloud of crimson-hued furies, barely sentient embodiments of wrath, came at her left, a storm within a storm. Attacking her right was a herald of Tzeentch, riding a chariot pulled by winged, howling screamers. The daemon of change, its flesh the deep pink of exposed muscle, held the reins of the chariot with one hand, while with two more arms it conjured the power of the warp, preparing to cast Stern into a sorcerous abyss.

She clenched her fists tight, the power building around her. She called on the fury of the warp, shaping it with the purity of faith. Then she turned, diving directly at the herald, unleashing her fury.

'Die, abomination,' she roared. 'In the God-Emperor's name, *die*.'

A torrent of light, blistering to the soul, blasted into the daemon. It howled in pain, and its spell exploded. Uncontrolled sorcery enveloped it and its abhorrent steeds. The chariot began to tumble, speed bleeding away, and then a geyser of lava fountained up, swallowing the abominations. They vanished in a conflagration of molten rock and blinding warp explosions.

The furies were caught by the edge of Stern's firestorm. Wings sheared away and daemons spiralled down into the eruptions below. The others swung around, the swarm trying to get at her from behind. She turned, her righteous anger far from sated. Stretching out her arms, holy light leapt from her fists and lightning crackled from her eyes as a nimbus of shattering force surrounded her, and then launched itself forward. The furies screamed, their wrath turning to uncomprehending pain, until they fell as ash, and the ash disintegrated into scarlet sparks of warp-stuff.

Stern flew on, faster now, rushing with the momentum of combat. She weaved around the largest eruptions. Her shell preserved her when she passed through the magmatic blasts she could not avoid. She streaked through a world wracked with convulsions. Nothing was solid. Mountains were sinking. This portion of Parastas had returned to the moments of the planet's shrieking birth.

This is your doing, an insidious voice whispered within her head. *You called this destruction upon this world. This is what the abominations will do to stop you.*

'This is judgement,' Stern replied out loud, her voice vibrating with power. 'Parastas has fallen. Its people turned from the Emperor. Now it pays for its apostasy.'

While all else succumbed, the Shrine of Saint Aphrania would not. That would still be standing. It had to be.

And it was.

The Mountain of Faith Eternal loomed ahead. Deep in the volcanic chain, it rumbled with tremors, but had not yet erupted. As she drew closer, she saw rockslides cascading down its flanks. The ocean of lava had risen to almost a third of its height. Wreathed in smoke and ash, it still towered over every other landmark.

On its rounded peak, the Shrine of Saint Aphrania weathered the cataclysm. It was a squat, brooding structure, its massive walls surrounding the dome that concealed the tomb and reliquary. The saint who slept within had been a visionary and a conqueror, and her monument was even more single-minded in its fortification than the Sepulchre of Iron Sleep. That monument, to the west of the volcanoes, was where Stern had been forced to establish her base, and where she had gathered the relics she had rescued from destruction. The Shrine of Saint Aphrania was ten times stronger. It was designed to hold off a siege that would never come, and protected no one but the dead.

Only the siege *had* come. The invaders clustered along its ramparts, their obscene forms seeming to dance in the hurricane winds of fire and cinder. The abominations had taken the fortress. The holy relic she sought was their hostage. And squatting astride the dome was the worst of the monsters to have come to Parastas. It was a bloated, suppurating, corpulent mass. Internal organs bulged outward from the huge lesions in its gut. It carried a gigantic, rotten, rusting bell in one hand, and a blackened axe, the blade pitted and oozing, in the other. It greeted Stern's arrival by rearing up, flames sliding off its viscous flesh, and spreading its arms in welcome.

'Come to me, thrice-born! Let the rulers of two fortresses meet! Come, and receive the gifts of a present, generous god.'

The daemon had a name, and Stern knew it. She knew it because of the seven hundred within her, the seven hundred Sisters and their knowledge. Because they had fought so long and learned so much of the Ruinous Powers before they had fallen, she knew the daemon too. This was a Great Unclean One, and his name was Thylissix, the One Who Gnaws. He was the spreader of cancers, the sower of tumours. At his presence, flesh and bone devoured themselves. But Thylissix attacked much more than the body.

'Accept the embrace of the Grandfather. He will never abandon you!'

Thylissix found special delight in the canker of the soul. He harvested the blisters of doubt, and the oozing pustules of despair. But while Stern knew this daemon, he knew her too. He attacked while there was still a distance between them, seeking to prise open her faith and set the rot loose inside. He offered her an obscene mirror, drawing connections between them, and then presenting a contrast. His god was always with him. His was the god of perpetual giving.

'You will always be worthy. You will always be rewarded.'

Thylissix shouted with welcome and joy, but Stern heard something quite different behind the daemon's words. She heard pain. She heard anger.

'You are desperate, filth!' Stern shouted back, closing in. *'You should be!'*

The tremors on the Mountain of Faith Eternal intensified. It was stirring to life in order to die. Steam blasted up from opening craters. The walls of the shrine shook and split, hurling daemons down the mountainside and into the cauldron.

Thylissix raised his great bell and swung it. A muffled yet deafening toll resounded over the volcanic chain. Each peal was louder than the eruptions, and sounded like a corpse striking lead. The bell swung, and the ash in the air turned to flies. They battered upon Stern's shield, buzzing and biting. Each insect was a fragment of doubt, and millions surrounded her. The shield blackened. The light became dirty. Heat and corrosion reached for Stern.

'Hear the call of the Grandfather! Hear the wonder of his promise!' the daemon shouted.

His bell tolled and tolled and tolled.

Stern saw nothing but the night of flies. She sensed the arc of her flight altering. Her stomach dropped. She was falling. Tumbling into the waiting, lethal embrace of the Great Unclean One.

'No,' she hissed. 'You will fall to me, abomination. I am the invader now. I am the threat, and you, Thylissix, cannot hide your fear.'

The flies could not touch her. The doubt could not touch her. She had lost the favour of the God-Emperor, but she served Him yet. She always would. He was the Father of Mankind. There could never be a capitulation to the Grandfather of Disease.

Stern summoned the light again. She felt the power of the warp surge through her body, her mind, her spirit. She moulded it with the outrage of faith, then sent it out to burn the One Who Gnaws.

The bell tolled, but the flies vanished, incinerated by the psychic blast. The bell tolled, and the ash-that-was-flies swirled around her, becoming the vortex of a storm. The buzzing horrors could not approach her. They burned when they drew near.

Thylissix raised his terrible axe.

Stern's excoriating beam hit him in the thorax. The daemon staggered, roaring in pain. The bell dropped from his hand. It bounced against the dome. Where it hit, the rockcrete rotted and turned soft as sponge. A portion of the roof disintegrated. The bell rolled down, struck the wall, rotting it too, and then rolled over the edge of the mountain. It plummeted into the eruptions. When it vanished, its final peal was a shriek.

Thylissix swung the axe. His blow was weakened, his aim off as his other hand clutched the open wound. The side of the blade smashed through Stern's protective shell. It struck her like a wall and hurled her down the base of the dome. She hit with the force of an artillery shell, punching a crater into the dome and the breath from her lungs. Masonry exploded around her, and her armour thrummed.

Stern screamed in agony, her body now a single mass of pain. Worms crawled over her armour, probing for cracks, probing for weakness, their movements a sinuous questioning. *Now? Now? Are you weak here? Do you doubt here?*

She gave them her answer. 'No!' She took hold of the pain, made it hers and answerable to her alone, and she rose to her feet.

Thylissix howled. The wound in his chest was a huge one, and it was spreading. The daemon's flesh was black. Instead of putrefaction, it was the black of incineration. There was no joy to be found in the festering of an injury. There was only the pain of dissolution, the agony of a form losing its hold on the materium.

'You will beg Grandfather Nurgle for the balm of his gifts!' Thylissix roared. He readied the axe once more.

The mountain shook and the shrine canted suddenly, staggering the One Who Gnaws.

Stern flew upward, away from the rising lava. She was the lightning of faith, and she concentrated the power into the blade of her sword, Sanctity. Thylissix swung his weapon. The attack was weak, foredoomed. Stern struck. Blazing with light, she dragged Sanctity upward, into the wound. Flesh parted. Tumours rolled, burning, down the torso. She flew upward still, slicing into the neck, and into the obscenely soft jaws and skull.

Thylissix screamed, his agony becoming slobbering, broken syllables as the sword cut his tongue in two.

Stern flew higher, faster. She was a meteor now, shooting skyward instead of down, a rising angel.

The daemon fell silent. His head parted. The two halves lolled on opposite sides. The great, hideous body fell. Stern flew above it, then paused, hovering, to see the purging complete. Already disintegrating, Thylissix slumped away from the dome and collapsed on the walls, crushing more daemons beneath him. His mass became a semi-coagulated liquid, his skin its too-weak crust. He flowed over the walls, bringing them down. Stone and abomination became a gelid wave. Lesser daemons struggled, drowning in the eldritch putrefaction. More crevasses opened in the mountain, and the first streams of lava emerged on the peak, omens of the eruption to come. The flow burned the corpse and the abominations trapped within it. Very quickly, the enormous foulness shrank, its essence returning to the dark corners of the warp that had spawned it.

The mountain shook again. Cracks spread over the dome.

Hurry, Stern thought. The shrine had already well rewarded her faith. If she tarried and lost the relic within, the sin would be hers.

She shot down through the gap opened by Thylissix's bell, the psychic power crackling off her armour bringing light to the interior of the vault. Lesser daemons surrounded the marble tomb in the centre of the floor, and she fell upon them in fury. She hit the ground with an impact of thunder, and a shock wave of incandescent psychic energy exploded from her, flash-burning the horrors where they stood. For a few moments, their carbonised bodies were motionless, echoes of the statues erected by the penitents around the Sepulchre of Iron Sleep. Then they collapsed into blackened dust.

The eerie silence was broken as huge, jagged wedges of stone thrust up through the floor, steam hissing between them. Chunks of the dome and the upper walls fell, smashing to splinters.

Hurry.

The centre of the chamber was still intact, the tomb and its reliquary untouched. But they would not be for long if she did not hurry.

Stern ran towards the tomb, leaping over the chasms opening up in the floor. The dome shook again, and the heat was rising. Angry red light shone from the depths of the mountain. Another tremor was almost strong enough to knock Stern off her feet.

She reached the tomb. Its sanctity was so strong that the upheavals in the chamber faded into the background of Stern's awareness. She knelt before the memorial of the great saint. The marble tomb depicted Aphrania lying with her hands clasped around her sword, her eyes open as if commanding those who looked upon her to take up her cause for the God-Emperor. Though this was a tomb, no actual remains were here apart from the relic itself. Aphrania had died in combat. That her skull had survived was the first of the miracles.

The reliquary case was fixed to the sarcophagus, just past the head of the statue. It was a cage of gold and armourglass. Inside, the skull of Saint Aphrania rested on a cushion of violet silk.

'Holy Aphrania,' Stern prayed, 'I have come to take you from this place. You have been vigilant over Parastas. Now it is I who needs your sight. You, who are worthy of the Emperor's grace, grant me your intercession. Allow me to see by the God-Emperor's light. Let me perceive the path I must take to redeem myself and prove myself worthy of His guidance once more.'

The tremors eased suddenly, as if the saint had commanded a moment of calm.

Stern removed her helm and her gauntlets. The front of the reliquary was hinged, and she opened it reverently. She paused, her hands a few inches from the skull. It was dark grey. The centuries lay on it, invisible yet weighty. In the dimness of the chamber, where the only light was the pulsing red of the rising lava, the eye sockets of the skull were dark and deep beyond fathoming.

'You can see,' Stern whispered. 'Even now, you can see. Grant me this boon, that I may serve the Emperor as I should. Forgive me, now, as I presume upon your sanctity.'

Stern reached for the skull and picked it up.

She held it with both hands. She stared into its black gaze.

Nothing. No visions came to her. She saw nothing except old bone. She felt nothing except the slight weight of the skull in her hands.

'Please...' she begged. 'Emperor. Father of Mankind! Will you not speak to me at last?'

The skull, aged to parchment fragility, crumbled to dust.

Stern howled. She sank to her knees, the fragments of bone spilling between her fingers. The chamber lurched again, but she didn't care. She closed her eyes, burying her head in her hands. She keened, her cry utterly inarticulate because there were no words for this grief, this guilt, this despair. She was beyond redemption. Somehow, she had sinned so profoundly, departed in so irredeemable a way from the Emperor's design for her, that there was no returning to His grace. There was only darkness, now. No visions would ever come again. No blessing of purpose. No guidance to show her how to fight for an Imperium that believed she was a monster and worse.

She cried out with all her soul. Her psychic identity reached out for the dream currents of the warp. Abandoned, she accepted her punishment and embraced the nothingness that awaited. She would not seek to see past it any longer. She would not delude herself into thinking forgiveness would come. She had been arrogant without knowing it, prideful to believe that her path had been so clearly and irrevocably delineated.

Then a great *nothing* came for her.

Her breath froze, silencing her cry.

The nothing *moved.*

The nothing *advanced on her.*

The blankness was something more than an absence. It was a monstrous *presence*. It was suffocating, smothering, a total blank, yet a blank that had something close to a substance. It was active.

This was not about her penance or her sin. This thing, this *nothing,* was not aimed at her. It was terrible, all-encompassing. The totality of the *nothing* showed her a truth so awful that she had never contemplated its possibility. Perhaps she should have seen it, in this long century and more that she had fought on world after world, desperate for any sign from the Emperor. Everywhere she went, the Ruinous Powers revelled in triumph. Everywhere she went, she faced civilisations plunging into darkness. Nowhere had she found any other active forces of the Imperium, beyond the desperate, lost remnants on those worlds. Every provisional victory had been one that she and Kyganil had had to forge on their own.

All that evidence, and she had not seen. She had not seen, because she had faith. Who, with faith, could conceive of this truth?

Who could believe the Imperium was gone?

Who could believe the *God-Emperor* was no more?

That was the truth of the *nothing.*

There could be no other explanation for a void so complete.

Stern rose. The tremors were shaking the chamber again, more and more violently. Steam filled the space, and the heat was unbearable. The floor trembled and split. The tomb of Saint Aphrania tilted to one side as its dais slumped. Stern looked at the ancient reliquary.

'What must I do now?'

There was no saint to hear her. There was no miracle to be granted. Not any more.

It was time to leave.

Stern donned her helm and gauntlets once more. She formed the psychic shield again, blocking the worst of the heat. Wreathed in spirals of warp lightning, she rose from the buckling floor. Gathering speed, she flew up through the hole in the dome. The entire shrine shook, the tremor so huge that the walls seemed thin as parchment, brittle as glass. Stern looked down briefly as she climbed higher. The peak of the Mountain of Faith Eternal fell in on itself. The largest volcano on Parastas, and the longest to slumber, was finally awake. The crater opened, swallowing the shrine and the daemons that remained on its walls.

The memorial to Saint Aphrania disappeared. It had lived only a few moments longer than the relic it had held.

Stern turned away. There was nothing more to see here. She had to go higher. She sensed the need for one more confrontation to complete the growing truth in her soul.

She climbed higher and higher, leaving behind the raging land. She flew through incandescent clouds of ash and burning gases, into the dark storms over the volcanoes. Driven to fury by the concentrations of ash, lightning struck in every direction. Violent thunder merged with the deeper cracks and roars of the eruptions below. Winds buffeted her. Cyclones sought to pull her into their spirals of destruction.

She kept climbing.

For a long time, she suffered a different sort of blindness. She could see nothing in the darkness of the storms except for the flashes of lightning and the glow of the burns. She was surrounded by a maelstrom of destruction, one without direction and without features. She had no sense of where she was going, or how far remained until she arrived. Her path was concealed from her. It was a fit punishment, and she accepted it without complaint. She withstood the attacks of the storms and climbed, always higher.

Finally, she broke through the top of the clouds. Below her was the billowing black and red of the ash storms. Above, she looked into clear night. Below was the wound that the erupting volcanoes had cut into the flesh of Parastas. Above, cutting across the firmament, was the greatest of wounds.

She had thought the Emperor had forsaken her, that she was being punished for her failures, or perhaps, at last, for being the unclean, warp-tainted thing that she was.

He had not abandoned her. He had not fallen silent. He was gone.

What was the rift? Had it done more than conceal? Was it truly a wound, the mark left by that which had destroyed the Imperium and its father?

She looked at the atrocity in the void. Her soul recoiled to gaze upon it.

'This is substance,' Stern said to herself. 'That is not *nothing*.'

The rift had made things vanish. Half the galaxy was on the other side of it, invisible to her. But it blotted out what she wished to see through its overwhelming presence. It was Chaos. It was the immaterium spilling over all boundaries into reality. It was destruction.

It was far more than nothing.

And it had been present for more than a century.

Suspended between the sight of two horrors, Stern turned her inner eye back to a third. To the smothering *nothing*.

Darkness. Void. Annihilation.

Approaching.

The *nothing* had swallowed the Emperor and His Imperium. And it was not done. It was still hungry. It was closing in. It would not be done until the galaxy entire was devoured. Perhaps it would not be sated even then. *Nothing* was coming, and it brought a final, endless, empty night.

It was too vast for her to see its contours. That was why it had been so easy to think it all a blankness directed at her. She sensed the movement now, though. She sensed the *cold*.

'Emperor, I will fight on in your name until my last breath.'

She would confront the *nothing*. She did not know what it was, much less how to fight it. But she would struggle for this small, unconsumed part of the galaxy. She would struggle, with all the fury of her faith, to avenge the God-Emperor.

In the darkness between maelstroms, she had found her path.

II

THE FIELDS OF THE PENITENT

The Valkyrie *Xenos Bane* dropped Dagover and his squad a mile from the base of the tower. There had been no response to vox hails as the assault carrier had made its descent through the atmosphere, and Dagover had decided not to risk even the appearance of making an attack run. The troops who disembarked with him were veterans of the defence forces of four different worlds. They did not have the skills of Dagover's initial crew. They had, though, fought and survived on worlds overrun by daemons. What they lacked in training, they made up for in resilience. And they were all from worlds that had been visited by the sacred terror. Their combat readiness and stoic determination could not conceal the soul-deep eagerness in their eyes. They were all converts to Dagover's quest. Like Granz, they believed the goal was within sight.

Xenos Bane left them on a patch of level ground. It had not always been so. The low, shattered walls surrounding the area showed that a towering mausoleum had once stood here. The surface under Dagover's boots was smooth, blackened glass. The ground vibrated with the distant rumble of volcanoes in the east. Their wrath turned the horizon into a pulsating sunset. There was no combat here, though. Nor was there any detectable within miles of the landing site.

'Peace reigns here,' said Irvo Werhig, looking around. He was the sergeant of the squad. His face was a mass of burn tissue, and his single eye stared with a fanatic's commitment.

'I'm not sure *peace* is precisely the right word,' Dagover said. He had heard wails coming from nearby when they had landed. They were growing louder. 'It is true, though, that the fighting here has stopped.'

'This is her work,' said Werhig, and there was a murmur of agreement from his troopers. '*She* has been here. This is her work.'

'We'll know soon enough.' Dagover began the march towards the tower.

The structure loomed over the landscape, much higher than any of the monuments surrounding it. Many of them had been destroyed in the battles that must have raged over the area. Their rubble had been hammered flat. Some had been sheared away, as if they had been stalks of wheat before the passing of a monstrous scythe. Not everything had been destroyed, though. Some smaller tombs and statuary were still standing. And as he made his way through the ruins, he saw that there was new construction happening.

The wailing filled the air with a thick miasma of repentance and despair. The people of Parastas came into sight. Some crawled in the direction of the tower, raising pleading arms as they cut their flesh to bloody rags over the shards of rockcrete. Others cowered, facing the same way, abasing themselves and gabbling incomprehensible prayers. Their fear and their shame were clear, though. Many, many more were at work on the new statues, whose details came into focus as Dagover approached.

'Who are these people?' one of the troopers asked.

'Heretics,' said another, raising her plasma rifle.

'Hold your fire,' said Dagover. There were hundreds, possibly thousands, of the desperate, howling people. They were ignoring the squad, though. 'Do not let them distract us from our purpose.' He also needed to study them more closely. There were things to be learned here.

The trooper was right. The people were heretics. They were covered in blasphemous tattoos and scarification. Unholy runes defaced their flesh. Their bodies bore the marks of fealty to the Ruinous Powers. Yet there was no rage here, no dark celebration, no worship, as he would have expected it. The reverse was true, he saw, as they passed the first of the statues. It had been carved from a broken column. The work was as crude as it was unmistakeable. It was a depiction of a daemon at the moment of its destruction. The horned abomination's maw was wide in fear, its arms outstretched in agony. Its lower limbs looked as if they were melting into stone. The heretics had created the graven image of defeat. The same was true of the next statue, and the next. The figures multiplied the closer the squad came to the tower. It was as if an army of daemons had been petrified, and all their doomed faces were turned towards the tower.

'This is not worship,' Dagover said. 'This is repentance.'

The crowd grew thicker as the squad advanced. The wailing was deafening. The people tore at their flesh with their nails and with jagged stones. They whipped themselves. They laboured on statues, they wept, they begged and they howled. The night shook with their desperation. They sought forgiveness.

They had not received it.

The tower was a colossal fortress-sepulchre. A high, forbidding wall of rockcrete and iron surrounded a structure that rose as a step pyramid, from whose peak a tall, rounded spire emerged. The top of the spire was encircled by a parapet, which seemed to look down at the land with brooding judgement. The structure was black, its sculptures a brutal, remorseless symphony of mourning, remembrance and calls to penitence and duty. Martyrs and heroes, rendered in immense proportions and wrapped in death shrouds, had their gazes turned to the horizons. There was no mercy to be found in them.

The penitent cultists held back from the wall. Fearful, they left a wide space between themselves and the sepulchre's gate. Those at the forward edge of the line stretched their arms out, begging for that which would never be given, but they did not take another step forward. None of them even glanced at the inquisitor and his troops.

Dagover paused at the edge of the open ground and smiled grimly. 'Look,' he said to the squad. 'See this boundary that the heretics cannot cross? That is the demarcation line where need finally encounters a level of fear that it cannot surmount.'

'Perhaps some tried, and their fates have taught the others that fear,' said Werhig.

'Perhaps,' Dagover said. The ground between the penitent and the wall was wide open. The shrines that had been here had been utterly destroyed in the battles that had surrounded the tower. The ruins were powder and loose stone. Dust eddied in the mournful wind. 'But I think the repentance we see is a result of the destruction that occurred here and elsewhere. I do not see any bodies before us. It is not the fear of retribution that holds these people back. It is awe. At its most fearful.'

'Then we who have been saved by her have nothing to fear,' Werhig said. He took a step forward.

Dagover reached out, the articulations of his long arm grinding softly. He touched Werhig's shoulder and the sergeant froze. 'Wait here,' he said. 'We do not wish to risk our approach being misinterpreted.'

Werhig blanched and stepped back. 'No, my lord.'

'I will go alone,' said Dagover.

He started across the shattered plain. The cries grew even louder.

The penitent saw him now. They saw him doing what they dared not. Did they envy him? he wondered. Or did they fear the retribution that would now come?

He walked slowly, boots crunching slivered rubble. The gate loomed before him, its relief work depicting a single kneeling, shrouded figure. Its hands were clasped and raised, offering the Emperor the force of its grief, compelling the onlooker to take up the torch of duty.

The gate was closed but did not appear to be barred. Dagover took hold of one half and pulled. His armour's servo-motors strained, and with a slow grind, the gate opened. He entered the gloom of the passage running through the wall. The other side opened into a narrow courtyard. The sepulchre loomed over Dagover, its walls marked by the maws of hundreds of vaults. Carved into the massive entrance doors was the same figure that had been emblazoned on the gate. Its features concealed by the hood, it faced outward now, as if demanding to know if the viewer had followed its example.

Dagover tried the doors. They, too, were unlocked, and he passed into the sepulchre. There was illumination here, albeit dim. Lumen torches, mounted every twenty feet along the walls, cast a funereal glow over the interior. The shadows at the edges of the light were deep and still as grief. Vaulted corridors branched off the main one, each holding rows of crypts ten storeys high. Dagover advanced towards the centre of the monument, the sound of his footsteps echoing back at him.

At length, the corridor ended at an immense chamber, its shadowed roof hundreds of feet up. Narrow stone staircases cut down to each landing of the stepped walls. The crypts were beyond counting, a vast hive of the dead. Dagover looked up, and saw the shaft of a column extending skyward from the centre of the chamber's ceiling. The effect was dizzying, the spiral of lumen torches in the spire a distant thread of cold stars.

On the floor of the chamber were the tombs of cardinals, vying to outdo each other with the complexity of their bronze and gold ornamentation. In between the tombs were piles of books and reliquaries. These were objects that had been rescued, over time, from the rubble of destroyed monuments, he realised. The struggle for Parastas had not been a short one, and it was not over yet.

This was why they had been able to catch up with *her*.

A shadow moved. It was silent. It was just enough of a disturbance in the stillness of the sepulchre to draw Dagover's attention. That was, he was sure, precisely the intent. He turned to his right. An aeldari warrior crouched on a tomb a short distance away, power sword in one hand, pistol aimed steadily at Dagover.

The inquisitor recognised the type of armour worn by the alien. It was sleek, engineered for maximum agility. The coat the aeldari wore was flowing, its collar high. The effect was theatrical, a performance. This was a Harlequin. Dagover had killed more than one over the years. But he had not come to do that here. And the colouring of the Harlequin's gear was unusual. It was dark, devoid of the markings that would have identified the aeldari's troupe. It was battle-scarred too, its elegance eroded by long years of combat.

Dagover stretched his arms and opened his hands. The gesture was symbolic of his purpose, not his ability. Though he was not holding a weapon, he could easily punch through stone. 'I must speak with her,' he said.

'Do you, human? You declare this role for yourself upon this stage?' the aeldari said. 'But what of our leading lady? Are you so certain that you perform together? *Must* she speak with you?'

'I hope she will.'

'Many have regretted that hope.'

'I do not think I will.'

The aeldari's blank expression was as eloquent as a shrug.

Light descended from above, silver-white light that cut as sharp as a blade. Dagover winced and looked up, squinting. There was a figure in the centre of the light. Psychic energy crackled around the silhouette, lightning emerging from the dark centre of the storm. The figure dropped slowly from the shaft of the spire, and pulled the shimmering, pulsing, dangerous light inside itself, gradually containing an energy whose purity was lethal.

Boots touched the marble floor a few feet from Dagover. A woman in dark, battered power armour stood before him. Her hair was white as death, and for a few moments her eyes were even more so. An awful white, the blank white that was the overflowing of power. Tendrils of lightning flickered in their corners.

Her very gaze can destroy, Dagover thought.

The Sister of Battle looked at him. She had less of an expression than the Harlequin. She might have been a statue. She might have been the cold of the void.

'You should not have come here,' said Ephrael Stern.

III

THE DESTROYER AND THE PREDATOR

The man was a reptile.

She must be wary.

Stern eyed the inquisitor. It had been a long time since one had found her. She supposed she should not be surprised one was still looking for her. She had grown used to their obsessive pursuits, and with all other meaning in their lives gone, their obsessions might be all they had. Still, she was bored with these witch-hunters. The Inquisition was not a threat to her any longer, not after her second death. Not after she had embraced the full flowering of her power.

She had given the inquisitor his warning. Now, with tedious inevitability, he would ignore it. He would attack, and she would have to deal with him. Once, she and Kyganil would simply have stepped into the webway, leaving another officious, blinkered fool behind. But she felt held on Parastas, as if her task here was not finished. She did not know where to go. She did not know how to fight the *nothing* that had come for the Emperor, and soon would come for everything else.

So she would not run from this man. Nor would she kill him. She would not kill a loyal servant of the Emperor. She would have to remove him from her path, though.

If he was corrupt, then the task became easier – and it would be easy to believe the worst of this man, with that death's head of a face emerging from the power armour, and those inhuman optics instead of eyes, concealing whatever remained of his soul. Stern knew the flaws in quick judgements, though. She had been on the receiving end of many.

'You are wrong,' the inquisitor said. What remained of his natural voice was a serpentine rasp. The vox-amp in his gorget magnified it into a phantom, echoing growl. 'I am exactly where I should be. I am where I have been destined to stand. Hail, Chosen of the Emperor. Hail, Thrice-Born.'

That was unexpected. Stern had never imagined those words being spoken by a servant of the Inquisition. Still wary, she said nothing.

'I have been seeking you for a hundred years and more,' the inquisitor continued. 'It must be with the Emperor's grace that I see you at last.'

'The Emperor's grace,' she repeated softly. Hearing those words from another's lips wounded her anew with fresh grief. At the same time, she resented the inquisitor's manipulations. He was choosing his words well, telling her what he thought she wanted to hear.

She sensed Kyganil tensing, as alert to a trap as she was. The inquisitor's words of welcome made her far more suspicious than the usual anathema. 'Why have you been looking for me?' she asked.

'Because the Imperium needs you.'

'The Imperium.'

'Of course.'

She grunted. 'I see. You come with offers of absolution, do you? Promises of reconciliation with the Adepta Sororitas?' A promise she would not believe. She was a psyker, tainted by the warp, and a heretic in the eyes of all Sisters of Battle. They would not welcome back an unclean, twice-resurrected being.

The man's smile was an awful thing. Hooks pulled his lips back, revealing teeth filed to points. 'No,' he said. 'I make no such promises. Who would even believe I had the power to make them a reality? You would not. Anybody who did believe that would be of no use to me. No. I am here because I know what is needed. *You* are needed.'

She shook her head. 'Do not lie to me. I know that the Imperium is gone.'

The smile vanished. 'It is wounded. It is not gone.'

The man's sincerity gave her pause. His faith was unbroken. A needle of shame pierced the wall of her grief.

'How do you know?'

'The alternative is unthinkable.'

She sighed. 'You do not know what I know.'

'I have seen worlds where you have passed, and the faith in the Imperial creed is renewed. Worlds that stand against the darkness that has swept across the galaxy with the coming of that rift. They have new hope, and new light. Some of their citizens have travelled with me in my search for you.'

'And *who* are you?'

'I am Lord Inquisitor Otto Dagover of the Ordo Xenos.'

'Xenos,' Stern repeated. She turned to Kyganil. 'Stand with me, old friend,' she said. If Dagover believed the ordos still existed, then he was an enemy.

The aeldari moved to her side. Though he did not sheathe his weapons, he lowered them, showing how little the threat of the inquisitor mattered.

'Ordo Xenos,' Stern said again. 'Then, Inquisitor Dagover, the friendship you see before you is blasphemous in your eyes, and we must be destroyed.' She took in the nature of Dagover's cloak. Her lip curled in disgust and azure sparks snapped from the ends of her fingers. 'Have Kyganil's kin become part of your war attire? Are you seeking to provoke his attack?'

The reptile smiled again. 'I come before you as I am so that there can be no secrets between us.'

Kyganil's expression did not change, but Stern sensed his sour amusement. She shared it. If an inquisitor promised to be open, the secrets he was hiding must be immense. 'Go on,' she said, her voice neutral.

Still that awful smile. 'I see that you do not believe me. I am not offended. I would not believe me either, were our positions reversed. Nevertheless, I maintain that I have no quarrel with your companion.'

'You appear to be a poor servant of your ordo then, inquisitor.'

'To the contrary. I am a clear-eyed one. I understand the difference between means and ends. It is the ends that matter.'

'That is a dangerously radical position. It is an invitation to corruption.'

'That is true. When I said I was clear-eyed, it is because I must be.'

He had no eyes at all, Stern thought. Dagover looked at reality through Mechanicus constructs. He must despise his flesh and seek to conceal his soul. She wondered what, exactly, his conception of clarity was.

'You said you have been searching for me for over a century. That surprises me.'

'You are used to being pursued by the agents of the Ordo Malleus.'

'I am.'

'I have friends of that calling. It is through them that I first heard of you. Their records were useful, if misguided. That is the problem with so many of the Ordo Malleus. When you are consumed with being a hammer, everyone begins to look like a witch.'

'You saw something else.'

'I did. I saw a great weapon.'

She wondered how strategic his candour was. 'I am not a tool for you to use.'

'Of course you aren't.' And again, Dagover smiled. 'I was looking for you before the darkness came. I have seen what you have done since. You have pushed the darkness back. I know you can do even more. The Imperium needs you more than it ever has before.'

Dagover's confidence in the existence of the Imperium continued to give her pause. She knew what she knew. She had seen the *nothing*. Yet Dagover's belief gave him a surety of purpose she envied, even with her commitment to avenge the Emperor. No doubt, that was what he wanted. 'In other words,' she said, 'you plan to wield this great weapon you say I am.'

Dagover shook his head. The effect was uncanny, a grub squirming on metal. It was difficult to believe his skull was still connected to anything of the flesh. 'That was my first intention, yes. Doing so is second nature to me. It is what I do with the Deathwatch squads under my authority.'

He paused, as if gauging Stern's reaction. She gave him none. She would not let her guard down. If anything, his openness about his work as an inquisitor made her even more wary.

'You said you would know if I lied,' Dagover said. 'Do I?'

Stern did not know if he believed she could tell. She wasn't sure she believed him at all. She had no doubt that at least some of what he said was true. The question was whether he was being honest in the service of a greater lie. 'Go on,' she said.

'I still think you are a powerful weapon, but your purpose is greater than I supposed. You are the Chosen of the Emperor, and your hour has come.'

'You are deluded,' she said, and she did not hide her sorrow. Fervent belief or manipulative flattery, Dagover's words meant nothing. 'The God-Emperor is...' She trailed off. She could not bring herself to speak the supreme blasphemy, even if it was true.

Dagover misunderstood her. 'None of us can see His will. The

Astronomican is gone. The Imperium lies in darkness. Surely you realised this in your travels?'

'I have spoken to no one but Kyganil for more than a hundred years,' said Stern. On world after world, she had struck, purging the daemons until the local defence forces were able to take up the campaign anew themselves. All of this she did at a distance from the citizens. She and Kyganil were pariahs. They had been for a long time. She had not realised until the Shrine of Saint Aphrania how truly alone she was. How truly alone they all were.

'My ship has not been able to travel in the warp for over a century,' said Dagover. 'My journey has been long, though the distances involved have not. I am fortunate that the worlds you have saved have been near-neighbours. But I should not say fortunate. I should say that my journey has been destined.'

'I would expect you to say that.'

'Justifiably.' Dagover was unperturbed. 'Yet consider the odds against our meeting. And here I am. Will you tell me why you are here? It is because your stay has been prolonged that we are speaking now.'

Stern exchanged a glance with Kyganil. The Harlequin remained resolutely silent. This was her decision to make. He would not interfere in her interactions with other humans. Stern hesitated. She had little reason to confide anything at all to an inquisitor. Yet this one had come in peace, and was speaking as no other ever had. Except one. Silas Hand, long-dead, whose spirit had also vanished from her visions.

She could not trust Dagover. She also could not ignore the possible importance of his presence here.

And the reptile spoke of hope.

'Come with me,' she said.

Dagover followed Stern up the stairs along the chamber walls, and then the great spiral of the spire. Kyganil disappeared into the shadows. Dagover suspected he was not far away, and would reappear suddenly if Stern decided the inquisitor was a threat after all. He had known, from the records he had seen, that Stern had an aeldari ally. He had been prepared for the xenos' presence. He would be happier if he could put a plasma shot through Kyganil's brain and be done with him. But that would ruin what he was trying to accomplish here, so he kept his hands carefully away from his weapons.

Though the climb was a long one, it was effortless for Dagover. He kept up a steady, mechanical pace. His power armour moved at his will. He was barely conscious of the vestigial flesh within any more. At the same time, watching Stern, he felt the chains of gravity as never before. He knew that Stern deigned to rise through the tower by the mundane intermediary of stairs out of a form of courtesy to him. Gravity had no sway over her. The grace of flight and the fury of annihilation were hers to command. The power was barely contained inside her. Now and then, minute ripples of psychic lightning flowed down her cloak and armour. The sight of her chilled his blood. He had forgotten what it was to experience terror. He savoured the sensation with wonder.

Stern was silent as they climbed. Dagover did not try to lure her into conversation. She would speak when she was ready. Prodding her would lead to resentment, and resentment would not lead to trust.

They climbed past hundreds of vaults. The honoured dead of the Imperium rested here, their final sleep undisturbed as yet by the wars that shook Parastas. The tremors of the volcanic eruptions thrummed through the stone of the great sepulchre. It did not threaten the structure. It underscored its eternal strength.

Midway up, Stern broke the silence. 'You said you had no quarrel with Kyganil,' she said. 'Yet you wear that cloak.'

'True on both counts.'

'That position is too fraught to be simple pragmatism.'

'Pragmatism is never simple,' Dagover said. 'Too often, those who lay claim to it are lying about the matters of faith that have determined their position from the start.'

'I am glad to hear you say that. What is the truth of your position? I can see, perhaps, why not being in the Ordo Malleus means that you do not automatically seek my extermination. That distinction is not enough, however. Be clear, inquisitor. Where do you stand?'

Dagover had hoped they would not reach this point so soon. Given how Stern had been branded a heretic and a witch, and been condemned to death by the Inquisition, he doubted her views were in line with the most conservative currents of the ordos. Even so, he could take nothing for granted, except, perhaps, the strength of her faith itself. Where faith took her, he could not know. What stances she agreed with, and which she condemned to fire, he could not know. The best he could do was guess, and hope that he did not guess wrong.

She had asked him a direct question. There was no point in lying, since he did not know what answer would please her, if any. In the past, he had sometimes taken a perverse pleasure in stating outright what many who shared his convictions kept secret. He felt no pleasure now. His convictions had not altered, but the galaxy had, and the new realities held up a painful mirror to his beliefs.

Well then. If he still believed what he had believed all his life, he must hold fast to his convictions and speak them now.

'I believe the old order of the Imperium cannot stand,' Dagover said. 'I believe that too much is stagnant, ossified, and rotting. I believe that gangrenous limbs must be amputated if the body is to be saved.'

His use of the present tense had a marked effect on Stern. She gave him a sharp look. He had struck home, though he did not know how.

'You are a Recongregator,' Stern said quietly.

'You have dealt with others of my faction, then.'

'No. Not directly. I know of you, notwithstanding.' Then even more quietly, as if speaking to herself, she said, 'I know so very, very much.' She raised her voice again. 'You are a destroyer.'

'Of what needs to be destroyed, for the good of the Imperium.'

'This warp storm that seems to have consumed everything. The extinguishing of the Astronomican. Does that give you satisfaction?'

'Throne, no!' The denial was torn out of him. His voice box struggled to convey the rare expression of emotion, and the sound was a dismal braying. 'I seek the renewal of the Imperium, not its destruction. We have strayed so far from what the Emperor wished for us. Finding our way back to His dream will mean great sacrifice. But this, Sister Superior… this is not the destruction that leads to renewal. My fear is that this is the darkness we Recongregators foresaw as inevitable if the Imperium were not renewed. My fear is that everything I have done has been for nothing, and that everything is too late. My *hope* is that you are proof that this is not so.'

'Your hope may be forlorn, Inquisitor Dagover.'

'I don't think so. You are the Chosen–'

She cut him off. 'Do not call me that again. It is not true. If I have been chosen, it is for damnation, because I was not worthy.'

When they reached the top, Stern approached the eastern parapet with Dagover a step behind her. 'What makes you think you are not worthy?' he asked.

'The Emperor has turned away from me.'

'As He has from us all.'

'Our plight is far worse than that.'

The howls of the heretics rose from far below. The cries circled the peak of the spire. The miserable choir had begun shortly after Stern had made the sepulchre her stronghold. It had not ceased since then.

'They call out to you,' Dagover said. He sounded impressed. 'By your actions, you have created an army of the penitent. They have erred, and now they see their crimes against the Emperor for what they are.'

'Do they? Or do they simply fear me?'

'Can you parse the difference between fear and repentance? I cannot.'

'The distinction is irrelevant. They can receive no forgiveness from me.'

'They do not deserve it, of course,' said Dagover.

'They do not. And I am not worthy to give it. But there is also none to be had.'

'What is your purpose here?' Dagover asked. 'You have one, I assume, beyond warring against abominations. You have no lack of choice for worlds afflicted by daemonic incursions.'

'When I came here, I was seeking to regain the Emperor's favour. No matter the means or the lengths I had to go to.' Stern spoke quietly. The words were difficult to say. She had told Kyganil everything, but this would be the first time she revealed the terrible truth to another human. She had chosen to do so with the spectacle of the penitent lost before them, a mirror of their own hopeless state. Yet there was something about Dagover that made her want to find hope, even though she knew there was none to be had. As she began to open up, to someone who would fully understand the loss and need she felt, she experienced a shameful relief.

'You think there is something on Parastas that will help?'

'I thought there was. I came here to save the relic of Saint Aphrania. Her skull was in a shrine to the east, there, where the mountains erupt. I came for Saint Aphrania in the hope of salvation. The Emperor came to her in visions, and because of those visions, she led a crusade that reclaimed a score of systems for the Imperium. I sought a miracle from her, Inquisitor Dagover. I hoped, through her, to see the light of the Emperor once more. I sought a renewal of my greater purpose.'

'Which is what?'

Again, she thought about how much she trusted him. She did not. At all. Did that matter? No. It did not. She had never hidden her calling. Many had not listened, when she had tried to tell them the truth, but that was their failing. 'I hold within me the collective knowledge of seven hundred Sisters of the Orders Pronatus. Their knowledge and their faith. What they learned of the Ruinous Powers must be preserved. To that end, Kyganil has been guiding me to the Black Library.'

'A xenos construct. You would hide the knowledge you carry from human eyes?'

'There is no safer place for it.'

'You have been a long time in getting to your destination.'

Stern gave Dagover a sharp look. 'Do you mock me?'

He showed his pointed teeth. 'Only with the intention of helping you see clearly.'

She refused to be baited, if that was what he was trying to do. 'The journey has been long because I have lost my way, and so has Kyganil. Too many of the routes he would have taken are closed. And I...' She hesitated. Dagover gave every impression of being the last person in the galaxy to inspire confidences. Yet somehow, that was what he had coaxed from her. Perhaps it was the fact that he seemed to have no illusions about himself that made her want to share in that certainty. 'Where I once had visions, I saw nothing. I thought that was because of my unworthiness.' She raised her arms, letting lightning dance along her fingertips. 'Because I am touched by the warp. I *am* unworthy. I *am* tainted. But I have had a vision once more, and seen the true nature of *nothing*. The Emperor is no more. The Imperium is gone. Emptiness and cold, consuming and purposeful, comes to devour everything.'

Dagover was silent. Stern watched him. He looked out over the broken memorials and the desperate penitent below. His withered face was unreadable.

Stern read it all the same. 'You are about to try to convince me that I am wrong.'

'I believe you are. I *must* believe you are. I do not think the darkness that has engulfed the Imperium is a result of the Emperor finding all of us unworthy. I believe the Imperium has been unworthy of Him for a long time. Isn't it possible that you are cut off from Him not by your failure, but by the warp storm that covers half the sky? Or by this *nothing* of which you speak?'

'I have encountered warp storms before. They have never cut me off from my visions.'

'You never encountered one on this scale, though. No one has. Everything has changed, Sister Superior, but it is not destroyed. I have seen too many planets, planets that *you* saved, rejoicing in their faith in the Emperor despite the darkness, to believe that. And I believe your goal must change too.'

Stern favoured his remark with a short, bitter laugh. 'It has. I have no purpose but to fight, for as long as I can, to avenge the God-Emperor. Only I do not know where and how to begin.'

'Then think on this. Is my presence here not a sign from the Emperor, a sign that He still has a path for you to walk? I, too, have lost much of my certainty. *My* path narrowed until all that remained of it was finding you. Having done so, I am at a crossroads. I must find my way forward. I think that, perhaps, I begin to see what it might be. My task may be to help you find your way again.'

'That is a very convenient epiphany, inquisitor,' said Stern.

'It is,' Dagover admitted. 'I do not expect you to take it on faith.'

If he was joking, she was not amused. 'Do not trifle with me about matters of faith,' she warned.

'That was not my intent. Quite the opposite. But come with me. We will fight for the Imperium, and the Emperor. For its renewal, and in His name, and by His will, not in their memory. Again I say that I have caught up to you at this juncture for a reason.'

It was Stern's turn to be silent now. She thought over Dagover's argument. He was being insistent that their meeting was fated, that there was still something to fight for. She wanted to believe him. She wanted to believe there was another way of interpreting her vision of the *nothing*. Dagover was here, now, offering hope at the precise moment she needed it most.

Would she be a fool to accept? Would she be playing into his grasp?

What grasp? What could he force upon her?

It was not what he could force upon her. It was what he could manipulate her into doing.

But she was wary. She knew what he was. The more foolish choice would be to reject the possibility of hope he offered.

'I will travel with you,' she said at last.

'I am glad.'

She looked out over the wailing damned below, towards the thunder of the volcanoes. She had destroyed many abominations, but she had not ended the incursion on Parastas. There was nothing that could be saved here. But there was desecration that could be prevented. 'What is the nature of your vessel?' she asked.

'The *Iudex Ferox* is a battle cruiser.'

'Is it still combat worthy?'

'It depends on the nature of the combat. It still has some of its capabilities.'

'Can it still carry out Exterminatus?' Stern asked.

Dagover regarded her for several seconds, absolutely still. When he laughed, it was the sound of vocal cords scraped over a saw blade.

* * *

Stern walked through the great hall of the sepulchre with Kyganil. She stopped before each of the relics she had saved during the months of the struggle on Parastas. She kneeled, murmuring her thanks to the Emperor and His saints. 'I am unworthy of your blessing, Father of Mankind,' she whispered. 'I do not ask that you hear or answer. I ask only that I be proven wrong about what I have seen. I ask only for a true purpose in your name.'

One of the relics was another skull. It was the head of Cardinal Fehervald, whose preaching enflamed the faith of a hundred worlds. After his death, the touch of his skull had been seen to heal wounds. The head was a relic of inestimable worth. She lingered before the reliquary chest after praying, hoping that she was making the right choices.

'Are you reconciled to these objects' destruction?' Kyganil asked. 'They are the markers of the acts of your culture.'

'Reconciled? No. I acknowledge that inevitability, though.'

'I wonder about the value of this temporary salvage.'

'There are no venerated objects in aeldari culture? No relics whose destruction would cause you pain?'

Kyganil bowed his head, accepting the point. 'I am thinking of our circumstances, and those of this world. One way or another, the preservation of these relics was always going to be a passing thing, a small collection of moments. A brief turn against the tides of fate, and no more.'

'Measured by eternity, is that not true of any salvation?'

'It is.'

'Then why fight to preserve anything at all?'

Kyganil looked sorrowful. 'True. That is the question we perpetually confront.'

'We cannot act with the view of our impact upon eternity, old friend. There is already too much that seeks to make us despair.'

Stern turned back to the remains of Cardinal Fehervald. 'I saved this when I could, because to leave it to ruin would have been a sin. A tomb of oblivion will now come for all these relics, and I will give them the respect of a proper farewell.'

Kyganil nodded again, and they walked on through the rows of salvage.

Despite her words, Stern's prayers felt like too little. Nothing she did felt like enough. The emptiness where the sense of the God-Emperor had been was too vast, too complete. Even if the Emperor still reigned, that did not change the fact that she had fallen from grace. What act by any mortal could possibly be an atonement? And if the *nothing* was not what she had believed, what was it?

What terrified her was the prospect that she had been right all along, and that it was Dagover whose hope was deluded.

When she had kneeled before every relic, Stern went with Kyganil to the top of the spire to look at the repentant masses for a final time.

'Better a holy cremation than a corrupted existence,' she said. The small population of the shrine world had, as far as she had seen, completely turned its back on the Emperor. To claim renewed faith because of their terror of her was not sufficient. There was no one on the planet worth saving.

The sky in the distance glowed black and red. Though it was twilight over the Sepulchre of Iron Sleep, the region of the volcanic chain was trapped in an endless, blazing night. No light from Parastas' weak sun could cut through the thick, warring clouds of ash. The rage of the mountains set the darkness on fire. The horizon pulsed an angry red. The peaks were jagged silhouettes, the fangs of a wrathful land. Stern imagined she could almost see the swarms of abominations cavorting on the slopes, revelling in the torment of Parastas. In her soul, she could hear the chanting of the cultists at the base of the mountains, wretches still singing their praise to foul gods, praying to be spared incineration by lava and burning clouds. Praying too, to be saved from the being of light and slaughter that had pushed them back and back and back until they had to seek shelter in the land of fire.

On this day, she would show them how little their heretical prayers were worth.

'The bombardment is almost upon us,' she said to Kyganil. She had chosen to remain on the planet until it came. The cyclonic torpedo would hit the mountains, and there would be time to leave the Sepulchre for the *Iudex Ferox* before the destruction reached her.

'Do you believe the words of Inquisitor Dagover?' Kyganil asked.

'I do not know yet if I believe anything he says. I trust him only as far as his most recent action. Set aside what I believe, though. What if he is right in what *he* believes? And what if it is no longer my duty and my fate to reach the Black Library? What then? If my destiny has changed, perhaps yours has too.'

'To what?' Kyganil murmured. The words were so soft. Behind their whispered calm lurked a terrible weight. Kyganil had needed Stern as much as she had needed him. They were both outcasts. Their callings had taken them on journeys that had them shunned and worse by those they fought to save. They had both found meaning in their lives by giving the other meaning.

'My hope is that soon, I will know my path once again. And I hope that clarity for one of us will be clarity for both.'

Kyganil glanced up at the sky. There was a break in the clouds over Iron Sleep, and the foul, discordant light of the enormous warp storm was visible at the zenith, slicing across the void like a festering wound. 'I would welcome a return of clarity,' he said. 'We have been long without it.'

Stern followed his gaze. A few stars shone faintly in the darkening evening, their light dimmed and tainted by the warp storm. One of them moved. It was the *Iudex Ferox*, approaching its firing coordinates.

'One way or another,' Stern said, 'a form of clarity is about to break upon us.'

She and Kyganil donned their helms.

Stern did not see the moment that the battle cruiser fired the cyclonic torpedo. She saw the weapon, though, as it tore through the atmosphere. A spear of light rent the clouds. The diagonal streak burned through the air, the flash so quick and searing there was barely time to register what it was. Yet Stern felt a dizzying rush, a sense of tipping deliberately over the edge of an abyss.

Surely, this fall would have meaning.

The torpedo hit in the midst of the volcanic chain. Day – lethal, destroying, consuming day – broke over the landscape. The world flashed white. Stern winced, even with the shutters of her eye-lenses shielding her sight from the full burn of the flash. As the initial burst began to fade, and details of the land returned like the broken lines of an unfinished tableau, the sound came, and with it the wind. The roar of the explosion was the crack of a great ending. The eruptions of the volcanoes were mere sighs in comparison. The wind, furious and burning, slammed into the sepulchre's spire. The tower wavered in the gale. It rocked back and forth, cracks running up its entire length. Stern leaned forward into the wind, her feet planted firmly. Kyganil was at her side, bearing full witness with her of the cataclysm she had called down on Parastas.

The land heaved. Monuments danced and fell. The volcanic chain became a single eruption. Fireballs as big as cities built upon each other in a crescendo of destruction. A red wave rose, climbing twenty miles high, cresting, and then rushing forward. It was lava, surging from beneath the crust like blood from the burst heart of the shrine world. The wave swept over the land, a flood of annihilation. The shrines that still stood in its path vanished, drowned and melted beneath its advance.

'Where are your prayers now?' Stern raged at the heretics. She could not even hear herself. The cultist army at the base of the mountains was gone. The greatest height and strength of the wave would have faded before it reached the region around the Sepulchre of Iron Sleep, but it was high enough that the penitent would see what was coming, and know it for judgement.

'This is all the forgiveness you deserve.'

Where the torpedo had hit, the land writhed. Billions of tonnes of rock evaporated, melted, and twisted in the grip of monstrous tides. Mountains fell. Peaks gaped open, parting like a leviathan's jaws. Where daemons had held their revels and gathered their armies, there was only the furnace of a dying planet.

Soon the lava would reach the Sepulchre of Iron Sleep, and the sanctity of the relics would be preserved by purging fire.

She hoped her despair would die here too.

IV

THE PATHS

Stern wondered if she was looking at a reptile triumphant.

In Otto Dagover's study aboard the *Iudex Ferox*, she and Kyganil stood before the seated inquisitor. She wished the lizard had eyes of flesh. The lenses that looked back at her disguised his soul. The hook-assisted smile was there, and it could, perhaps, have been read as complacent, or merely grotesque. Dagover's flesh was so ancient, so much a skin about to be sloughed off, that all but the most pronounced emotions were impossible to read.

No doubt, Dagover liked things that way.

He presumably liked having the silent, repulsive servitor present. It was in one corner of the study, motionless. It served no purpose that Stern could guess. Neither she nor Kyganil had commented on it. Dagover could do as he willed on his ship, as long as she did not sense that he was working against her.

Stern wondered what victory she might have handed to Dagover by coming aboard his ship. Would she have reread her destiny if he had not urged her to? Likely not. She could not see any alternatives. Whatever the truth about the coming *nothing*, she had to fight it. And travelling with Dagover felt like forging a link to the hope that the Imperium still existed.

Dagover seemed willing enough to assume a victory regardless of her hesitations. 'So,' he said, 'you have chosen the new path of your destiny.'

She did not answer him directly. 'The darkness that approaches is a threat to us all. It will consume everything. It must be stopped. That is my task. I will not presume to claim that I know my destiny.'

'Very wise of you,' Dagover said with his dry croak. The hooks on his face twitched his lips. 'Very humble and pious.'

Was he mocking her? That would be unwise. Power crackled at her fingertips in warning.

'What, then, of the Black Library?' Kyganil asked.

'Do you see a way forward to it?' said Stern.

'I do not,' Kyganil confessed. 'It seems farther away than ever before. Every webway route I think should bring us closer is blocked.'

'Then we cannot go, for now.' The words sounded like *forever* in her head.

'More signs,' said Dagover. 'More and more signs that you should not go at all.'

'I would expect that to be your interpretation,' said Stern.

'Of course it is. Because I am right. What value would there be in bringing that knowledge to this place, so inaccessible to the very peoples that need the knowledge most?'

'There, the wisdom of the seven hundred would not be lost, should anything happen to me.'

'Have you given any thought to how the knowledge held within you is to be extracted?'

Stern and Kyganil exchanged a glance. 'I have,' said Stern. 'We have discussed it. We do not know, though I am prepared to make whatever sacrifice might be required.'

The grunt that emerged from Dagover's voice box was clearly contemptuous for all that it was an electronic noise. 'How pointless.

Can you not see how pointless this is? Why do you resist what is so clear?'

'Clear to you.' Though she knew where he was going with his logic.

'It should be clear to all. *You* are what can be done with that knowledge. *You* are what comes of that wisdom and power. Do you wish me to believe that you carry such power against daemons, and that you have been born three times, only so that you can make this potential vanish? The potential is realised in *you*.'

'You insult me if you think I have not thought of this,' Stern said coldly. 'And of where following this path might lead.' Dagover did not understand the corruption of power, or else he did not fear it. Either possibility made him dangerous.

'Yet you have used your power. For centuries. And you must use it again, against the threat that you have foreseen.'

'On that, at least, we must agree,' said Kyganil.

'I do not know what this danger is,' said Stern. 'All I can see is the all-consuming *nothing*. It is immense.' She paused, and looked significantly at the aeldari and at the Ordo Xenos inquisitor. 'It will devour the galaxy if it is not stopped. So great a threat is beyond what any one species can fight.'

Kyganil's face remained impassive. His eyes sparked with bitter amusement. 'This is not an auspicious place to be discussing alliances,' he said. He gestured, taking in the skulls mounted on the walls of the study.

Dagover made a sound that might have been a laugh. 'Do not let me stop you,' he said.

'You would in other situations,' said Stern.

'No doubt. But not this one. I believe in the danger you have seen, Sister Superior. We have seen too much that has happened to the Imperium in this past century not to imagine another great cataclysm.'

Stern turned back to Kyganil. 'I know this is a lot to ask.'

'You ask only what is necessary, as you ever have.'

'Is there still someone among the aeldari to whom you can speak?' Kyganil was as isolated as she was. Dagover, though, was proof that the isolation was not total.

Kyganil nodded slowly. 'Yvraine,' he said. 'I believe I can find Yvraine. We have had dealings in the past. My ties with her are not broken. She understands the role of the outsider.'

'Excellent,' said Dagover. Stern would have sworn that his eye-lenses gleamed eagerly. 'Let us go at once.'

In all their years together, Stern had never seen Kyganil laugh. He came very close just then, his eyes widening in utter disbelief. '*You* are not coming,' he said. It was as close to sputtering as the aeldari had ever come.

'I think I am.'

'You are not,' said Stern. 'Consider who you are. Your presence would kill any possibility of an alliance before the first word had been uttered. You will wait here for my return.'

'Is that a command?' Dagover's rasp sounded dangerous.

'It is a statement of fact. Unless you have another destination you plan to travel to in my absence.'

Dagover was silent for a moment. 'You do not trust me, Sister Superior.'

'I most certainly do not, inquisitor.'

Stern and the aeldari left his study. At some point in the minutes that followed, they vanished from the *Iudex Ferox*. Dagover had given orders that they be kept under constant, but discreet, surveillance. Officers, distressed at their failure, contacted Dagover over the ship's vox as soon as they had lost sight of the pair and could not find them again.

'They'll be back,' Dagover instructed them. 'Watch for their return.'

He drummed a set of metal fingers on his desk. 'They've entered the webway,' he said to the corpse of Velthaus. 'They did it from inside a voidship. That aeldari is both promising and a threat.'

'Why do you think the aeldari is both promising and a threat?' came the toneless question.

'He appears to have determined his destiny as being shaped by hers. Which means, by my reckoning, he has subordinated himself to her will. That means his abilities are, for now, at the service of a warrior of the Imperium. Stern has a great deal of influence on him. That makes him useful, xenos or not. The question is how much influence he has on her. That was not an issue before I found her. It is, now. I grieve not to be travelling with them.'

'Why do you grieve not to be travelling with them?'

'This is a missed opportunity, despite the risks involved. Think about how much I might have learned, going so deeply into the aeldari realm. It is also a setback.'

'Why is it also a setback?' the corpse asked.

'Because now Stern is completely away from my influence, and completely in aeldari territory, and she is obviously ready to listen to them. If she is right about the scale of the coming threat, then it is good that, through her, we can have a line of communication with that xenos race. Good, with reservations. It would be better if I were there.'

'Why–'

'Silence.' He'd had enough of Velthaus' questions. He continued to address the servitor, though. Doing so helped him clarify his thoughts. 'She does credit me with pointing the way to a new understanding of her destiny. That is important. I am associated with a transformative point in her life. No one shakes that off easily.'

'No one?' said Velthaus.

Dagover stared at the servitor. He had told it to be quiet, hadn't he? Maybe he had thought the words without saying them. But the echo was wrong. It didn't follow the pattern of phrasing, the only pattern the servitor was capable of.

Dagover rose and approached Velthaus. He peered into the dead man's eyes, looking for something he knew could not be there, a sign of the inquisitor's living self.

The servitor returned his gaze with its blank, unblinking absence. There was no one there.

'Did you speak?' said Dagover.

'Why did you speak?' said Velthaus.

Dagover took a step back, uneasy. The pattern was correct. Yet the question felt too pointed.

'Silence.' Dagover spoke clearly, deliberately, marking the fact that he did, leaving no room for ambiguity. And then again, for good measure. 'Silence.'

The servitor said nothing.

What had just happened? Had anything happened?

No. Nothing could have. He had made a mistake. That was all.

But the servitor's unprompted question whirled through his mind. *No one? No one? No one?*

No one could shake off the transformative moment. Not Stern. Not him, either.

Dagover thought again of his first sight of Stern in the Sepulchre of Iron Sleep. He remembered how he had felt, to see a being of such overwhelming power. He had tried to shove aside the soul-deep vertigo that had assailed him. He had acted as he had planned to do.

But the vertigo was still there, deep inside.

Who was changing whom?

The servitor was still, yet the voice in his head belonged to Velthaus.

Who was exerting what influence?

He would have to make sure he knew, he thought. He must be watchful.

It seemed to him there was another voice, very close and terribly far, that urged him to do the opposite – to give in to the vertigo and let himself be carried towards the great flame of Stern.

'Where are we?' Stern asked quietly.

'From one world of holy memory to another. Indeed. I think that Yvraine being here is the reason I was able to find her with relative ease. The art of the dance we now perform is strong, for us to see it so clearly.' The aeldari paused. 'Tread carefully, Thrice-Born. You are a human treading on sacred ground.'

'I will.'

They were in a long wraithbone hall. The walls curved outward from the floor, and then came back together to form an elegant, pointed vault. The lines of the hall gave Stern a sense of flow. No matter which direction they walked, she would feel as if they were being carried along, as if the hall were the embodied essence of a river's current. Kyganil looked around reverently. A sense of the sacred radiated from the walls. In a manner that Stern could not define precisely, she sensed a kinship between the nature of the wraithbone and herself as a vessel for seven hundred souls.

Two guards were walking towards them from one end of the hall. They had left their posts before two large doors. They wore the crimson armour of the Guardians of the Ynnari. Kyganil bowed slightly as they approached, palms open and arms apart, his blades sheathed on his back. Stern followed his example. As he had said she should, she had left her weapons back on the *Iudex Ferox*.

'The Visarch has told the Herald of Ynnead of your coming,' one of the guards said before Kyganil could address them. She was looking at Kyganil, but speaking Low Gothic, implying that Stern was the one actually being addressed.

'Will she receive us?' Kyganil asked.

'She awaits you now.'

The guards turned around. Stern and Kyganil followed. As the guards approached the doors, they opened silently. The guards stopped at the threshold. Stern and Kyganil passed into the throne room beyond. Its ceiling was much higher than in the hall. It rose to the same pointed vault, the room lifting the eyes involuntarily to its peak. Stern found her impressions of the room shifting from one moment to the next, depending on which point she happened to be looking at. At first, the wraithbone designs conveyed a sense of clarity and light, and the thought that, if Stern could just find the right viewing position, she would see to infinity, in time as well as space. But some of the other lines were darker, more jagged, and she conjured her memories of Commorragh and its games of sensual violence and night.

The aeldari seated on the throne united these contradictory feelings. She was swathed in crimson and black, her face sternly forbidding. Her eyes glinted with hard judgement and the hint of coal-dark perversity. She looked first at Kyganil, and then at Stern as they approached. Her eyes narrowed slightly, as if in pain, as Stern drew near. The evaluating gaze with which she favoured Stern was a long one, and carried on for several seconds after Stern and Kyganil stopped a few paces from the throne's dais.

'Your power announces your arrival,' Yvraine said to Stern. 'It is a psychic nova. I have rarely seen its like.'

Stern bowed her head. She said nothing. Yvraine was clearly musing, not in the mood for conversation just yet.

'I wonder if you know the danger you represent,' Yvraine said.

'To the enemies of what I fight for, I think I do,' said Stern, sensing an opening now.

'Perhaps. And perhaps neither you nor they fully understand that either. Perhaps no being does, not even the gods. What would you say to that?'

'That I must be watchful not to let such words lead to hubris on my part.'

Yvraine smiled coldly. 'Quite so. Quite so.' She turned a palm up, and the gesture wordlessly changed the subject. 'I had thought I had heard the last of a need for an alliance with the humans for some time. It seems I was wrong. Must another be sought so soon after the last?'

'The last?' Stern asked, puzzled. She glanced at Kyganil, who looked just as confused. At least, she noted, Yvraine had not referred to humans as *mon-keigh*. That had to be a good omen.

'I would have thought I had done more than enough to help your race, Thrice-Born.'

'I'm afraid I do not understand.'

Yvraine cocked her head, amused. 'No, you don't, do you? Then I will be more direct. Was it not enough for me to assist in the return of Roboute Guilliman?'

The floor seemed to heave beneath Stern. Her balance was suddenly more precarious than it had been in the Shrine of Saint Aphrania. She grappled with what Yvraine had said. The words were fragile. Their meaning was too great. 'Guilliman,' she said. 'Guilliman has returned.' She almost wept with gratitude. Dagover was right. The Emperor still watched over the rest of the Imperium. Nothing else could explain the return of the Avenging Son.

Yvraine leaned forward slightly. 'Then you know nothing of what has transpired on the other side of the Great Rift?'

'We do not, Herald of Ynnead,' said Kyganil.

'Then the reason for your presence here becomes much more interesting.'

'Does the Imperium still exist?' Stern asked, torn between hope and dread.

'It does. Its state was desperate. I believe it still is.'

Stern nodded. The Imperium's extremity must have been terrible for Guilliman to awake.

'But it endures,' said Yvraine. 'When I last took my leave, it endured.'

'You have my thanks for this news.'

Here, Yvraine turned to Kyganil. 'Now tell me why you have sought me out.'

'For the reason you spoke of when we entered, Herald of Ynnead. Once again, the aeldari and the humans must stand together.'

'Against what?'

Kyganil looked at Stern.

'There is something approaching,' said Stern. 'A nothingness of terrible vastness. I do not know much more than that, but I am sure that, if we do not stop it, it will consume the galaxy.'

Yvraine said nothing for a long moment. Finally, she asked, 'This is a vision you have had?'

'It is. For a long time, I did not know it was a vision. The absence is so huge, so suffocating, that I believed I no longer had any visions at all. When I perceived the absence truly, even then I did not understand what it was.'

'I see.'

Yvraine rose. At the same moment, a wraithbone column emerged from the floor in front of the throne, its base an unbroken part of the whole. It took the form of a braided stand. At its crown was an orb that shone a pure white. 'Come closer,' Yvraine said. She stepped off the throne's dais and stood in front of the column.

Stern walked forward until they were facing each other across the orb. This close, Stern felt as if just beyond the edge of her hearing, there was a great choir of souls.

'Give me your hands,' said Yvraine. Stern obeyed. 'Now seek your vision.'

Stern closed her eyes. She barely had to open herself up psychically. The nothingness rushed to seize her. Her breath stopped. All was black and cold and numb. The blackness was eternal, swallowing stars and souls forever. She could not see its boundaries. It seemed infinite, and to be growing at the same time, stronger and stronger, finality upon finality, the last of all curtains to fall.

She jerked out of the vision and saw that Yvraine had released her and taken a step back.

'Enough,' said Yvraine. 'I have seen what I need.'

'Do you know what it is?' Stern asked.

'I do not. I shared your vision. That is all. The danger is as great as you say.'

'Then you understand the need for an alliance,' said Kyganil.

Yvraine looked at them both steadily. 'How do you imagine this will come about? Do either of you have the standing of an ambassador?' The question was not really a question.

'No,' said Stern. 'Until you told me, I did not even know that something of the Imperium endures.'

Yvraine was silent again, her eyes shadowed, as she thought. 'Know this, exile of Cegorach,' she said at last. 'When the time comes, you will have my aid.'

Kyganil bowed to the Herald. 'You have my thanks.'

'And mine,' said Stern, bowing too.

'Yours, if not that of the rest of your race,' Yvraine observed.

Stern could say nothing in answer to that justified remark.

'Where will you go now?' Yvraine asked her.

'I do not know. I must seek the point from which the nothingness will spread, but I do not know where to begin looking for it.'

'On that point, I cannot assist you.' Yvraine turned once more to Kyganil. 'And the help I give rests upon a condition. The condition is the task I give you now. You will seek out your former Harlequin kin. Find a Solitaire. You will do this as your part of this bargain. Then I will fulfil mine.'

Kyganil bowed again in obedience.

'Then we are done,' said Yvraine. 'Go now. We have paths that await us all.'

Kyganil brought them back to the *Iudex Ferox*. They stepped out of his portal and into an empty cargo bay in the bowels of the ship. It would be a few minutes at least before Dagover knew of their presence. The bay was deep in shadow. It had been damaged in battle, and fallen into disuse. There was no light except for a single emergency lumen strip, still emitting a bruised red glow from the base of the walls. The deck above had collapsed diagonally across the space. The bay was a chamber of wreckage and shadows. It was a poor place for a farewell. At least they had their solitude.

'We have walked far together, Thrice-Born,' said Kyganil.

'A journey I could not have made without you,' said Stern. 'I shall miss your wisdom and your blades.' She smiled. 'It will be a challenge to grow used to travelling exclusively by human means again.' The words were banal. Anything she said would be after so many years of companionship.

They clasped forearms. 'I will hope our paths cross again,' said Kyganil.

'I have faith they will,' Stern said. Everything about their friendship, from its beginning to its duration, was so unlikely that meeting again seemed the least of improbabilities. 'But we move as fate demands.'

'We do,' Kyganil agreed.

'Do you think we have performed well?' Stern asked, shifting to the Harlequin's idiom, paying tribute and respect to what he had taught her of his ways and faiths.

Kyganil smiled. 'Magnificently,' he said. 'Especially for so small a troupe, so often deprived of any audience, perpetually without the proper one.'

'By your side, the art was its own reward.'

Kyganil placed a hand over his heart and bowed his head. 'Well said, Thrice-Born. It has been the great honour of my path to perform beside you.'

'As it was mine to dance beside you.'

'Then I bow to you, until the curtains rise to reveal us to one another once more.'

'I bow to you in the same hope.'

Stern stepped back, giving Kyganil space to summon his portal to the webway. He gestured, and a frame of air around him shimmered. They looked at each other one last time, holding on to the link of solidarity. Kyganil stepped into the portal. His image shimmered too. Then the air cleared, and he and the portal were gone.

Stern did not move right away, contemplating the loss of the fellowship of the xenos she trusted with her life. She was left with the company of the human she did not trust at all.

Then she left the cargo bay. She walked towards the bridge, sure that one of the inquisitor's officers would meet her momentarily. It had already been several minutes since she and Kyganil had returned. Dagover knew she was back. If he claimed otherwise, she would not believe him.

'Will this suit your needs?' Dagover asked.

Stern walked across the threshold of the chamber the inquisitor was offering as her quarters. It was on the same deck as his study, a short distance from the bridge. It was one of the chambers attached to the cloisters. It was sparsely furnished. There was an iron cot, a shrine taking up most of the forward wall, and little else. It was a religious cell.

'You had Ministorum priests aboard?' Stern asked.

'You sound surprised.'

'Given your radicalism, I am.'

'My faith in the God-Emperor is not open to question.'

'I did not say that it was. But the Ecclesiarchy is suspicious of the unorthodox. As I happen to know.'

Dagover gave an electronic grunt. 'Priests and a prayer conclave have not always been part of this vessel's complement. They have been sometimes, though.'

'When it suited you politically.'

The hooks spread Dagover's lips into a smile. 'I leave the exegesis of my decisions to you. They were with me when last we departed a world before the great warp storm tore the sky. They did not survive the century. I think, for many of them, a crisis of faith weakened them in combat.' He walked slowly around the room. 'That is the past. Will this chamber do?'

'It will.' Its proximity to the bridge was useful. Its proximity to Dagover's quarters was, she guessed, useful for him. That made no difference to her. She presumed she would be under perpetual observation.

'Very well,' said Dagover. 'Now we have the question of our destination. I am disappointed the exalted figure you consulted had no helpful suggestions.'

'I believe in the Emperor and His guidance.'

'As do I, Sister Superior Stern, as do I.'

She did not think he was mocking her. She was willing to believe his protestations of faith. What she wished she could discern was his underlying purpose. But the reptile was as unreadable as ever.

And then he said, 'Guilliman,' and his face changed. He seemed to be looking past Stern, at an object of wonder.

Was he acting? she wondered. *Was he genuine? Or was his genuine display a strategy in itself, its purpose to win her trust?*

There was no way to know.

'Yes,' Stern said. 'Guilliman.'

'You believe this to be true?'

'I think it would be a strangely pointless lie, coming from an Ynnari.'

'It is an event that gives one hope,' said Dagover.

'It does.'

'Yet I think, too, of how close to the brink we must be for him to return.'

'As a Recongregator, do you not feel vindicated?'

'Perhaps.' The rasp was barely louder than a whisper. 'I have fears, though, Sister Superior. I have fears that my vindication will come to feel like the mockery of fate. Or that I will discover that my faction did not act fast enough, or forcefully enough. I need to know.'

'So do I,' Stern told him. 'But the darkness is what I must fight. If the struggle takes me farther away from what remains of the Imperium, then so be it. If that is a condition that is unacceptable to you, tell me now.'

'It is not,' said Dagover. 'We will go where we must.'

She was relieved, and she was disturbed that she was relieved. With Kyganil gone, she was dependent on Dagover and his ship for transport. She did not like the idea of needing the inquisitor. She felt uneasy and wary in a constant, gnawing way that was foreign to her after so long in the trusted company of the aeldari.

'Where, though, must we go?' Dagover asked.

'I will seek the guidance of the Emperor.'

'You sound confident that you will receive it.'

'I am.'

'Much has changed in a short time.'

'It has.'

The smile crept over his face. It looked like victory. 'Then we have cause to rejoice. I will leave you to it.'

The lizard in power armour walked out of the cell.

Stern closed the door behind him, sealing herself in gloom.

Candles flickered on the shrine, casting moving shadows over the bronze sculpture of the holy winged skull. Stern kneeled before the shrine. She fixed her gaze on the sockets of the skull. This was not a relic that would crumble at her touch. It was a symbol. It could be destroyed, but what it represented could not.

'Father of Mankind,' she said. 'Forgive me for my weakness. Forgive me for not seeing what I should, and for believing you no longer protected your children. Though I am not worthy of your blessing, I am your servant eternally. Show me what you would have me do. Grant me the wisdom to know how best I must serve you.'

She closed her eyes and bent her head to her clasped hands. The darkness that came to devour the stars enveloped her once more. She could barely breathe. The nothingness sought to consume everything. If she did not fight it, she would vanish in the suffocating black.

'You are not everything,' she growled at the nothingness. 'You will be defeated.'

She did not have the strength to see past it. The black future swallowed all the times to come, and it crushed the present. She strained against it, but it was like trying to hold back the tidal wave of a terrible ocean. She started to drown.

'I will not despair!' she cried in prayer. 'My greatest strength is not my own. It is the strength of the God-Emperor that will stand against this evil.'

It was not for her to see the way. It was for her to believe that she would be shown the way.

Her duty was to have faith.

And she did. Her belief in the God-Emperor sang in her heart. The shrine before her gave her a way to concentrate her thoughts, and powerful as symbols were, it was still just a symbol. Monuments and rituals served their purpose, but they fell away to insignificance before the essence of faith itself. That was what she offered the God-Emperor now.

She gave herself to the totality of belief. Without reservation.

She believed. She *became* belief.

Her identity vanished, yet the darkness could not absorb her, for Another had claim over her.

And in this state, for a tiny, blessed fragment of eternity, the dominion of the nothingness receded. It had not yet arrived, it had not yet consumed all, and so something came through to Stern.

A name.

A place.

A beginning.

Severitas.

Stern found Dagover on the bridge. 'Severitas,' she told him. 'That is where we must go.'

'What is there?'

'Our destination.'

Dagover cocked his head. 'Are you bandying words with me?'

'No. I am telling you what I know, and nothing more.'

'Very well.' Dagover leaned over the tacticarium table. 'Severitas,' he muttered, and called up a hololithic map of the galaxy. A rune pulsed yellow over a planet in the sector. 'Interesting. In close parallel to our current position, but on the other side of the rift, as far as I can tell.'

'Your map is incomplete,' Stern commented. It only showed a rough approximation of the huge warp storm's location.

'We do not know the full extent of the rift,' said Dagover. 'We have mapped what we have been able to determine, but there is too much we don't know.' He extended an arm and tapped Severitas. 'I should have said that I *think* this planet is on the other side of the rift. But there is a fair bit of guesswork involved.'

'It is not in the storm. Of that I am sure.'

'Good. I am trusting your visions not to send us to a world consumed by the warp. We are still faced with a problem. Somehow, we have to cross that rift without the benefit of the Astronomican.'

'True. So we will.'

'I'm eager to know how you think we will do so.'

'With the guidance of the God-Emperor,' Stern said. She turned away from the tacticarium table and looked at the viewports. The *Iudex Ferox* was still in orbit around Parastas, and the planet's arc dominated the perspective. The atmosphere was dark with volcanic ash, hiding the death throes of the world. 'We should turn to confront the rift,' she said. 'There is nothing more to confront with Parastas. The justice of the Emperor overtakes the abomination and the heretic.' Let the penitent strive for forgiveness in their final moments. It was still not hers to grant.

Dagover gave the orders, and the battle cruiser pulled out of its orbit, slowly turning its bow towards the wound in the void. The warp storm was a barrier that stretched to the infinite. The only way to defeat it was to go through it.

Even at this distance, the storm's roiling unreality was corrosive to mind and soul. The crew of the *Iudex Ferox* instinctively turned away from its sight. Stern made herself look at it.

The Emperor protects, she thought.

That belief gave her the strength to study the monster.

'This ship is warp-worthy?' she asked Dagover.

Shipmaster Avaxan looked at her in horror, then at the inquisitor. 'My lord...' she began.

Dagover cut her off. 'It is,' he said. 'Though entering the warp without a guide would be suicidal.'

'We will have a guide,' Stern said simply.

She stared at the horror. Convulsions of nightmare colours flowed into vortices of madness. Tendrils as large as worlds reached out from the rift with the uncanny hint of intention. The rift was Chaos given form. Avaxan was right to fear it. Even a close approach was to gamble with insanity.

'We must go,' Stern intoned quietly. 'We must cross. I know you will guide us. I know you will guide me now. My faith is absolute and unswerving. Show us the way, Emperor. Show us how to be true to our duty to you.'

Her eye kept being drawn to the same point in the warp storm. It was centred in the viewport and was the nearest point in the rift to Parastas.

The position began to seem significant to her. She focused on that point, and on the cyclone of warp matter she saw there. The stuff of unreality swirled in a vicious spiral, drawing her mind in. Her sense of the bridge and of her body diminished. Her awareness centred on the spiral, on the rush of non-matter going around and around and around with hideous force, luring, seeing, summoning. She was about to plunge into a maelstrom tunnel.

The cyclone called. And she knew, as her heart swelled with certainty, that they must answer.

'That is where we enter the rift,' she said, pointing.

'There?' Dagover had few inflections, but his delay in answering showed his astonishment.

'There.'

'The ship will be torn apart, or worse,' said Avaxan. 'We do not even have our Geller field operating at full capacity.'

'The Emperor protects,' Stern told her.

'He does. He does. But...'

'Then have faith in Him, shipmaster.' Energy crackled angrily down her cloak. It ran along the deck, sparking against workstations. The lumen strips on the bridge flickered briefly.

Avaxan paled and looked helplessly at Dagover.

'You are certain?' the inquisitor said to Stern.

'I am. Our path to Severitas takes us through that point.'

Dagover hesitated. 'You understand our caution,' he said. 'There is nothing to suggest we should take such a dangerous step.'

'Nothing except faith. The Emperor protects, inquisitor. The Emperor also commands. We have a duty. It is on the other side of that rift.'

Dagover said nothing. He looked back and forth between Stern and the viewport.

'Is this not what you expected or planned, inquisitor?' Stern said quietly, so only Dagover could hear. 'Did you expect you were simply taking on board a new weapon?' He started to answer, but she did not give him the chance. 'No, I should not underestimate your machinations. But you did not expect to have the direction of your ship commanded in this way.' Again he opened his mouth to speak, and again she cut him off. 'I have no sympathy for you. Your hopes and needs are not relevant. Nor are mine. We are the agents of the Emperor. Nothing more, and that is more than enough. We must seek to do His will, and that is all.'

They stared at each other in silence. Then Dagover said, just as quietly as Stern had been speaking, 'I wonder which of us will seem the bigger fool when the immaterium tears our ship in half.'

'The days of my folly have passed,' Stern snapped. 'Is that not what you wanted? Or is that what you fear?'

Dagover broke away from her stare. He raised his voice. 'Shipmaster, set course for the position indicated by Sister Superior Stern. Prepare the warp drive. May the Emperor protect us.'

Stern stayed on the bridge, on the strategium's platform, during the entire journey from Parastas to the rift. She lost track of time. It might have been days of travel with the plasma drive. The abomination of the warp storm grew larger in the viewport, and then the cyclone of madness expanded, becoming a terrible eye, and a call to immeasurable depths. Dagover ordered the shutters closed to safeguard the sanity of the crew. Pict screens struggled to present hololithic approximations of the horror that the ship approached. Stern ignored them, staring straight ahead, as if she could see through the shutters. In her mind's eye, she perceived the churning spiral.

Dagover came and went from the bridge. She was barely aware of his movements until he approached her and said, 'We are ready to make the jump.'

'Good.'

'We are risking much.'

'No. We are doing what is commanded.'

'If you are right, my crew will fear you even more than if you are wrong, I think.'

'Their fears do not concern me.'

Dagover's harsh electronic chuckle scraped across the bridge. 'In this, Sister Superior, we are alike.'

'Warp drive ready, lord inquisitor,' Avaxan called.

'Make the jump, shipmaster,' said Dagover.

Stern closed her eyes and welcomed the plunge into the vortex.

PART TWO
IMPERIUM SANCTUS

V

SEVERITAS

Somewhere ahead, north of their position, past the tangled hulks of the manufactories, the road sloped uphill, and at the top of the hill was the Cathedral of Saint Thecla the Unyielding. The cathedral, with its walls, defences and position, would be a strongpoint. They could make a stand there. They could withstand a siege for some time. Perhaps long enough to re-establish communications with the battlegroup and escape the trap.

Dominion Klavia of the Order of Our Martyred Lady resented the fact that she was thinking of defence and escape. Her natural instincts in battle were to charge at the forefront of the advance, to be the blade that first sliced into the enemy. She could not change the impossible, though, and she had the wisdom to know when she saw it.

'Vox!' Canoness Commander Macrina called. She was a few steps from Klavia, leading the run with the Dominions, while the Rhinos of the commandry rumbled up along the flanks of the Battle Sisters, blocking some of the incoming fire from the manufactories. 'Tell me you have something!' She listened for a few moments, then cursed.

'Anything?' Klavia asked. She had to shout to be heard over the clamour of the pounding of bolters, the roar of flamers, and the unending thunder-and-lightning attacks from the cultists' lasguns and heavy stubbers.

'Battle Sister Eluned says there was a brief signal. Maybe a ship entering orbit. Then nothing again. She cannot be definite.'

A stream of las cut into the road just ahead of Macrina. She returned fire with her bolt pistol. Her shells exploded against a shadowed catwalk leaning over the road. Bodies fell, and flames spread along the promethium conduits. More blasts built up, running rampant through the huge complex. Klavia heard the screams of heretics in the growing conflagration.

It wasn't enough. There were thousands of heretics, infesting the complexes like vermin. And more were coming.

'Curse this world,' said Dominus Odilla, marching in lockstep with Klavia. 'Curse it for what it pretended to be.'

'It pretended well,' said Klavia. She swept her storm bolter to the right, blowing apart a crowd of heretics that tried to rush the Adepta Sororitas from a loading bay. The road narrowed up ahead and made a sharp turn to the right. The forge complexes were so large and packed in that they formed an arc across the road at that point.

'What odds there's an ambush ahead?' Odilla asked.

Klavia grunted. 'You mean all of Severitas isn't already an ambush?'

She was not exaggerating. From the moment the strike cruiser *Rectitude* of Battlegroup Kallides entered the orbit of Severitas, the Sisters of the Order of Our Martyred Lady had entered the jaws of the trap set for them on the planet. They had not known it right away. They had responded to a cry for help from the surface. Vox traffic indicated a loyal population grappling with a cultist insurrection. The size of the uprising was clearly beyond the strength of local defence forces to deal with. But a strategic insertion by the Adepta Sororitas would turn the tide, and reclaim Severitas firmly for the Imperium. This was the sort of world that warranted the flexibility built into the battlegroups of the Indomitus Crusade. Severitas was valuable. It was a powerful forge world, and its salvation would result in reinforcements of weapons, vehicles and ships being supplied to the crusade.

One commandry of Sisters of Battle was going to be more than enough.

Only the vox traffic was lies. Everything about Severitas was a lie. The depth and scale of the deception was in itself as much a sign of the enemy's power as the sheer numbers of the foe. Severitas was a fallen planet. If there was a loyal population here, Klavia had not seen it. The commandry had landed at the space port, all signs pointing to this as a secure landing site and good staging point to take the fight to the heretics. Instead, the Adepta Sororitas had found themselves surrounded by the devotees of the Ruinous Powers.

Orbiting Severitas were its shipyards. It had no completed vessels, but there were enough shells with functioning engines for the second part of the trap to close. Moving in uncanny concert, a score of hulls broke from their moorings and closed on the *Rectitude*, a swarm of battering rams. The attack was so sudden, the half-built ships so close, that the strike cruiser had no chance. Its guns saw off a few of the attackers, but it might as well have been trying to defeat a meteor shower. When it died, its destruction was a bright fanfare of explosions in the sky.

The ground forces knew what had happened because the crew of the *Rectitude* managed to remain in vox contact until the end. But the communications were broken, erratic, and grew worse and worse by the second. Once the disguise fell from Severitas, the planet crackled with uncontrolled warp energy. It streaked through the clouds like sorcerous lightning, abolishing certainties. It unleashed storms where rain rushed upward from the ground, and the winds were full of howling voices. And it enclosed the planet.

The *Rectitude*'s astropathic choir attempted to send a distress call before the catastrophe claimed the strike cruiser. It failed. There had been no contact with the battlegroup since the mission had begun. It was possible that the prolonged silence from the *Rectitude* and the Order of Our Martyred Lady might be noticed. It was just as possible that by the time that happened, the circumstances and location of the battlegroup would preclude aid being sent.

The commandry was alone. It would be alone until the struggle on Severitas was decided one way or the other.

The initial surprise of the ambush had been costly. The commandry had barely a hundred Sisters of Battle left. A hundred against millions.

The cultists were armed, and they were organised. They had taken up positions everywhere in the manufactories along the route the commandry was following. When the true nature of the situation on Severitas became clear, Macrina had formed her troops into a wedge and driven hard, the thrust of a holy spear, through the initial rush of heretics, and deep into the canyons of metal, heading for Saint Thecla. The cultists had responded, turning the huge forge complexes into honeycombs of firing positions. The Order of Our Martyred Lady advanced through an unending stream of las and stubber fire. The farther the Sisters of Battle went, the more they encountered mines and heavier weapons.

The forges were all still active, even if nothing was being produced by them. Massive chimneys belched fire and smoke into the sky. The walls vibrated with the roars of the furnaces inside. Flaming gas and steam vented from the snaking tangles of iron conduits. Bristling with attackers on their catwalks and at every window, the manufactories seemed to Klavia like corrupted beasts, straining to tear themselves free from the chains of their foundations and hurl their mountainous bulks at the commandry.

They were less than a hundred yards now from the turn.

'We know what the blasphemers will seek to do, my sisters,' Macrina voxed to them all. 'We will smash through them with the strength of righteousness. Hold fast! The road turns twice, and then we shall have a straight run to the cathedral. We shall see our fortress soon, and then the heretics will truly have cause to fear us!'

When Macrina finished speaking, Klavia heard the new sound. It was hard to make out at first as anything different from the crack and rattle of weapons fire, the deep rumbling of the forges, and the snarl of the Rhinos. Very soon, it was loud enough for her to be certain. 'Enemy vehicles approaching,' she warned. The growl of the engines was pitched higher than those of the Rhinos, and sounded maddened, the vehicles as corrupted by Chaos as the humans who drove them.

For the enemy's motorised reinforcement to be audible before coming into sight, it had to be a large contingent.

'By the Throne,' Macrina snarled, 'we are being tested on this day. We shall hit harder and faster, then. There is not much more than a mile to the cathedral.'

The Canoness charged forward, firing as she ran. The Rhinos picked up speed, and the commandry rushed down the narrowing roadway. They sent a wall of shells ahead of them.

'They think to ambush us!' Macrina shouted. 'What difference can a few guns more make? Onward, sisters! Onward, in fury!'

The formation raced for the turn, defying the enemy guns. Bolters and flamers raked the façades of the manufactories, annihilating heretics. The air was choking with the smell of spent fyceline. Black smoke rolled in between the walls, further reducing the visibility of the dim late-afternoon light.

Then the day blazed white. Klavia staggered, momentarily deafened by the force of the concussion. Demolition charges blew out the hearts of the manufactories to the left, right and ahead. Furnace shrapnel tore through the walls. The slices of glowing metal flew across the road in a slashing web. Sisters of Battle fell, decapitated, cut in half, impaled and burning. Tides of molten ore burst from the shattered façades. They collided in crashing, incandescent waves, and formed a raging flood in the street. With the groans of dying giants, the huge complexes leaned forward, their structural integrity gone, and the collapse began.

'*Pull back!*' Macrina roared. The order was unnecessary, in that there was no other option, and every warrior of the commandry was already retreating back up the road, trying to stay ahead of the burning river. The order was needed, because it took away the shame of the retreat.

Klavia ran up the road. She and her fellow Dominions were slower, weighed down by their heavy weapons. She would sooner die than abandon her storm bolter. The weapon was sanctified, anointed in the holy oils that were held by the sacred armament font in the convent of the Order of Our Martyred Lady. While she lived, it would not be destroyed by a flow of ore, or fall into the hands of the filth she and her sisters fought.

And the filth were dying too. Cultists screamed in agony, incinerated, smothered and drowned at the same time. Many others were blown to sprays of blood and fragments of flesh by the explosions. Hundreds more were going to be crushed in the collapse, and already those close to the foundations were crying out as thousands of tonnes of rockcrete and metal folded in on themselves and came down on the heretics.

Though they were losing thousands to the unfolding cataclysm, the cultists were also triumphant. They did not care about their brethren. They cared about the disaster reaching for the Sisters of Battle. From their positions high on other manufactories, they shouted in ferocious joy and hate.

The Adepta Sororitas retreated from the enveloping disaster, running back into even more determined fire. Behind them came the roar of the falling structures and the molten ore's monstrous serpent hiss. The destruction was hungry for prey. The avalanche of wreckage caught a Rhino on Klavia's right. For a few moments, the vehicle remained visible under the fall of rubble, its wheels spinning futilely. It was held. Before its driver could escape, the river of ore swept over it, turning the vehicle into a crematorium.

The heat pursued Klavia. She could see little except a thick cloud of dust lit orange. Her sisters were vague shapes in the bellowing inferno. She could not see the enemy. She fired all the same, aiming high for where she knew the other complexes must be. If she was to die now, God-Emperor grant that she take a few more of His enemies with her.

The rumble reached its deafening climax. The manufactories were down, and their fall pushed the molten ore forward in a surging wave. Klavia lunged ahead. Adrenaline fought with exhaustion. Faith in the Emperor, and the determination to serve Him well, won the day. She moved faster, keeping just ahead of the killing heat, her face blistering and cracking. She ran through the dark, suffocating, glowing limbo.

There was a change in the movement of the vague silhouettes that were her sisters, a shifting in a current. She turned with them, and hurtled along another road. This one went uphill. In another minute, the commandry had left the worst of the dust behind, and the river of ore flowed away below.

The position was still not a good one. The enemy fire was growing stronger again, and the sound of the engines was still drawing nearer.

'Defensive posture,' Macrina ordered. 'Ring of sacrament!' With the remaining Rhinos creating a wall at both ends of the street, the Sisters of Battle formed a circle, blasting at the cultists' firing points, holding down the attackers for the moment.

'Sister Keyne!' Macrina called. 'Can you find us a route?'

Battle Sister Keyne worked her way close to the Canoness. She held a data-slate and was looking at a map of the region. 'They've cut off the main approach to the cathedral,' she said. 'The other options are circuitous and much more narrow. Barely wide enough for a single Rhino.'

'They want us in killing zones,' said Klavia. 'They think to eliminate our strength.'

'They're doing it well,' Odilla muttered.

'The enemy vehicles will be here soon,' Klavia added.

For the first time ever, she saw Macrina hesitate. The Canoness had no good options to choose. They could make a stand here, and be ground down, or advance into ambushes they could not survive.

There was no way forward to victory.

'Prepare to make them pay,' Macrina said.

Then this would be where they fought to the last, Klavia thought. This was where they would stand against a world.

More and more guns opened up against the Sisters of Battle. Cultists swarmed out of the manufactory bays, emboldened to have their foe cornered, willing to die by the hundreds just for the chance to sink their blades into the Emperor's most faithful warriors.

At the head of the street, a corrupted tank appeared, flames belching from the spines that covered its hull.

Then, before Klavia could see it clearly, the tank exploded.

A beam struck it from above, a beam of something far purer and more lethal than light. The flash lit up the gloom of Severitas, turning the vast bulks of the manufactories into negative images. Klavia winced from the glare. Burned onto her retina was the image of the tank erupting, its cannon flying end over end to embed itself high in a conduit of the complex to her right. The impact set off a chain of explosions through the manufactory, ones that the heretics had not prepared. Fire bloomed with purifying anger, scorching sniper positions.

The triumphant cries of the heretics turned into screams.

And then there was a roar from the skies, and a Valkyrie came in low overhead. It unleashed two Hellstrike missiles. They slammed into the manufactories on either side of the Sisters of Battle, punching deep before exploding. The complex on the right was a promethium refinery, and the entire building turned into a fireball, a raging pyre for the heretics. The gunship passed through the flames of the destruction and turned its multi-laser on the cultists massing at the lower end of the street.

There was another tank there, and it blew up before the Valkyrie arrived, struck by another blast. The killing power hit again and again, working its way back up the road, tearing open the walls that were still standing, seeking the cultists within. The cries were now wails of fear. The Order of Our Martyred Lady no longer came under fire. The heretics who were still fighting had another target, and they were desperately trying to bring down the source of their terror.

In the searing light of the blasts and the fire, it took her a moment to see what they were shooting at. The source of the beams that were annihilating the heretics was a blinding sphere. What Klavia saw was something like light, but its true nature was very different. It filled her with unease.

'Sorcery,' Odilla said beside her, her jaw tight.

'A loyalist psyker,' Klavia said.

'Maybe.'

'Our rescue does not mean we should take anything at face value,' Macrina warned.

'The Valkyrie bears the symbol of the Inquisition,' said Klavia.

'I saw that,' Macrina answered. 'Stand ready, sisters,' she voxed to the commandry. 'Hold your fire until my command, but do not drop your guard. Nothing is certain.'

Nothing, Klavia thought, except the extermination of the heretics in this region. The screams began to die out. For the first time since the order had landed on Severitas, the flood of enemies was staunched. There were more, countless more, but at this moment they were not able to reach the scene fast enough to replace their dead brethren.

The Valkyrie came back, making another strafing pass. There was little for it to do. Enemy fire fell to sporadic bursts, silenced immediately by another of the psyker's blasts. The display of power made Klavia feel almost as uneasy as Odilla looked, though she welcomed the respite. It was as if a star had descended to the surface of Severitas and was annihilating the foes of the Emperor with coronal storms.

And now the gunfire ceased. There was no one left to kill in the immediate vicinity. The sphere diminished in intensity, then winked out. The Valkyrie came in for landing at the top of the road, dropping slowly over the wreckage and bodies where the tank had been. The figure who had been in the centre of the sphere descended too, her cloak and her white hair billowing in the wind that blew towards the manufactory fires. Her armour was battered, it and her face bearing the scars of battles beyond counting. Yet it was unmistakably marked with the red-and-black livery of the Order of Our Martyred Lady.

Klavia stared as the figure alighted on the ground. 'I do not understand,' she said. Odilla was shaking her head in incomprehension.

Macrina, though, looked at the woman with disbelief, and with hate. 'Ephrael Stern,' she spat.

Klavia had never known the Sister Superior. In the commandry, only Macrina was old enough to have seen Stern. Every Battle Sister knew the name, though. All knew the judgement that had been rendered against her by the Inquisition, and the shame of her memory cast a long shadow over the Order of Our Martyred Lady.

'Heretic,' Odilla hissed.

Heretic. The word made Klavia's blood run hot with fury.

They had killed heretics by the hundreds on this day. This heretic, though, embodied the word with much more awful significance. Ephrael Stern was far, far worse than the cultists, weak-minded civilians who had been tempted away from the light of the God-Emperor by the Ruinous Powers. Ephrael Stern bore the armour of the Adepta Sororitas. She wore the livery of that which she had betrayed. There were no words that could encompass the full scope of her treachery.

The Battle Sisters of the commandry trained their weapons on Ephrael Stern.

Dagover descended from the Valkyrie and strode down the slope towards the confrontation between Stern and her long-lost sisters. He hurried to get there before someone pulled a trigger. Stern was standing with her arms apart, palms open. 'That doesn't make you less of a threat,' Dagover muttered under his breath. After Stern's display of power, it was hardly going to matter that she was not wielding a bolt pistol.

So this, he thought, was to be the hard part of their journey.

He was still trying to process the voyage through the warp storm. Getting from Parastas to Severitas had been uncannily easy. He would have been reluctant to take the *Iudex Ferox* into the warp at all, given its condition. What he had done, if he was honest with himself, was place his faith in Stern's faith, and so he had committed himself to an act of utter madness. According to all the lights of his understanding, the battle cruiser should have been destroyed the moment it plunged into the vortex. Instead…

Instead…

What exactly had happened?

He did not know. His impressions were confused, partly because he had trouble accepting what had happened. He had just as much difficulty trying to grasp the implications.

The *Iudex Ferox* had shot through the storm like an arrow through air. As if they were destined, fate-commanded. The phrases haunted Dagover, and he could not shake them. Nor could he put aside the memory of what he had felt during that journey. He had felt tiny, ridiculously unimportant. Even the ship barely mattered. Only Stern mattered. A great power had determined that she should pass through that enormous storm, and so had seized the ship, parted the ocean of the warp, and dragged them all through to the other side.

A great power. Why did Dagover not want to give it a name? *His* name?

Dagover did not dare. He could not remember when he had last felt reticent about anything. He did now.

Stern was much more than he had hoped. She might be even more than he feared.

Dagover did not like experiencing awe.

He might have to get used to it.

In time. First he had to deal with a situation that was unquestionably beyond Stern's ability to defuse. There was nothing she could say that would allay the suspicions of her order.

That task fell to him. Otto Dagover was to be the voice of reassurance. How strange.

But he now lived in a galaxy where Guilliman had returned. Clearly, everything was possible now.

Stern looked back at him as he approached, her face impassive. She was seeing her sisters for the first time in far more than a century. How long and how deeply, Dagover wondered, had she thought about this reunion? She must have known it would begin this way. Did that hurt any less?

Whatever emotional agony she was suffering, she had submerged it. She was waiting for him to speak, to effect the reconciliation.

That was not his specialty.

But the forging of the right alliance, at the right time, for the reasons he deemed right… That *was* his specialty.

'Please lower your weapons,' he said, taking one step ahead and to the side of Stern. 'They are not needed here.' He did not extend his arms. Their inhuman length made them more sinister than reassuring.

'Who are you to make that decision?' the Canoness asked. Her dark skin was deeply lined. There were many, many decades of experience behind the eyes that evaluated him.

'I am Lord Otto Dagover of the Ordo Xenos. It is a privilege to meet you, Canoness Macrina of the Order of Our Martyred Lady.'

Macrina's eyes narrowed, displeased rather than impressed that he knew who she was. His name didn't help, either. 'Dagover,' she said. 'I have heard of you. I have heard rumours of the warriors you bring into the Deathwatch.'

'Loyal servants of the Emperor, all of them.'

'Mutants. You have kept company with the Black Dragons.'

And Adeptus Astartes far more mutated than they were. But Macrina did not seem to know about them. So that was something, at least. 'Yes, I have,' Dagover said. 'And at least one member of the Adepta Sororitas, the Canoness Errant Setheno, has done the same. But I do not believe your doctrinal differences with me are what matter at this juncture, Canoness. You may not like what I represent. You are not alone. Few do. You are, however, obliged to acknowledge my authority.'

Macrina said nothing.

Dagover gave her his smile. He knew how disturbing it was. That was as it should be. He did not want her to see him as ingratiating. Being an uncanny figure was useful to him. Be they friend or foe, it was always better to keep them off balance, because friend or foe, they could shift from one to the other with the wind of circumstances. Even when he wanted to inspire trust, it was better for the subject to be uneasy too. He thought he was achieving this end with Stern.

She was certainly making *him* uneasy. The experience was a new one. It was not altogether welcome.

'I have seen the works of Ephrael Stern,' Dagover continued. 'I have seen legions of abominations fall before her. We have come from the other side of that warp storm.' He pointed up, to the sight of the rift, just as huge and baleful as it had been from Parastas.

'You crossed the Cicatrix Maledictum?' Macrina asked before he could continue. Her Battle Sisters stirred uneasily.

It was the wrong kind of unease. He was committed, though. 'Is that its name?' he asked, putting as much curiosity into his electronic voice as he could.

'You have come from the Imperium Nihilus,' Macrina said, her tone cold. 'That provenance marks you as suspect.'

'If you have not been there, who are you to judge?' Dagover shot back. 'You have not seen what I have seen. You have not borne witness to the acts of Sister Superior Stern.' He was choosing his language carefully. *Works, acts.* He was building up to the most important word. It was not one that Macrina and her Sisters would accept this day, or the next. But he was preparing the imaginative soil for this idea. 'She guided us through the Cicatrix Maledictum without harm. It was as if the hand of the God-Emperor Himself carried us through, and brought us here, to Severitas, to the very place where she would find her order in its time of need.'

'It is a bold thing to say that the Emperor commanded your arrival,' said Macrina.

'I believe it would be bold to affirm He did *not*. Bold, ungrateful, even, I am tempted to say, *sacrilegious*. Does anyone here have any doubts as to what would have happened if Sister Superior Stern had not come to you at the very moment that she did?'

Dagover took the risk of pausing after his question. He won his wager. Macrina had no immediate answer. The silence was heavy with meaning. It was a telling victory, he thought, and so he took advantage of it to speak the crucial word. 'I tell you, Sisters of the Order of Our Martyred Lady, that Ephrael Stern is not corrupted. I tell you that she is a *saint*.'

Stern had remained perfectly still while Dagover had been speaking with Macrina. Her head lowered, her hands parted, without realising it she had presented the perfect image of the point he had been leading towards. The air driven by the hunger of the fires stirred her cloak and her hair. That was the only movement. She might have been a marble idol.

Her appearance was perfect, Dagover thought.

When he uttered the word *saint*, though, she turned her head sharply. She glared at him, eyes flashing with righteous anger. 'I make no such claim,' she said, her voice hard with the very sanctity she denied. 'I am no saint. I am a psyker, tainted by the warp. I am tainted to my core. Do not blaspheme by calling me a saint.'

Only the truly saintly would deny their sanctity, Dagover thought. He stopped himself from saying those words. That would be going too far, much too far. He must not push the Sisters to a point they could not go. 'I make the claim for you,' he said instead. 'I am your witness.'

Stern shook her head. 'I am a servant of the God-Emperor,' she said. 'Nothing more.' She spoke softly, though her voice carried over the background roar of flames, and the gathering rumble in the distance of engines and heretic cries. 'All I seek is to do His will, and to fight for Him where His will takes me.'

'You do not see the arrogance of declaring that His will brought you here?' Macrina demanded.

'I see arrogance in believing that our journey was possible by any other means,' she said.

There was another silence. Dagover let it stretch. They had said what needed to be said. Anything more, and they would be going in circles.

Macrina gazed at Stern and Dagover in turn. She was still wary, hostile. But she was not ordering an attack on the heretic. She was having doubts. Thinking about what Dagover had said.

So, clearly, were the other Sisters of Battle. Some of them were looking at Stern with wonder in spite of themselves.

Good. There was a lot Dagover had to learn, and quickly, about the situation here on the other side of the Cicatrix. An organised, well-armed commandry of the Sisters of Battle pointed to the continued existence of the Imperium in something like a recognisable form, though. If Stern was to be used to her full potential, she could not be having to fight to prevent her execution for heresy or worse. Even if a second execution would be any more permanent than the first. He had to work to see her integrated back into the Imperium's machinery, however tenuously.

Dagover waited another few moments. The sounds of the approaching enemy grew louder. Stern had destroyed many, and bought the commandry some breathing space, but the window for action was narrowing again. 'The true heretics are closing in again,' he said. 'We must move and fight.'

Reluctantly, as if she had been hoping for divine revelation to make clear what she should do about Stern, Macrina nodded. 'The Cathedral of Saint Thecla the Unyielding,' she said, pointing north. 'We can hold back the enemy there, and make our plans.'

'With your permission, Canoness, I will annihilate any heretic who stands in your way,' said Stern.

Her lips pressed tightly together, Macrina gave another curt nod.

Stern turned north, towards the burning tanks. Light gathered around her as she rose into the air once more.

Dagover watched the Sisters of Battle. He had called Stern a saint. They would be thinking about that now, as they watched her. He willed them to look at her, to try to deny that she was a saint. Try and fail.

The aura around Stern became blinding, and then she shot forward, a spear of holy fire.

VI

SAINT THECLA

The fortified Cathedral of Saint Thecla the Unyielding was a massive block of ferrocrete. In its brutal strength it was, Stern thought, a fitting tribute to the warrior whose name it bore. It rose from the peak of its hill like a basalt extrusion. It was spireless, and its walls were five hundred feet high, sheer and black, their blank faces broken only by turret holes. It was half again as long as it was wide, and the sole entrance was in the eastern side. The façade here was rounded, and dominated by an immense sculpture of the God-Emperor's winged skull. The east face was the prow of a blunt, battering ship, which was ready to descend from its heights and crush the apostate and the heretic beneath its dread weight. Demolisher cannons on the parapet aimed their judgement at every quadrant. The Cathedral of Saint Thecla was the shock maul of faith. It demanded everything of the worshipper, and granted nothing. In a galaxy without mercy, Saint Thecla herself had taught, the true servant of the Emperor must also be without pity, impervious to human frailty. A soul must be of iron, or be destroyed.

Though it seemed the entire population of Severitas had succumbed to heresy, the cathedral had not been defaced. Its great doors had remained shut. It was as if it had risen above the cauldron of apostasy that raged in the streets below its hill. The heretical tides had rushed around it, but since it had been abandoned, the fallen hordes had chosen to ignore its existence. With no need to attack, they had avoided the sacred ground.

The situation changed as soon as the commandry of the Order of Our Martyred Lady entered the cathedral, but by then it was too late. The Battle Sisters had their fortress.

The heretics should have destroyed the strongpoint when they had the chance. Stern gave thanks they had not. She thought, too, that perhaps they had never been able to, that the cathedral had been preserved by the Power they had betrayed.

'Yours is the will that protects, God-Emperor,' she murmured, kneeling in prayer. 'Yours is the will that commands.'

She had taken a prayer cell in the crypt of the cathedral. There were barrack cloisters off the nave, and the vestry was a command post with a grav-lift running directly to the battlements. Though Macrina had made no attempt to imprison her, recognising the futility of doing so, Stern had respected her suspicions by removing herself from the centre of things as much as possible. In the cell, she was isolated. No Sister of Battle need see or hear her unless they chose to. She would not impose her presence on planning sessions. She trusted Dagover far enough to presume he would keep her informed.

If she was to earn her place back into the grace of her sisters, it would be on their terms. She would do what had to be done to save them, just as she would do what had to be done to save the Imperium from the doom that haunted her visions.

The sound of guns reached down into the crypt. Muffled by walls twenty feet thick, it was almost gentle, a deep heartbeat. Another attack had begun. She would be needed again soon, but she would not dishonour her sisters by racing to the battlefield prematurely. They knew how to fight a war, and how to repel a siege. They would summon her when it was time, as they had three times already since they had taken possession of the cathedral.

She would practise humility, and she would wait.

Their terms. Her return must be on their terms, or it would fail.

While she waited, she meditated, and she prayed for guidance.

And all the while, the visions were growing stronger. With increasing frequency, it took a conscious effort to hold them back, to stop them from overwhelming her, a black wave of freezing *nothing* swamping her consciousness. The horror was coming closer.

'How must I fight it? Where will it come from? All my being is at the service of your will. Guide me, God-Emperor. Guide me to the field of this battle.'

Wheresoever she was commanded to go, though, for now she was trapped on Severitas. After so many years of travelling the webway with Kyganil, it was a jolt to have to adjust to no longer being able to depart any world at a moment's notice. The evil on this world had to be defeated first. By any means possible.

'You have sent me here for a reason, Father of Mankind. I accept the task you have placed before me. I will not fail. This is my vow. In your name and by my blood, my sisters and I will purge Severitas of the heretic.'

If they let her.

She looked up at the sound of footsteps approaching her cell. She rose to greet her visitor. She expected Dagover. He had been the only one to come to her so far. Macrina still refused any but the briefest of direct communications with her. If Dagover resented being made the go-between, he did not show it. He seemed amused.

The visitor came into view in the dim light of the crypt. It was not Dagover. It was one of the Dominions, Klavia. Her short crop of white hair stood out even against the ghostly pallor of her complexion. An angry red scar ran down the side of her neck. She was solidly built, as if born to carry a storm bolter. Stern had noticed her at the first encounter with the commandry. Klavia was one of the few who had not looked at her with hatred.

'Pardon the interruption, Sister Superior,' Klavia said.

The courtesy almost snapped Stern's heart in two. 'No apology is necessary, Dominion. I am honoured by your visit.'

'I...' Klavia grimaced. 'There is something I must tell you, sister. I have been watching you at your devotions.'

Stern nodded slowly. 'I have been aware of someone there. More than once.'

'You said nothing.'

'If this person wished to speak with me, then they would. If not, they would not. I am glad you chose the former.'

'I do want to be clear. I was not spying on you. Or at least, that was not my intent.'

'I did not think it was.' Stern wondered if she should smile reassuringly. She realised she did not know how. She was long out of practice with that skill. She might look like Dagover. Stern contented herself with keeping her voice soft. 'Is there something I can do for you, sister?' she asked.

'I wanted you to know that you are not alone,' Klavia said. 'I believe in you. I am not the only one.'

Stern closed her eyes for a moment in gratitude. Then, concerned about what Dagover was trying to do, she said, 'When you say that you believe... not, I hope, that I am a saint.'

'I believe you are not a heretic,' said Klavia. 'I believe that you follow the Emperor's will.'

That was not exactly a denial, but it would do. 'Thank you, sister,' Stern said. 'Thank you. To follow the task the Emperor sets for me is my one desire.' She sighed. 'It can be so very hard to know His will.'

'Do you have visions?'

'I do. Too often now they are a burden more than a guide.'

'Then how do you know His will?'

'I am not always sure of it. A sense, sometimes. An intuition.

Sometimes I must deduce it when the visions do not clearly point the way. Especially now.'

'Why now?'

'My visions are all the same. They are of a coming horror, an all-destroying *nothing*. With every passing day, the visions grow stronger. This *nothing* is drawing closer. I believe it will consume the galaxy, sister, if it is not stopped. That is the battle the Emperor has set before me. There can be no other reason for these visions.'

'I see.'

'Tell me. Is it true that Guilliman has returned?'

'He has.'

'And the Imperium still stands?'

'It does, by the Emperor's will, and by the might of Guilliman. He returned in the hour of our greatest need, and now he leads the Indomitus Crusade.'

'Tell me of this crusade.'

'The Order of Our Martyred Lady is part of it,' Klavia said. 'The largest crusade since the Great Crusade is taking back the Imperium from the darkness that would consume it.'

Stern listened carefully as Klavia described the scale and might of the Indomitus Crusade, and what it had accomplished thus far. Bit by bit, Stern understood what had happened to the Imperium during the century of darkness. So much had been lost and destroyed. For another doom, much like the one announced by her visions, to fall upon the Imperium was too much.

No. Never too much. Whatever came, they would triumph. It was the will of the Emperor.

'Yes,' Stern said when Klavia had finished. 'Yes.' She spoke half to herself, and half to the Dominion. 'What comes is monstrous, but we have the strength to fight it. This crusade. The means are before us. This is how the obliterating *nothing* must be fought.' With every word, the certainty took hold of her. It was the same one she had felt when she had told Dagover to take the *Iudex Ferox* into the maelstrom of the Cicatrix Maledictum. The path that had taken her from Parastas to Yvraine and to here was more than fated. She was on the journey the Emperor had commanded. She had been brought here to join the Indomitus Crusade, and through that great strength to fight the *nothing*. She focused on Klavia once more. 'We must leave Severitas,' she said.

Klavia gave her a sour smile. 'I agree, Sister Superior.'

'I know.' Stern offered a tentative smile in return. 'It is easily said.'

Klavia showed Stern how much she believed in her. It was through her intervention, more than Dagover's, that Macrina grudgingly asked her to meet. Stern joined Macrina and Dagover in the vestry. Maps of Severitas covered the huge table in the chamber. The architecture of the cathedral was sombre, solemn. Even in the halls of worship, the cathedral embodied brute strength. It was a redoubt of the faithful, and had no patience for ornamentation. The same was true of the vestry. The walls were dark, the furnishings massive and functional. In one corner of the room, a Battle Sister worked with a vox-unit, struggling to re-establish contact with the *Iudex Ferox*.

'Still intermittent?' Stern asked. The vox had become very erratic during *Xenos Bane*'s descent from orbit.

'Worse,' said Dagover. 'No contact at all since our arrival at the cathedral.'

'And your greatest strength is depleted.'

'It is.'

Macrina looked questioningly at Dagover. She had given Stern no greeting on her arrival. She had simply stared at her coldly, and moved to the far side of the table.

'The *Iudex Ferox* was capable of Exterminatus,' Dagover explained. 'No longer. It launched its last cyclonic torpedo against Parastas.'

'So even if an evacuation were possible, we would have to leave this planet in the grip of corruption, and the Ruinous Powers triumphant.'

'Quite,' said Dagover.

'That is not acceptable,' said Stern.

'On that point, I will agree,' Macrina said, though there was no warmth in her tone.

'Severitas must be purged.' Stern would not countenance the idea that her path had brought her to her sisters only to abandon this world.

Dagover chuckled. 'I have never known the Adepta Sororitas to be adherents of the art of the possible. So be it.' He waved a metallic arm. 'There is no choice anyway, if we cannot contact the ship.'

'Will your crew not send a search party?' Macrina asked.

'No doubt they will. How well will such a party fare?'

'Destroyed if they do not find us,' said Stern. 'Trapped with us if they do.'

'There is something else,' Dagover said to Macrina. 'What is left of my astropathic choir suffered a massive psychic blow when we entered orbit. The level of warp interference around Severitas is powerful. We cannot contact the ship, and the ship cannot contact anyone else.'

'The enemy on this world is more than a heretical populace,' said Stern.

She saw a grimace flicker across Macrina's face before she nodded. Agreeing with Stern caused the Canoness physical pain. 'The cultists are too organised,' she said. 'Their assaults show coordination and planning. And the deception that lured us to Severitas was too well done.'

'Too powerful as well,' said Dagover. 'To conceal the true nature of an entire world, and then to seal it off at will... The question, then, is who is in command?'

'They are our target,' said Stern.

'One we have not found.'

'What scans were you able to do?' Macrina asked Dagover.

'Very few that were useful. We were able to find the heat signatures of your combat from orbit, but they were just spikes in a sea of static. Auspex readings became clearer as we descended in the Valkyrie, but then the range was too limited.'

'So we must look for ourselves,' said Stern.

'Look where?' Macrina snapped. 'Do you think to search the entire planet?'

'I have faith we will not need to,' Stern said quietly, and Macrina's left eye twitched, a wince in the face of what the Canoness took as a rebuke. 'The attacks are coordinated. The fact of coordination will carry within it signs of its origin.'

'What do you propose?' Dagover asked.

'That you and I fly sorties.' She turned to Macrina. 'We will not abandon the Cathedral of Saint Thecla. Like her, we shall not yield.'

'We can hold back a siege without your help.'

They could not break it, though. Stern nodded and kept silent.

Dagover was studying the map. 'I agree with the Sister Superior. I can see no other way forward. We may be at this some length of time, though.' He waved an arm over the maps. 'The geography of the city and of the land means there will be certain inevitable dispersions and concentrations of the enemy.' He looked at Stern. 'If it were possible to go beyond the city, that would help, but we cannot.'

The contiguous land masses of Severitas were covered by a single population centre, a complex of forges that sprawled for thousands of miles in every direction. It covered plains and valleys and mountaintops. Only the deep, angry, polluted oceans marked its boundaries. Severitas the world and Severitas the city were one and the same.

'In what direction do we even begin?' Dagover continued.

'The heavy armour seemed to make its initial approach from the east,' said Macrina.

'Then that is a beginning.'

'We will not be alone in our search,' Stern said. 'The Emperor protects. The Emperor guides.'

The wind blew hot with smoke and ash against Stern's face as she flew beside *Xenos Bane*. She and Dagover left the Cathedral of Saint Thecla the Unyielding in a grimy dawn, after Stern had assisted in throwing back another wave of cultists. The heretics had to regroup, and build up their strength before another attack. Stern and Dagover took advantage of the window to try to read the currents in the flow of reinforcements.

They went high over the city's forges, keeping below the ceiling of smoke and ash so the ground was always in sight. Stern flew with the Valkyrie more than a couple of miles to her left. She could just see the searchlights of the gunship from her position. She and Dagover were within line of sight of each other. Vox communication was working for the moment, but she did not trust it. Even over this relatively short distance, Dagover's voice kept breaking up in her vox-bead.

At first, their search seemed like it would bear no fruit. The cultists closed in on the cathedral from all quarters of the city. Stern headed east, and she saw more and more tanks, the farther she went.

'Guide me, God-Emperor,' Stern prayed. 'Show me your enemy that I may destroy them.'

She had to resist the temptation to engage the armour when she saw it. This was not a time for skirmishes. They would slow her, bog her down fighting an endless supply of foes.

'The heretics' army is very well supplied,' Dagover voxed. He had

noticed the increase in armoured vehicles too. *'My pilot is relaying their positions to Canoness Macrina.'*

'Good.' The commandry would have to launch some strikes out of the cathedral. There were tanks with heavy cannons heading that way. Even the walls of Saint Thecla's were not invincible.

'The forges of Severitas are busy,' Dagover commented. *'More evidence of the power behind the attacks. It is worrisome that they are still operational.'*

'They will provision the heretics with weapons until the cathedral is destroyed with everyone in it,' said Stern. She paused, sweeping her gaze over the horizon. Everywhere, the city pulsed with the monstrous chants of the apostate, and the endless pounding and grinding of the forges at work, steam and fire blasting up from the chimneys like the irregular exultations of a ritual. To the east, though, the light from the fires burned more brightly. Not every manufactory in Severitas still functioned. Sectors of the sprawl had fallen dark, turning into smouldering ruins. In the east, there was fury.

She flew on, and as she travelled east, she saw the light more clearly. The blazes of fires mixed with a different glow. Crimson and violet, it was an aurora with the qualities of an oil slick. The light twitched and oozed over its domain. Its source was miles away yet. The ground rose in that direction until, at the horizon, the manufactories crowned a high, rocky plateau. The cliffs were dark, shadowed by the glow above them, a brooding menace in the sunless dawn.

'That light over the plateau,' said Dagover.

'I see it, inquisitor. That is what we seek.'

'The commandry will not be able to travel that distance, even with your help.'

'I know.' There would be millions of heretics between the Sisters of Battle and their goal. 'Let us try to learn what and who is there. If need be, return to the cathedral without me.'

As she spoke, a wide line, bright as a stream of molten ore, extended down the height of the plateau. Shortly after the forward end reached the base, the rear pulled away from the peak. The light dimmed somewhat, turning into an angry orange shot through with streaks of blood red. The light pulsed, and Stern detected a regularity to its rhythm. It felt like something was marching west.

'Do you think that is a response to us?' Dagover asked.

'It may be. If so, the greater foe shows us its hand.'

Stern flew towards the glow. *Xenos Bane* kept pace, and narrowed the distance between them. They arrowed east, and the glow brightened. The streets between the manufactories filled with shouting cultists. There was a new intensity to their charge, a revelry at the prospect of the fight to come. A cluster of high chimneys a mile wide blocked Stern's view of what was coming. The smoke billowing from them was so thick, it brought the choking cloud cover down low enough that the tops of the chimneys disappeared in the murk. Stern dropped lower, making straight for the linked complex of manufactories. She planned to fly between the chimneys.

The complex exploded before she had the chance. A series of massive blasts tore the core structures open. Walls flew out, a wind of rockcrete fragments. The chimneys jerked up, as if trying to launch themselves skyward. They buckled, their heights breaking up, and they fell on themselves, the columns of a temple of fire collapsing into the cauldron. A storm of dust and smoke enveloped Stern. The wind and heat of destruction buffeted her. For long moments she was blind, and she hovered in the grey-and-red maelstrom. She coughed, her psychic shield no defence against the grit-filled air. Her lungs felt as if they were caked in clay.

'Pull up! Get us above the dust!' she heard Dagover shouting at his pilot. The engines of the Valkyrie screamed as the gunship fought for altitude.

Stern cleared her eyes. Shapes moved in the dust cloud below her, and things brighter and larger advanced through the blazes of the ruined manufactories. She drew closer. She was ready to fight whatever vision was now materialising before her.

She was wrong. She was not prepared for what she saw as, driven by the wind, the worst of the dust cleared.

The dead of the Order of Our Martyred Lady had returned. The corpses of Battle Sisters marched again. They were burned, mutilated, dismembered. Their armour was riven by gaping holes. Their faces were grotesque. Some had been flayed to the bone. Some glistened with exposed muscle, their jaws hanging wide with unspeakable hunger. Still others were just recognisable as the Sisters they had been, but their features were distorted by the abominations that now resided in their bodies. The horrors sang as they marched. The sounds that issued from their throats clawed at Stern's soul. They were parodies of the human, each voice torn in two. One part squalled like an infant. The other was the high, fluting, worshipful praise of a dark god.

Limping heavily at the back of the mass of bodies was a worse horror yet. Some of the corpses had been so badly damaged that they were now fused together. Monstrosities with three legs and four arms and two screaming heads. The creatures shambled forward, waving limbs that had become one with their weapons.

Stern looked down upon desecration itself. The mockery and insult to the saintly dead took her breath away.

Behind the possessed corpses came larger monsters. They were things of conduits and pipes and half-molten rockcrete. They were portions of the manufactories turned into daemonic engines. The industry of Severitas had come to foul life. Huge assemblages that had been twisted into a simulacrum of limbs walked heavily, punching craters into the street with every step. Steam and burning gas jetted from their joints. Their heads were open furnaces, skulls without eyes, shaped around maws that gaped wide, vomiting fire and smoke. As they advanced, the sightless heads turned this way and that, unleashing their burning rage on the world around them.

'Throne!' Dagover cursed over the vox. *'Shoot it down, blast you! Don't let it get–'* His voice disappeared in a burst of static.

Stern looked for *Xenos Bane*. It dropped out of the clouds, control lost, spiralling towards the ground. A daemonic engine held it in its talons. The creature was winged, an aircraft transformed into a blasphemous image of a drake. Its torso burned with its internal fires, and its reptilian jaw unleashed the flames over the cockpit of the Valkyrie.

It was a heldrake. Even as the attack began, she began to see the signature of the threat. Daemonic engines. Many of them, and possessed corpses. Her rational analysis of the attack took place at the same time that her heart swelled with horror.

The gunship's weapons fired to no effect. The heldrake clung to the top of the Valkyrie and perched to the rear of the cockpit, out of range. It smashed its claws through the fuselage and began to tear the ship open.

'Dagover!' Stern shouted. She launched a searing burst of light at the abomination. Silver fire scorched the heldrake's back. It screamed but did not release its hold.

Xenos Bane plummeted.

As if in answer to her shout, the corpses of the Sisters of Battle looked up at her, and the blind manufactory monsters swivelled their heads in her direction. The creations of ruin paused in their march, and in their song.

The dead Sisters pointed at Stern and screamed. A wave of hate and loss and hunger for retribution swept over her, stunning her with a force that felt like the actual souls of the Battle Sisters shrieking at her, a new collective of the dead coming to take vengeance because she had failed them. The limb-weapons fired, and the manufactories unleashed the full force of their flames. Burning rage enveloped her.

The world vanished in a sun of pain and the screams of the dead.

VII

THE SONG OF RETURN

The thunder of the explosions rippled across the sea of manufactories just as Klavia exited the grav-lift and joined Macrina behind the cathedral's parapet. To the east, the morning gloom flashed brutal red. It looked as if fire and blood were erupting from the centre of the manufactories at the limit of Klavia's vision. Stern was still visible for a moment before the fireballs engulfed her, a blazing star in the distance. Then the star dropped and vanished. At almost the same moment, she saw the streak of engines twisting down from the clouds.

The explosions kept growing, and they grew closer. Klavia squinted, trying to see through the waves of fire and smoke to the movement within.

'It looks like the very city is walking,' she said, hoping she was wrong.

'It does,' said Macrina. 'Something large is coming. Our enemy attacks with true purpose now.'

'Because our foe encountered a force that needed this response,' said Klavia. She kept her tone respectful. She wanted Macrina to know what she believed. It was just as important to her that she not sound insubordinate. She did not want to challenge the Canoness or chide her. Klavia wanted her to understand, to see what Klavia and more and more of the other Battle Sisters did. She wanted Macrina to see the saint.

'You may be right,' Macrina said quietly.

Those few words were much closer to a conversion than Klavia could have expected. She said nothing in response, worried she would choose the wrong words and change Macrina's mind again. There was hope, though. Even the most suspicious of the Battle Sisters could not have fought the besiegers again and again at Ephrael Stern's side and not seen the power of her faith, and the ferocity of her commitment to the order.

There was hope, as long as Stern had not fallen. Klavia gazed into the distance, willing that star to appear again. Instead, the maelstrom of fire and dust and smoke kept advancing, and it was coming fast. She still could not distinguish the huge shapes that seemed to be causing the spreading explosions. They were vague, hulking, darker movements in the clouds, bursting with sorcerous flame.

Ahead of them, other foes came faster. She caught glimpses of daemon engines at the edge of the cloud. The monstrous silhouettes of forgefiends and maulerfiends, hated and familiar from other battles, marched towards the cathedral. At the forefront came the infantry. Another vast mob of heretics streamed through the streets. Many were caught in the destruction wreaked by the behemoths behind them, and they shrieked in ecstasy as they ran, burning and dying with unholy curses of victory on their lips. In the centre of the mob, there was a tighter formation, its details still shadowed by the smoke. Her eye kept going to that group, though. Something called her attention, and chilled her blood.

The forgefiends reared back and fired. Their forelimbs and necks ended in fanged cannon maws, and their warp-tainted projectiles streaked at the cathedral roof. Eldritch blasts shook the battlements. Klavia leapt backwards as the wall in front of her crumbled away, stone turning into worms and then back into rubble as it plummeted to the cathedral square.

The Demolisher cannons opened fire once again. They sent their massive shells into the streets, striking the leading edge of the enemy tide. Roads and buildings that had already been reduced to rubble exploded once more. Huge geysers of wreckage roared skyward and new craters appeared, their edges overlapping with the scars of the previous barrage. A shell struck a forgefiend square in the thorax as it prepared to fire again. The monster disappeared in a conflagration fuelled by its own furnace. A terrible howl of daemonic hatred tore the air.

In the distance, the flames rose high, blotting the horizon. There was no sign of the star of hope.

The Demolishers set up a slow, heavy drumbeat of annihilation. The cannons recoiled in their mounts with the pumping movement of giant pistons. In between the deafening booms, and cutting through the screams, howls and rumbles of the enemy, came a song. It should not have been audible over the cacophony of war. If the things that sang had still been human, it would not have been.

'Throne,' Macrina cursed. Her wince mirrored Klavia's.

Klavia's instinct was to cover her ears. She resisted the impulse, tightening her grip on her storm bolter instead. There would be no blocking out a song that was more witchery than actual sound. It became a twisting fist in the centre of Klavia's being. Her lips pulled back in spiritual pain. The most terrible thing about the song was the familiarity. The inhuman chanted and wailed, yet there was a core, rotten and transformed, that spoke to Klavia with a hideous, tragic kinship. It called to her. It mocked her. It summoned grief that she did not yet understand, though it tried to drown her.

'I know you,' she whispered in agony. 'I have heard your voice before. I loved you once.'

Each word sung fractured the last, making them into razors. She wanted to weep. She thought blood was about to run from her ears.

It was an effort to move. The song tried to hold her in place. It tried to smother her in despair.

But she had to move. Something was flying at the tower, an abomination of metal and warpflame, a winged and taloned horror. The heldrake opened its jaws wide. The screams of the tormented soul of the being that had once been the machine's pilot scraped across the parapet. A corrupted autocannon extended from its gullet. A stream of shells cut over the roof, blowing up one of the Demolisher turrets.

Klavia and the other Sisters of Battle trained their weapons on the heldrake, stitching its torso and wings with bolter fire as it completed its strafing run. Anger and pain tinged the booming screams. It flew past the cathedral, banked, and came back for another pass.

And the song from below grew in intensity. The enemy was closer. Hundreds of cultists had been obliterated by the cannon strikes. Thousands more came on. The song came from the mass in their centre.

Klavia was tracking the flight of the heldrake, so she did not see what had closed in below. Macrina did. She was facing Klavia, and the Dominion saw her eyes widen in furious horror.

'This must not be!' Macrina shouted. Then she gave orders as she ran for the grav-lift. She called Klavia and half the Battle Sisters on the roof to her side, leaving the rest to defend the battlements and maintain the Demolisher barrage.

They were twenty-strong, those who crowded into the grav-lift. Klavia kept silent as they descended and Macrina spoke to the full commandry by vox-bead. The Order of Our Martyred Lady was going to launch a concerted attack to the east.

From above came the screams of the heldrake and the rattling thunder of guns. The sounds of the battle grew muffled as they dropped away to the ground floor of the Cathedral of Saint Thecla. The dread song, though, was just as clear, just as sharp and twisted a blade to her heart. In the faces of her Battle Sisters, Klavia saw the same agony she felt. Macrina's eyes burned with hate.

'What you will see must be destroyed,' she said. 'Do not hesitate. Attack with the greatest fury of faith. Attack to purge.'

Most of the rest of the commandry was in the cathedral's nave. Its rear doors were open, and beyond them was a vehicle bay, where the Rhinos rumbled, the engines revving and ready to charge into the heretics.

'For the Emperor!' Macrina shouted, taking the lead and beginning the advance even as the cathedral's outer doors ground slowly open. 'For Saint Katherine!'

'For Our Martyred Lady!' her Sisters of Battle cried.

They surged out of the cathedral at a run, at Macrina's command opening fire before they could even properly see the foe.

'Straight ahead!' Macrina called. 'Focused fire on the centre. That is what must be destroyed first. That is what must be silenced!'

The melody was more intense than ever. And when Klavia finally saw what the heretics flanked, when she finally saw the reanimated corpses of her sisters, the song attacked her with renewed force and with a new, cruel multiplicity of pains. It sank claws into her, shooting the cold of sorrow to her core. It surrounded her, smothering her with despair. It laughed at her, mocking all that she held to be true and holy. The sight of her former sisters was part of the song. The corpses, dragging limbs or shambling in fused, patchwork monstrosities, laughed and screamed and chanted their dark praise. Sound and image were part of the same assault. The reality of this horror gave the song its full power.

Klavia cried out as she pulled the trigger. She shouted in grief and anger and revulsion and all-consuming agony. The mass-reactive shells slammed into flesh. Explosions blew skulls to ash, but the dead kept coming. Ectoplasmic glows throbbed from the stumps of necks. The abominations that inhabited the corpses, turning them into puppets of flesh, would not release them willingly. The once blessed ceramite armour that had protected the Battle Sisters as they brought sword and fire to the foes of the Emperor now held possessed forms together in the face of the attacks.

After a wide strafing salvo, Klavia trained her storm bolter on a single monster as it closed in on her. It was one of the patchwork atrocities. Two torsos had been crushed together, the four arms flailing blades. It hopped forward on three legs. The two heads had been fused so that one seemed to be growing out of the screaming jaws of the other. A third head, the only remnant from yet another body, grew out of the flank, its teeth chattering in clicking, angry hunger.

Klavia's shells punched holes in the creature, and the first few hits severed one of the arms. Daemonic ichor, flickering with foul energy, burst from the wounds. The thing howled. The lips of the top head tried to form words. Six eyes trained on the Dominion, taunting and hating.

'Kuh...' the monster stammered. 'Kuh... kuh... kuh... Klahhhhh... *viahhhhhh!*'

The voice was part of the choir of the unholy song. It was also the sound of the familiar made terrible. Klavia knew the voice. It made her recognise the face too, which was so grotesque in its expressions, the flesh stretched to tearing point by the being inside, that she had not seen her sister until now. It was Sister Superior Menefreda, who had led her squads in a hundred battles, and whose voice raised in prayer had been as strong as a choir in itself.

Klavia winced at the cry, and her aim faltered. The emotional attack ahead of the physical one was devastating. The patchwork lunged at her. Its remaining arms reached for her in a bladed embrace.

'Saint Katherine, lend me your strength!' Klavia spat. She jumped back and brought the storm bolter up in an arc, hammering open the monster's fractured power armour. The abomination stumbled. Roaring in grief, shouting Menefreda's name, Klavia poured shells into the monster's core. They unleashed explosions that would have torn open the plating of a Chimera. The voice of Menefreda screamed in pain.

It was not Menefreda. The cries were lies, all lies.

'My sisters died in the purity of battle!' Klavia shouted at the monster. She fired until the body came apart once and for all, collapsing into a heap of burned flesh, bone fragments and shattered ceramite. There was a shriek of rage at the last, and there was nothing human about it at all. Diseased light flashed before Klavia, and the abomination that had gripped the body of her sister was gone, banished back to the infernal reaches of the immaterium.

Klavia did not release the trigger. As the monster fell, she sent the stream of shells into the one behind it. She advanced again. Righteous anger coursed through her veins, shielding her from the crippling grief. There were perhaps fifty of the returned Sisters advancing on the cathedral, half of the number who had died in the initial battles on Severitas. Without losing her aim, Klavia flicked her gaze above the monsters for a moment, towards the horizon she could not see, where the bright star of Ephrael Stern had vanished.

Were the rest of them there? Were they all attacking her?

There were no answers to be had. There was only each moment of the battle. Every heartbeat called for another decision. March forward or step back? Fire on one attacker to destroy, or strafe many to delay? Every decision was the pivot between a next heartbeat or a final one.

Odilla had joined Macrina in the nave, and the two Dominions marched in lockstep, Macrina's storm bolter and Odilla's flamer a synergy of destruction. Fire consumed the creatures as the shells broke them apart. Bit by bit, the abominations fell and the surface of Severitas was purged of their presence.

Odilla roared in concert with her weapon. Her jaw was wide, muscles quivering, as if her fury were too huge to be released in her cries. At the head of the advance, Macrina shouted her encouragement to her commandry, calling the Battle Sisters to acts of sanctified extermination.

Klavia loaded another magazine into her storm bolter. Odilla covered her by sending a powerful stream of ignited promethium into the reanimated Sisters ahead of them.

'Their ranks are smaller,' Klavia said as she resumed firing. She spoke to give Odilla hope, and to remind herself that she was awake, and that this nightmare must end.

'They should not exist,' Odilla gasped. The strain of forming words scraped her voice raw. *'They. Should. Not. Exist!'* And she sent her flames washing over once beloved figures as they surged forward, their terrible song a more devastating weapon than the blades they wielded.

Klavia saw one sliver of mercy in this dark day. The Battle Sisters that the abominations killed did not rise in their turn. There were limits to the reach of the foe who had committed this atrocity. And limits were the doorway to defeat.

'We will prevail!' Klavia shouted over the hammering of her weapon. 'Hold fast, sister. The Emperor protects!'

'The Emperor protects!' Odilla repeated, her shout of faith dangerously close to a shriek of desperation.

The jaws of despair gnawed at Klavia too. If she hesitated to destroy the risen Sisters for even a second, she would be lost. The pull of the trigger was an act of defiance against the unspeakable.

But as the song ate at her, seeking to break down her defences, she thought of what Stern had said about her visions of the monstrous *nothing*. There was something coming that was worse than this, worse than the perversity of Battle Sisters turned into walking blasphemies. Klavia had believed Stern's words before. Now she felt their truth resonate with renewed urgency.

A galaxy that could permit the horror before her was depraved beyond prayers. An all-destroying *nothing* was not just easy to believe. It was to be expected. It was inevitable.

'*We will stop you!*' Klavia roared. She hurled her resolution and her promise into the teeth of annihilation.

VIII

THRICE-BORN AND RISEN

Falling. Burning.

No up or down, only the fire, only the song, only the embrace of horror.

Burning. Falling.

No up or down, but the atrocity was reaching to embrace Stern. The dead Sisters of Battle would claim her. On Severitas, the hope of sisterhood had been revived in her.

Now you shall have it.

A voice without sound or words, the voice in the fire engulfing her, the voice of the horror that was the Ruinous Powers.

Be one with your sisters, Thrice-Born, for they are reborn too.

'NO!'

It was a single word. But it was a real sound, a shout like a breakwater against the wave of the daemonic song. In the word was Stern's power, her strength. It was a denial of Chaos.

'EMPEROR!'

One word. The affirmation of faith, of power, of purpose in this universe. It was by the Emperor's will that she had come to Severitas. It was by His will that she fought here, now, in this very second, at this very space.

By His will, she would destroy these abominations.

And with the invocation of the God-Emperor, she no longer

fell. She flew. She did not know whether she flew at the ground, the sky, or into a ruined manufactory. It did not matter. She flew with her faith. As the light of sanctified psychic energy exploded out from her once more, she felt as if she had *become* her faith.

She attacked, though she could not see her enemy. She became a spear of light through the firestorm around her. She fired a psychic blast ahead of her, and this too seemed more to her than before, a sword of faith launched at whatever enemy would dare to stand against the will of the Emperor.

She passed through another explosion. This one, she had caused, and the pain of passing through it felt clean, purging. It was a disruption of the attack on her, and then a disintegration. In another moment, she was clear of flame, in the open air, and she could see again.

In her wake, she left one of the walking constructs. She had blown apart its forge skull. The huge monster staggered without purpose, its pipeline arms flailing at the stump on its shoulders. Flames, ore, daemonic ichor and warp energy erupted uncontrollably from the neck. The fountain shot twenty feet into the air, and then the molten liquid within it fell back, coating the body. A shrieking aurora surrounded the hulk, eating into its form. Chunks of metal fell away. The body lost coherence. It took another few steps, and then it collapsed with a boom, crushing and burning a score of the risen Sisters of Battle beneath it.

As Stern turned her attention to the reanimated creatures, they called for her. All the strength of their song focused on a single point, on her. A spear tip forged from the monstrously familiar and the inhuman desire pierced her heart. Preparing to attack, she had let her defence slip, and no psychic shield could block the sound. The pain and the grief turned the world dark. It was only for a moment, but her flight turned into a fall. She hit the ground with an impact that shattered pavement.

The risen Sisters shouted their welcome of hunger. Grimacing, Stern pushed the pain away and stood even as the mob fell on her. They attacked her with blades. They flailed at her with broken limbs and hands hooked into claws. A few still had guns and fired clumsily. Bolter shells cut through other corpses and slammed into her armour, throwing her sideways. The daemonic song screamed into her ears, into her head, into her heart. *One of us, one of us, one of us, one of us!* The grotesque mockeries of Sisters of Battle were what so many believed she was, and what she had been told she was for so long. These monsters confirmed it. They embraced her. They clutched at her with greed, seeking to drag her down and make her part of their foulness. The song struck home, and so did the knives. Blades and words were one. Her armour was no defence, and the risen, distorted reflections of what she had so often feared she truly was, stabbed her again and again. Icy, burning pain slid between her ribs, into her chest, between her shoulder blades. The abominations stabbed, and they stabbed, and they brought her to her knees in a pool of her blood.

'Never!' she cried. She could not die here, not with her task unfinished. She could not let oblivion claim her when a greater oblivion threatened everything. 'I am the wrath of the Emperor!' In faith she rose, and she whirled violently, slashing with Sanctity, severing limbs. 'Return to the abyss from which you came!' she shouted.

She tore open the veil to the immaterium.

She launched herself into the air at the same moment, struggling against two of the monsters clinging to her. The rip in the real became a maelstrom on the ground, and a hurricane wind rushed into its maw, dragging the risen Sisters with it.

Stern was still so close to the rift of her creation that it tried to pull her in too. Holy fire rushed over her. The obscene creatures screamed and fell away from her, to be swallowed by the vortex.

The rift began to close. The remaining Sisters, their song diminished, shrieked with anger, reaching up for her. Another walking manufactory forge loomed over her, its footsteps shaking the ground with seismic force. Its massive arms grabbed at her. It launched a flaming attack from its head.

'You have no dominion here!' Stern hurled herself through the flames. She swung Sanctity upward. A blazing beam of psychic energy turned it into a weapon thirty feet long. It sliced vertically through the body of the daemon engine, cutting it in half. The giant's flames died with its scream. A flood of burning ichor fell upon the remaining corpses.

'You are nothing!' Stern shouted at the abominations that remained. 'In the Emperor's name, I will tread upon you in my anger! By the Emperor's will, I shall trample you in my fury!'

The right of destruction was the Emperor's. The anger was hers. The pain the mere existence of the risen Sisters caused in her was tremendous. Their claim to kinship struck her where she was most vulnerable. She embraced the pain as she unleashed an inferno of blasts on the creatures. They howled as she ended their song forever, and she howled back at them. She could not escape the torment that came with destroying forms that still resembled Adepta Sororitas. She did not seek to. The agony was the pain of salvation. Its presence was the reminder that she was *not* one of the damned.

There was only ash below her now, the ash of corrupted flesh eddying in wind-driven spirals. To the west, the conflict still raged, and she could hear the distant fluting of that awful song.

Blood coursed from her wounds. Her body throbbed in an agony she could not afford to acknowledge.

More daemon engines were marching from the direction of the plateau. So many. So many foul creations unleashed by the force that resided in that stronghold.

Stern's eyes narrowed. Between the engines and the risen Sisters, there was a pattern. She began to see the truth of what opposed her.

She would think through that truth later. On the ground not far away, the heldrake was tearing open the fallen Valkyrie.

'Dagover!' she called, streaking downward.

Dagover crawled out of the smouldering wreckage of *Xenos Bane*. He struggled to keep his head clear through the novelty of pain. So little flesh remained to him that sensations of any kind were rare. He would not have survived the crash if more of him had still been human. As it was, his skull throbbed from the impact. His face burned and wept with open wounds. His vision kept blurring, the optic connections fighting to stabilise.

His machinic limbs obeyed the commands of his brain after a few moments, and he was on his feet again. His movement caught the heldrake's attention. It turned from ripping apart the Valkyrie's ruin. Before it could attack, Dagover fired his plasma pistol at its eye. He shot it as if it were a living beast, and it reacted as if it were one. It howled in anger. The scream, a fusion of the machine and the daemonic and the human, they who had once been the pilot instead of the prisoner, staggered Dagover. His aim wavered.

The heldrake reared over him.

A beam of psychic fire struck it in the neck, tearing open its plating and releasing a flash of incandescent ichor. The heldrake launched itself into the air, its autocannon unleashing a continuous barrage.

Dagover watched the daemon engine and Stern meet in mid-air. A storm erupted above him. Crimson and silver flame clashed. Stern's figure was tiny next to the heldrake, but the light that surrounded her was brighter than the monster's, and it grew wider, even brighter, and angrier. Dagover's bionic eyes tried to adapt to the glare's ferocity. It was like staring into the death of a star. The heldrake banked sharply, trying to catch Stern in the stream of its fire. She closed with it as if she thought to tear it apart with her hands. Dagover made out the narrow line of her powerblade. Stern hit the heldrake in the neck again. She plunged the blade through the plates. A shock wave rippled outward, and Dagover winced as if he had been hit.

As if the sword were much longer than it appeared, with a cry of wrath and a flash of even more brilliant, terrible sanctity, Stern decapitated the heldrake. Its scream silenced, the body fell broken to the ruins in the street.

As Stern descended towards Dagover, he glanced at the shifting ash that had been the resurrected Sisters of Battle.

That act of destruction must have come at some cost to her, he realised. Yet she did it. That was information worth probing.

'Your pilot?' Stern asked when she landed.

'Dead on impact,' said Dagover.

They were in an island of calm in the storm of war. In the direction of the cathedral, the day burned. To the east came the sounds of machinic howls and heavy footsteps.

'The enemy is determined to stop you,' Dagover said.

'You mean *us*,' Stern corrected.

'No, I mean *you*. These attacks, in strength and kind, are designed to stop one particular threat. Without you, the masses of heretics would, in the end, have prevailed against your sisters. You are the threat this assault has sought to vanquish. It has failed. Keep going east. You have the advantage. Destroy this army.'

Stern looked east. She saw, through smoke and fire, the shapes of more daemonic engines. She wanted to erase their existence. She wanted to make them pay, not just for their own abominated being, but for the crime of the risen Sisters. Though there could be punishment for that sin, there could never be expiation, not even if an entire heretical population was blasted to dust.

She turned back to Dagover. His cadaverous face regarded her with its expressionless eye-lenses. *Destroy the army.* She wanted to. There had been a taste of vengeance when she had annihilated the heldrake and the walking forge. The taste was not unwelcome.

It was also not what was needed from her.

Was this what the inquisitor wished her to become? A killing machine that he manipulated to his ends? No. That was not what she would be. That was not what the Father of Mankind commanded her to be.

'Cut through the enemy like a scythe,' Dagover urged quietly. 'Blast through it until you reach whoever stands behind this.'

'No,' Stern said.

'This was our purpose.'

'The situation has changed. The Order of Our Martyred Lady needs me now. And I have to get you back safely.'

'So then we do this all over again?'

'The enemy's supply of heretics may be almost inexhaustible. But I will see to it that there will never be another body from the ranks of my sisters to resurrect.'

'Is that a wise use of…'

Stern jumped into Dagover's hesitation. 'My resources? My power? Me? I am not merely a weapon. I am not a destroyer, and nothing else. The Emperor is our salvation. There must be something to save. Even, I think, in you. Or we are no better than the daemons we fight. So I will return to save my sisters, and I will keep you alive as well.'

'Even me?' the living skull asked sardonically.

'Even you.'

They headed back west, Stern protecting Dagover as they cut through the mobs of heretics towards the front lines. Most of the cultists were focused on advancing towards the commandry.

'You claimed I was the target,' Stern said to Dagover. 'Why does the army not turn on me now?'

'Because it has failed in its goal to stop you. I think there is another prize to be won.'

Dagover was close to being a walking tank. There was barely any human left in his armour to kill. He could hold his own, and when they reached the battlefront, Stern left him to seek her sisters. The forgefiends and the manufactory horrors were hitting them hard with flame and a storm of phosphor shells. The Sisters of Battle fought in the midst of a blinding, incinerating ocean. The heretics died in droves, their bodies forming huge pyres as they ran in the way of the fire of the engines, or were cut down by the Adepta Sororitas. Enough got through and survived in the cauldron to hurl themselves at the Battle Sisters.

It was the other half of the risen Sisters, though, that were the greatest threat. Their assault was a spiritual one even more than it was physical. The unholy song sapped the strength of the soul and left the warriors vulnerable to other attacks.

Stern saw something else as she flew low over the struggle. Though the Battle Sisters of the Order of Our Martyred Lady who fell were not rising again as abominations, the cultists were dragging their bodies away.

'Sisters!' Stern cried. Warp energies gathered around her and she braced herself again for what she must do. 'Leave the resurrected blasphemies to me! Let me take your pain! Let it be mine alone! Fight instead the enemy that has dared use this horror.'

She plunged into the middle of the walking corpses. Those closest to her burst into flame at her touch. The others, howling their song of woe and welcome, rounded on her.

'No more!' she shouted. 'There will be no more of you! You end *now*!'

She burned them. She burned the images of her sisters. She burned the images of what she was said to be. She burned them for the sake of a true sisterhood, and the promise of something to save.

IX

WALKING WOUNDED

When the Sisters of Battle retreated to the cathedral, they left behind them thousands of dead cultists and a score of smouldering daemon engines. The commandry had blunted the assault. For the moment, there were no other monsters in sight, and the cultists kept their distance from the Cathedral of Saint Thecla, gathering again to await the command for another attack. There would be no more resurrections. The abominations were ash. The bodies of the dead had been returned to the cathedral for holy rites, or cremated on the battlefield.

Stern returned to her cell in the catacombs of the cathedral. There was no time to rest, no time to heal. Her wounds had clotted, but they were deep. All she could do was pray for the strength she needed to take the fight to the enemy's stronghold before another siege wave began. She descended the stairs. Before her mind's eye were the faces of the Sisters of the Order of Our Martyred Lady. They were more haggard than they had been after any of the other battles on Severitas. They bore the psychic scars carved there by the risen corpses.

Klavia was waiting for Stern by the door to her cell. The Dominion's eyes were anguished. The manner of her gaze made Stern uneasy.

What was Stern? It was *always* that same question, whether it was Macrina, Dagover, Klavia or herself asking. All had different answers. All had answers except her. She did not know the truth.

'Be strong, sister,' said Stern. 'We have had a victory today, hard as it was.'

'It does not feel like one.'

'We will not see any more of those abominations. The dead rest. Their souls have always been with the Emperor. Their bodies are at rest now, too.'

'They should never have existed,' Klavia said with a shudder.

'No. They should not have. But their corruption came after death. There was no fault, no lapse, on the part of our sisters. We did not see their souls coming for us.'

Klavia nodded. She clearly wanted to believe Stern's reassurance more than she actually did.

There were so many terrible things that were possible. But they were words that Stern did not say.

She was a thing that was possible.

'The enemy cannot attack us like that again,' Stern said. 'Remember that, and that the Emperor protects.'

'The Emperor protects,' Klavia repeated. 'He does indeed.' She looked hard at Stern, her eyes shining. 'I am glad to be reminded.'

Stern watched her go, then knelt in her cell. She had not been there long, her prayers hardly begun, when she was interrupted. She looked up, surprised to see Macrina.

'Canoness,' she said, and bowed her head.

'The next attack is coming sooner than we had hoped or guessed,' Macrina said. 'There are more daemon engines on the march. Will you come to the vestry? We must decide on our new strategy immediately.'

'I will,' Stern said. Macrina's tone was neutral, but she had come instead of Dagover. The flush of hope warmed Stern's veins. That was the strength that she needed. She was ready.

* * *

Dagover was waiting for them in the vestry. If he was surprised to see Macrina arrive with Stern, he did not show it. They gathered around the great table, looking down at maps they already knew too well.

'We have been stymied,' said Macrina.

'I disagree,' said Dagover. 'We have confirmed that the plateau to the east is the enemy's stronghold. I believe it was our approach that triggered the escalation. The foe sought to destroy us, and Sister Superior Stern in particular. The attempt failed, and the most significant weapon in our foe's arsenal has been destroyed.'

'True,' Macrina granted. 'I give thanks to the Emperor that we will no longer encounter our sisters in such a desecrated form. The daemon engines that are making their way here are not insignificant, though. Enough of them, and they will breach the cathedral's defences.'

'Then we must defeat the true foe before that happens,' said Stern.

Macrina looked at her. 'How?'

'By finishing what we began. We have not retreated, Canoness, and we are not in a stalemate. We know where the enemy is, and that is where I will go.' Stern turned to Dagover. 'Alone, this time. I will confront and destroy him.'

'*Him*,' Dagover said. 'You know something the rest of us do not?' He did not sound as if that idea pleased him.

'You are Ordo Xenos, inquisitor. You have not fought as many forms of the Ruinous Powers as I have. In making war against them, I have come to know the nature of daemons, their worshippers, and all of their degree. The patterns are more visible to me.'

And there had been a cost for this knowledge, Stern thought.

'The presence of so many daemon engines, and the nature of what happened to the fallen Sisters of Battle suggests the actions of a Master of Possession.'

'Yes,' Macrina said slowly. 'Yes. Your reasoning is sound. But the scale of what is being done here is colossal. If you are correct, then this is a Master of Possession whose power is truly monstrous.'

'I believe that is the case,' said Stern.

'You plan to confront him alone?'

'I see no other choice.'

'A massed advance,' Dagover suggested. 'We do not act separately this time.'

'No,' said Stern. She bowed to Macrina. 'I mean no slight to your commandry, Canoness, when I say it would be too slow. I can get to the plateau faster on my own.'

'This is our fight too,' Macrina said coldly. 'Do not think you can take it from us. We were lured here, and we will not be spectators.'

'It is interesting that you, and therefore *we*, were lured to this particular location,' said Dagover. 'A point on the planet so close to the centre of power.'

'The closer to the centre, the greater the power,' said Stern. 'This is where our enemy has the greatest chance of victory.' She turned to Macrina. 'Canoness, I would never dishonour the order by suggesting it stand aside. But I *must* go alone. Think of how many means of attrition and distraction the enemy could use. Advancing on the ground, we could well be truly stymied. Our foe has an inexhaustible supply of troops. Too far from the shelter of the cathedral, and there are limits to what any of us could do to stave off defeat.'

Macrina scowled, but did not contradict Stern.

'If the Order of Our Martyred Lady makes a stand here,' Stern continued, 'then it still takes the battle to the enemy. You can fight long and hard in the cathedral. The forces against us will be divided by two targets, as they were earlier, but you will be in a stronger position.'

'And your position?' Dagover asked. 'Will it be stronger?'

'That is irrelevant,' said Stern. 'It is what is necessary. It is what I am called upon to do.'

X

POSSESSOR

The Lord of Severitas strode the length of his ramparts, watching the coming of night. There were threats to his reign out there. He knew that one would almost certainly come for him before dawn. The knowledge did not concern him. He felt no need to think about it. Instead, he enjoyed the death of another day, and revelled in the power of the faith of others.

He held the faith of millions in his grasp. It coursed through his veins. It made reality dance to his command. Its nimbus crackled down his cloak, flashing crimson and violet and blue and green as the cloak billowed in the wind. At each step, he tapped the rockcrete of the rampart with the tip of his staff. When he did, the surface twisted. For a brief moment, he walked upon flesh, and it screamed in pain.

Varak Ghar sighed with pleasure. He flexed his arms as if rolling the shape of faith from shoulder to shoulder. He gloried over its possession. The setback his forces had suffered earlier in the day was so trivial that it was barely an irritation. If his victory had not come then, it would come tonight, or the next day. He rather liked the delayed gratification. He could savour the slaughter a little bit longer.

Faith was an engine. It was the greatest of engines. Next to it, Krezen Pak's creations were trivialities. They were amusing, and they were useful, but they were nothing without the daemonic life that Varak Ghar gave them when he tore up the veil to the warp and brought in the entity that would give movement and volition to a construct. The engines were one physical extrusion of faith. They were but the iceberg tip of the power the Word Bearers Master of Possession commanded.

The corruption of Severitas was his masterwork, a culmination of millennia of labour and study. It was here, finally here, that he had harnessed the collective faith of a population. So much energy, so much power, was contained in belief. How many cults had he founded, on how many worlds, before he had discovered the precise teachings that would accomplish what he sought? He had lost track. In the end, he had achieved his goal. He found the words, the shaping words. The revelation of Chaos spread through the population, and the people turned to the worship of the true gods. In the way they worshipped, they made Varak Ghar their intercessor. They believed that it was only through him that they received the blessings of the gods. And so all their energy of belief was directed to him, seeking his favour, his blessings of power.

Millions of prayers. Millions of rituals. All of them centring on Varak Ghar. With every prayer, he grew stronger. The faith of Severitas flowed through him like an electrical current, unending, ever-blazing.

He possessed an entire world.

But a challenger had come, and she refused to be stopped.

He would have to show her the error of her ways.

Bootsteps approached from behind. Varak Ghar growled under his breath. He moved to the parapet and stood still, looking west. He resented having his solitude disturbed, especially by Krezen Pak.

'Are you indulging in victory before you have earned it?' the Warpsmith asked.

Reluctantly, Varak Ghar turned his head to gaze at the other Word Bearer. He was a full head taller than Krezen Pak, and the great, curled horns of his skull added still more to his height. The Warpsmith's features were hidden inside his crowned helmet. The red glow of his eye-lenses shone balefully from its shadowed crevices. His eight clawed mechadendrite limbs moved restlessly, a signal of his anger.

'Victory has already been earned,' Varak Ghar said. 'It is certain. It is written.'

'It did not look written yesterday. It looked anything but written.'

'You are bitter over the loss of your trinkets. Your horizons should be broader.' Krezen Pak was a mere labourer. His daemon engines were nothing without the entities that Varak Ghar summoned. What the Warpsmith made was useful, but only to the extent that the constructs were endowed by Varak Ghar's creative flame.

The mechadendrites twitched. The claws snapped. 'My engines–' Krezen Pak began.

'Had better do what I ask of them,' Varak Ghar interrupted, reminding the Warpsmith of his place.

Krezen Pak refused the lesson. 'You should ask more of yourself,' he said. 'What of your creations? What of those corpses that were going to hand us victory in a single march?'

Varak Ghar shrugged. 'They would have, if not for the greater enemy.'

'If not... If not...' Krezen Pak snarled. 'If not for her, the Adepta Sororitas would have been destroyed days ago. You did not need to reanimate them then. You did so in answer to the one who came to save them.'

'I did,' said Varak Ghar. 'That is true. Everything I have done and everything I have commanded for quite some time has been in answer to her. Her coming was foretold.'

'Then why does she still live?'

'To make her death all the more satisfying.'

Krezen Pak's limbs scraped and tapped against the crenellations of the wall. 'I am not satisfied.'

He never was. What of it? Varak Ghar cared little for his satisfaction. Krezen Pak was here to serve him. 'And?'

'I would prefer to stop her before she reaches this position.'

Varak Ghar shrugged. 'Your preferences are what they are.' And they were irrelevant.

'You are too certain. We have not fought the likes of her before.'

'We have not. I wonder if many of our brethren have. We came to Severitas, we took it, and then the omens of her coming began. We are here for a purpose. The gods have tasked us with her destruction.' *Glory upon glory. Glory upon glory.* He kept his pleasure to himself. If Krezen Pak was too lowly to understand it, he was too lowly to share in it.

'Beware your arrogance, Master of Possession.'

Varak Ghar growled. His fingers tightened around his staff, but he held back from striking the Warpsmith. This was not the time. He was confident in victory, but he was not a fool. There was work to be done. 'Very well,' he said, when he had calmed himself. 'What would you do? The new assault on the cathedral is already underway.'

'Destroy her there if we can.'

Krezen Pak's stupidity was beyond tolerating. Varak Ghar would have to rid himself of the fool before long. 'What?' he asked acidly. 'Do you imagine I have given orders that she be left untouched?'

'Send all the engines in. If they do not kill her there, she will encounter them between the cathedral and here.'

'Oh, very well. Do as you please.' What did it matter? Let the Warpsmith have his way, and he would leave Varak Ghar in peace for a time. If Krezen Pak could not see that he was repeating the very tactics whose failure he had decried moments ago, let that be on his head. There was a chance a greater mass of weapons might succeed. Varak Ghar would be disappointed if they did, though he would accept that as the will of the gods. More likely, though, the engines would weaken her. She would not be able to see the greater trap waiting for her.

The flesh on Varak Ghar's skull had petrified thousands of years before. It resembled a cracked, grey clay coating over bone. He could not smile. Yet he could still feel the sensation of pleasure that would have made him smile. He felt that now. Tiresome as he was, Krezen Pak did serve a purpose. Varak Ghar saw now that the greater effort on the ground below the plateau would be the prologue to his personal triumph. Krezen Pak was his tool always and forever, even when he tried to go his own way.

How perfect were the dictates of fate!

'Go on then. Release the engines. Let her play with them.' He was careful to show disdain. It would not do for Krezen Pak to think he was acting according to Varak Ghar's wishes after all.

Deny it he would, but the Warpsmith was Varak Ghar's possession too.

To the west, on the hill of the Cathedral of Saint Thecla the Unyielding, a star rose, piercing silver in its baleful purity.

'There,' said Varak Ghar. 'She comes. I think we will put an end to things.'

As the star flew towards the plateau, Varak Ghar stretched out his hand. His grasping fingers closed, and his will reached down to the tens of thousands of his followers near the base of the cliff. He had given them their faith, and now he demanded it back. His jaws opened in the ecstasy of power as he seized the strength of collective faith for himself.

Beside him, Krezen Pak was silent.

The Warpsmith felt awe, then, Varak Ghar thought. *That was good. He should.*

* * *

Stern passed over the heretics closing in once more on the cathedral. They chanted their unholy prayers louder than ever. No human tongue should have been able to form those poisonous words, those malefic syllables. Stern heard the same song that the risen Sisters had proclaimed. The memories that it summoned were dangerous, and poisonous to the soul. In the midst of the heretics came the daemon engines. Maulerfiends crushed celebrating cultists beneath their feet. Heldrakes screamed in the falling night, and flew towards the roof. There were more of the giants carved out of manufactories, walking cauldrons striding forwards to the siege.

The assault was massive. Not a wave but a tide, an ocean coming for the Sisters of Battle. The commandry was fierce, and the walls of Saint Thecla's were colossal. That would not be enough. Not in the long run.

She could stop that engine. And the one after that. She could hold back the tide.

No. She could not. She would be a single breakwater against a storm surge. The most she could do was briefly delay the crash. There was only one way to stop the enemy. Only one way to win. She would not be helping if she stopped to fight. If she did, she would be the one being delayed. She would be making herself the guarantor of the enemy's victory.

She grimaced in pain at the thought of what she was leaving her sisters to face, and she flew. But as she did, she realised how naturally, how easily, she had thought of the Sisters of Battle as *her sisters.* The joy gave her strength. It submerged the pain of her wounds. And she gave thanks to the Emperor for guiding her to this moment.

She turned her gaze from the swarm of heretics and monsters. She rose higher, and the cultists became ants below, an undulating movement in the darkness, obscured by smoke and briefly revealed by flame.

She focused on the plateau. The true enemy waited there. He had held Stern and her sisters back until now, but in doing so, he had shown his hand.

'Guide my flight, Father of Mankind,' she prayed. 'Make me your spear, that I may pierce the heart of your foe.'

Faster, higher. She flew on the wings of sacred wrath. The plateau came into sight. Streaks of fire led from its base, the marks of the daemon engines' passage. Until she was about a mile from the base, the heaving insect carpet of the heretics was still below her. Then the landscape changed. It stilled. All the daemon engines had passed, making for the cathedral. Stern was surprised, though, that the thronging of the heretics seemed to have stopped completely.

The stillness felt ominous. There was something in the air, something dark, as if great sorcerous currents were at play, so huge they were almost beyond perception.

She flew lower, and saw that this sector of the city was not deserted. The roads were clogged with bodies. Thousands upon thousands of corpses surrounded the base of the plateau. They lay frozen in the agonies of death. They were desiccated, hollowed out, like the husks of wasps.

On her guard, Stern headed up towards the top of the plateau. The sensation of flying through a field of power grew stronger. It was a feeling of being pulled, not spiritually but physically, as if a tremendous will were seeking to yank her soul from her body.

An immense action was occurring. It had drained the essence from every heretic for a span of miles. Stern wondered if her foe could really be what she had surmised. Could what she saw be the work of a single being? Could she hope to defeat him?

Yes. Because it was not she who would defeat him. It would be the God-Emperor, acting through her.

Stern reached the peak of the plateau. Before her, a fortress brooded. It was a patchwork, and it was a unity. It was a conglomeration of desecrated chapels and twisted manufactories, forced together to create a bastion of the Ruinous Powers. Flying buttresses and ore conduits entwined like sinew. The fortress looked like a flayed beast, its muscles exposed.

The central block was the height of the Cathedral of Saint Thecla. It was wider than the cathedral. Its wings, two-thirds as tall, extended for a mile to the north and to the south. They curved inwards at their tips, the daemonic architecture turning the ends of the fortress into talons. Chimneys thrust out of the fortress like spines, belching foul, black smoke. There were no windows, except near the crown of the central mass. Two wide, jagged apertures pulsed red, the eyes of madness.

Beneath the eyes, the entire middle of the façade was densely packed with grilles that opened and closed, unleashing geysers of flame. They formed a single, gargantuan maw. The fortress seemed to look back at Stern, and welcome her arrival in its own right.

She streaked towards the crown, Sanctity held before her, its blade shining in anger. Then all the grilles opened at once. A wall of flame thundered up at the sky. The fortress roared. It *roared*. It lurched, a thing given abhorrent life and motion. Its wings tore themselves up from the ground. They reached around for her, so huge they blotted out the world. She shot up, racing for freedom, but the fortress was too vast, and too quick. With rockcrete and metal screaming and grinding like a mountain rockfall, its terrible embrace came for her.

Talons a hundred feet long slammed together, and seized their prey.

XI

THE BLOOD OF FAITH

Dagover kept asking himself how this would end, and what he still hoped to achieve. He struggled to see what, exactly, he thought he was reaching for, even in the midst of the siege.

The cannons roared from the battlements of Saint Thecla's. Crater upon crater opened in the street. The bodies of the heretics, reduced to fragments and blood, turned the shattered streets into a swamp of gore. Daemon engines, hit full-on by shells, blew up, taking scores of cultists with them.

The cannons weren't enough. Nothing could be enough. The Sisters of Battle were engaged in a war of delay. Dagover knew it, even if they would not admit it. Macrina fought for any fragment of time she could get. And so, in a defensive war, she went on the offensive. She launched sorties out of the cathedral gates to drive back the enemy and gain a little bit more time. Dagover joined them. All the while, though he never took his attention off the killing of the foe, the questions haunted him.

How did he think this would end?

There could be no true ending. He did not expect there to be.

No, that was sophistry. What was his goal? The struggle to stay alive in the Imperium Nihilus must have dulled his faculties. He had found Stern, but what had he achieved?

He feared he was a pawn of her fate more than anything else.

Was he any closer to harnessing the power she represented? He did not think so. The failure was shameful. He thought of his Deathwatch kill teams. He thought of the Adeptus Astartes from cursed Chapters he had forged into squads. They fought the xenos foes of the Imperium, but every skirmish, every victory, had been calibrated to the greater need of the Imperium. The needs, that Dagover, as a Recongregator, conceived of them.

Everything was different now. The Imperium had nearly been destroyed. Was this the cleansing fire he had worked for, the annihilation of the corrupt order that would open the way to renewal and the chance for the Imperium to become what it should always have been?

Guilliman had returned. Was that a sign of what he hoped? Perhaps. He did not know. There was so much he did not know. Cut off from the Inquisition for more than a hundred years, he carried with him the ordo's authority, but not the real power that came with information.

And what of Stern?

He had to admit that he did not know how he hoped to use her in the new reality. Or even if he could. He had only the sense that power like hers could and should not be left unchannelled, unsupervised. Wherever she went, she triggered power struggles. That was true before the Cicatrix Maledictum, and it would be true now. There were factions that would want to destroy her. He could not let that happen.

He almost laughed at the arrogance of the thought. *He* could not let *her* be destroyed? Was that even a possibility?

He didn't know.

Once they left Severitas, what then? He did not know who was using whom any more.

That was the most profound admission of ignorance he had ever made to himself, in his entire life as an inquisitor. Stern would no doubt tell him that he found her, and that he brought her to Severitas, for a reason. So had he become merely a player in the arc of her fate after all? That was not good enough.

As if he had a choice.

In his heavy power armour, Dagover might have seemed more like a Kastelan robot than a human being. He marched with the Dominions, a hard jab of a fist into the heretics. They headed out of the gates with a Rhino. Its storm bolters, joined by the heavy bolters and flamers of the Sisters, scythed through the corrupted. Dagover incinerated them with his plasma pistol, firing with quick, contemptuous movements. The heretics were a legion, but they were easy to cut down. Individually, they were no threat. As a mass, they were stymied by the perfect formation and discipline of the Adepta Sororitas. Two squads cleared the gate of enemies, then separated left and right to purge the environs of the walls.

Dagover kept pace with Klavia. As one of the first to have embraced Ephrael Stern as a sister, Klavia interested him. He observed her as they fought. All the warriors of Canoness Macrina's commandry visibly bore the spiritual wounds inflicted on them by the risen Sisters. Their faces were haggard, their sunken eyes burning with the anger of traumatised grief. In Klavia's eyes, though, there was something else. It was in the eyes of some of the other Battle Sisters too, and more and more of them all the time. But it was in Klavia that Dagover saw it most vividly, and it was Klavia who had first believed in Stern. There was a brightness in the midst of her grief and anger. A brightness like new iron being forged, the shine of faith rewarded, of a warrior who had found new hope, new cause, new and glorious fury.

Klavia had the face of someone who had witnessed a saint. Stern recoiled from the word. Yet she would have to confront it. She would have to shoulder the burden. The word was too powerful to be shed or claimed by an individual. The saint had little say in how the title was bestowed. The perception had begun. It would grow. It would inspire fierce passions, for and against her.

There were so many variables at play. Some few, Stern might be able to influence, if she truly understood what was happening. But the perception of sainthood lay far more in the hands of the observers. Dagover prided himself in understanding all this very well.

He might not be able to influence Stern directly. How she was perceived, though, that was another matter.

He saw possibilities. He saw potentials. They were embryonic still, and that was for the good. He would need to oversee the gathering currents of sainthood carefully.

He might yet be more than a pawn.

But first he and Stern and the Sisters of Battle had to survive and escape from Severitas.

The squad made it a third of the way around the perimeter of the cathedral. The Dominions no longer had the extra firepower of the Rhino with them, and a maulerfiend closed on their position. It charged over cultists, barrelling straight at the squad and the wall behind the Sisters. Klavia held up a fist and shook it back once. The squad obeyed, retreating several steps so abruptly that the maulerfiend's attack run took it in front of the squad instead of through it. The beast snarled, swiping a massive claw at the squad. It missed, and instead of turning to attack, it leapt at the cathedral wall. The claws punched into the rockcrete as if it were flesh, and the monster began to climb.

'Bring it down!' Klavia shouted.

If the maulerfiend reached the roof, already besieged by two heldrakes, it could wreak havoc with the Demolisher cannons.

The Dominions trained their heavy weapons on the daemon engine while the rest of the squad held back the heretics. A precise stream of heavy bolter shells slammed into the abomination's right foreleg. Dagover added plasma blasts to the attack. The combination of shell detonations and superheated gas blew apart the lower part of the limb. With an outraged roar, the maulerfiend lost its grip on the wall. As it started to fall, it leapt back from the cathedral, dropping like a meteor into the centre of the squad. It crushed Dominus Odilla on impact.

The squad scattered, Klavia roaring in grief and anger, the warriors throwing themselves out of the way of the raging behemoth. It parted jaws with teeth of razor-edge metal. Burning ectoplasm jetted from its throat. Dagover's power armour was suddenly too slow, too cumbersome, and he fell trying to get out of the way of the daemonic fountain. He spun as he dropped, and his right shoulder caught the edge of the ectoplasmic burst. The plating curled and bubbled. Ceramite worms twisted on each other, verging on unholy life before flaking to ash. He landed on his back, looking up at the maulerfiend as it turned its attention to him.

The daemon engine ignored the renewed attacks on its flanks. It gaped at Dagover, the red of its eyes shining with bloody hunger, and prepared to unleash its unholy liquid warpfire a second time. Dagover had no chance to escape. Trapped, he raised his plasma pistol and fired into the beast's maw.

His shot exploded in the monster's throat just as it fired. A massive internal blast convulsed it. The maulerfiend reared back, its remaining forelimb thrashing madly, flaming ectoplasmic bursts shooting out of its neck, boiling ichor pouring down its flanks and scoring its plates. Black and red flames shot out of the shattered orbits of its eyes.

Dagover's articulated arms dragged him out of the way. The squad reformed, and the Battle Sisters of Our Martyred Lady turned their weapons on the skull and neck of the maulerfiend. Blind, it heaved its bulk in an attempt to crush its tormenters through sheer rage and luck.

It failed. The attack blew away its lower jaw and severed its neck. The head dropped to the ground dead metal once again. The body kept thrashing, though, spewing ichor and ectoplasm in every direction. The walls of the cathedral ran with molten blood. The heretics caught in the unholy rain burst into tortured flame that screamed louder than they did as their flesh bubbled like wax.

Dagover rose to his feet again, and retreated with the Sisters of Battle. They had done what they could here, and they pulled back towards the gate, leaving the maulerfiend to its final, agonised contortions. They were barely out of range when the spreading internal damage hit the critical point and the huge body of the daemon engine exploded. A dazzling blaze of corrupted red and green lit the cathedral, the expanding sphere of warpflame consuming cultists and filling the night with inhuman screams.

Dagover's optic lenses struggled to translate the sight. His vision stuttered, and the traces of burning, reified Chaos reached through to his mind, making him gasp in pain. At the same time, he grinned in satisfaction. This felt like a concrete victory, one that would do much to hold the cathedral's position and stymie the enemy forces until Stern could complete her self-appointed mission.

His satisfaction lasted precisely as long as it took to fight back to Saint Thecla's main gates. Just as the squad arrived, there was a massive rumble in the east. It sounded as if a mountain had entered the war. The plateau was hidden by distance and the chimney spires of the manufactories, but the sky over where Dagover knew its position to be lit up, red like the sunset of an angry god.

'Has she succeeded?' Klavia asked as they marched inside the covered courtyard and the gates began to close. Her voice was hollow with sorrow, and desperate for hope.

Perhaps, Dagover was about to say. But then the rumble was echoed by a colossal, triumphant roar from the mobs, and his optimism drained away.

In the minutes that followed, the heretics staged their most concerted push yet. There were still many daemon engines out there, and the cultists' assault had no end. They were coming in the hundreds of thousands. They could no longer be pushed back. They ran unheeding through cannon and bolter fire. They scrambled over their dead. The Demolishers might as well have been firing into an ocean.

Macrina met the returning squads in the nave. She came fresh from defending the roof. Her face was smeared with ash and burns. An angry tear was open in one cheek, the blood barely staunched by a medi-pad.

'No more sorties,' said the Canoness. 'They have served their purpose. The enemy presses us too strongly now. We must not open the gates again.'

'That barrier will not last long,' said Dagover.

'No, but it will hold long enough for us to prepare for the next phase of our defence. Saint Thecla's is designed to purge the heretic inside its walls as fully as outside.' Macrina pointed up, to the galleries lining the nave. They went all the way up to the roof, and ran around the entire perimeter. They gave access to the scores of turret positions. 'When the heretics enter, they will come here. The guns in the turrets are on rails. They will back out of their outer wall emplacements and turn their fire on the interior of the cathedral.'

'This nave will become a kill-zone,' Dagover said, admiring the rigour of the followers of Saint Thecla. They had made the building constructed in her honour as unyielding as she.

'We shall not suffer the heretic to live,' said Klavia.

Dagover and the returned squads took their places in the turrets. The commandry had suffered so many casualties during the siege that there were barely enough warriors now to operate all the guns and still defend the roof. Positioned two levels up from the nave, Dagover climbed onto the circular platform of an assault cannon. He rotated the gun, and the platform tracked out into the gallery. He aimed the barrel down into the nave and waited. He looked around the nave, as more and more of the guns were turned inside. Close to half the turrets had given up holding off the heretics from the exterior. The breaching of the gates was about to happen, and it was time to be ready for the invasion.

The inevitable marched closer and closer to the heart of Saint Thecla's. Even if Stern succeeded, there was no certainty of victory. If she failed, though, defeat *was* certain.

Dagover thought of the rumble and the foul red light in the east. He worried that he had already witnessed the disaster, and that now he was just waiting for its ripples to sweep him and the Order of Our Martyred Lady away.

His fears were confirmed with the breaching of the gate. The ripples had arrived in the form of explosions and crashes, louder because they were closer, though not as deep, not as profound, as the eruption over the plateau.

Seconds later, the heretics poured into the nave. They came in like a flood of rats, clawing and trampling each other in their eagerness to invade the holy ground. They had stayed away from it until now. They had left the cathedral empty and untouched before the Sisters of Battle had come to Severitas. Its sanctity had been a deterrent. No longer. Their desire to vanquish and destroy the commandry was too strong. And perhaps, Dagover thought, they sensed that their greatest foe was gone, that a saint had fallen, and now everything was open to them.

He opened fire. So did the other assault cannons. Shells and slaughter turned the air in the nave into a choking mix of blood and burned fyceline. The slaughter was enormous.

But the tide kept coming, unending, unstoppable.

* * *

Stern woke, surprised to find that she had not died a third time. Her vision cleared reluctantly, and her temples throbbed with a war drum's painful beat. She could not move her arms or legs, could only turn her head a few inches to the left and right. She was held, her arms outstretched, by a mixture of iron and rockcrete, both of them bending like muscle. She was inside the fortress, ten feet up from the floor, in the grip of its wall, embedded in the flesh of the monster.

The chamber was vast, lit a sullen red by the grilles of hundreds of forges, which covered the walls like an insect's composite eyes. The fires within them were unnatural, the flaming madness of the warp encroaching on the materium, sorcery contained by the metal bars, waiting for its master to call on it again.

In the centre of the chamber, a concentric series of circular iron platforms rose to a central dais. Two Word Bearers stood on the platforms, looking at her. At the peak, presiding over the room with the majesty of command, was the enemy she had expected to find. The Master of Possession held his staff like the symbol of his reign. A step below him was a Warpsmith, his pincer limbs and mechadendrites hovering around his body with slight but restless motions.

She was not dead. She was a prisoner. Why was she still alive?

She still clutched Sanctity in her right hand, though she could not see the blade. Her fist and the sword were completely embedded in the wall. She strained. There was no leverage to be had. No movement possible.

The Master of Possession struck the dais with the end of his staff. The boom reverberated through the chamber like a funeral bell. It was a call to attention. Stern granted him her full concentration. And all her hate.

He wanted her to look at him. To see who had captured her. Very well. She would. She would look at the being she would destroy.

Every moment she breathed was a moment she could use to find a way to free herself and fight back.

'Let us be known to each other,' said the Word Bearer. 'I am Varak Ghar.' His horned skull nodded dismissively at the Warpsmith. 'That is Krezen Pak. And you... you are Ephrael Stern.' Though she did not react, Varak Ghar tilted his head as though she had expressed surprise, and he was pleased. 'Yes, your name is far from hidden from me. There have been whispers through empyreal halls and chambers of nightmare about you. Ahriman still seeks you. Fallen daemons curse your existence. I am *very* pleased to have you as my guest.'

Krezen Pak said nothing. He looked briefly at Varak Ghar, then back at Stern. His stance shifted slightly, as if he were bracing for combat. Stern wondered whether it was she or the Master of Possession he was more wary of.

Varak Ghar strode down the platforms and crossed the floor to look up at her. He cocked his head. 'I know your name. I know what you have done. I know *who* you are.' He raised a finger. 'There is something I do not know. And now we have the opportunity and the time to resolve this question. I don't know *what* you are.'

Stern attempted to lunge forward, spitting at his feet.

'I am your bane,' she growled.

'Of course you are.' Varak Ghar made a noise like bones scratching against stone. It took Stern a moment to realise this was his laugh. Unease raced up her spine.

'You are a foulness in the gaze of the Emperor. You are traitorous filth. Your end has come.'

'I would have been deeply disappointed to hear otherwise. And yet here you are, and here I am.' He gestured, taking in their relative situations. He looked around the chamber, as if seeking a doom that someone had misplaced. 'As banes go, you leave something to be desired.'

Stern struggled again to free her arm. She might as well have been a fossil encased in a mountainside. And the prison was more than physical. The sorcery that had given the fortress motion flowed through the wall. It concentrated around her like a fist. When she tried to summon her own psychic strength, the colossal power in the fortress tightened around her and shut it down, a constrictor serpent cutting off her breath.

What it did not seal off from her was the vision of the nothingness. The black, cold, monstrous absence was closer than ever. It pressed upon her mind and her soul. Its weight was more awful than that of the wall. It was an absolute ending. She was held, helpless. She could not fight the dread approach, and it seemed to be coming faster and faster.

'I am your loyal subject, God-Emperor,' she prayed. 'My life is yours to command. I have no purpose but your purpose. Guide me now, and give me the strength to be the arm of your will. I know you have not forsaken me, for my task is not yet accomplished. I must give action to your will. Your commands are with me now.'

'Faith,' Varak Ghar hissed. '*Faithhhhhhhhhh.*' He pointed an accusing finger. He raised his staff in anger, and the power in the walls crackled around Stern, burning her, trying to silence her. 'Do you know what has caught you? *Do you?* Faith. *Faith.* An act of faith gave life to stones, and seized you from the skies.' He stretched out his arms, his free hand grasping as if he would seize the galaxy. 'Behold the full power of faith!' he shouted.

The walls trembled. The floor of the chamber canted to one side and then another. Stern felt a monstrous *heave* from below. The fortress was rising again.

'The God-Emperor is with me,' Stern whispered to herself. 'I shall not fear.' Yet she felt the dread that came from being held by such awesome power. And she struggled harder against her bonds, her wounds bleeding afresh.

'This is the strength of the faithful, of those who follow the true gods. The gods of Chaos! This is the belief of Severitas made manifest!' Warp lightning snarled around his cloak. 'The faith of millions flows through these walls, and the walls walk!'

The chamber rocked with a slow, heavy, ponderous rhythm. The fortress was marching across the plateau.

Fire burned in the dark sockets of Varak Ghar's eyes. His stare never left Stern. 'But what are you?' he said, speaking more softly, more to himself than to her. '*What are you?*' A snarl of frustration. 'You are a being of faith, misguided though it is. And you have come here, now, to my planet, to my monument of faith. Where your sisters of faith have come too. This is far beyond chance. You agree, I'm sure?'

Stern did not answer him. 'Make me your blade, God-Emperor,' she prayed. 'Make me the fire of your wrath.'

'What say you, Warpsmith?' Varak Ghar asked. 'There must be meaning in her presence, must there not?'

'I would see meaning in her destruction,' Krezen Pak growled.

'Oh, so will I. So will I. But the true meaning of her end can only come with the full understanding of her presence *now*.'

Varak Ghar's frustration kept breaking through. Stern kept praying, the words of faith and loyalty coming automatically, while another part of her mind, inspired, fastened on the Word Bearer's displeasure. It was important. She saw that with sudden conviction. She began to look for deeper meaning too. She sought the reason for his anger. After all, he had her trapped. She was at his mercy. She could barely breathe, let alone attack him.

'You are here for a reason,' said Varak Ghar, turning back to her. 'You must be a revelation, or the harbinger of one.' He paused, his tone growing thoughtful, insinuating. 'I think you and I are one in this opinion. Yes, yes, we are. Do not try to deny it.'

She did not respond to him. She maintained her litany of faith.

'If we agree on that,' said Varak Ghar, as if she had conceded the truth of his words, 'then there is much more we should explore together. You must see the potential here. Perhaps you wonder *what* you are too. Perhaps the gods have brought us together so you will see properly at last. Your obedience to the False Emperor has blinded you. Open your eyes. Open your soul. Listen to the words of true revelation.'

His temptation was pathetic. He couldn't possibly think she would succumb to such a blandishment. Why was he attempting it, then? What did he really hope to achieve?

He could not truly believe he would corrupt her.

Unless he needed to believe it.

And then she focused on the real question. Why was she still alive?

She paused in her prayers. 'Why haven't you killed me?' she asked, calmly, as if debating the traitor on an obscure point of doctrine.

His hesitation was minuscule. It was also telling. 'You will be a prize,' he said. 'A prize to present to the gods. A saint of Chaos to inspire despair in the souls of the Imperium.'

He was wise. He answered her truthfully. He really did seek her corruption, and was only just beginning his campaign. But though he spoke the truth, she saw the equivocation behind it. She saw the real truth, and smiled.

Why hadn't he killed her?

Because he could not.

He had *tried.*

The revelation of his failure sent new strength coursing through her veins.

There were no bodies on the floor of the nave. The relentless barrage of the assault cannons did not leave anything intact enough to be called a corpse. Instead, there was a swamp, a rising morass of pulverised flesh, blood and bone erupting into geysers with each new impact. The heretics charging in had to wade through the remains of their fellow apostates, the sludge thick and clinging, slowing them down and leaving them even more vulnerable to the hammering shells.

Multiple turrets turned their focus on the first daemon engines that appeared in the doorway. The maulerfiends were too large to get through more than one at a time, and they too were slowed by the fanatical rush of the cultists. First one, then another, fell to the turret fire. Their explosions washed the nave with warpfire, boiling blood already several feet deep, and they collapsed the walls of the entrance.

But even with rubble clogging the way in, and with the punishing hail of the assault cannons, the heretics advanced. The swarm of rats spread into the cathedral, filling the halls with the disease of their presence. Scores died every few seconds, but their deaths shielded others who found their way onto the stairs and up to the galleries.

The defence of the interior of the cathedral had two faces now. While the Battle Sisters on the turrets fired into the main wave of the attackers, other Sisters in turn defended the turrets. Klavia held off the enemy, stopping the cultists from reaching Dagover's gun. The gallery was narrow, constructed that way so the gun platforms could move quickly between exterior and interior positions, and to create a bottleneck for besiegers. Klavia kept up a steady, precise rhythm of shots with her heavy bolter, wasting no shells, yet giving no quarter. She measured her use of energy and ammunition. There was no end in sight to the invasion. The war would only end when the heretics finally overran the Sisters of Battle, or when Ephrael Stern triumphed. Klavia accepted these two outcomes as articles of faith. She knew the ammunition would not last forever. She knew precisely how many clips she had left, and knew, down to the second, how much longer she could keep firing at this rate. She knew when her and Dagover's position would most likely be overrun.

But she also knew, with her soul, that Stern would destroy the enemy who had taken Severitas from the light of the Emperor.

'Coming around,' Dagover called.

Klavia crouched, backed up a few steps and mounted the platform. Dagover swung the assault cannon away from the nave, rotating to fire down the gallery. His turret was closest to the staircase, and there was no risk of taking down another gun emplacement. The massive shells blasted through the swarming heretics, dropping huge fragments of the cathedral's masonry on the enemy and blocking the stairs for the time being. More time gained. Another few precious minutes.

Klavia took advantage of the respite to reload her heavy bolter. 'Victory is close,' she said to Dagover as he rotated the gun back to the slaughter in the nave.

'Your certainty does you honour,' Dagover replied, his electronic rasp tuned loud to reach her over the thudding concussions of the assault cannon.

'Your doubts are unwarranted, inquisitor.'

Muffled explosions sounded from below. The cultists were blasting through the rubble. They would be entering this end of the gallery again soon. From the other end, the rattling of bolters and roar of flamers signalled the ongoing invasion of those positions.

'Perhaps they are.'

Klavia did not interpret Dagover's words as agreement. 'We have seen the coming of a saint,' she said. She raised her weapon, ready for the next wave of the attack. 'She would not appear, merely to be defeated. The Emperor would not permit so futile a tragedy.'

'I hope you are correct,' Dagover said, noncommittal as he methodically turned heretics into pulp.

'The great tumult we witnessed outside may well be the beginning of her triumph.'

Dagover did not answer right away. Then he said, 'If it were, I think we would already know.'

The walls and floor already shook steadily from the turret barrage. But now a more violent tremor swept through, growing in power and intensity. Klavia settled her stance against the rocking. It felt as if the ground beneath the cathedral were struggling to rise up and throw Saint Thecla's from its back. The vault of the galleries cracked. The rubble in the stairwell gave way, and the cultists surged forward again. The tremors hurled them from side to side. Some crashed into walls and fell. Many died as they reached the gallery, yet they were singing their praise to their foul gods with even greater fervour than before. They were caught up in a violent ecstasy of faith. They barely seemed to know if they were alive or dead. Their praise and their attack were one and the same.

Klavia sent her shells into the building horde, killing and mutilating several with every shot, all the while fighting to keep her balance. The event in which the cathedral was caught kept growing larger and larger.

'This does not feel like victory,' Dagover grated.

Before Klavia could answer, a force reached into the cathedral. It passed through like a gale, like lightning, and like hungry claws. It stole her breath. Her heart seemed to stop, then beat violently. The force blew against her body and scraped inside her soul. It pulled at her too, a monstrous undertow, the tug of a devouring vortex.

Klavia cried out, though she had no breath. The sound was weak, a bare groan from the depths of her chest. Yet it was real, present, her defiance given voice. Then she was struggling to draw another breath.

She never stopped shooting. This was her other defiance against the force that tried to pull everything out of her. And she won. It failed. It released her and passed on.

Dagover grunted. He staggered, though he held on to the assault cannon. Klavia heard psychic pain in the electronic voice, but he too shook off the grasp of the unseen hand.

The power seized the heretics. It devoured them. They stopped mid-charge and screamed their praise. They convulsed, consumed by an ecstasy beyond pain, reason and belief. Lightning arced from their eyes, and then they shrivelled in on themselves, their skin turning brittle and cracking, flaking off into ash. They turned into husks, all of them. The roaring of the daemon engines ceased. The monsters screamed once and then collapsed, silent and dark.

Klavia and Dagover stopped firing. So did all the turrets in the cathedral. There was no one to fight. The chanting of the heretics ceased. There were no throats to give it voice any longer.

But there was no silence. In the wake of the gale of power, the tremors grew, and the thunder of a tortured city became deafening. The walls of the cathedral shook and swayed. The floor heaved upward, fissures splitting wide open.

Klavia staggered. The entire building seemed to tilt to one side. She and Dagover fell against the gallery's railing overlooking the nave.

The roof of the cathedral groaned. The fissures running up the walls met in the centre, and the collapse began. Huge pieces of the roof fell into the swamp of blood.

And the tremors grew, and grew, and grew.

XII

THE SACRED TERROR

Stern flexed. She leaned forward, feeling the matter of the fortress strain to contain her. The sorcery coursing through it recoiled. A burning force wrapped itself more tightly around her.

'You will not hold me,' she hissed at Varak Ghar, and the wall began to crack. She pushed back at the suffocating vision of *nothing*. She would not let the apprehension of cataclysm stop her from fighting it, and she would not let it defeat her in the battle before her. She felt Sanctity thrum with renewed power. The sword gathered more strength from her, and it began to burn through its prison. She could move her wrist. Only a few inches from side to side. Enough, though, for her to begin to cut away at the interior wall. A beast had swallowed her, and she was going to claw her way out of its belly.

Varak Ghar stared at her, motionless. 'No,' he said. 'I will not hold you. I will claim your faith and turn it to the true gods.'

Stern bared her teeth at him. 'I hear your desperation, traitor. You are lying to yourself.' She redoubled her physical and psychic efforts. She pushed against the matter and the witchery, and they began to crumble.

Varak Ghar snarled. He raised his staff. 'Your destiny is here, Thrice-Born,' he said. 'Your fate is now. Your fall is now.'

The staff blazed. Its light was the colour of worm-riddled rage, suffused with the sensual pleasures of despair. The light filled the chamber. It consumed Stern's vision until she could see nothing else, and then it took on forms. They were vague at first, indistinct shapes crawling and leaping her way. As they gathered definition, the light dimmed, but the chamber did not return. Stern was as immobilised as ever, as trapped by the grip of the fortress, yet she was also suspended in the maelstrom of a storm. Darkness and red the shade of a volcano's fury surrounded her. The storm howled and roared with the mad lightning of the immaterium. The storm hated her. It hated what she was, and she felt the dizzying conviction that the storm knew what she was more profoundly than she did. It was less her physical self that it sought to destroy, than the essence that it perceived so clearly.

The shapes sent to destroy her emerged from the crimson darkness. Daemons of the four powers of Chaos crawled and leapt and slithered through the storm towards her. Glistening pink abominations, some bulbous and some muscular, shouted prophecies at her in a language that her mind could not understand, but which spoke directly to her soul with terrible insinuations. Sinuous tempters danced through the lightning, lithe and lethal, their very movements a song of dark delight and the promise of the full, shattering experience of the sublime. Horned crimson monsters ran at her, swords raised, screaming an anger that, in its purity, sought to graft itself to her own rage and twist it to the ends of ruin. And with the tolling of bells doleful and joyful came creatures of disease, rotting with plenty, viscous with life. With them, her being would spread, becoming legion. They would drive dread thoughts across the galaxy, her squirming hopes quickened to new births.

She could not move. Yet she was not defenceless. She looked at the daemons with the righteous hate that was the gift of true faith. She shaped her hate into the light of the Emperor's wrath. The power rose within her, her flesh prickling and then burning with its force, her blood roaring in her ears. Then as the daemons came closer, she unleashed a sphere of implacable, relentless purity. Daemons screamed and burned at its passing. A bloodletter that survived leapt for her, brandishing its sword, and when it struck her, she felt only anger in its holiest form.

'You dare?' Ephrael Stern roared, but the daemon was already doomed. It had begun to burn as soon as it had touched her. It recoiled, screaming, and the fire consumed it to ash.

More and more daemons gathered. They circled her, calling and snarling and singing and chanting. Flouting whistles and deep, reverberating refrains swirled out of the storm at her. The dark music of Chaos wanted her soul. It wanted her in its dance. But she refused. She sent out wave after wave of faith. Abominations cried out and vanished, but more and more came. They could not approach her, but they would not retreat. They would harry her until they had her conversion.

Gradually, a voice detached itself from the greater choir. It was Varak Ghar, whispering in her ear, knocking at the door to her soul. 'You think this is a stalemate. You think you have stymied the will of the true gods. You think you can maintain this struggle forever. Perhaps you even believe that you will, in the end, prove stronger. That there is a limit to the foes that will confront you. Is that right? You will break them? Then break your bonds? Then break me?'

She did not answer him, but to every question, she thought *yes*. She would do all these things.

'You are wrong,' said Varak Ghar, as if he had heard her. 'You do not have eternity to struggle towards victory. You cannot erode a wave. You have no time at all. Listen to the passage of the moments. One and two and three and four, lost to the past. One and two and three and four, gone forever. One and two and three and four, and how many of your sisters have died since I began to count? One and two and three and four...'

He was right. She struggled against the bonds of the hidden fortress, against the force with which Varak Ghar held her. He was so powerful. He was more powerful than she had imagined, even with everything she had seen.

How? How? How is he so strong?

If she did not free herself, if she did not destroy him, then the Sisters of Battle of the Order of Our Martyred Lady would be lost.

'Do you ask why you are here? Do you wonder why fate would bring you to Severitas, where you find your sisters only to lose them? Do you rage at the irony of futility? How can existence be this senseless?'

She tried to jerk her head away from the words. They were striking too close. She could not escape them. They sank in, deeper, deeper, the wounds bleeding freely.

As if sensing her injuries, the dark *nothing* closed in too. The shadow of the future was not of the warp. It lurked behind it, a separate evil, a different doom, but she was not fighting it while she was trapped here, and it marched forward, closer, closer, closer.

'Existence is not senseless,' Varak Ghar whispered. 'I bring you the Word of truth. I bring you revelation. It was not chance that carried you here. It was fate. It was destiny. You *are* here to see your sisters destroyed, because then you will be free. You will become what you were meant to be. You were cast out by your kind, and you did not understand. You were killed twice, and you did not understand. You are here because at last you will understand what you are. What you will do. What must be.'

'Emperor, you are my guide,' Stern prayed. It was hard to speak. It was hard to think. The daemons brayed and laughed and sang, drowning her out. 'Show me the way forward. Show me your will. Father of Mankind, hear my plea and show me your will!'

'Silence is your answer.' Varak Ghar's words, serpents, coiled around her. 'My gods do not give me silence. My gods answer. The true gods hear and reward.'

'I seek no reward, God-Emperor. I seek only to serve your will.'

'What will?' Varak Ghar asked. 'Do you know it? Do you see it? Is it clear to you? It is not. It is your hope, always frustrated. It is hidden, a thing to guess at, a thing for the venal and the ambitious to invent and manipulate. Think how often the will of the False Emperor has been used against you. Think how you suffer in ignorance. You will never see it, because it is not there to see.'

Stern cried out, shouting without words against the doubts that Varak Ghar was seeking to insert like shards of glass into her being. She refused them. Yet the truths embedded in the Word Bearer's lies cut and sliced. She was trapped. Time was passing, slipping into oblivion. Her sisters were dying. And the nothingness was coming, the nothingness she had thought herself destined to fight. She thought she had been following the Emperor's will, but she had never seen it clearly, only been convinced that she knew what must be done and where she must go.

She had been proud. She had behaved as though she were a prophet.

'You were wrong,' said Varak Ghar. 'You have been wrong about everything. You are here to see the truth.'

She shouted, reaching with her soul for the Emperor, reaching with the full strength of her faith. The words of the traitor echoed and re-echoed in her mind, inescapable, louder, the peal of a terrible bell.

You will never see it.

It is not there to see.

You are here to see the truth.

You are here to see the truth.

The tolling of the bell brought forth revelation.

She was here to see the truth.

If she was here, it *was* because the Emperor willed it. She had not come to be embraced by her sisters. She had come to save them. She was not on Severitas to call to the Emperor and pray for His answer. She *was* His answer.

She could not see His will because she *was* His will.

She was His sword, and she was His judgement that had come for Varak Ghar.

Her shout became a roar. She could not be held. She could not be imprisoned. The Emperor's will would not be defied by the likes of the Master of Possession.

Her roar was the thunder of judgement, and the holy wrath now erupting from around her dwarfed the storm. It was terror incarnate. The chanting of the daemons turned into screams. They tried to retreat, but there was no escape for them. There would never be. They burned, and the storm burned, and Varak Ghar shrieked in rage and pain, and the sacred, purifying, unforgiving fire of the Emperor was everywhere, radiating from her being, an execution and a sun.

The fire passed, and she was in the chamber of the fortress once more, and she could move. The psychic blaze of faith burst from her again, and the wall of the fortress writhed. She leaned forward and pulled with her arms, and the wall began to tear. Metal and rockcrete shredded like rotting muscle. The tip of Sanctity's blade pierced through the prison, its light a new flare of the sacred.

Varak Ghar had staggered back a step. He was motionless for a second, hunched forward as if winded. 'No,' he said. 'This will not be permitted.'

'You have no say,' Stern snarled at him. 'This is the passing of your sentence.'

Krezen Pak rushed forward, his mechadendrites lunging at her with snapping claws. She yanked her right arm completely free and slashed at them with Sanctity. The powerblade severed the claws of the metal tentacles with a furious burst of lightning. The lightning snaked back along their flailing lengths, staggering the Warpsmith.

Varak Ghar mounted the platforms to the top dais once more. 'The judgement here is mine!' he shouted.

'Then pass it,' said Stern, and she burst free. She dropped to the floor, trailing ichor and sparks from the wall. She fired a quick burst from her bolt pistol at Krezen Pak, forcing him onto the defensive, as she marched up the platforms, steadying herself against the slow, rocking gait of the walking fortress.

Varak Ghar grasped his staff with both hands. He raised his head, looking far above Stern and beyond the walls.

'You are mine!' he shouted. 'Your lives are mine. Your faith is mine! I gave it to you! *I claim it now!*'

The movement of the fortress turned violent. The hundreds of grilles belched fire, and the temperature in the chamber spiked, becoming infernal. The walls glistened. They glowed red. They glowed white. They began to run.

A monstrous wind blew into the chamber. It came in from every direction and knocked Stern off her feet. A psychic cyclone surrounded Varak Ghar. The roof of the chamber spun in its pattern, and then irised open. A pillar of dark, nightmare light, forged from beams arcing in from around the horizon, descended on the Master of Possession, and he welcomed it.

Stern got to her feet, but could not advance against the wind. Varak Ghar stood tall, laughing in glory as he fed on the pillar of coruscating flames. He looked down on Stern, his eyes smouldering with infinity. 'BEHOLD!' he thundered. 'THIS IS FAITH! THIS IS THE FAITH OF BILLIONS, AND IT IS MINE!'

With an unhurried gesture, Varak Ghar reached towards her. She was already rising off the ground, her psychic shield in place once more. The walls and floor of the fortress, molten now, mimicked Varak Ghar. Waves and peaks and whiplashing stalagmites rushed at her. Krezen Pak screamed, submerged by the rising lava of metal and stone.

Stern shot upwards, escaping their grasp. She launched a psychic blast at Varak Ghar, but the pillar deflected the strike.

She needed room to fight him. She had to find air, and deny him the use of his possessed structure.

Stern streaked through the gap in the ceiling and into the night like a comet. The darkness quivered and screamed with the manifested spiritual energy of an entire population. Varak Ghar's hunger was all-consuming. The more his followers gave, the more he summoned. Stern felt a world shudder as a ragged hymn of praise was torn from every human essence.

The fortress was changing shape. It had been walking on its wings, its form a lumbering, heavy arch. Now it melted in on itself, turning, and rose higher and higher, a pillar of twisted construction mirroring the pillar of belief. Misshapen windows and fiery grates spiralled around its height. The twisting structure screamed with the throats of tens of thousands, and still it grew. It held Varak Ghar on its peak. He was a nexus of flame and magmatic creation.

'YOU CANNOT FLEE A WORLD!' he bellowed.

'You are the one who flees!' she answered. She flew down at him, bolt pistol firing, a spear of psychic force striking ahead of her at the Word Bearer. Varak Ghar shifted his staff minutely, and her attack exploded harmlessly before him.

Tremors shook the plateau. The earth screamed, and the plateau rose, becoming part of the pillar, a mountain twisting upward with sudden agony.

Stern retreated, flying higher. The land beyond the plateau began to turn too, the vortex spreading wider and wider. The great, towering smokestacks of the manufactories fell into the spinning ruin. The city and its millions of corpse husks hurled itself into the cyclonic upheaval. The influx of souls was so torrential that it covered the entire sky, a dome of reified belief contracting around the lightning rod of the pillar. It blocked all paths. Stern's room for manoeuvring shrank.

She attacked Varak Ghar again and again. He repelled the psychic blows with barely a glance.

The dome contracted more and more. Soon it was less than two hundred feet across. The psychic force of billions was coming, and she would vanish like an insect in a bonfire.

The Master of Possession laughed. 'YOU SHOULD HAVE ACCEPTED YOUR FATE. THE FAITH OF ONE IS NOTHING TO THE FAITH OF ALL!'

Yet she was here, and she was the Emperor's will.

The faith of one.

Varak Ghar fed on the faiths he had created.

And she saw.

'You wield the faiths of others! They are not your own. You created a lie, because your faith is weak.' She arrowed down again, her course sure and true. This was not a war of the faith of one against the faith of billions. It was one faith – strong, pure and absolute – against a fractured one. 'YOU DOUBT!' she roared.

Her accusation hit Varak Ghar with the force of a sentence passed. Stern saw the fissure in the pillar of flame, the flaw in the construct of belief. She shot through the cyclone and plunged Sanctity into the skull of the traitor.

In his final second, before the night erupted with annihilating light, Varak Ghar faced the monster of judgement and screamed in terror.

XIII

SAINT

What had he witnessed?

Dagover walked slowly down the hill from the gaping ruins of the cathedral. His optics still pulsed uncertainly from the aftermath of the nova-sear of light that had silenced Severitas and ended the tremors. The Battle Sisters of the Order of Our Martyred Lady marched together. Less than a third of the commandry had survived. They descended the hill in tight formation, their tattered banners flying in the ash-strewn breeze.

He held back from them, keeping his distance.

The landscape was utterly transformed. The cathedral's hill was riven by crevasses and rockfalls, but its changes were minor compared to what lay beyond. The globe-spanning city on Severitas had fallen. Saint Thecla's was split open, but most of its walls still stood. Everything else, from horizon to horizon, was destroyed. It looked as if giant hands had seized the earth, down to the bedrock, and twisted it up, dragging it high and then hurling it down. The plateau where the fortress had been was a smashed bowl, crumbling cliffs to the north and south the gravestones to mark where it had been.

Stern had done this. Dagover tried to process that reality. He stared at the levelled city. The air was grey with ash from the millions of shrivelled bodies. Stern had fought a being who had the power to change the shape of a world, *and she had destroyed him.*

That light, the light that had ended the tremors and brought the deafening silence that comes with the end of war. That awful, terrifying light.

Dagover wrestled with his own awe. His thoughts of controlling such a being seemed like a drunkard's folly. What was she? She was Adepta Sororitas. And she was what should be anathema to the orders. And yet... and yet... and yet...

Perhaps she truly was a saint. Perhaps he had done nothing but urge her towards the truth.

For the first time in his life, he experienced the full, soul-deep paralysis of holy terror.

He turned away from the Sisters. He would not wait for Stern's return. He could no longer conceive of controlling such a being. If he stayed in her orbit, his destiny would be swallowed by the immense gravity of hers. He had to pull away, for his own sake. Perhaps for his sanity.

He walked faster. Vox traffic with the *Iudex Ferox* had resumed with the destruction of the Master of Possession. He would call for another Valkyrie to retrieve him.

Faster. He left the Sisters of Battle behind. He did not look back.

Klavia rushed to the front of her sisters as Ephrael Stern staggered slowly towards them through the rubble. Stern's gaze was solemn with gratitude. Her armour was battered. It looked as if it had been gouged open by giant claws. The wounds inflicted by the returned Sisters, the wounds that had no chance to heal, bled freely. Her face was scorched with unnatural burns. She stumbled, pain shivering through her frame.

'Sister!' Klavia ran forward. She embraced Stern, and then dropped to her knees in front of her. So did most of the commandry.

'No,' said Stern, her voice weak. 'No, sisters, my sisters, you must not. Please stand.'

When they would not, she kneeled herself before Macrina. Klavia watched, holding her breath. The Canoness hesitated, uncertain. It was not suspicion that held her back, though. Klavia could read her face plainly enough. It was awe. Then, tentatively, she asked Stern to rise, and embraced her too.

Stern wept.

And then she fell.

And she did not move.

EPILOGUE

REVELATIONS

On the bridge of the Adepta Sororitas strike cruiser *Iron Penitence,* Stern kept watch before the primary viewport. She had been standing here, moving rarely, for two ship's cycles. They were drawing near to where fate had appointed they must go, to where the *nothing* would come. It was closer than ever before. The premonition of its arrival was the pressure of a hurricane behind her eyes. And she still did not know what the cataclysm would be that would bring the *nothing,* nor how it would be fought.

But it was coming soon. Very soon. That much she knew.

With the death of Varak Ghar, the warp interference around Severitas had ceased for now. Astropathic communication had become possible once more, and Macrina had sent out the call to the Indomitus Crusade's Battlegroup Kallides of Fleet Primus. Coordinates had been relayed, and, with the *Rectitude* lost, the *Iron Penitence* had come to rescue the task force.

Macrina had taken point in the debates that Stern's presence had triggered. It was her arguments, and the testimony of the other Sisters of Battle, that had paved the way for the commanders of the *Iron Penitence* to listen to Stern, and to her warnings of the cataclysm. They had agreed, with reluctance, to deviate from their assigned path to this point. The course alteration had been a relatively minor one. Stern doubted she would have prevailed otherwise. But again, fate had ordained the circumstances. And she no longer wondered about her instinctual knowledge of where the next struggle would occur. She and the Emperor's will were one. Her path was clear.

Her wounds had finally had time to heal. She was strong again, though her frame still throbbed where the unholy daggers had stabbed her. The pain, she thought, was the reminder of her taint. It would prevent her from the prideful sin of believing in her sainthood.

Macrina joined her at the viewport. 'We have arrived,' Macrina said. 'Or nearly. But there is nothing here.' They were in the deep void. The nearest system was Xendu, and its star was no more than a point in the dark. 'Is there something we should be searching…' Macrina began.

She did not finish.

It came. The *nothing*. The void outside the viewport did not visibly change. But a wave came down on the ship – a deluge, a weight, a spiritual suffocation so absolutely heavy that the *Iron Penitence* might have been broken upon the bottom of a planetary ocean. For long moments, Stern thought she was blind. She did not know if she stood or fell. She had no voice. There was no sound. There was only the arrival of an all-conquering, all-consuming blankness.

The ship shuddered. Klaxons erupted on the bridge. Someone nearby was shouting about the Navigator, that the Navigator was screaming, and that direction was lost.

Stern forced herself to breathe. It took a conscious effort. It was a shock to take oxygen into her lungs and not water. When she breathed, she could see and hear again.

Macrina was standing, but barely. She held herself up by leaning against the viewport. Most of the bridge crew had fallen, and the officers were dragging themselves up with difficulty. Everyone was moving as if in the grip of a fatal lethargy.

'Damage,' the shipmaster said. Her words came slowly. 'What damage?'

There was no response at first. Then the auspex officer said, 'No structural damage, shipmaster.' She gasped, then spoke again. 'But the astropathic choir is silenced.'

'Silenced? Silenced how?'

'Our psykers have been shut down. As if there were pariahs everywhere on the ship.'

The bridge was silent, except for the chattering of terminals and the machinic movements of servitors. No one said anything. Stern looked from face to face, and saw the same strain on everyone from the auspex officer to Macrina.

They were all struggling through the *nothing*. It was draining everyone, psyker or not. It was infinitely stronger, and more total, than any human pariah.

Stern rushed from the bridge. Even as she pounded down the corridors towards the chamber of the astropathic choir, she felt, at the back of her mind, a sense of wonder that she *could* run. She was pushing through the suffocation of the *nothing*. She had the strange sensation of being able to sprint underwater.

She burst into the chamber, and confronted a vista of suffering. For the astropaths, it seemed the end of all things truly had come. The pain of the crew on the bridge was trivial in comparison to what Stern saw here. The psykers had staggered from their tiered pews and fallen to the floor of the vaulted hall. The choirmaster had collapsed behind his pulpit. His mouth opened and closed soundlessly, his eyes were wide, staring blanks, and his face was blotched white and blue. He was a man drowning. The other astropaths clawed at the air, dragging their fingers as if the *nothing* that surrounded them were a tangible thing, and they struggled to tear through and breathe once more. Many, like their choirmaster, were silent in their agonies, as if death had already taken them, and done so with such ferocity that their corpses still echoed their last pain. Others still had their voices, and the moans of desperate horror rose to the vaults, so piercing the statues of the saints should have been weeping.

The cataclysm had come. The *nothing* of Stern's visions was here, but the task force was here too. The Imperium still stood. The time to fight had come.

But how? How, when the *nothing* had ripped away the power of psykers? Without her warp-tainted power, how would she fight?

Yet she felt no pain.

Yet she had run.

She felt the suffocating blankness, yet she did not feel helpless.

And then.

And then, oh so glorious.

And then…

Stern gasped as the vision began. It started with light, gold and shimmering. It limned the edges of everything around her, and it came *from* her, from deep inside, from her soul, from its very core…

No. No, that was wrong. The source was something even more profound. It spoke *to* her soul.

The light grew. And with it came thunder, the thunder of the birth and death of stars. The light turned into the lightning of nebulae, and it was still gold, purest gold.

The gold of a throne.

The thunder. The thunder was a voice, a voice too great for sound, too vast for words, though words formed in her mind, words placed by a force that was sanctity itself.

Be thou my sword.

The thunder was in her. She *was* the thunder. She *was* the lightning. This was the decree of that great will.

Stern took a breath. She took hold of the lightning. She grasped the thunder. And as the vision faded, she felt the power, her power, that terrible strength that had always been hers, that she had always believed was the taint of the warp. The astropaths flailed in the dark silence that had befallen them, but she blinked, and lightning flared from her eyes. Shimmering power ran down her arms. It flashed from her fingertips.

Behind her, someone gasped. Stern turned around, the flames of strength racing over her shoulders.

Macrina had followed her. The Canoness stared at her. 'How?' she said. 'You, too, are a psyker!'

'No,' said Stern, awed before the revelation that she had almost perceived when she fought Varak Ghar, but which she could not have truly seen and understood until now, here, at the coming of the catastrophe. She was not a psyker. 'The Emperor protects. The Emperor is my strength.'

Faith. Her might, *her power*, came from faith. And faith was the terror she brought upon the foes of the Emperor.

She took a few steps past Macrina. 'Now,' she said to the unseen enemy, to the author of the *nothing*. 'Now. I am here. Fear me.'

THE TRIUMPH OF SAINT KATHERINE

DANIE WARE

PROLOGUE

SORORITAS

'They've got behind us!'

Dropping to a combat-crouch, shield in hand, Katherine strove to see through the smoke. The broken streets were filled with soot and floating grit, with fragments of fluttering banners that still smouldered at their edges.

The cultists were raving and fearless. They'd come on in a rush, torching everything and slavering as they burned. The very air seemed scorched, rippling with heat and fervency. But Katherine's sacred armour defended her; the air she breathed was pure. She was still standing; her Sisters were still standing. The relic they bore was safe. She could not see them clearly – only the curves of their pauldrons and helmets that glittered with reflected fire – but she could hear and feel them, their closeness and unity.

Their faith, and the Litanies that carried it, echoing even now in the wake of her Sister's warning.

'Walk with us, O Emperor!'

'They are taint and foulness,' Katherine replied, her tone lit with rage. 'And we will show them no quarter.'

Stone dust drifted in hot winds, obscuring her vision further. Beside her, her closest Sister gave a curt, merciless nod, and they kept moving. There was no need for conversation. They were the army's heart and courage, and they knew what awaited them. Knew the death that they must deal.

'In His name!'

Around them, they could see little. Rising convection currents confused their preysight, and the shattered streets were both endless and maze-like. Flitting like shadows, the cultists were many, gleeful with unconstrained violence. They flickered past ruined shrines and through splintered windows, round tumbled corners and across heaps of still-steaming rubble. In many places, the ancient spires and statues had crumbled completely, giving the foe cover to both advance and retreat. Unlike so many of their kind, Katherine had realised, these had tactics; they thought, planned.

And that made them dangerous.

'Be wary,' she told her Sisters.

'He is with us,' a voice answered her, unshakeable.

From somewhere close: howling. The sound was eerie, shockingly inhuman. Her skin prickling, Katherine raised a gauntlet and they stopped, trying to place its source. It circled them in waves as if their enemy had some interlinked witch-mind. As they turned to try and locate it, it grew louder, becoming a battering, an onslaught of pure noise. It assaulted their ears, tried to stick its curious, taloned fingers into their thoughts.

Katherine prayed, her tone a smoulder of determination.

'Walk with us, O Emperor. Bring us your rage, your strength, your light.'

And there, upon the heels of her prayer, a vox-bark of stern orders – the Jaguar himself, Major Owai Haro of the 16th Gavera. Command HQ were behind the Sisters, but they, too, were responding to the cultist incursion.

'Platoons one, three, five, defence point delta.' Haro was one of those steel-haired infantry veterans who knew exactly how to manoeuvre his company. *'Haija, I want every Sentinel we have!'*

'Sir!'

'Walk with us, O Emperor. Bring us the righteousness of wrath!' She prayed for their souls, for their weapons, for the hammer of their strength. She prayed for the spirits of the Sentinels and their pilots. For–

'Renagi, give me range!' Haro, again. *'And fire!'*

Heavy weapons bellowed, cutting off her thoughts. There were mortar detonations, the cracks and rumbles of falling stone, thicker billows of smoke, eddied by the resulting currents. The ground shook.

The cultists' howling climbed to a shriek. In defiance, there came the barks of sergeants' orders and the crack of the troops' las-fire. Scarlet flashes, streaking out through the murk. The mortar thumped again, loud through the thickening air. She heard the faint servo-whine of the running Sentinels. The smoke stirred again, the floating fabric whipping to spirals.

With a roar, another building came down.

'They move left!' a Sister's voice came over the vox. *'We must stay with them!'*

Another Sister shouted her battle-rage, the sound of her hymnal an outright challenge. More howling came in its wake. Daring her. Daring all of them. The smoke grew thicker, choked with soot.

Her visor clogging, Katherine repeated, 'Bear left! We must keep the relic with company command!'

Agreements returned to her like prayers, and the Sisters were moving in a low, swift run, their purity seals fluttering and the relic suspended between them. Armoured boots stamped on cratered roads, the noise their celebration of His presence. The shadows over their heads were their floating cherubim, prayers carried aloft, their wings wafting the darkness to a deeper, stirring gloom.

A chime of ancient hymnal rang from their vox-hailers, loud enough to reach the soldiers around them.

'From the lightning and the tempest!'

'Advance by sections, give covering fire!' A sergeant's vox-shout was barely audible over the racket. Glimpsed between broken walls, the moving platoons were no more than flak-armoured shades, tiny, red-firing spectres that ran, and dropped, and ran again.

A Sentinel came past them, eerily quiet at full speed. In the vox, a Sister cursed. They kept moving, staying with the main force. But–

'Hold!' The order came from another of the Sisters' unit, her voice suddenly tense.

They had come to the end of their cover. Ahead of them lay an open, flagstoned square. In its centre stood a vast plinth and two stone feet, both broken off at the ankle. Behind this rose the soot-stained front of a mighty cathedral, its towers shattered, its steps cracked and stained. Its front doors had been wrenched from their hinges and cast aside; its mosaic flooring was pitted with explosive damage. Katherine could just see its pews, piled roughly into a central, defensive barrier–

Without warning, the cultists' yammer fell away, leaving a sudden, hollow silence. At the outer edge of the building's forecourt, the Sisters stopped. Listening.

Somewhere, lasers cracked and spat. The mortar boomed again. Another building crashed down, all thunder and dust. Screams cut like glass, human and mortal and laden with dread.

Around the Sisters, nothing moved.

Chills went down Katherine's back – but she ignored them. He was with her and she was not afraid. Behind the huge feet, the front wall of the building was carved into intricate archways, layers of designs that radiated outwards from its empty door. Saints stood in alcoves, every one of them foully defaced. She tried to look, past the feet, past the pews, to see what was waiting for them. Her hands tightened on sword and shield.

Instinctively, the unit pulled closer together, shoulder to shoulder, all facing outwards and defending the relic at their centre. Over them, the cherubim still hovered, sinister with vigilance. Bell-tower hollows watched them, each one an enemy eye. The stone was covered in grime, like the black smudges of some spreading disease.

'Throne.' One of the Sisters muttered a curse. 'I know they're there...'

'Hold,' Katherine told her. 'He is with us.'

Another Sister voiced the Litany, her words laden with tightly controlled fury. 'Our Emperor, deliver us!'

'There!' The youngest of them extended her arm, pointing. The cherubim shifted, their banners flapping in the heat.

Katherine stared, her heart in her throat.

The cultists were not in the pews. The air wavered, and they were suddenly visible, lurking behind the plinth, and amongst the edges of the outer buildings. There were a hundred of them, a thousand. Many wore robes, which danced in the heat-currents, burned or torn at their edges. Others wore fragments of scrounged gear, a lot of it Militarum, some of it even bearing the Gavera's distinctive Jaguar insignia. And there were *things* with them, things looming, things stalking on stick-thin legs, things with eyes and teeth in all the wrong places. Some of the daemon-things had mandibles, or great jaws dripping with slaver. Others had bloated bellies, muscled arms, hands that dragged on the floor or that ended in pincers or claws.

The Sisters were surrounded. The monster throng had stopped, letting them see it, count it, fear it.

'From plague, temptation and war!'

There was no need to call an order – without hesitation, six bolt pistols opened fire. Weapons barked, rounds howled, detonations of flesh and ooze splashed at the symbol-gouged stone.

Dozens of monsters died, dozens more fell injured and screaming.

The noise blended with the cries of the still-moving. The Sisters added noise of their own, the harmonised chime of their hymns drowning out all but the loudest of the incoming horde.

Pressure began to build in Katherine's mind. Again that sensation that someone – something – was trying to gain entry to her thoughts, trying to prise open her skull like some box of ill-gotten treasure.

'Our Emperor, deliver us!'

She cried her prayer and kept firing. Beside her, a Sister stopped to change her magazine, and the reload flowed around the formation in perfect synchronisation, each Sister in her turn, no words being spoken.

He was with them. He spoke through their movements, their voices. They were the heart of His army; its soul and its mettle, and they would stand at its very core.

Pistols and voices howled His rage.

'From the scourge of the Kraken!'

But the things cared not for His wrath; they were still coming. As more fell, hundreds seemed to take their place as if the foe knew that if they took down this unit of Sisters, then the entire force would falter and eventually fail.

And they, too, moved with a bizarre and fluid rhythm.

In the vox, a Sister said, 'We were correct, there is a single focus to this force. Something controlling them.' Her voice was low, with the odd, guttural catch of one unused to speaking. 'We will break through the enemy lines. Find it, take it down.'

Katherine looked for a break in their ranks, a flaw, a figure in command, but there was nothing, only the onslaught of mutants that came ever closer, and yet more creatures that piled in from behind. Most had crude hand-weapons, some bore spurs of bone that stuck from their flesh. But there were others with–

'Defend the relic!'

Katherine did not know who had spoken. The monsters were upon them now and there was a colossal, mutant beast standing over her, its thin legs bowed, its gangling arms muscled and with fists like hammers. It drove a blunt, fingerless hand at her and she moved, raising her bolt pistol and shooting it clean through the eye.

But behind it came another, and a third.

'We must break out,' the quiet-voiced Sister said. 'Find this commander.'

But they could not. They were completely encircled, each fighting for her life, her faith. Voices raised in the hymnal, a blend of song and shout, and laden with vehemence. From somewhere, the barks of the platoon sergeants could still be heard. Soot still clogged Katherine's visor. She could not spare a hand to wipe it away. Instead, she shot and shot again, brought two more creatures crashing down. Around the Sisters, the wall of death was beginning to grow.

And then, to her side, a Sister staggered to her knees, buried below the creature that had leapt upon her.

'Stand!' Katherine bellowed. She shot the beast in the face, kicked it aside, then covered her Sister with her shield.

The Sister was regaining her feet, but the monsters had seen the breach and they were there already, crowding at the gap. The other Sisters tightened their defence, moving sideways, but it was too late. One of the creatures had ducked through and was reaching for the relic.

'Our Emperor, deliver us!'

Howling, Katherine did the only thing she could.

She turned to take the monster down, but in doing so, she exposed her flank to the pack that now filled the concourse. Only for a moment, but it was enough.

A bone blade went clean through the side of her gorget. Into her throat. Gagging, her own blood hot on her skin, in her mouth, she crashed to the floor.

But that could not be. She must stand, get back to her feet. She must…

Thumping feet, close, that familiar servo-whine. The ground shook. A boom of heavy weapons and the front wall of the cathedral crumpled like parchment, its defiled saints lost.

Through the billowing mess, the Sentinel was half-unseen, its head tracking back and forth, its weapons firing. Beside where Katherine struggled for life, the downed Sister was back on her feet, shouting, fighting furiously.

Katherine tried, she *tried* to get up. She tried to get her boots under her. But the wound was open and fluid coated her gorget and pauldron; she could feel it, thick and sticky down the inside of her armour. Her vision was blurring, her legs would not hold her. Her knees were like water.

'From the blasphemy of the fallen…'

She must *stand*.

The Sentinel stalked forwards. The rest of the front wall came down in a thunder of rubble.

And why could she smell incense?

Her Sisters were shouting, but the vox was hollow, a world away. Above her, the sky and the cherubim spiralled in patterns. The smoke made no sense. Where was that smell coming from? She needed to understand it, that warm, soft scent of the Convent Prioris, of the great cathedral, and home…

And then, she saw Him.

MONSTER

Lance-Corporal Gideon Mase had a lho-stick, a packet of rations, and a mess tin of recaff. Well, not 'recaff' exactly. They'd mixed it with something, and it tasted like boiled mud... but that was what the quartermaster issued, and moaning was heresy.

Mase's little hexi-stove was still burning, a tiny blue flame like some miniature beacon, and he'd sat his weary arse down on the boot-pounded dirt beside it. Broken buildings towered all around him, many of them heaped into makeshift defences, but here, the ground was flat.

He took a long drag on the stick, and blew out a plume of grey. It was late, and finally quiet, thank the Emperor. The sky was dark, and drifting, settling clouds of soot and stone dust were everywhere, getting in his eyes, his mouth, his hair, his kit.

He took another drag on the stick, and coughed up black gunk.

'Nice.' His squadmate Kewa nudged him with a battered, camo-covered elbow. She was a small, wiry thing, her eyes tired, her face dirty. Like him, she had the rich, purple-black skin of Uvodia III, and her hair, once shorn and dark, now more resembled the tangled filth of Kiros. And of this endless bloody war.

His recaff was too hot, and he scalded himself on the metal. 'Shit!'

The 16th Gavera, known to themselves as the 'Jags', had been here on Kiros for almost a Solar year, fighting back and forth, and back and forth; a grinding, endless tedium that never seemed to change. The foe attacked, slobbering forwards, screaming and shrieking; the Jags skirmished out and drove them back. They were an infantry company, stationed on the outermost edge of what had been Kiros' capital city, and way too bloody far from home.

It defied Mase's understanding: Kiros had no value. It had been an Administratum world, a world of hab-blocks and endless, featureless dormitories of cubicles and tiny offices, their grubby walls inscribed with bureaucratic mottos about the holiness of diligence. Great cathedrals had spiked free from its regulation skyline, along with massive statues and cloud-scraping bell towers that rang the sacred hours of far-distant Holy Terra. Mase's briefing hadn't included specifics, but as far as he knew, they were the only things notable about this backwater world. There was nothing here even worth fighting over.

At least, not until…

He stopped, glanced round, and coughed again. A second lungful of muck spattered his chin.

'D'you think it's real?' he muttered, half under his breath. 'The holy text, I mean?'

'Watch it,' Kewa told him, grinning. 'You know we're not supposed to speculate.'

'They were talking in the officers' mess,' he said. 'About some new horror from the warp. It's here to claim it first – or destroy it.' Wiping his mouth on the end of his sleeve, he scowled and looked furtive. The platoons had driven back the afternoon's assault and were now on downtime. Many had already started on bivvies and bedrolls, slinging their ponchos from the remains of the walls, or just wrapping themselves up and going straight to sleep. The metal leg of a patrolling Sentinel caught the faint reflection of the platoon HQ lumen; a distance ahead of him, he could make out the floodlights and field emitters that defended the front line.

Mase leaned in, lowering his voice further. 'I think that's why they're here,' he said. 'To face it.'

'You think they can?' Kewa asked him. In the tiny light from the hexi-stove, her dark eyes shone. 'I *saw* them, earlier today. They were at the centre of the line, right in front of the cathedral where the plinth is. Fighting like nothing I've ever seen. And they're no bigger than we are, not really.'

Mase was still watching round them. He hissed at her to lower her voice, then said, 'I thought they'd be huge. Like Space Marines.'

'Nah.' Kewa grinned, winked. 'I saw one of them, once, too. Did I tell you that? On Aldana, just standing there, like some...' She shrugged. 'Colossus. He didn't move or anything...'

She tailed off as the sergeant came into view. The man still wore his webbing, flak and helmet, but his rifle was slung.

'You two all right?' he asked them. His dark skin was filthy, his stone-coloured camo-paint lost under layers of soot. 'Mase? Kewa? Injuries? Kit failures?'

'Can we go home, yet, sarge?' Kewa asked.

'Ask the commissar.' The sergeant gave them both a sarcastic look, and strode off to the next group.

She snickered, then lowered her voice once more. 'They were amazing, Mase. I saw them, cutting their way through literally swathes of monsters. Dozens, hundreds of them. It was incredible. And they *sing*. It's enough to make your hair stand on end. Watching them...' She shivered. 'It was like watching some perfectly blessed war machine.'

'You're jealous,' Mase realised, grinning.

'Yeah, maybe a bit.' Her expression turned rueful, and she shrugged. 'What must that be like?' She was looking out across the site now, past the gleam of a waiting tank. 'That kind of kit, that kind of skill? Do you think the Emperor really speaks to them? Do they get scared, feel pain, the same way that we do?' She stopped, staring at the semi-darkness. Ends of lho-sticks gleamed, and the occasional hexi-fire. Conversation and hints of weary laughter floated out across the evening wind.

'You just said they were human,' Mase told her. 'I'd been told they were eight feet tall and bit the heads off heretics.'

She snorted. 'They aren't like Space Marines. The Sisters of Battle are like... I don't know... Like watching faith fighting, like holiness incarnate...'

She tailed off, watching the sergeant as he came back into view. He passed them, going the other way, and she turned back to her dumped webbing, rummaging through it. Mase could see the frown on her face, like there was something she wasn't saying.

He didn't press, it wasn't his business. Instead, he blew steam and soot off his recaff and wondered if it was cool enough to drink.

The Adepta Sororitas, the Sisters of Battle. *Here.*

Speculation had been forbidden but still, his curiosity burned like the hexi. They had come to end the war, said some. To find this holy text, to deny and slay this great beast – whatever it was. To purge the taint from this world, to rebuild its churches and cathedrals, all the way back to its filth-choked sky...

Despite the officers' command, stories had flared through the troops like spreading fires. Conjecture had been rife, percussion shocks of expanding whispers... though if the sergeant heard you muttering, you were likely to get the toe of their boot. But – so many tales! Tales of a hundred battles, a thousand legends! Truly, the Jags were blessed, they and Kiros both.

Kewa had found her own hexi and was opening it out, reaching for its block-fuel. His recaff still too hot, Mase took another drag on the lho-stick.

He'd heard the stories, of course he had. The Sisters had their own procession, fearsome and wondrous, an icon at the heart of the battle. There were six of them, their armour black, and they bore the very saint herself, the bones of Holy Katherine. A flock of cherubim circled them like a moving halo, bearing prayer-banners and other things, things Mase did not know. And the darkness... they said that the darkness, the very *clouds*, fled before them like a thing defeated, like a receding tide.

Where the Sisters strode, they carried His light, the light of Sol and of Terra, and the foe *cowered*... The thought made his heart race and his breath catch – surely, now, the end of this war must be in sight? The long-beleaguered Jags had a sharp point to their blunt hammer, the strength of blade, bolter and holy benediction–

He caught himself, calmed his thoughts. Kewa's irreverence was known – it had got her in trouble before – but they both needed to watch themselves. He saw all your thoughts, after all, every last flicker.

Perhaps, Mase thought, the Sisters could see them, too.

The idea made him shiver. His lho-stick burned his fingers and he swore, flicking its end in the hexi. Beside him, Kewa was cooking her ration pack, soot and all. She whistled through her teeth, a tuneless rendition of a Militarum marching song.

They sing...

And it was not just the procession. There were other Sisters here too: squads deployed to protect the Militarum's flanks. Their armour was likewise black, their cloaks red, and they fought fearlessly, hurling themselves at the foe. He'd seen them earlier, from the corner of his eye, seen them move like...

Again, he caught himself. A distance away, only visible by the light of its electro-sconces, was their Order's battle sanctum, sacred and off limits, the towering cathedral one of the few buildings still half-intact. It was defended by four faceless, armoured figures, and he worried that they would hear if he thought too loud.

He put a hand to the talisman in his jacket. It was a little thing, a carved effigy of the Emperor that he'd made himself, when he'd been stuck in a mudhole on the Salyon moon. It gave him hope – made him believe that they could win this. In the end.

He was taking another tentative sip when the monster struck.

It came out of nothing, as if born from the darkness. And it fell upon Kewa, ripping her clean in half. Hot gore slicked Mase's skin.

Casting her shredded pieces scornfully aside, it leered down at him, grinning. By His name, it *stank.*

For the tiniest moment, Mase gawked.

Then: mayhem. Reflexes swift, he was shouting the alarm, hurling the still-steaming recaff, mess tin and all, into the thing's face. With instincts drilled into him from years of training, he went straight for his lasrifle, always at his right-hand side. Shouts and movement came through the darkness; the rest of the platoon were on their feet, already running. In the vox, the sergeant was barking orders, questions, but he was too far away.

Everyone was too far away.

But, with His blessing, the recaff had been enough, just enough, to make the thing pause. It had claws and a grotesque face, semi-human, but teeth in all the wrong places. Its skin was rotted and sloughing off where the liquid had burned it; its compound eyes were red and swelling. It hissed at him, but he had the rifle now and was bringing it up, ready to fire.

He was too close. He smacked the rifle-butt neatly into its claws, and it grabbed and pulled, snarling.

Still on his arse, Mase scrabbled backwards, trying to reclaim the weapon. He shouted into the vox, 'Mase! To me! To me!'

Alarums blared, and the patrolling Sentinel's lumens flared in his direction. There was the distinctive click-click of its weapons tracking – though it surely wouldn't fire at its own campsite.

A second, bigger floodlight snapped his way, dazzling. And–

By the Emperor!

He saw her, he *saw* her, right there, like a vision: an armoured silhouette, the glare behind her. Her helm shone, her black armour glowed at its edges, her red cloak billowed as if she were framed by blood.

A Sister of Battle.

He had no idea how she'd got there; she was surely a miracle. But He had seen fit, for whatever reason, to spare Mase's humble life.

'Get back.' In the vox, her voice sounded young, but it was impossible to tell. The bolter in her hand shone like His blessing as she raised it and blasted the thing full in the chest.

Fluids splattered, the hexi went out. Mase managed to scrabble to his feet, freeing his rifle at last, but she was already between him and the beast. The rest of the platoon had stopped dead.

'Hold your fire!' The sergeant barked the order, but the command was unnecessary. The Sister was too close to the beast.

She ignored them. The thing was still moving, still hissing. Ichor dripped from its body, its mouldering skin. A burst of hymnal came from her, as bright as the bolter's flare; she shot again, and again. It slashed at her, once, twice, with two heavy, claw-tipped arms. Scrapes screeched across her armour.

What in His name *was* this creature?

But she did not pause, her song did not falter. She pressed forwards, pace by pace, indomitable, shooting it again, again, again.

It did not retreat. Its teeth closed on her helm, skidded off. The claws flashed at her pauldrons, putting dents in the ceramite. She shot it a fifth time, a sixth, and finally, it began to weaken, its knees giving way.

'Sarge?' A shocked voice came through the darkness.

'Full perimeter defence!' The sergeant's bark was edged. 'Don't let any more through!'

Mase, gawping, had stopped, his rifle clutched in one nerveless hand. The thing was struggling, still trying to slash at her legs as it went down, but she was a flare of cloak, a wall of armour. As she moved, the floodlight picked out the scraps of parchment fixed to its surfaces, each one inscribed with a prayer. Her bolter glinted like resolution.

At last, the thing tumbled. With a grim resolve, she put one black boot on its shoulder and shot downwards, right in its face. It spluttered, gagged, and went still.

Nothing moved. The sergeant stood silent, staring; Mase could see his filthy, shocked face in the harsh glare of the floodlight. His shadow angled out along the ground, hard as determination.

The Sister, still not paying them any attention, kicked the thing over, put another shot into its skull. Then she turned to where Mase stood, his hands still wrapped round his unused rifle as if it were the only thing that made sense in this insane world.

'Are you hurt?' she asked him.

'I…' He had no idea what he was supposed to call her – milady, ma'am? Did she have a rank? He could see no recognisable insignia. 'No, Sister.' It seemed to be the safest thing to say.

'Good.' Her helm moved and she was looking down at Kewa, shredded like so much fabric. In the rush, Mase had not looked at her and suddenly he faltered as her loss, the nearness of his own miss, hit him like a fist in the temple.

He found himself on his knees, throwing up a stream of sooty bile. Kewa's eyes were glass, empty. Dirt was already settling in them. And her torso…

He looked away, and tried not to throw up again.

'Do not be concerned,' the Sister told him gently.

He glanced up, blinking.

'She died facing the foe,' the Sister said. 'She stands before the Throne in honour and in His grace. You should grieve for her, as is proper, but have no fear for her soul. Her time of strife is done, and she may rest.' There was a burr of pain in her voice, human, and oddly touching.

Numbly, he nodded. 'Yes, Sister. Thank you, Sister.'

'All right, lad.' The sergeant's hand came down on Mase's shoulder. 'Fun's over. Sister, we owe you our gratitude.'

'It's why I'm here, sergeant,' she said. 'A service will be held at twenty-one hundred, Terran standard. With what you have just witnessed, I will expect you to attend.'

'Thank you, Sister,' the sergeant said, again. He poked a boot at Mase, and Mase belatedly remembered his manners.

'Yes... thank you, Sister,' he repeated. 'I will... ah... attend, of course.' He was stuttering. Was he supposed to salute her? He made the effort to stand up, though his legs still shook.

The sergeant was already shouting. 'All right, listen up! Perimeter defences doubled! And I want to know how in the name of the Emper... ah' – he remembered himself – 'how that thing got through here!'

'They crawl,' the Sister said. 'Belly down in the darkness, and slithering. They are cunning, and can affect both your mind and your heart. Be vigilant, sergeant, and hold Him in your thoughts, always.'

The sergeant offered an aquila salute. 'Understood.'

'Know that He is with you, on Kiros, and all across the galaxy.' She paused, and Mase almost heard her smile. 'The battle for this world will not go on forever. We are here to see it ended.'

The sergeant returned, 'Sister. Ave Imperator.'

But Mase could say nothing more, had nothing more to say. Rather than looking down at the remains of his fallen comrade, he watched the Sister's armoured figure as it turned, taking in the sight.

The odd burr of pain was back in her voice as she said, 'His blessing upon you.'

And then she walked away, her black armour still shining as if it carried His very promise.

Careful not to make it audible, Mase let out his breath.

The sergeant raised an eyebrow. 'Don't let it go to your head, son,' he said. 'Find a gunny sack, and we'll put Kewa with the others. And you heard what she said – you be at that service!'

'Sarge.'

A couple of his platoon-mates were lingering, questions on all their faces, but they could wait. If Kewa lay with Him, then he owed it to her memory to tend to her properly.

Turning from the battered Militarum soldiers, Sister Avra felt a stab of regret.

She belonged to the Order of Our Martyred Lady, and her death in combat was expected, the highest honour. But not here, not now. Her life had been refused, and instead, her sacred black armour was scratched and dented. The damage pressed inwards, hard lines of failure against the padding she wore. She knew she should return to the sanctum, but there was a coil of hurt in her heart.

Understand your instincts, child, her schola tutors had taught her – had it only been two Solar years before? *They come from Him, they are your teachers, and they will show you much.*

She walked on, a prayer on her lips, seeking His wisdom. Avra's Order were the faithful of Saint Katherine, deployed to Kiros to end the war. The mission was not unusual, but when she had learned the full brief, about the presence of the saint herself...

In His name, she could never have dreamed of such a blessing!

The Triumph of Saint Katherine, the saint's very bones, borne in holy and ceaseless procession, out across the galaxy – it was *here.* A beacon of courage, guarded by six Sisters, exemplars and representatives. They were chosen by Him to stand with the saint and to carry her strength forth, to proclaim her name and His light!

In the chapel of the *Sword of Bridiga*, Avra had fallen to her knees, unworthy, blessed, elated, overcome. Her heart had rung with song, a threnody that may have been either celebration or lament. She prayed, humbly but with longing, that she may even see the saint for herself – she and her Sisters were taking turns as honour guard.

And she'd prayed, even harder, for the chance to offer her life.

Stepping past the scattered bivouacs, mess tents, armouries, communications hubs, she used her preysight to watch for more of the crawling beasts. The company enginseer flowed past her, ducking from her way, though his attendant servo-skulls and mechadendrites all turned to follow her. Like everything else, his red cloak was covered with soot. Somewhere, soldiers' voices were raised in raucous song. It was a hymn, but sung as only the Militarum could manage.

She controlled a twitch of a smile. Avra had been raised on Fura IV, bleak and severe. Her father and brother had been Third Furan Rangers, but her mother had given her life for her family, dying in childbirth as Avra's brother was born. Avra had been six, her mother's death a moment of great questioning and even greater, unshakable faith. Even now, Avra ached to be worthy of such sacrifice...

Ached to be worthy of her saint.

Fully identifying her curl of disappointment, she paused, chastising herself for the unworthiness of her thought. Her life was not hers to discard, even in battle. Her death was His, in His hands, at His will. Her martyrdom would happen as He decreed, in the proper time, and in the proper place.

Walk with us, O Emperor.

Her thoughts calmer, she glanced around. Her restless, introspective walking had taken her to the outermost edge of the encampment, within blessed sight of where the Sisters of the Triumph of Saint

Katherine had established their own sanctum – taking over a tiny local chapel, its walls and tower all mosaicked with shattered ceramic. It was beautiful, brightly coloured and unique. Its minute windows shone with the light of the saint within.

Avra dropped to her knees, her gauntleted hands tracing a fleur-de-lys on the front of her armour. She had never thought she would be this close, had never dreamed that she would witness this hallowed miracle, let alone be blessed enough to walk behind it.

She intended to bow her head – but the windows flared with His light, and the sight before her was lost.

She stands upon a battlefield, ablaze with wrath and fury. She wields a blade that carves limbs and heads and flesh. She bears a great shield against which the foe shatters, tumbling in dust and fragments. And those fragments fuse together, each one melding with its fellows. They become stones, become rocks, become walls.

Become the crystal glassaic of a great cathedral's windows.

Fire bathes her; it flares from her armour, from her very heart. She burns, but the pain is good, like the purity of total immolation. In the flame-light, the glassaic windows are brought to life, every one an image. In one: an agri world, rippling with crops. In another: a convent, quiet and secluded. In a third: the kneeling forms of Sisters, robes pooled upon a flagstone floor.

And there are more: a man, radiant with dark power and terrible authority. Trust and truth that char right through, like fluttering pieces of fabric. The sickening lurch of a terrible, soul-devastating betrayal.

And then more: a duel, upon which the galaxy waits.

The windows cannot contain the images. They waver and melt, and their running, puddled colours reflect the clouds. They become steam, and are gone.

And still, she burns.

But now, her agony is glorious. She becomes a hymn, raised to a darkness-filled sky. Buildings burn, pillars of smoke rise as if they hold up the very clouds. Further and further spreads the maze of burning streets, stretching back to impossible distance. It is all about her, but she is its hub and its centre and she stands, she always stands…

The shield is back in her hand, but now, she bears her sword in the other. She slays the rising monster. The young soldier is her brother for whom her mother died, her still-youthful father; he may be but one tiny speck upon the surface of the Emperor's Hammer, but he matters. *They all matter.*

Comprehension hits her like a blaze of truth, like a bone spur.

She feels her gorget give, feels that cold spur as it spikes sideways through her throat. As it carves out the side of her neck. Her flame gouts, wild and fervent. Her song hits its crescendo, with power to shatter walls. The monsters cower before her.

The song is her requiem.

She feels her carotid artery as it bursts, feels her lifeblood pouring forth. It is His greatest blessing, His answer, the thing she had come seeking.

'Thank you,' says her fiery heart. 'Thank you.'

She smells the faintest wisp of incense.

Then the flame flares dazzling, and she burns away.

SISTERS

Cool air, the gentle drift of stone dust. A hand on her forehead, the harmonies of a long-familiar hymn.

'Sister.'

Avra's throat was dry and her chest burning, her head pounding with pain. In the blur of awakening, her mind was still overflowing with a richness of dreams: with immolation, with the crescendo of hymnal and glory, with melting glassaic-crystals that showed the sunlight of some strange and far-flung world.

With a bone spur, driving hard through the side of her throat.

Uncomprehending, she raised her gauntleted fingers to the hole in her gorget... Metal scraped on metal. There was no hole.

But...

She started to sit up. A strong hand caught her wrist, steadying her. There was a ring on its middle finger, a steel band inscribed with prayers.

'You are well, Sister. You will find no injury.'

The voice was female, older, both gentle and severe. And it had an odd catch to it, something Avra couldn't quite define. Was that... curiosity?

A frisson ran through her; she shook off the help and sat up fully. The movement made her belly turn over, made a further slew of images tumble through her thoughts. Sisters, kneeling upon a flagstone floor. A yellow sun, angling slantways through the windows of an ancient convent. Ceramite boots, circling one another in a legendary duel…

Her frisson became a chill, a prayer like pure shock. That had not been a dream. That had been a–

She stumbled on the word *vision* like it was blasphemy.

From the desire to be extolled, O Emperor, deliver me…

She was only Avra, just a younger member of her Order. She had passed her Trials of Ordination just two Solar years before. She had no rank, no beads of merit, no mighty deeds to her name. She was not worthy.

And yet… had she really seen…?

Her soul shivered at His closeness. Awed, almost fearful, she whispered the prayer in her heart.

'From the need to be glorified, O Emperor, deliver me…'

'You do not question His will, Sister.' The soft, severe voice spoke again, brooking no argument – without realising, she'd spoken the prayer aloud. 'You are Katherine, ever-martyred and ever-chosen. In our battle today, we lost our beloved Sister of that name, and now you are returned to us once more, to take your place in the sacred march.'

Katherine.

The name went through her like the spur of the monster. Blinking, she ground herself into proper focus. Her helm was already off; her short, brown hair matted with sweat. She turned to see where she was.

Stopped.

Around her, holding her within its bright, mosaicked embrace, was the Sisters' tiny sanctum. It was hollow, offering no pews, no pulpit, no organ loft, no statues. And it was open to the sky, its roof long gone. Field-emitters kept the soot at bay, though the clouds were lifting now. In places, Kiros' stars shone down at her, clear as a blessing.

She sat up further, turning, catching her breath. At the head of the altar steps, where the Sol-facing window should have shone in glassaic and glory, was a hanging depicting His sacred presence, His blade in hand, His head haloed in bright thread that caught the pale gleam of something laid below. The hanging was new, had presumably been brought by the Sisters to sanctify their place of rest. But she *had* seen Him–

That thought was too much. It spiked like a sore tooth, sending sharp sensations thrilling along her nerves. She shied away.

From the hunger for mortal praise, O Emperor, deliver me...

Instead, her gaze found the source of the light. From the top of the altar steps, there fell a cloth. It cascaded down steps of stone like black water, a fiery heart upon it. And there...

From the need to raise myself...

By the Throne!

There, upon the cloth: a casket, shining with its own soft glow. Her awe peaked, breaking over her like the Font of Ordination itself. Her heart hit her chest like a hammer; she found herself staring, tangled in wonder, in the tiniest threads of denial.

O Emperor, deliver me!

The casket was open, its edges hung with banners of the Sisters' Orders. She could not see what lay within, only that it shone and that the chapel seemed hushed about it, as if the stone had silenced itself in reverence, its walls leaning forwards in veneration. A great, shining banner hung at its head, and red and white petals surrounded it, scattered on the stone.

Reflexively, pulled by strings of pure faith, she stumbled upwards from her pallet, and came to her knees. Her head was already bared. She shuddered as the dream touched her again.

Her heart, burning.

Her chest hurt with remembered pain.

The bone spur. And incense...

There was no incense here. The air smelled of blood and sweat and metal, military smells. But still, she could only gaze. Rapt, captivated.

Saint Katherine.

She bowed her head, her tears overflowing and spilling down her cheeks.

'Be at ease, Sister.' Her companion had stepped back, letting her take in her surroundings. Now, she came forwards once more, her boots black on the flagstones. 'We welcome you, in His name.'

Still not understanding, Avra looked up at the ceramite-clad figure. 'Why...?' She wanted to ask, *Why am I here?*, but she couldn't finish the question.

The unknown Sister dropped to one knee beside her, also bowing her head. Her armour, too, was fully black, with her red cloak all soot-stained and ragged at the hem. She was older, Avra saw, perhaps in her forties. Her hair was blonde and greying, cut short; her face was soot-stained, lean and lined. And her left eye had been replaced by a sacred augmetic, carved with the same prayers as her steel ring. It whirred gently as it focused.

She saw Avra looking and gave a smile both gentle and edged. 'You know who we are,' she said.

'Of course.' Avra's words were a whisper. 'But I don't...'

I don't understand. What has happened to me?

'He has shown you, child, has He not?' Answering the unspoken question, the Sister's words had a faint insistence, like a pointedly raised eyebrow. 'As He has shown us. The vision of our founding, the duel that shaped the Imperium. It is not your place to doubt His will.'

Avra turned back to the blessed casket. Looking at it, a great well of feeling rushed up in her heart, as if the black flow of the altar cloth was not water, but promethium, fuelling the fire that still burned, *burned,* in her chest.

You know who we are, Sister.

Of course she did, she knew them like she knew her own name, like she knew the sacred recitations of the schola: Saint Katherine had been martyred by the witch-cult upon Mnestteus, yet she led battles still, borne across the galaxy to wherever the need was greatest. It was her Triumph, her march unending, her sacred coffin carried by six Sisters, each a representative of a different saint...

But this was different – not words upon a slate, not even a statue revered within a cathedral. Avra could *feel* it, *feel* the saint's sacrifice and glory, *feel* her honour and courage. And layered with those feelings came the monster with the bone spur, cutting sideways through her throat.

Tears stung her eyes, and the images misted, blurred, became one.

'I am not worthy.' The words were a sigh.

'That is not for you to say,' the Sister told her, with a calm vehemence. 'Your life as Avra is ending.' The words were almost intoned; they flowed out through the chapel's quiet with the delicacy of a choir's first notes. 'The Sisters of our march come to us from the Orders Pronatus, but you, child – we are in need, and you have clearly been chosen. From the morning, you will be Sister Katherine, called to replace our Sister of that name who fell to sacred martyrdom at the strike of the ancient foe. She has answered His word and given her life in defence of her Sisters, her saint, and of those who follow where we lead. She stands now in His grace, her duty fulfilled.' The Sister's augmetic eye whirred again, a flicker of red in its depths, and her smile deepened. Her other eye was yellow, like Sol's light, like the precious amber effigy Avra's father had so loved, passed down from his father and his grandmother before that.

'My armour...' Still struggling to assimilate the vision, the dream, the pain, the change, the huge weight of this expectation, Avra looked down at the dents that the beast had left.

'You bear badges of both combat and distinction,' the Sister told her. 'And there will be time for the sacrament of repair. We stand upon the edge of hostile territory, and our Sisters still hold holy vigil. As night deepens, they will come to greet you themselves.' Her augmetic whirred again. 'This is an ancient ceremony, and one you will respect.'

Unable to speak, Avra nodded. Prayers flared in her heart, warming her like the Sol-yellow sunlight of that long-lost world. She looked up, daring to raise her gaze to His image.

But He was too much. Shivering, she dropped her chin once more.

'I am Sister Lucia,' the Sister went on, 'of the Valorous Heart. And it is ever my sacred task to greet you, as with shared vision, I honour your pain in mind, and in flesh, and in soul.' A faint smile. 'Do not doubt your worthiness, my Sister. Such would be blasphemous, would it not?' She raised her human eyebrow in an expression that might have been either humour or reprimand. 'Once again – it is His will that you are here.'

Sister Lucia, she thought, catching up – like Katherine, one of the original Daughters of the Emperor, the companions of Alicia Dominica from the convent of San Loer. They who had faced the heretic Vandire...

His name brought a prayer of shock from her lips, asking forgiveness, even as her mind flashed dream-images.

Sisters kneeling upon a flagstone floor.

Yellow sunlight, slantways through convent windows.

A duel of legend.

I did see..!

She shivered again, soul-deep and awestruck, resisting the urge to scrub the water from her skin. Despite Lucia's assurance, her own powerful sense of unworthiness remained: *no, I cannot possibly!* But Lucia's face bore the same gentle severity as her voice, and it tolerated no uncertainty. There was a long, pale scar down her left cheek, running under the augmetic. And if Avra remembered correctly, her Order would consider the loss of her eye His blessing.

Had not Saint Lucia herself lost both her eyes to torment?

She, too, had been chosen.

From the desire for wealth and glory, O Emperor…

Still praying, Avra steadied herself. She unfolded to her feet, her damaged armour clattering in the chapel's quiet. For the first time, she became aware of the noise outside – the camp was still out there, the singing thinning now, the Sentinels still patrolling – but this tiny chapel offered blessed sanctuary and they seemed like a world away.

Slowly, her boots thumping like heartbeats, she ascended the steps. Lucia stood back, understanding, leaving her to her moment. Avra stopped before she reached the top; knelt before the bones of the saint, all robed in white and laid upon a bed of scarlet. They shone, their warmth like Sol's blessing, and He stood above her almost fondly, like a father, defending her repose.

And, though the black sockets of His daughter's skull stared sightless at the open roof, that same gleam came also from within.

That Avra had been honoured to see this! Her breath caught on more tears.

Cherubim hovered watchful, augmetic eyelids clicking, though they had laid their supporting chains aside. Glinting in the soft light, they carried the faintest edge of menace. Yet she also felt their welcome, and they did not touch her.

You are worthy, they seemed to say. *You sought to lay down your life for an infantryman. For the love and memory of your family. For your Sisters. Stand, child, you shall bear sword and shield in strength and faith, the shield that guarded Alicia Dominica herself. And you will not lay it aside.*

Avra bowed her head, tears of humility pouring down her cheeks.

'Remove your armour,' Lucia told her. 'It will go to your Order's sanctum. And you, my new Sister...' She glanced sideways, smiling. 'You must attain your clarity.' Her augmetic whirred, focusing on Avra's still-pale, tear-smeared face.

Avra nodded, again. She had yet to find words for the sheer scale of what had happened to her.

Lucia smiled, making her scar crinkle. 'Do you recall the night before your Ordination, Sister? Where you lay upon the floor and you offered your life to Him?'

Avra nodded again. 'Of course.'

'Now,' Lucia said, 'He calls upon you to do this once more. You will hold your vigil, here and alone. You will reflect upon the vision that has been shown to you, understand it, and contemplate your place as part of our sacred march. As we have said, there will be no room for doubt or unworthiness, come morning and muster.'

Avra nodded a third time, removing her gauntlets so she could reach for the fastenings on the armour.

Still watching her, Lucia continued, 'At oh three hundred hours, Sister Superior Aliaah of the Order of Our Martyred Lady will step up her squad, and they will take our place as honoured guardians. We will join you for sustenance, and prayer, and to offer you our Sisterhood and support.' Her smile deepened. 'And we will embrace the Service of Tales, that you may understand us better, and walk with us across the galaxy.'

'Tales?' Dropping her pauldrons, Avra was faintly surprised.

'What else?' Lucia told her. 'You do not face your fears alone, Avra. We have all known what it is to stand in this place.' She took the pauldrons, the chestplate, each piece of the armour as it was handed over. Two young, black-armoured Sisters, their faces lowered, had appeared at the doorway. They carried a sacred chest between them, marked with the fleur-de-lys and ready to take the items back to the sanctum.

Avra looked at them, realising they were no older than she was, that...

No room for doubt.

With the newly arrived Sisters to help her, she removed her leg-plates, kicked her way out of her boots, then stood there in her padded underarmour, suddenly sweating in the full, thick heat of the Kiros night. Lucia nodded at the young women, and packing the chest, they bowed and vanished, back out of the doorway to the safety of their Order...

Her Order.

Avra paused, feeling exposed and very alone. Her armour had been so much a part of her, she felt acutely vulnerable without it. Yet now, she could feel the presence of the chapel upon her skin, the touch of the saint, and of her glow. They felt like the heat in her heart, like its warmth and light was already reaching out, touching the resting, sleeping, guarding Militarum, all the way across the site.

Bringing them His courage, for the dawn.

With a sudden rush, she found herself anticipating the morning, and full muster. But that rush was not anger – it was new, and strong. It felt more like a great anticipation, flowing up through her body, out through her limbs. As she knelt upon the steps, her face bathed in the casket's glow, she found herself thinking back to her home. Thinking about her father. Thinking about the medals he'd kept in that tiny steel box, along with their grandmother's effigy of Saint Celestine. She remembered him crying, though she'd been too young to fully understand why – tears of pride, courage, honour and worship...

And *loss.* She'd been nine when her father had given his life to the Emperor; her brother had been three. But they'd wanted nothing more than to follow his example, to take up arms in His service... She and her brother both, so young and eager, their eyes shining – they'd been the last, lingering reminders of their mother, and they'd headed out to almost certain death.

As if in response to her thought, she heard the voice of a shouting sergeant, the bellow stentorian and familiar. He could easily have been her father, or her brother Talan, conjured from her youthful memories...

She raised her gaze to the casket, to the great banner that rose behind. Above her, a star constellation glittered past the chapel's fractures. She thought it was The Warrior, His eye on her.

Maybe she *had* been chosen? The thought felt daring, but crept through her like the warmth of Sol itself.

'Begin your vigil, Sister,' Lucia said softly. 'And have no fear. We will watch, and we will return.'

Before her Ordination, Avra had spent a last night in her novitiate's robes, prone before His likeness, her arms outstretched and her face down, praying for the morning. And now, she did the same – without her armour, clad only in her padding, she lay belly down on the black cloth that covered the hard, broken angles of the steps.

She remembered her father's tears, the confusion of feelings that had gone with them.

And they flowed down her face, also.

THE SERVICE OF TALES

Outside the Sisters' tiny sanctum, the noise of the camp was loud – the noise of massed humanity.

Descending the front steps, Sister Lucia was assailed by a wave of sound and motion – voices, orders, feet, shouting. Before her lay the front line of the forward defences: a long, piled wall of broken stonework, a rank of heavy weapons. Tall towers had been built, rebuilt or repurposed; floodlights glared from observation points; juts of vox-antennae spiked at the darkened sky. She could see scatters of infantry, lying in silence upon the wall tops, their lasrifles at their shoulders.

Beyond the defences, the remaining streets had been completely flattened, twisted with wire and layered with charges. It was the no-man's-land that neither side should cross without being observed... But the foe did not rest, as the attack last night had proven. They were always alert, always pushing, always seeking to destroy. Far out there, somewhere in the thick warmth of Kiros' night, their fires still burned.

At the base of the chapel steps, an armoured figure stood like some forbidding stone statue, broad curves of ceramite shining black in the floodlights' glare. She bore a tray of scarlet petals in her hands, a bolt pistol at her hip.

Over the vox, Lucia said softly, 'Our new Sister begins her vigil. She is worthy, is she not?'

As yet, Avra did not have the clearance for their vox-channel. That, and her name – they would come when she'd completed her journey.

'She's very young.' The severe, almost monosyllabic response came from the chapel's rear, from Dominica herself, an icon of armour and unyielding strength. She faced the light of far-distant Sol, watched over the sleeping army. 'Barely blooded.' Her tone was deep, measured. 'And while her fears of unworthiness are honest–'

'We all shared her vision, Sister,' Arabella replied, her tone gentle but its insistence clear. 'There can be no doubt.' She faced south, her hope and light in what had once been the chapel's cloisters and garden. 'Only we see the sacred convent, and only we–'

'I have seen the blessed vision,' Dominica said, her tone a growl, 'every time a new exemplar has joined these ranks. And I say – her youth bothers me. And she is not Pronatus.'

Voices shouted across the camp, borne on hot wind. Lucia turned, but Silvana, facing north and the ancient graveyard, said, 'It is nothing.'

Deceptively mild, Arabella was still speaking. 'Does my youth worry you also, Sister?'

'You are proven, are you not?' Dominica asked her.

'I would certainly hope so.'

'Guard your tone, Sister.' Dominica's voice was a warning.

'Avra has been chosen, and will show us her strength.' Lucia spoke across them both, her words calming. 'We will all tell our tales, as is proper, and she will offer a tale of her own, that we may know her heart. And you, Sister Arabella, you will show the proper respect.'

'Yes, Sister.'

The five of them fell silent, looking outwards to both camp and foe. From the front lines, the shouting voices grew louder. A floodlight swung through an arc, making shadows scud swiftly sideways, like fleeing ghosts. From the steps, Lucia watched the guarding infantry, a wary shift that went through their deployment as they leaned eyes into rifle-sights, peering out over wire-tangled gloom. Flicking through the vox-channels, she listened in for a moment, then returned her attention to her Sisters.

'Major Haro reports movement,' she said. 'Tower delta, though not yet within range. Sentinels are deployed, but they have no orders to engage.' She paused, then went on, 'The major believes there will be another incursion, such monsters as we have already seen – foetid and foul, warped humanity, twisted beyond mental or physical tolerance.' She paused, added, 'Still screaming with their own pain.'

Mina snorted. 'Combat will be welcome. I dislike this waiting.'

'Agreed,' Silvana said, the faint sound of a smile in her tone. 'The great monster is come, and it will seek to thwart us. Tomorrow, we will slay it, and push for victory.'

Arabella muttered, but said nothing further. Lucia understood that she still smarted from the reprimand.

Dominica commented, ending the discussion, 'We will complete our vigil, and commence the Service of Tales. I need not remind you that we stand at the heart, even here, and we will not relax our vigilance.'

'Sister.' The agreement flowed out around the unit, and they settled to their posts, the preysight in their visors working. They had no auspex, but a tell-tale green flicker came from their guardian squad.

'Sister Superior Cico,' Dominica said to them, softly. 'You will keep us informed of any movement or order.'

'Yes, Sister.'

Silence. Tension. A whisper of prayer across the vox, flowing from Sister to Sister with a harmony that belied their previous disagreements. Regardless of their differences, they stood united in His grace and in the face of the ancient enemy.

Another Sentinel padded past them, heading out to scout the darkness. Briefly, it crossed the sky, a black shape against the stars. Orders sounded in its wake, and a second wave of alertness flickered through the waiting soldiers.

Her hand closing round her steel ring, Lucia felt its pinprick of pain, a tiny shock of alertness and focus. She and her Sisters worked in a flawless, fluid harmony that required almost no communication. Their shared visions bound them, mind to mind and weapon to weapon – every Sister knew her role and every task neatly overlapped into the next.

Arabella had the gift for teaching such harmony, Mina for their squad commands and Silvana for their larger, tactical decisions. But it was Dominica that was their commander and elder, and all other tasks began or ended at her word. She was the ultimate Sororitas warrior, the perfect Sister. At times, Lucia had wondered if she, too, understood His terrible knowledge, but she had never asked.

Some things, she mused, were best left alone.

'Sister Avra.'

The words were as sharp and sudden as the stamp of Dominica's boot. The sounds cut at Avra, severing her thoughts. She found herself almost falling, tumbling from a place of prayer and holy meditation, a place that was already vanishing, even as she tried to move.

She was chilled and stiff, but such hardship did not matter. Had she seen… had she seen the saint herself? Again, that distant world, those Sisters kneeling on stone? She had no recollection of a second vision, but her prayers had taken her out of herself, carried her away from discomfort and into the vastness of His presence and expectation.

'Stand up, child,' Dominica said, more gently. 'We bring nourishment and support.'

Her body aching from the steps' hard edges, Avra creaked unsteadily to her feet. The Sisters made no move to help her. Lucia watched her with a faint, almost analytic whir to her augmetic. It was deep night, and the heat had faded at last; Avra found herself shivering. She was hungry and her mouth was dry as sand. She felt empty, not only physically, but mentally, emotionally. She felt as if she had cast her soul upon the steps of this tiny chapel, left it for His approval.

For the saint to bless, as she chose.

She staggered and, this time, a gauntlet caught her elbow – Arabella, she thought, helm off in His presence, as was proper.

'Easy, Sister,' she said. 'Your muscles will protest, but you will move more freely, in a moment.'

She was young, Avra realised, barely older than Avra herself. Her complexion was very pale, with a sunburned strip across her nose. Her sweat-soaked blonde hair stood up like a nimbus in the casket's glow. But her smile – she had an expression like the rise of a star, brilliant and compelling. It was inclusive, warm. And something about it made Avra like her immediately.

Perhaps it was His hope, so radiant in her face.

The other four Sisters had sunk to one knee upon the steps, a perfect row of bowed shoulders. They were all heads bared, their armour limned by the saint's light. As they stood up and turned around, Avra saw their faces for the first time.

Sister Lucia, she had seen before, with her scar and her augmetic eye.

Sister Mina: square-jawed and dark-skinned, her black curls cropped short. She too bore a facial scar, cutting inwards from one ear and stopping just short of her mouth. And there was a tangible authority to her, a solidity and strength that made her seem like the very stone.

Sister Silvana, pale skin and very black, smoothly glossy hair. Her cheekbones were blade-sharp and her eyes as blue as gemstones. Her black armour gleaming, she seemed to shine like the edge of a knife, a sharp blade of courage. She was, Avra thought, very beautiful.

And Dominica…

The ultimate Sororitas, her responsibility carried like huge, dark wings. Tall, rangy, slender to the point of being wire-thin, her face was lean and hard-edged. Her skin was dusky, her short, dark hair flecked with grey. She was easily the oldest of them, but her expression was as hard as the steps' corners, cold and judgemental. When she met Avra's eyes, Avra almost flinched – but she held both her ground and her gaze.

Slowly, Dominica nodded, like the younger Sister had passed some sort of test. 'Good,' she said. Then, 'Are you well?'

The question meant more than just her physical discomfort.

'Yes, Sister,' Avra answered her. She stretched her shoulders, winced, let herself smile. 'I am glad to have taken this time to search my heart.'

'Pain teaches many things,' Lucia said gently, casting a raised-eyebrow glance at Arabella. 'Walk, Sister. It will hurt, but your blood will move more swiftly.'

Muffling an unworthy groan, Avra did as she was bid, her muscles protesting the motion. Gradually, she was able to move more freely.

In the middle of the chapel, Arabella had opened a large chest, this one marked with the banners of all six Orders. From it she produced, with suitable reverence, six mats, which she laid upon the floor. From the same box, Lucia was breaking out rations, opening packets and offering a tiny piece of each to a carved effigy at the mats' centre. When this was done, she came to kneel, lighting an electro-candle and letting the warmth of its flame spread through the tiny building, making its odd ceramics shine.

'Come.' She indicated a mat. 'There is enough space for all. We are Sisters, are we not?'

Mina eyed the makeshift refectorium with wariness. 'We should rotate a guard, Sisters–'

'There is no need,' Dominica answered her. 'We are guarded by both His might and by the blessing of the saint–'

'And by the troops outside,' Arabella said.

'Desist.' Dominica folded her arms and glared down at the younger Sister. 'This is a ritual both sacred and ancient. I do not wish to enact stern discipline, but I shall, if you do not show the proper respect.'

Privately, Avra wondered what form such action would take – the fact that this perfect unit of Sisters did not work in pure accord was shocking and, oddly, quite reassuring. As reassuring as the peeling skin on Arabella's upturned nose, as the familiarity of saying Grace.

They were all like you once, her thoughts told her. *Even Dominica. They, too, shared your vision.*

Sisters, kneeling upon a flagstone floor…

Her vigil had shown her much, but still, that single image was powerful enough to be overwhelming. How was she supposed to live up to such expectations?

She took the rations as they were passed to her, whispered the prayer, and listened as Dominica began to speak.

'You know who we are, Sister, and the roles that we take in defence of the relic we bear.'

The others had fallen silent, each kneeling on her mat. Outside, the noises had faded again, a world and a galaxy away. Floodlight tumbled through the front doorway, leaving an arched and angled shape across the floor, but it did not stretch as far as the steps. If Avra looked up, she could see that the clouds had cleared. Kiros' three moons hung visible, now: tiny tumbles of uneven rock, too far above the planet to shed any real light.

She lowered her chin, and listened.

'It is our task to march across the galaxy entire,' Dominica said. 'You know this from your studies. Across time and void and fear and warfare, we bear our most holy saint to the places where she may bring His blessing. I say to you, my Sister, that you must accept this responsibility and forge it to a weapon of faith, to courage and leadership that will surpass all you have known before. You will stand at our forefront, and you will stand to your full height and capability. I will drive you hard, make no mistake. I am a difficult taskmaster and I brook no errors. But I will ensure that you become worthy of bearing Katherine's shield and sword, and of leading our march across the galaxy.'

Lucia was nodding, though she said nothing. The faces of the others were watching: Mina with intent, Arabella with a serious honesty, and no sign of her previous humour. Silvana was holding a chant, very soft, a faint whisper of unfamiliar music. It was not Grace; it was something that Avra did not know, and it chimed through the stone with a sound that was almost eerie.

Dominica looked around at all of them, met each of their gazes in turn, turned back to Avra.

'This is the Service of Tales, where you will meet each of your new Sisters, and where we will remind you of Saint Katherine's Wars of Faith. Each of us, in turn, will offer a story of our saint's endeavours, at a time when she reflected the courage and soul of each Order. These tales are what bind us as family, as Sisters in – as well as of – Battle. Thus you may understand us, and the sacred nature of our march.' She held Avra's gaze. 'And when this is done, you will offer us a tale of your own, that we may understand you also.'

She paused, still watching Avra's expression, though Avra said nothing.

'Do you have any questions, Sister?'

Her thoughts still tumbling with amazement, Avra felt her own unworthiness loom large. Refusing to give it voice, she shook her head.

Dominica said, her deep voice gentle, 'You will respond when I speak to you.'

'I...' Avra gathered her wits. 'No, Sister, no questions.'

'Very well, then,' Dominica said. 'Sister Mina, as our champion, you will commence.'

And so, the Service of Tales began.

THE TALE OF MINA

'Be welcome, Sister Avra,' Mina said. Her voice was strong, and though the words were intoned like ceremony, they had the familiar, clipped tones of the tight disciplinarian. 'I am Sister Mina of the Bloody Rose. I am warrior and champion. It is my sacred task to guard you, to defend our faith and courage, to stand forth and slay the foes of His light. Where the enemy walk, I bring them death. I forge my rage by the hammer of my faith, and I slay His foes, wherever they may be found.' She paused, her dark eyes twinkling, and her voice softened. 'My Sisters and I defend the sanctum, and our most holy saint.' A twinge of humour, almost. 'And so will you, from the breaking of tomorrow's dawn.'

Her tray of petals lay to her left side, her bolt pistol to her right. The air across the floor stirred tiny flakes of scarlet, fluttered them in miniature tornadoes. It teased the very edges of her blood-red cloak.

'My Sister Dominica has explained the nature of this ceremony,' she said, still with that faint twinkle. 'It has been enacted many thousands of times, down through years and centuries, in worlds and wars across the galaxy entire. Its purpose will become clear, as it unfurls.'

Avra watched her, unspeaking.

'It falls ever to me to begin,' she said. 'And to tell a tale of strength and combat, as befits my Order.'

'Tell on, my Sister,' Dominica said. Voices called outside, but they were a world away, muted by the sanctum's expectant quiet.

Mina took a moment to compose herself, and began.

In among the gravestones, Katherine paused.

Above her towered tombs, the pitted grey faces of a myriad memorials, each one leaning sideways as if too weary to stand alone. The air was thick and pale with fog; it obscured her vision and made her armour shine like a promise. Wary, she barked an order over the vox.

Behind her, her surviving Sisters stopped. They were a mess, only three of them remaining, and Sister Kemra was limping on a suspected broken ankle. But they could not, would not fail in their mission. The Nakemaran war banner lay here, somewhere, abandoned but not forgotten. Its fabric might be long-rotted, but its pole, styled like a great spear, still awaited them – possibly this sarcophagus, or in the next. And as they searched, He would show them the way, whatever pitfalls might lurk in their path.

High over their heads, rows of lumens made soft, blurred hazes of the white mist. Unseen themselves, they shed little light upon the unused walkways of the Sukato cemetery. She did not know how many years – centuries? – it had been since the feet of man walked here…

Or the feet of woman.

Across the vox, Katherine and her Sisters' voices chanted softly, twining in harmony across the planet's ever-present night.

'Domine, libra nos.'

Men under arms… forbidden. Katherine was a Daughter of the Emperor, Adepta Sororitas, a warrior of His grace and of the blessed Ecclesiarchy. And she and her Sisters were here to honour their duties as soldier and as zealot both–

* * *

'Zealot?' Interrupting, Dominica had one graceful eyebrow arched almost in her hairline. 'Interesting choice of word, my Sister. We have spoken of this before.'

'But we are zealous, are we not?' Her tone short, Mina sounded irritated at the interruption. 'And such a trait is surely a virtue? It carries us out across the void, to slay the heretic, the xenos, the ancient foe.'

'Get on with the story,' Lucia told them, faintly impatient. 'We have many tales to tell, and neither morning nor muster will wait.'

Mina's scarlet armour rattled as she settled herself once more. A breath of quiet sighed out through the little chapel, and she continued.

In the wraith-light of the mist, they moved, their visibility minimal, but all their senses alert. The silence of the place felt heavy, eerie; it hung about them like cobwebs, thick and cold, concealing every threat. And soon they heard the sounds start once again, noises too tiny to be dangerous, yet insistent in their pursuit.

A chill rolled out ahead of them, like a harbinger.

'They're coming again.' Sister Kemra's voice was a whisper. It caught on her weariness, on the faintest tremble of exhaustion. She had not slowed them down, but her limping gait was a constant reminder of her injury. 'By His light, is there no end to them?'

'We know not,' Sister Xara said, her voice flat with anger. 'But be they legion, we will fight through them nonetheless.'

Katherine said nothing. She gripped her holy shield in one hand, her bolter in the other. Carefully, she scanned the surrounding ground with her preysight, but the planet was bitterly cold and the low body temperature of the creatures made them difficult to see.

Yet the noise still danced behind them. Something small was skittering between the gravestones' ancient feet, something that came with a scuffle of claws on gravel. Even as Katherine turned to look for it, it vanished again.

'Why are they even here?' Sister Kemra asked. 'On a world of so many tombs, we surely expected an assault of the necrons. Or...' She stopped, out of words. 'What do they want?'

'Us, and dead,' snapped Sister Livia, at the rear. 'We keep moving.'

'These tombs belong to the Imperium, and to Him,' Katherine said softly. 'There are no necrons here.' She gave a second order, and the squad headed forwards once more.

Yet Kemra had a point, she realised. This was Jelena, lone planet of a darkening star. It was a world of almost pure night, far out from its sun, the orbit of its large and singular moon leaving it in semi-permanent eclipse. The moon was close enough that its weight was almost tangible, a vast rock suspended in the sky by His will and might alone... If the mist cleared enough for them to see it, they would see also its ever-present corona, and the world's only daylight.

Jelena was a world of the dead, all but uninhabitable, a place where the Imperium had brought the bodies of its heroes to lie in state. Tetricus the Great lay here, or so the briefing had told them, and Dama herself, the Liberator of Pius IV. So many names, lying silent, gently rotting into a soil that now grew with nettles and great tangles of creeper. However mighty they may have been, they all now occupied the same six feet of Jelena's soil. And however tall their monuments, they still tumbled forgotten, pulled down by the ravaging weeds...

Katherine stopped, chastising herself sternly for the unworthy thought. Tetricus and Dama, all of these great heroes, they now stood in His light, in the presence of the Golden Throne. It was only their mortal remains that lay here, gently disintegrating–

That skitter, again. Close, this time, flicking from side to side as if moving faster than thought. Playing with them.

'Vigilance, my Sisters,' Katherine said softly, raising her shield.

Over the vox, the Sisters offered assent. They moved forwards carefully, weapons gripped and ready, auspex and preysight alert. That scuttle was oddly visceral, as if it touched some primitive, nightmare terror. Several of the squad had shuddered at their first encounter – they'd been ambushed almost at their landing point by a horde of the things, each one a yard at the shoulder, and breaking loose from a ring of sarcophagi. They'd flowed forwards like iridescent water, their fangs bared, their weapons extensions of their many arms. Three Sisters had been slain, Kemra injured, but the squad had thrown back that initial assault, shooting without mercy, blasting the creatures to fragments. The Sisters had scouted the empty tombs, but no further sign had remained.

Until now.

Softly, Sister Livia raised the Requiem, her voice pure as cut glass. It was a holy celebration of the dead that lay here, a sanctification. And it was a clarion call – not yet the full rage of battle joined, but a warning.

Her arms spiking with gooseflesh, Katherine echoed her Sister's stanzas, and they kept moving, searching for the place where the banner was held.

Guide me, God-Emperor. Under the crystal sound of the hymn, she prayed silently for His light. *My eyes are but mortal.* Her prayer was internal, the words in her heart. *Pray, bless me with your truth.*

'Hold,' Sister Xara said, over the vox. 'We have a change in terrain.'

Katherine stopped, turned. To their right, the maze of gravel pathways dropped sharply, tumbling down a short flight of steps to a series of grave-lined trenches, every flagstone carved with ancient lettering. They were hard to make out, but she thought that the stones bore names, faded and lichen-choked, or were etched with symbols, skulls and weapons and military insignia.

Some were adorned with offerings, perhaps placed by long-dead family – badges, skulls, the rotting stalks of flowers.

It was a vast, half-walled labyrinth, stretching outwards into the fog. But He guided them still, and they would follow His wisdom.

Briefly, she wondered how many of the scuttling creatures lurked here, but she did not voice her concern aloud. This was no place for fear, only for battle. For victory. For the success of their mission. And her Sisters' watchfulness was strong.

The others had joined Livia in the rise of the Requiem, gaining now in passion and intensity, offering rites for this world of the dead.

'You know, our Emperor, the secrets of our hearts!'

Katherine felt her blood stir, a shudder of rising adrenaline. 'We will proceed,' she commented softly, out over the vox. 'Bear right, and trust in His guidance.'

They shifted deployment, allowing Katherine and her shield to the front, Livia to the rear with her heavy bolter. Their boots scraped down the stairs, skidding on the worn-smooth stone, and they went onwards.

Mist oozed round them, seeming almost to thicken as they pushed their way through it. Above them, the lumen-lights were no more than a blur. Under their feet, the flags bore more names: Valgus, Mallia, the Lord of Catalus Prime. Katherine continued to sing the Requiem, for all those who lay in rest here, and for the courage of her Sisters.

The scuttle came again, somewhere to their left. Instinctively, they paused.

A split second later, another one, to the right. Then again, to the left; again, to the right. The noises were louder, closer, and – thanks to the trench – now on a level with their shoulders.

The Requiem softened to a thrum of pure threat, allowing them to listen. Needing no order, the four of them had moved to a compass formation, four weapons pointed in four directions. Katherine was facing forwards, her bolter aimed along the trench of gravestones. Ahead of her, there waited what looked like a clearer space, though the haze-blur of the lumens made it difficult to see.

Another scuffle. Behind them, this time.

'Xara,' she said. 'Location?'

Xara had her auspex in hand, and was moving it in a slow arc. At ground level, everything was still smothered in loops of the spiking creeper, thrown around the leaning graves as if to tug them all the way down.

'Where are they, Sister?' Katherine said, urgency in her tone. 'How near?'

Over the vox, Sister Kemra spoke a prayer, her voice deep and quiet. Livia still sang the Requiem, the notes chiming through the cold air. The hymn pulled the four of them tight together, and they watched, blessed by His praise.

By blade and bolter, by shield and armour, by heart and courage. Whether these were early invaders, or left over from some previous battle, the Sisters would exterminate all of them. Return this world to His grace.

Beside Katherine, the auspex blipped green, blipped again. From the corner of her eye, not letting go her vigilance, she glanced down at the screen – saw one dot, two, three. Four, five, ten, twenty. They were not coming closer. They seemed to be…

Spreading out.

'They're moving all round us,' Xara said, echoing Katherine's thought.

Sister Livia continued to sing, the sound ghostlike in the stillness. Slowly, Xara moved the auspex back again. The blips were still there – too many to count. The screen was swamped with green flashes.

'What are your orders, Sister?' Xara said. 'Do we take our stand here?'

'I still can't see them,' Kemra said. 'There's too much vegetation in the way. And curse this awful light!'

Carefully, still not moving, Katherine looked all around them. She was seeking a defensible position, something more secure than being out here in the open, the creeper-smothered ground at almost neck level, the things able to get close and then leap for the Sisters' faces...

'Let us make for the opening ahead,' she said. 'The light there is stronger, and will give us a killing ground. And we may be able to gain the security of a standing tomb, something in which we can take cover–'

'Take cover?' Interrupting the flow of Mina's story, Sister Silvana sounded startled. 'My Sister, this is surely a fictionalised part of this tale? You imply that Katherine herself *fled* from her foe?' The shock in her tone was tangible, a sharp echo in the chapel's quiet. Outside, a shadow passed the tiny windows, a Sentinel perhaps, moving dark against the lumens.

Mina gave her Sister a stern look. 'To find a tactically advantageous position is not fleeing, my Sister, but surely practical sense. A Sister can better serve His will if her defences are well placed. There is no sagacity in dying needlessly – certainly not without taking as many of the enemy with you as you can.'

'You speak of Saint Katherine herself,' Silvana said, her tone cutting. 'Our Martyred Lady, and in her very presence.' She dropped her voice, almost as if she expected the saint to hear her. 'And you skirt dangerously close to insult, my Sister.'

Mina inhaled sharply, her dark face flushing.

'Sisters, please.' The calming voice was Arabella's, cutting across the other two. She extended a quieting hand to each of them. 'We do not squabble amongst ourselves, and certainly not in the presence of our most hallowed saint. Nor of our soon-to-be Katherine' – she smiled, though the expression had a definite edge – 'who must learn of each of us, and of the Orders we represent, and learn well. Perhaps, Sister Avra' – she turned, still with the smile – 'you should speak on this matter yourself, you who will carry her very shield?'

Avra swallowed, her mouth dry and her heart fluttering. The saint was a strong presence, almost a physical touch, as if she could feel the coffin's glow upon her skin. Above it, the cherubs hung watching, their wings stirring the air, their eyes clicking as if they recorded every word.

Carefully, she said, 'Surely, my Sisters, we each follow His path as it has been taught to us?' She was surprised to find authority in her tone – just a touch, but enough. 'Yet Sisters we remain.'

Dominica was nodding at her, the woman's lean, dark face sternly approving. 'Well said, my new Sister. Silvana, you may tell your tale in your proper place. Mina, continue.'

Sister Mina looked around at the five of them, their faces touched by the electro-candle, their hair shining with the light of the saint herself.

'Very well,' she said. 'But I request no further interruption.'

The circle of her Sisters remained quiet, and after a moment, she went on.

'We will make the tyranids come to us,' Katherine said. 'Sister Livia, on my command, give covering fire.'

'Understood.' At the rear, Sister Livia had the heavy bolter aimed backwards down the trench.

'I'm seeing even more,' Xara said. In her hand, the auspex had a ghostlike green glow, diffusing through the mist. More and more blips were covering its screen, flickering in silent eagerness. 'If we're going,' she said, 'we need to go now.'

'Livia, prepare to fire,' Katherine said. 'The rest of you, move on my command. And *fire!*'

Loosed at last, the heavy bolter thundered into a full suppression. Termagants squealed, creeper shredded, flesh and leaf both splashed out across the semi-dark. Ancient gravestones cracked and tumbled. As if compelled by the noises, Katherine broke into a flat run, her shield in front, lifted to catch the things as they threw themselves at the trench. Behind her, Kemra and Xara both ran with bolters in hand, each one watching to her side. Kemra's gait was uneven, but she did not slow down. At the rear, Livia ran backwards, spraying rounds as she went.

Greenery tore; stone exploded into dust and rubble, or crashed to the ground as it split clean in two. Bio-forms screamed and scuttled. There were eruptions of ichor, fluids slicked vine and soil.

At the front, one termagant threw itself at Katherine. She caught it on the shield, then slammed the shield, hard, against the wall of the trench. The creature slid to the floor, its long body shattered, its limbs splayed and broken.

She was still running, already catching the next. Behind her, twin bolters barked fury, one to each side. At the back, the heavy weapon continued to thunder, roaring His rage. The 'gaunts hurled themselves at the Sisters' faces but the squad was moving too fast.

'From the lightning and the tempest!' Sister Xara howled a prayer, and took a leaping creature clean out of the air. Gore splashed against the side of Katherine's faceplate, but she did not slow down. Any moment, that clear space would come into better view. And if there was no tomb in which they could take cover, then at least the creatures would be bereft of their concealment...

But as her view of the crossroads cleared, she saw two things.

The first was the huge side wall of the great cathedral, its glassaic windows shattered, and diamond fragments still dangling from the old lead lighting.

The second was the *beast.*

It was huge, bigger than the scuttling termagants, hunkered

down like some terrible guardian and it stood utterly still, all but indistinguishable from the stone about it. Writhing tentacles hung from its face, tasting the air as if hungry. And it had two great, scythed talons raised above its head.

It hissed at them, a sound like glee made manifest.

'It was waiting for us,' Kemra said, her tone bleak. 'They herded us to it.'

'It matters not,' Katherine responded. 'They will die just the same.'

Behind the thing, the cathedral wall reared like some vast, dark cliff face, its flint cobbles studded with more gravestones, each engraved with names. No light came from within, but the overhead lumens were brighter here, and the Sisters could see the plinths and feet of ancient, broken statues, some of them clearly depicting warriors in armour.

Abandoned it might be, but this place still belonged to Him – and they would purge the xenos from its grounds.

Katherine barked, 'Move to the centre. Then compass defence!'

The shout was almost unnecessary; the Sisters were still moving, still shooting. The heavy bolter was at the wrong side of the formation – Katherine needed the bigger weapon to face the creature – but they could not afford the shuffle, not now. She raised her shield, aimed her bolter over the top, and fired. Around her, muzzle flashes blazed outwards through the fog.

Her shot struck the thing in the shoulder, cracking the carapace, spilling fluid. The beast lowered its head at her and seemed to taste the air with those grotesque tentacles, as if getting the measure of its opponent.

'By the light,' Katherine told it, her voice half threat and half prayer, 'this is hallowed ground, a place of His faithful. You do not belong here, accursed creature. And you will face His wrath!'

Behind and to each side, Kemra and Xara were still shooting, controlled bursts aimed at a sea of incoming, scuttling chitin. The clearing's moss-grown flagstones were alive with movement.

And at the rear...

The heavy bolter barked continuously, loud and sharp, a full and merciless suppression. Knowing her Sisters were safely behind her, Livia moved the weapon in an arc, cutting through swathes of the incoming tyranids. They shrieked and rattled, scuttling sideways, running each other over, but they could not escape the relentless batter of incoming rounds.

Or the rage of the Sisters that accompanied them.

'Our Emperor, deliver us!'

In front of Katherine, the great beast cared not for the deaths of its minions. It uncoiled like some huge spring, raising its spines further and rearing high.

But Katherine did not fear it. Crying defiance in His name, with the words of His Litany on her lips, in her heart, she slammed her shield full into its face. One great scythe, then the other, hit the incoming metal and skidded, screeching as they struck. Like a blade, the awful noise sliced through air and mist and hearing.

'Begone!' she raged at the beast. 'This place holds the sacred lives of Terra's servants, their sacrifice and memory. It is no place for you or your kind. I am Katherine of San Loer, I am His word and His weapon, and I say, by the Emperor, *you will not stand here!*'

In the chapel, Mina's cry rang like a bell tone. It brought a shiver to Avra's skin, a flurry of gooseflesh like ice down her spine. All six of the Sisters had paused at its force, at the passion and rage in Mina's voice. In the light of the electro-candle, her dark skin had the faintest reddish glow, like her very fury made manifest.

Overcome by her own ferocity, the Sister of the Bloody Rose bowed her head. From outside, there came the faintest noise of engines. In the chapel, there was a moment of profound silence.

Then Dominica said softly, 'You do well, my Sister.' Her voice was very deep, a touch like rich cloth. 'You do our blessed saint great honour. We know the tale of the lictor at Jelena, yet to hear it in your voice is to live it once more, to see and purge the xenos taint from its sacred grave-trenches and from those they hold. Take a moment, if that is what you need.'

Mina stayed where she was, her head still bowed. Arabella had tears in her eyes; Avra could feel her own eyes tickling, though she blinked the water away. Silvana gripped Mina's armoured shoulder in a gesture of solidarity.

'Forgive me,' she said. She added no explanation. The words did not need one.

'Between us, my Sister,' Mina answered her, looking up, 'there is nothing to forgive.'

Dominica was nodding, and her face had the faintest edge of a smile. It was stern, almost a smile of pride, and she looked around at the others, watching each in turn.

Like the rest of the Sisters, Mina had removed her gauntlets to eat, and now she picked up one of the Bloody Rose petals in her fingers, holding it so it shone with the faint red glow of her skin. Turning to Avra, she said, 'Thus do I ask you a question, my new Sister, one of several that you will answer, during this service. I seek to understand your fury. Do you celebrate its presence, and use it to serve Him?'

Avra thought back to the schola and to what she knew of each saint – as Saint Lucia had been tormented and had lost her eyes, so Saint Mina had been Alicia Dominica's champion… And it had been Mina's boots in the vision, fighting that terrible, epic duel.

Again, that shiver. The two years of her service seemed suddenly very short, but Avra said, 'I fought the drukhari, within the jungles of Udon Gamma. They took my Sister, and endeavoured to manipulate our squad, to force us to stand down. It was our rage that drove us, and we slew them all, proclaiming victory in His name.'

Beside her, Sister Lucia was nodding, though she did not speak.

'Good,' Mina said. 'In its place, Sister Avra, anger is His greatest blessing, given to us to lift the heart and to make it race, to endure pain, to raise such a cry that He may hear our very voices, if it pleases Him to do so. Your rage will make the foe know fear, and drive them forth.' She too smiled, her square face softening, and held out the petal. 'Hold to your anger.' Her dark eyes searched Avra's face, though if she saw the sparkle of unshed tears, she said nothing, she only went on, 'But never – never – let it consume you. Embrace it, use it as His fuel.' Her dark gaze flashed like a warning. 'Control it.'

'I understand,' Avra said. She took the petal and laid it to her right, like a talisman.

Nodding, not releasing the younger woman's gaze, Mina repeated, 'I am Katherine of San Loer.' Her words were gentle, now, more like song. 'I am His word and His weapon and I say – by the Emperor, you will not stand here.'

Avra nodded, letting the warm flush of Sisterhood spread through her cheeks.

And Mina continued with her story.

The lictor was vicious, and it carried an anger of its own. It was a scout, come seeking knowledge, and to claim the world for its kind. It carried the xenos' hive mind like some great and terrible galactic awareness. And it had lingered here waiting, learning all of Jelena's routes and consuming all of its dead. It knew of every Imperial tomb that pocked the planet's surface, that delved deep, deep into its skull-walled stone bowels. It carried the lore of the grave-world entire, perhaps even the location of the very banner that Katherine sought.

Again, it crashed its spines at Katherine's sacred shield, and again, Katherine threw it back. To her side, Xara was changing her magazine, the motion pure reflex; a second later, she continued to fire. At the rear, the heavy bolter raged with His voice, unstoppable.

But the smaller creatures were still coming, an endless mass of them, flowing like black waters that threatened to engulf the Sisters. Sister Kemra was struggling; Katherine could feel her slump as if the pain in her ankle had become too great to bear. She cursed, briefly, across the vox, stood on the other foot, and kept shooting.

Xara raised a cry, a shout of the ancient hymnal, and the great monster – almost as if it had heard – reared backwards again, ready for another slash. Echoing her Sister, Katherine shot it again and watched as its face exploded, gore covering the front of her helm.

It staggered, but still it did not go down.

Its cracked chitin still gleaming in the wraith-light, one spur slashed sideways; she blocked it, shot the thing again, this time in its belly.

Flesh and carapace burst. Still it did not fall. It hissed, again, that sound so like laughter.

At the rear, the heavy bolter clattered to a stop. 'Cover me,' Livia called, dropping to one knee to change the belt. Both Xara and Kemra followed the order without question, but the things were coming at them faster, now, closing around their feet and knees with pincers and talons and teeth.

'Make for the wall!' Katherine barked.

The three of them moved. Livia, cursing, was trying to feed the ammo belt into the heavy bolter, even as the creatures were scuttling to attack. She kicked at them, vicious and lethal, but the trickle of xenos was rapidly becoming a full-on flow. Stingers lashed at their armour.

And the beast was clever; it could see the opportunity. Even as the Sisters moved, it feinted at Katherine's left, then sprang to her right, intending to go past her.

Seeing it, she raised bolter and shield, aiming a round at its already mangled face, needing to throw it back. She half-caught it, the round hitting its jaw and taking the edge of its face clean off, the shield knocking it sideways. The momentum of its leap interrupted, it fell, squalling and kicking, lashing in fury. Instantly, Kemra turned her bolter on the downed beast, while Livia still covered the rear.

But the thing was smart. And Kemra was on one foot. Even as she aimed the bolter, the great monster slashed her ankle out from under her.

With a startled curse, she fell, half atop the downed lictor. Instantly, the smaller creatures assaulted her, teeth bared as they came. She tried to get her arms under her, her good foot, but the lictor was beneath her still and it drove one talon clean through her armoured back. Her scream was liquid and crystal, and it rang through vox and mist, shattering Katherine's hearing.

At the rear, Livia was up, heavy bolter reloaded and held in both hands. With a cry of hymn and pure outrage, she loosed the full might of the weapon, shattering the swarming creatures in their droves. Katherine was still shooting, her shield taking monsters from the air, even as they leapt.

Kemra, on the ground, was still fighting. Spitting prayer and blood and savagery, unable to shoot the thing as it was still half under her, she pulled a krak grenade from her belt.

'Go!' she said.

Katherine took one look, and understood. She bellowed, 'Move!'

There was no need for explanations, they were Sisters and they understood. The hymns would come, as would the grief, in their proper place. But now, with the lictor held down by Kemra's armour and fury, with the seethe of smaller creatures already trying to claw and stab and bite their way through to flesh, the three of them reached the wall.

Livia spun, the heavy bolter in her hands, ready to clear the space entire, but there was no need.

The detonation was enough.

Mina let the last words fall, and the silence of the little chapel enfolded them all. Outside, the noises of the camp had stopped, though the floodlights were still bright and watchful.

Avra let her tears overspill, understanding that they carried no shame. The light from the coffin bathed them all, touching their faces like gentleness.

'A worthy tale, my Sister,' Dominica said. 'And told as befits a warrior. Though we have heard this tale many times, each time we hear it anew we learn more about its teller, about ourselves, and about our most holy saint.' She looked around at the group, paused at the water that streaked Avra's face.

'There is no need for tears, though we comprehend. And this is a proper place for such things. As Adepta Sororitas, we endure much. And we embrace that endurance that we may praise Him with our fortitude, and with what pain and loss can show us.'

The others murmured agreement. Lucia's face was uplifted, watching the glitter of moonlight, of the tiny, faraway stars. Her augmetic eye glowed with the vehemence of her thoughts, and her scarred expression seemed carved in lines of stone. Avra wondered what she thought, and Dominica, it seemed, had noticed it too.

'What say you, my Sister?' she asked.

'It is time for my tale, I think,' she said. 'As rage and pain are Sisters, and walk often hand in hand.'

'And in both, we praise Him,' Dominica answered. 'Go on, my Sister, and tell us the story of your heart.'

THE TALE OF LUCIA

To Mina's right, Lucia took a moment to inhale, drawing in breath like she could draw in the saint's very light. The cherubim shifted, watching and recalling every movement.

Turning the engraved steel ring on her finger, she said, 'I have already bid you welcome, Sister Avra. I am Sister Lucia of the Valorous Heart. I am strength and clarity. I am the anvil upon which the hammer shatters the enemy. I carry the sins of the Daughters of the Emperor. I comprehend anguish, of the flesh, of the heart and of the mind. I seek no easing to my own suffering. But' – a flare in her augmetic eye – 'I will not tolerate the torture of the innocent, nor the presence of the foe. Like my Sisters, I defend the sanctum, and our most holy saint.'

To her side, stood against the wall, the icon of the Valorous Heart shone with a light like blood. Its glow touched her skin, her armour; glittered from her augmetic.

'Before I begin my tale,' she said, 'please understand' – she smiled at Avra, her scar crinkling – 'that this is perhaps not the tale you expect.' She lowered her chin, and both eyes focused on Avra with a penetrating intensity. 'It is a tale of many layers, and it can teach many things.'

A sudden shout came from outside. A shiver of alertness went through all six Sisters, but the shout did not repeat, and after a moment Lucia went on.

'Pain is both brutal and subtle, my Sisters, and it can be the greatest teacher of all. If we comprehend it fully, it can teach us our strength, our faith... and our limitations.' A flare in her eye, like a warning. 'For we do have them, and it is a wise Sister that learns this, and that works always to best them. And pain can tie us, one to another, with bonds unbreakable. Not by fire, not by fear, not by warfare, not by pride or victory...'

The shout came again, but it had lost its faint timbre of alarm, and the Sisters did not move. All five of them were watching Lucia as she continued.

'And not by *loss*.' The iris of Lucia's augmetic whirred open, a flare of red in its depths. 'And no one understands pain,' she finished softly, 'like the Repentia.'

Repentia.

The word sent the faintest ripple through the chapel's chill. Avra had seen them once, only at a distance, but even that had left an impression, a burn-scar upon her mind. Those Sisters who had committed some unspeakable dishonour, some unthinkable disgrace – they were stripped of their name, their consecrated armour, their blessed bolter...

Before the Emperor, I have sinned...

Many such Sisters disfigured themselves, some act of shame or contrition; they took out their own eyes, carved prayers into their very flesh. And yet, the Repentia were also symbols of hope. Of *redemption.*

The shout came a third time, ending on a distant bark of military laughter. It seemed like another place, another life.

'Tell on, my Sister,' Dominica said softly, her voice very deep. 'And let us learn anew.'

Like Mina, Lucia had taken a moment to consider both herself and her narrative. Now, she drew in a breath.

And began.

* * *

In the very first days of the Order of the Fiery Heart, Saint Katherine made, with His blessing, two great friends. As she founded her Order, striving through its pangs of new growth, these two Sisters were inspired by her example. They stood at her side like pillars of pure tenacity, not only as companions, but as bodyguards and warriors. They loved her, and they resolved to follow her, even unto the darkness itself. Their names were Sarin and Mila.

Sister Sarin gave her life in the defence of the young Order, an act of selflessness and great honour. Yet Sister Mila was touched by a witch, and her spirit faltered. In her shame, she offered her life to Him in the only way that remained to her.

She Repented.

It was a moment unspeakable, and Katherine's heart of fire burned – she missed both Sarin and Mila greatly. But her Sisters both had offered their lives in His honour, and she resolved to carry their memories with her always, to fight her wars to remember them, and to anneal the new Order with the shed blood of its first members.

And so, drawn by a vision from the Emperor, Katherine left the Convent Sanctorum. Commanded always by His light, she crossed the galaxy alone, moving from ship to ship, from world to world – all the way to Segmentum Obscurus and to the fourteen tiny satellites of the great, red star called Thelys. Each of these was little more than a rock, an orbiting, tumbling boulder. Yet these had become the places where the conquered ships of the Imperium, and others, spiralled down to finally die.

They were junkyards, colossal beyond words, and none blessed by Him; they were not Mechanicus worlds, they bore no shrines nor temples, no prayers for quieting damaged machine-spirits, nor for offering them new life in the name of the Omnissiah. They were scavenger worlds, metallic, unhallowed and dark. From ork to heretek, from the minions of the Archenemy to the graceful hunters of the drukhari, opportunists dwelt here. Xenos and cultists skulked among them, seeking wealth and fortune. No one had laid claim to these rocks full of wreckage, yet still, they had many eager denizens.

And so Katherine, drawn by her vision, walked among the vastness of the carcasses they bore. *There is learning here,* He had told her. *And you must find it, my daughter. But your trials will be many.*

Long she walked, seeking His wisdom, the insight for which He had called her. She walked amongst angles impossible, amongst great decks like mountain slopes that reared up and away from her and far into the darkness, amongst twisted, shattered metals and shredded gantries and the remnants of destroyed machinery. She walked amongst huge holes blasted by great battles, amongst the debris of the ammunition. And she prayed for the spirits of these ruined ships, these mighty skeletons, all rust and corrosion. They towered like the greatest of cathedrals, echoing with their own emptiness. And noises ghosted still through their broken veins – hints of combat, cries of rage and pain.

Through all of it, Katherine walked without fear. She held His vision in her heart, and she walked with shield and bolter, searching for the place that He had shown her, and for the knowledge that lay waiting.

What she found, however, was something else.

Twining through the ghost-sounds, flawless in its crystalline harmony and making the very air shiver with its presence, there came song. Familiar, so achingly familiar – the words made her pause, her heart thrilling.

'A spiritu dominatus.'

The hairs on her neck stood on end. The voices carried tones of prayer, of hope, of loss, of courage unending. Amid the tangle of the rotting ships, she could not tell the source of the music, but she *knew* those words, knew them as if they had been engraved upon her skin...

After all, she had been there when they were written.

'Domine, libra nos.'

She prayed, 'Show me, my Emperor. Show me to where my Sisters sing.' And she returned the words of the Litany. 'From the lightning and the tempest...'

At her voice, the song fell from the air like He had torn it down Himself. And there – there! – at the end of a huge and dark and empty tunnel: a single, shining light. It was her vision made manifest, the light from her dream. It was the light He had shown her and, while it was not yet the wisdom she sought, it was as clear as His touch. This was where that vision had begun.

This was her guide.

Bolter and shield still in hand – there were dangers yet – she moved swiftly past the sagging walkways, past the rusting and terrible wounds, past the hatches of the saviour-pods, now half-buried in a century of rock... and there, she found the source of the voices.

Four of her Sisters.

Alone, abandoned. Unbroken.

Yet these Sisters were not in armour, not of any Order she knew. Their bodies were clad only in tunics, each shredded and filthy; their hands carried no bolters, only the great, toothed chainblades known as eviscerators. Each Sister had a shaven head, though their scalps were stubbled and their hair was growing back, patched and awry. And each had symbols carved harsh in her skin – wounds self-inflicted, that, by His decree, would not heal until their bearer died. One had no eyes. Another had no mouth, her lips stitched shut. And at their head...

Katherine's friend, one of the founders of her Order.

Mila.

Katherine beheld her shamed Sister and her heart flared with fire, burned with love and pity and horror. She had not thought to see her again. Not like this.

Upon seeing a Sister in armour, however, Mila had dropped to one knee, her head bowed as was proper. She was a mess, her scalp bloodied, her bared shoulders carved with half-healed wounds, her gore-blotched blade held out before her like an offering. Behind her, surrounded by the shipyard's corroding carcasses, the other three had also dropped to a kneel.

The four of them seemed held together by faith, by sheer determination.

'My Sister,' Katherine said, her tone a whisper. 'Mila.' There was hurt in her voice, for this was truly her family, her closest of friends. Yet she spoke no word of sympathy, only said, 'You fight as He has decreed and have no need for such gestures. You do not kneel to me, only to Him.'

Looking up, Mila met her eyes. And there was realisation like pain in her gaze – her understanding of Katherine's identity. But she said nothing, no word of plea or weakness; she just came to her feet. She shook with fatigue yet she sought no help, and Katherine did not extend her hand. The other three did the same, their eyes downcast.

'You should speak, my Sister,' Katherine said. 'While I understand that such is usually forbidden, there is a thing here that I seek, and I must have your knowledge.'

'Yes, Sister.' Still Mila did not raise her gaze. She was small, fierce and dark, and though her wounds pained her, she made no mention. She said, 'I alone among my Sisters will speak, and I say – we came here to Thelys to offer our lives in His name, and we have seen battle. Our mistress was slain by the enemy, great hounds of flayed flesh that assaulted us from both sides. We are the only survivors.'

'How?' Katherine's comment was pointed, and the dark woman flushed. The other three, their faces carved in scars, still kept their eyes downcast. Shame flushed through them all, tangible as a touch.

'A gantry fell from beneath us, and took us from the fighting. The fall was far, and there was no way to regain the battle, though we made the attempt several times.' She frowned, and Katherine could see the rust marks on her hands. 'We have come in search of death.'

'Then it is His will you are here, my Sister,' Katherine said, an ache in her tone. 'Mila.'

'My name was taken from me,' the Sister replied. 'Now, I am named Rue.'

The name was short and poignant, marking the difference that had come over her Sister. Her dishonour. But Katherine said only, 'And those with you?'

'They are named Grief, Sorrow and Regret. If you will accept us, Sister, we will fight by your side until He grants us – or refuses us – redemption.'

'I will accept you, and gladly,' Katherine said. 'Truly this is a place of darkness, and there is battle enough for all. Yet I would first ask you a question.'

'I will answer.'

'I seek knowledge, and it lies upon a command deck, high in the carcass of the *Blade of Sacrifice*. In my mind, there is an image – its deck is broken, its viewport shattered, its panels long perished. I must find this place that matches my vision.'

'This is the *Blade*,' Rue said. 'Though I know not the layout of the ship.'

'Then we should go upwards,' Katherine told her. 'And seek His blessing.' Katherine wanted to explore the wreckage, seek the place of her vision, but she knew the hounds of the enemy, knew that they had tasted blood.

And she knew that they were coming.

Lucia paused, and the weight of a long silence fell over the Sisters like a sacred cloth. Avra thought of her own vision, of the sheer might of His will made manifest, of the weight and responsibility of His blessing. She wanted to ask Lucia if the saint had felt the same thing, but it seemed impertinent, and she made herself wait.

Lucia's augmetic eye whirred as if she frowned, but none of the Sisters spoke. Even the outside seemed hushed, waiting.

A passing searchlight scudded over the floor, and she continued her tale.

The hounds knew the scent of the Sisters' blood, and of their faith. Such things track with their noses to the metal, never resting. Creatures of the enemy, their teeth are bared and dripping with bloody froth, their gazes like windows to the very warp itself. They ripple with snarl and muscle. And they never stop, never relent.

But Katherine had no fear and the Sisters with her had but one purpose. They hungered for battle, craving to lose their shame in His wrath and glory. His vision and will had brought them together, and they would neither flee, nor falter, in His name.

In His name, they would slay the creatures, here and now.

'Ready your weapons,' Katherine said, as if she were the Repentia mistress, exhorting them to deeds of valour. 'We do not run from these horrors. Instead, we will slay them where they stand. And once they are gone, then I will continue with my search.'

A rasp of eviscerators roared out through the surrounding death. Corpses of metal rang with the noise, a clear and clarion challenge. And again, the Sisters sang, their voices chiming with the grinding of their blades.

And a great snarl came in return.

The hounds had been following them, moving swiftly, pelting down the tilting tunnels, their slavering jaws agape. They heard the challenge and they set up a yammer, a howl of defiance that bit at the ears like red-hot teeth, that filled the mind with a tumble of skulls, with pools of gore still steaming. Fear washed ahead of them like a great, red wave, but the Sisters stood like a fortress of faith, indomitable. And the fear wave broke as it hit them, shattering to a splash and leaving them standing untouched, their blades still screaming.

The hounds closed eager, their eyes afire. The Sisters ran at them, still singing, carried by the word of His redemption.

'From the begetting of daemons!'

Katherine ran with them, taking shots with her bolter before the battle was joined. And then everything was a fury of tumbling flesh and claws and the slash and roar of the eviscerators, and the song became a shout and there were screams of pain and rage and of sheer, exultant savagery. Using her shield, she threw the hounds back, twice, three times, but each time they leapt forwards once more. One of the Sisters fell, her throat torn out by great white teeth, then another, a hound with its jaws across her eyeless face. But the hounds, too, were falling; they detonated in flashes of red fluid, in hisses of steam, and their remains burned the Sisters' exposed flesh, making them turn and slash in response...

Lucia stopped to draw breath. The little chapel was utterly silent, filled with the images of the fight, with the glow of the saint herself, the very warrior of whom they spoke. Even the outside seemed to have fallen quiet, as if captivated by the tale.

When the battle was over, three of the Repentia lay slain, their lives offered to Him and their redemption complete. Mila, however, was still standing, yet unaccepted by the Golden Throne. Her wounds were severe – bites to her legs and arms that bled copiously, making her stagger where she stood, her own lifeblood pooling at her feet. But Mila did not fall, and upon her scarred face was an expression of great humiliation.

'I should have perished,' she said, her eyes still downcast. 'But

I will not die of injury, of pollution, or of blood loss. I will die fighting, my blade in my hand.' A flash of her dark eyes, looking up from under her brows. 'I will attain my redemption, with His blessing.'

'There are battles aplenty, my Sister,' Katherine told her, again. 'We will seek them out even as I seek the wisdom that has brought me here. Let us find the command deck, and we will find your death as we go.'

And so, they walked. Before long, Mila began to falter. Her own red footprints followed her, counting down to her imminent failure. She shook with pain, but would suffer no sanguinator. Nor would she lean upon Katherine for support, and her hand did not release her blade. Soon, her agony became as loud as a cry. Katherine walked beside her friend, her own heart aching with grief, wanting to reach out to her, to offer her strength, to hold her by the elbow and keep her on her feet. To ensure that she made that final fight, and was able to perish in His grace.

The pain of Mila's wounds was terrible for Katherine to behold. Yet the pain of her failure – that was almost too much. For Mila to die, on her knees and without that final battle... Her Repentance would be denied.

Still they continued, climbing higher and higher through the ruin of the *Blade*. It creaked at them, stirred by the cold winds of the rock upon which it lay. In places, panels and wires sparked as they passed, as if the great ship's machine-spirit, also, was in pain and begging for their help. The ghost-noises continued, though no foe came close.

Mila staggered, her legs refusing to hold her. She made no word of complaint, just muttered the words of the Litany like a focus, a steel-cold grip of faith that held her to herself, enabled her to put one foot in front of the other. She held her blade tightly, though its point was no longer held high. And the hurt in Katherine's heart was like a tear, widening with every step that her Sister took.

Why had they not been attacked? It was His will, and they had only to bear it.

And then, Mila fell. Forwards, onto her hands and knees. She did not release her blade – such would have been a travesty, a sin beyond words – but her free hand left a perfect, bloody print upon the metal.

Katherine stopped, her blood burning. The bloody hand was a sign, an image from her vision. They were almost to the command deck. To the place of her vision, and to the knowledge that she sought, in His name.

'You must stand,' she said, her voice an order. 'You are Adepta Sororitas, a Sister of Battle. You are His daughter, a warrior trained, and you will *not* perish upon your knees!' She held out her hand, but Mila forestalled her.

'Do not,' Mila said. 'I am Repentia. I am forsaken. I will do this alone, or I will perish without His forgiveness.' She glanced up, and Katherine could see the face of her friend, see the battles they had undergone together and the memories that she had carried forth to her wars. The tear in her heart grew wider; she wished only to help, to reach out for those past days, to share them once more, to ensure that Mila attained His grace and met her death upon her feet.

With her free hand, Mila reached out for the edge of a gantry, and began to pull herself up. As she did so, she recited still the words of the Litany, and never had Katherine heard them with such timbre, never had she felt them like blows against her skin. Each one was like a drumbeat, like a shard of hard glassaic, spat through gritted teeth…

'Domine… Libra… Nos…!'

Each syllable was a fusion, its heat making Mila not resist her pain, but become one with its blessing. Allowing her to accept it, make it a bastion against her weakness, become charged with it, like adrenaline; use it to forge herself anew and to bring steel to her flesh and to her mind. Watching her rise back to her feet, Katherine felt a rush of pure wonder, of awe at His grace made manifest. She prayed, not the Litany, but words that tumbled with respect. She understood how pain gave resolution, but this... this was beyond her. This was something almost more than human.

Truly, this was His blessing.

'I will stand,' Mila said, 'until I cannot.'

And the words went through Katherine like a blade, making the tear in her heart ever wider.

Lucia paused for a second sip of water. Not one of the Sisters had breathed a word, though Avra knew that parts of her own Order had taken those very words and had made of them a symbol, a Litany of Resilience. Understanding their origin felt like a blessing in itself.

She watched Lucia as the woman continued.

Understanding now, Katherine did not offer her friend help. Mila walked like some Mechanicus creation, one foot before the other, relentless, driven, automatic. Fuelled by pain, she used its very presence to push herself forwards. Prayers came from her like sparks from gears, erratic sprays of words, but like her walking, they did not cease.

And Katherine felt her Sister's agony. It was empathy, and hope. It was their mutual days from the earliest wars of their Order. It was their training, and their cathedral hymns, and their evening games of Tall Card. It was the chiming of their laughter, and their voices raised in His praise.

And so, by His light and guidance, they at last found the metal ladder and the command deck of the *Blade*.

* * *

As she spoke, Lucia smiled at Avra. 'No words, my Sisters, can describe the sensation of finding His vision made manifest. It is a key in a lock, a touch of pure wonder, the utter perfection of His truth. And the command deck exactly matched Katherine's memory – as if she walked in a place of her own mind and heart. She had never seen it before, and yet she remembered it – its floor tilted, its control panels broken and hanging, the armaglass of its viewport shattered, and the precise lines and angles of its external view. We have known such moments, ourselves, have we not? Truly, they are the touch of His grace.'

'Tell on, my Sister,' Dominica said softly. 'We understand.'

Through the command deck's broken oculus, Katherine could see the surface of the tiny, nameless moon, black and pitted with craters. And buried within it, the pieces of all those shattered ships, great carcasses tumbled nose down, their hard angles blotting the faint light of Thelys' even tinier satellites. The thin layer of atmosphere was breathable, but only just, and long shadows moved across the deck, making its uprights leer like phantoms. But the memory, the knowledge that He had brought her here to find? While the surround matched her vision, she still did not understand.

And her searching was interrupted as Mila stumbled again to her knees. As if the thread of her endurance had finally snapped, she could not stand. She tried, tried again, attempting to lever herself upright with her eviscerator, but her legs simply would not hold her, her blood loss too severe.

Katherine had stimms, but she knew that Mila would refuse their help, just as she had refused everything else.

'Tell me,' Mila said, her voice hoarse. 'Tell me that you have found what you seek?'

Tell me that I have not striven in vain. Tell me that there is hope.

Katherine stood, carefully looking around at the ruined deck, at the command chair, at the walls of panels, the prayers and diagnostics, but nothing looked or felt right. There was something she was missing. Something–

The hound-snarl made them both turn round.

It was only the one, shoulders low and body skulking, but Mila's blood covered its snout and tongue, telling them that it had followed her very footprints, tracking her by the path of her pain. And one was enough.

Katherine raised her bolter, but Mila said, 'Do not.' There was a note of relief in her voice, a faint ring of triumph. 'This beast is surely the last survivor, and on this occasion, it is welcome.'

Understanding, Katherine let the weapon drop. She prayed aloud, her voice ringing through the ruins. And Mila joined her, their voices twining as once they had, so many years before. With an effort that made Katherine's heart rend all but in half, Mila finally forced herself to her feet. Held upright by her song alone, by the words of empathy and shared pain, she raised the eviscerator. Starting its furious rasp, she faced the beast.

Katherine stood back, the bolter still in one hand, her shield still held in the other, and watched.

The hound leapt.

Incredible, impossible, Mila slashed at the leaping creature. Her effort made her totter, and she missed it; it landed behind her and spun, its claws tick-tacking on the metal, its eyes afire, its teeth bared.

But Mila did not fear it, and while she ached for the clamp of its jaws, she would not, could not surrender. She bared her teeth in a snarl of her own, shouted the names of her fallen Sisters, of Grief and Sorrow and Regret, of other names that Katherine did not know. The beast watched her, sly and narrow-eyed, as if picking up the scent of her exhaustion. It slunk in low, and Katherine's hands tightened upon her weapons. But she could do nothing. In His name, her only task was to stand back, and to let her Sister, her friend, die.

Die, at the teeth of the enemy.

The hound leapt again, its jaws agape. Mila's grinding blade slashed, catching it on its shoulder, but it was not enough, not enough…

And in that moment, watching its jaws close upon her Sister's throat, so His understanding came to her. The final piece of her vision fell into place as if completing some great puzzle. This – this – was what He had brought her here to find. She was not here to discover some relic or remnant, but to learn a lesson of pain and truth.

As Mila's body fell, released in honour to the Throne, and as Katherine shot the last surviving hound, singing as it skidded and was gone in a gout of blood and steam, so she lifted her voice in celebration.

In His name.

'In His name.'

In the chapel, the Sisters echoed the blessing. Dominica was singing, her voice very soft but her rich contralto humming strong through the tiny building. Avra did not know the hymn, but Arabella joined her, a pure and crystalline soprano that made shivers flare down the younger Sister's forearms.

Lucia smiled at them both, speaking in rhythm with their song, 'As Sisters,' she said, 'we carry many weapons. We carry our bolt pistols and our sacred relics. We carry rage' – she glanced at Mina – 'and we carry other things within our hearts, each of which we will reveal, in turn. But pain…' She stopped, touching her augmetic eye. 'I was tortured by the aeldari, upon the fallen hive world of Mastark VI. Like Saint Lucia herself, I lost an eye to my tormentors and I did not surrender. And it was that very torment that blessed me with His vision, and that brought me here. I have served Him in this march for almost ten Solar years, and I have told this tale a total of six times, including today. My Sisters…'

Lucia paused, and carefully removed the steel ring that she bore upon her finger, holding it up to the light.

And in that moment, watching its jaws close upon her Sister's throat, so His understanding came to her. The final piece of her vision fell into place as if completing some great puzzle. This – this – was what He had brought her here to find. She was not here to discover some relic or remnant, but to learn a lesson of pain and truth.

As Mila's body fell, released in honour to the Throne, and as Katherine shot the last surviving hound, singing as it skidded and was gone in a gout of blood and steam, so she lifted her voice in celebration.

In His name.

'In His name.'

In the chapel, the Sisters echoed the blessing. Dominica was singing, her voice very soft but her rich contralto humming strong through the tiny building. Avra did not know the hymn, but Arabella joined her, a pure and crystalline soprano that made shivers flare down the younger Sister's forearms.

Lucia smiled at them both, speaking in rhythm with their song, 'As Sisters,' she said, 'we carry many weapons. We carry our bolt pistols and our sacred relics. We carry rage' – she glanced at Mina – 'and we carry other things within our hearts, each of which we will reveal, in turn. But pain…' She stopped, touching her augmetic eye. 'I was tortured by the aeldari, upon the fallen hive world of Mastark VI. Like Saint Lucia herself, I lost an eye to my tormentors and I did not surrender. And it was that very torment that blessed me with His vision, and that brought me here. I have served Him in this march for almost ten Solar years, and I have told this tale a total of six times, including today. My Sisters…'

Lucia paused, and carefully removed the steel ring that she bore upon her finger, holding it up to the light.

'As our blessed saint learned that pain comes in many guises, not just physical, but the pain of empathy, the pain of helplessness, the pain of grief, the pain of watching a loved one die… so we must embrace that pain. Physical pain is both the easiest and the hardest to bear. Like rage, it will anneal you and lift you to His grace. But shared pain, pain of the heart? Ah, now that is much harder.'

She held the ring out to Avra, who took it and turned it over. It bore more prayers, inscribed about its inside, and a tiny needle-sharp point that flicked in and out, depending upon how the thing was turned.

'Many of my Order bear these,' she said, 'as reminders that He will place great demands upon us, but also as reminders that we will stand fast in the face of those demands. Pain is focus, my Sister. It purifies us, and brings us to His grace.'

As she finished, the last notes of the Sisters' hymn died away, their echoes dancing out through the tiny building. Somewhere outside, engines barked and roared.

Dominica said, 'You have a query?'

'I…'

Briefly, Avra wondered how Dominica knew, but the bonds between the Sisters had been shown to be strong, and Dominica's perception was indeed powerful. Greatly daring, Avra gave the coffin a glance, looking at the glow of its light.

'Your visions, my Sisters. They have brought you here? All of you?' She found herself struggling with understanding that the bones in that coffin were not just an artefact; they were the very saint herself, the woman, the Sister that had walked these tales. That had founded her very Order and had carried her wars to the stars.

Dominica said, 'When one of our march is called to His side, another always takes her place. And yes, His visions bring us, bind us, and unite us.' There was something in her tone, some faint flex of tension, and Avra remembered the knowledge that Dominica was said to bear. That was one question, however, that she was not going to ask.

Instead, she said, 'I saw Sisters, kneeling upon a flagstone floor. They were–'

She couldn't finish. She knew what she had seen, but the enormity of it was almost too much.

'You must embrace the understanding.' The voice was Silvana's, that faint rasp of a woman unused to speaking. 'You have heard tales of rage, and of pain, and of how they are His blessing.'

Avra saw her catch Dominica's eye and the oldest Sister give a faint nod – permission.

'Sometimes,' Silvana said, 'new Sisters can be overwhelmed with the sheer size of this task. Not the wars that we spearhead, but the honour that we carry.' Her blue eyes were sharp. 'And you must stand to that honour, Sister, bear it without doubt, without faltering.'

Avra nodded. 'I understand.'

'So you do, or you would not be here.' Silvana's lips twitched.

'Tell your tale, Sister,' Dominica said. 'The light rises, and muster draws ever closer.'

THE TALE OF SILVANA

Kneeling to Lucia's right, Silvana's armour gleamed with the reflected light of the Simulacrum of the Argent Shroud, now folded in her lap. Her face seemed serene, yet it carried strong, hard angles, lines like absolute fearlessness.

'First, Sister, I will speak my welcome.' Her voice was soft, but it had a constant, odd scratch, almost as if something in her throat were rusting. 'I am Silvana, of the Argent Shroud. I was the first martyr, offering my life to ensure Dominica's survival, and it is my sacred task to take action in His name, pushing ever for the heart of the encroaching darkness. Too many lives are lost through chatter, through procrastination, through the inability to make a decision. You will observe that I do not like wastage, of either words or time. While it will be Mina's task to ensure your basic training, it is mine to make the larger military assessments. It is not our task to fight, but fight we will, if He decrees it necessary.'

'I understand,' Avra said.

'Perhaps you should voice your question, Sister,' Dominica said.

'My question.' Silvana appeared to think for a moment, though Avra would have guessed that the questions, like the ceremony, had been performed many times.

Outside, a sergeant bellowed for quiet; from somewhere, a raucous voice told him what he could do with his quiet, and Avra's lips twitched. She stopped herself smiling, schooling her expression to a proper reverence.

'My Sisters,' Silvana said, 'have spoken about rage, and pain. So my question to you is this – tell me of your courage, Sister. Tell me of your initiative.'

Once again, Avra cast her mind back to the schola, to her tutor and her data-slate, to the legends that she and her fellow novices had learned. Every Sister – be she Militant, Hospitaller, Dialogus or Famulous – was taught His lore, lessons of honour, discipline and courage. It was only when you were submerged in the font's holy waters, and then donned the sacred garments of your Order, that the greater legends were revealed.

Avra said, 'We faced the necrons upon Psamitek. The layers of their tombs stretched down to the heart of the planet's carven stone. They came upon us from a hundred positions and we could not hold against them. But, with my Sisters, I struck at their very heart, at the deathplace of their overlord. And thus, they faltered.'

'A good example,' Silvana answered. Her voice still burred, but there was a kindness to it, something different to Mina's clipped, practical tones, and yet different again to Lucia's gentle severity. A sense of kinship rose in Avra's heart and she closed her eyes, offering a prayer of thanks for the courage of these Sisters that seemed so powerful and yet so human.

'In my middle to later years,' Silvana said, 'I was an abbess at the Schola Progenium, honoured by Him to assist in the education of our younger Sisters Militant.' In the soft light from the Shroud, the lines on her face were shadowed and she looked almost girlish, but her stance and shoulders bore the weight of both wisdom and age. 'I used to say to my novices – we are Sisters both of, and in, Battle. We must learn structure, and manoeuvre, and warfare. We must learn restraint, and self-control. With prayer and faith, we must learn to use our anger, and our pain, to further His glory.'

The odd catch in her voice had faded as she spoke, and her tones became almost rhythmic, as if she recited some great poem or saga, some lore of times ancient.

'Yet there are times when a Sister finds herself bereft of such structure, or when she must rely on the keen edge of her daring. And this is the story that is mine to tell. A story of the Wars of Faith, of course, but a story of our saint's great and audacious courage.'

'We all have courage, my Sister.' There was the faintest catch to Mina's voice, a sound like an old disagreement, but Silvana only smiled at her. When Mina said nothing further, the older Sister continued.

'We have all seen battle against orks, have we not?' She raised a silver-grey eyebrow at Avra, who shook her head, though she remembered her classes well enough. 'They are everywhere,' Silvana continued, 'like some fanged and fecund plague. As fast as we purge them from one place, they invade from another, all noise and commotion. Their engines are loud, their voices coarse, their relentlessness – frankly – exhausting.' Again, that flicker of a smile. 'And, my Sisters, discipline is as alien to them as it is doctrine to us.'

Her smile moved back to Mina, less like an apology and more like an act of inclusion – a reminder that their shared Sisterhood was far stronger than any old flaring of discord. Avra was finding that she liked this quiet older Sister, with her voice still flowing like a song.

'And so,' Silvana said, 'my tale takes us to the great invasion of Tirzah Kai, and to orks without number. Stamping and shouting, mocking and murdering, flinging filth and fire. And slaying and eating the men, women and children of the planet's towns and villages – in truth, no words can do complete justice to the horrors of a greenskin invasion. Kai was a small world, little able to defend itself. It bore only the crudest of weapons and armour.

Its people worshipped an icon of His glory so ancient that it no longer even carried His face.'

She turned her own up to His likeness, her expression almost penitent. Her lips moved in a silent prayer, perhaps for forgiveness, and she went on. 'Yet He had blessed the world of Kai with a dark and buried wealth – with deposits of promethium deep within its core. And so, in His name, came the Adeptus Mechanicus, to build mines and to teach industry, and with them came the ever-proud soldiers of the Imperium, mustered to hold back the xenos tide.

'And at their core, even as we are today, stood Katherine herself, and her Sisters of the Fiery Heart.'

Silvana's blue gaze stopped on Avra, and the younger woman found herself blushing, though she was not sure why. Perhaps it was just the weight of the drawn parallel, and the responsibility that she now bore. It seemed that all of her new Sisters were insistent upon this point, each in her own way.

She accepted it, admitted her humility, set her shoulders to carry it.

And Silvana began her story.

Katherine and her Sisters were upon the world of Kai, stationed with company command, and at the very heart of the Imperium's counter-assault. Over them, warships streaked the skies with fire, their debris tumbling like meteors, amid rains of molten metal. Much of the planet's surface was a great ash-plain, pocked with craters. Clouds of grey dust billowed constantly skywards, filling the overheated air. Amid this endless, churning powder rose dark, rocky islands upon which dwelt Kai's people, defending themselves from not only orks, but also from the local predators: the vicious, many-legged carnivores that stalked relentlessly about them.

The xenos invasion was monstrous, a clash of human and greenskin in a vicious and terrible confrontation.

At the heart of the battle, Katherine and her Sisters defended Camp Righteous. Their armour was sealed against the clouds of ash, they bore flamer and bolter and hymnal, and they inspired the Militarum to greater and greater efforts. The rage of the orks came at the fortified camp many times, but the greenskins were erratic and unruly and their attacks fell apart, even as the Sisters fought them back. With Katherine's shield as their banner, the defenders held the camp against invasion.

But one does not presume to interpret the will of the Emperor, and there are times when He calls upon us in ways we cannot anticipate.

Silvana paused, again looking up at His likeness and sketching the sign of the fleur-de-lys upon the front of her armour. Outside, the ever-watchful Sentinels were moving again, and the faint whine of their servos crept through the chapel, reminding all six Sisters that their time was short.

Picking up the pace of her recitation, Silvana kept speaking.

The onslaught of the greenskins was unceasing, their numbers infinite. They soon surrounded Camp Righteous, spreading out to threaten camps Vengeance and Retribution, forcing their way even to the mineheads. And they were not only on foot. Their metal contraptions rattled and clanked, belching forth smoke and flames. There were bikes and trikes and buggies, all rasping with eager rage. There were larger contraptions that carried gleefully chanting orks into battle. There were other vehicles, larger still, that carried great siege weapons – unreliable yet devastating. And their constant roar ran around and around, the noise as unrelenting as the shouting of the orks themselves.

The soldiers were exhausted, and they began to make mistakes.

* * *

Listening, Avra found herself caught by the story. One of her squadmates had told her of orks, though not in planetwide numbers; the Sister had been aboard an old hulk, searching for an injured member of another Order... This was the first of the tales with which she could really identify, and it called to her heart with a thrum like Silvana's voice.

Told her that she understood this.

Could do this. In His name.

Faced by the soldiers' exhaustion, Katherine made a choice. A cadre of Sisters with her, she sought the Militarum commander and told him her intention.

'We must end this,' she said. 'I will take a small force and we will locate the warboss. When we have slain the creature, you will coordinate all three camps for a counter-attack, and the rest of this assault will falter.'

The commander was wise – he made no argument. He commanded his men and women to commence a full bombardment, every camp raining death upon its besiegers. With the orks thus distracted, Katherine and her Sisters departed in silence and in stealth. Their armour black against the planet's ash-filled night, they moved as silently as Sisters can, taking a careful route through the greenskin horde...

'Do you have something to say, my Sister?'

As Silvana had told her tale, Mina's expression had become steadily grimmer, darkening to a thundercloud. Dominica watched them both, saying nothing, but Avra was beginning to understand the odd, old flex of tension between these two Sisters. The Adepta Sororitas did not refuse to face the enemy – such was cowardice, unthinkable – and to 'sneak' through the greenskins' camp was tantamount to blasphemy. It refused their honour and calling, their role in His wars. It sent a shock through her blood, though she said nothing.

The others, it seemed, also understood. Lucia commented softly, 'Be at ease, my Sisters. We have all seen battlefields, and we all drive for victory. Sometimes He calls for extreme measures.'

'Such have been my schola teachings,' Silvana continued, her smile back in place. The light from the Shroud bathed her with an odd serenity, her armour glittering like black water. With a questioning glance at Mina, who held her gaze but said nothing, she went on.

The Sisters' silence was necessary – they moved to target only the warboss. His throne and minions were easy to spy – and to hear – through the morass. Orks lead from the front, the biggest always at their head, and they did not have to go far to discover him.

Blessed by the Emperor, the Sisters moved without detection. The orks were busy cavorting, shouting and fighting. They were loud, boastfully dismissive of the Imperium's barrage, of the tumbled fragments of the shattered ships, of the occasional too-curious predator. They saw only their own noisome machines, banged together from oddments of metal. They burned great campfires, their fuel carried by grots. They rode their noisy vehicles in wide circles, making clouds from the dust. In places, they had captured defenders and predators both, and the Sisters' stomachs turned. Yet He had bid that Katherine seek their warboss and she commanded her squad onwards. They dealt neither wrath nor mercy, and they eased carefully through the greenskin horde. By His blessing, they were not assailed.

Soon, they spied their target: the warboss himself, sitting upon a great and soiled throne. He was the loudest of all, and garishly clad. His shoulders and belly were vast, his fangs yellow and rotted. A line of skulls hung about his neck, and chunks of metal glinted in his ears. Even as the Sisters closed upon his location, they could hear him bellow the words of the orks' familiar chant.

But he was also wily, a sly intelligence in his burning red eyes.

As Katherine came close, so he pointed one muscled arm and roared, 'Humies!'

The word echoed loud through the little chapel and Silvana paused. The others had a tight feeling of anticipation, caught by the tension of the tale. Outside, the Sentinels had stopped again and the air was sharp and still.

But Silvana said, 'I, too, have faced orks. In great numbers. I was injured in mind and in body, and hence He led me to take my place at the schola, to teach a new generation of Sisters. Yet the injuries inflicted upon me would not leave me in peace, and while my body healed, my mind did not. And He came to me with the vision we have all seen, of the chapel and of our greatest Sisters kneeling within, and so I came here, back to the battle, to confront my horrors and to heal that mental scar.' She touched the Shroud like it was a talisman. 'Sister Avra, our new Katherine, be not shamed by our disagreements. As we fight together, each defending the Sisters to her sides, so do our skills and disciplines overlap and balance each other. Sister Mina is a proud warrior, she faces the foe head-on. It is my task to think in… broader terms. Sister Arabella will tell you more of our harmonies, but I say this – we overlap, each skill in its turn. And there are no odds that we cannot face, in His name. No force that can withstand us, in His grace. No enemy that we cannot defeat, in His blessing. We stand in the light of sacred Terra, and we bear the saint herself, her shield to defend us, her very sarcophagus to lead us – and each and every army with whom we stand – to victory. As you listen to these tales, remember that she who fought the Wars of Faith – she is *here*. With us. It is her glow that touches our armour. Her very strength that we bear.

'In His name.'

'In His name.' The Sisters repeated the blessing, the whisper shivering round the chapel like a faint breath of wind.

Mina was nodding, her expression now serious, approving. Dominica's lean, dark face had softened to a smile, and Arabella almost shone, her eyes as bright as electro-candles.

Lucia said, 'I hear you, my Sister. Injuries of the mind can be the worst of all to bear, but still, we fight on.'

'We fight on,' Silvana repeated, agreeing. 'No matter what the odds, no matter how deep the darkness, we fight on.'

She smiled, and continued.

And so, Katherine confronted her target. There, alone in the centre of that mighty greenskin horde, so our saint and her Sisters raised their weapons. They closed ranks, shoulder to shoulder. While they were vastly outnumbered, He was with them; He had called them to this very duty, and their objective was not to fight the army in its entirety, but to execute its boss. And to perish in so doing, if that be His will.

Seeing them, the boss was on his feet and stamping down from his throne. He waved his minions back, leering in horrific and toothsome glee. He picked up his huge axe in one massive, warted hand. He would slay these interlopers himself. A show of strength.

The Sisters confronted him, weapons raised. As they did so, the greenskins about them gathered into a ring, fangs bared and weapons bristling. Word of the Sisters' presence was flowing out through the ork camp like some susurrus of scorn, and more and more of the creatures were abandoning their posts and incoming, jostling and shoving to be able to see.

They fought amongst themselves, snarling and barging, but the warboss bellowed and they stopped, their fangs all bared. He came forth, opened his jaws as if to speak.

Katherine did not wish to hear his words. She barked the order, and the Sisters raised their bolters and opened fire.

But the boss was quick, fast indeed for a beast of such size.

Dismissive of the Sisters' weapons, he moved sideways, then lunged forth, slashing the axe at Katherine's shoulder, and strong enough to slice her through to the hip.

But the axe hit the shield with a great and mighty clang, and the greenskin crowd set to whooping and jeering. The sounds of engines and clattering metal had stopped, and more and more of the creatures were approaching.

With a greenskin's poor discipline, they had moved away from the camps, coming to see the fight for themselves. The commander's bombardment had ceased, and that, of course, had been a part of Katherine's plan. Over the vox, she said, 'We must buy the Militarum time, allow them to fully muster. Hold your fire, and we will play this warboss' game.'

The ring of greenskins was slavering and baying, but the boss had ordered them back. And Katherine's Sisters, too, ceased their assault, forming to a compass defence and watching in every direction.

Katherine herself challenged the warboss. And he grinned, his fangs still covered in shreds of flesh and gore.

He moved like some huge predator, his ears jangling with steel tokens. Around him, campfires glittered like gems, and fragments of burning metal still streaked down through the sky, like meteors of destruction. Katherine faced the huge beast without fear. Fastening her bolter, she drew her sword and, using her shield to defend herself, she cut at his shoulders and face. But the beast moved back, his face a foul and mocking leer.

The Sisters began to sing and the orks became louder, drowning out the hymnal with their rough, ragged chant. But the Sisters did not stop, their vox-casters chiming loud from their armour, and the orks faltered at their words, as if His very voice sang with them, bass and deep beneath their sacred harmonies.

Angered at his troops' weakness, the warboss slashed and slashed again. Katherine blocked with her blade and her shield. The creature was strong, but her sacred armour and strength were enough to withstand his brutality. She sought gaps in his defence, struck through them at the thing's muscle and hide. Yet the ork was armoured with heavy plates of rusted steel, and it did not look like he would slow.

Back and forth they fought, sword striking axe, axe striking shield. The beast used the claws upon his free hand to slash at her face and throat; he moved the axe to both hands and spun it like a staff to strike at her with the butt. But every time, her shield was too swift and she blocked the incoming attack, her feet skidding in the ash at the power of the ork's blows.

The fight continued, and the singing grew louder. The orks began to fidget, to glance at one another and snort with laughter. Blow and counter-blow struck and clashed. Katherine's armour took strikes from the axe; they were enough to almost knock her from her feet, but she stayed upright and fought on. She struck at her opponent's face, her blade taking one of the warboss' flaming red eyes.

At this, the boss stopped, blood seeping down his face and over his fangs. His own forces were starting to mock him, shuffling and grinning and nudging. He was losing status, and he knew it. Stepping back, he turned his head, ogling Katherine from his one good eye. He continued to leer, fangs bared; he ran his tongue over his own blood.

In the vox, Katherine said, 'We are out of time. Commander, are your troops set?'

The commander's voice responded, *'Yes, ma'am. Upon your command.'*

Once more, she drew her bolter.

At the motion, the warboss roared, 'Boyz! We *gets* 'em!'

Released to combat, the mass of slobbering greenskins threw themselves forwards. Few had firearms, fewer still the space to shoot, but that did not stop them. They loosed their rounds, injuring themselves and each other, stamping and trampling in their eagerness to get at the Sisters. They pulled each other down to the flattened-hard ash.

The boss himself advanced, still bellowing, kicking the smaller orks out of his way. Katherine barked her orders over the vox, one to the commander, one to her Sisters, but the Sisters' drill was good, their unity strong. They needed no commands to enact His will.

And they opened fire.

The boss roared as the first wave of xenos went down in a hail of rounds and flame, in explosions of flesh and blood and gore. The wave behind them staggered and slipped, falling over their own dead and dying. Uncaring, driven by savagery, they stomped their fellows down into the ash and came onwards, their eyes and weapons glittering. The hard pulse of their chant had grown louder, now.

Snarling, shrugging off the bolter fire, the warboss raised the axe over his head and brought it down, two-handed. It was a mighty blow, and it hit Katherine's shield with a *clang* that made her ears ring.

But the Sisters fought on. There were only four of them, Fiery Hearts all, and the whoosh and roar of one Sister's flamer detonated the ammo of the closest ork. The explosion was blinding, deafening. It bathed the boss in fire and blasted the smaller creatures back.

It was not enough.

The orks broke over the Sisters like an angry green tide, its foam-spray grey as ash. Yet the four of them stood like the very rock of Camp Righteous itself. Firing until their magazines ran down, they fought with fists and feet, and they stayed upright amid the rush. Katherine saw this from the corner of her eye; she was still focused on the boss, fulfilling His command and her own mission. She would behead this xenos army before she perished.

A mob of gretchin, each one no higher than her hip, were coming for her – more afraid of the boss than they were of the Sister. With a shout of prayer, she let off a full suppression with her bolter, blasting them backwards. Battering one out of the way with a slam of her shield, another with a well-aimed foot, she broke through their rank with ease.

Learning their folly, they fled, squeaking, and she faced the warboss once more.

In one part of her warrior's mind, she was still aware of her Sisters behind her, of the heave and struggle of the impossible odds they faced. She was also aware of the commander, barking vox-orders and deploying his troops. There was the rumble of tank tracks, the boom and thump of artillery. Fire streaked the sky.

At the back of the greenskin horde, some creatures were bawling warnings. Engines were coughing back to life, rasping into motion as the besiegers realised their mistake.

The boss snarled, smart enough to understand that he'd been tricked.

Katherine shot him, her full rate of fire, but he seemed indomitable, the rounds hitting the plates of his chest with myriad detonations. He juddered, but walked through her attack as if propelled by some demented, heretic belief. A round in his shoulder blasted flesh and bone; still, he did not stop. A round hit his upper arm, shredding the muscle; he moved his axe back to a one-handed grip. His blood still slid down his face from the missing eye, but he did not care. The vast ork kept coming.

And then, her bolter clanked empty.

Behind her, her Sisters were singing, tight notes of pure fury. They could not win this, but they would offer their lives in His service.

A cold hand in her heart told her: this boss was too powerful. She may fail this mission. And such was not permitted. In His name.

Over the vox, she said, 'Sisters, re-form to attack pattern zero-one. We will alpha strike the warboss. Weapons ready, and on my mark–'

'Which begs the question,' Mina said, cutting hard across Silvana's tale, 'why they did not do this in the first instance. If their target was to slay the boss, why did they not simply open fire? You are not telling me that one duels a xenos with honour?' The flare of disagreement was back in her tone.

'I said nothing of honour, my Sister.' Silvana's response carried its burr like an edge of annoyance. 'They bought the commander time to muster, and to hit the ork horde in the back.'

'Such is not the duty of a Sister of Battle–'

'Sisters, please.' Arabella tried to quell the disagreement, but Dominica caught the younger Sister's gaze and stopped her with a pointed look.

Avra looked from face to face around the group. She could sense that this was an old issue, resurfaced once more to accompany the familiar tale.

'We know the answer,' Dominica said. 'We have had this discussion many times.' There was authority in her tone, telling the Sisters to behave themselves. 'With the passage of vast time, so battle-stories are retold, and knowledge is distilled. Fact becomes tale, tale becomes legend, legend becomes myth. Our Sisters Dialogus are guardians of His sacred lore, but *we*' – the word was pointed – 'we are warriors. And it is not our place to question the sagas of our saint, whatever they may be. It is our place to learn from them. You, my Sister,' she said to Mina, 'you are a warrior without peer, a soldier foremost, and your thoughts are forthright, honest and true.

But you' – she directed this to Silvana – 'you are also a tutor. And you bring us a tale of great boldness, of an action beyond a Sister's usual discipline, and this, also, has its place.' Her tone was a warning. 'Be this fact, or legend, or somewhere in between, it exists to illuminate an aspect of ourselves. And, my Sister,' she said to Mina, 'we do not only think in straight lines.'

Mina inhaled, stung. The rest of the group had quietened, watching Dominica. The older Sister turned back to Arabella.

'When Sister Silvana's tale is done and her gift given, you will offer your story, to remind all why we stand together. And why, together, we are stronger than the total of our single parts.' Her dark eyes took in Avra. 'I will tell my tale after Arabella, and then, my new Sister, you will tell us a tale of your own.' Her lean face had turned watchful, almost assessing. 'Understanding, like the stories, comes in many layers.'

The others had subsided, demurring to her leadership.

'Silvana?' she prompted.

Bathed by the light of her Shroud and by the reflection that came from her armour, Silvana once again picked up the thread of her tale.

'We will alpha strike the warboss,' Katherine said. 'Weapons ready, and on my mark... *Mark!*'

The Sisters moved with perfect fluidity. Shifting from their compass defence, they re-formed to a single line, and opened fire at the huge bulk of the bloodied boss. Katherine was already moving, sideways and out of range. Taking the moment to reload her bolter, she checked the enemy to both sides.

The orks had been startled by the Sisters' sudden movement, and more and more of them were moving away, back to the rocky rise of the camp, and to the rumble of the incoming ranks.

But not enough... not enough.

Even as the four Sisters of the Fiery Heart assaulted the boss with faith and fury, even as the boss bellowed in pain as his flesh burned, as his face and skull were battered by the full rate of fire from the heavy bolter, so they were buried completely by the orks' assault. In their armour, they were strong, they could withstand the individual blows and attacks, but the weight of the entire force was too much. As the boss staggered to his knees, the line of Sisters was gone. But still, they sang. The vox was alive with their voices, refusing to submit.

His armour red-hot, his flesh cooking as it fused to the metal, the front of his face all but destroyed, the warboss could still snarl. And, with impossible might, he came back to his feet. His ruined mouth made one bellow, one stinking roar that cut through the boiling mêlée.

'WAAAAAAAAGH!'

Katherine did not comprehend, but his forces did. Still commanded by the boss' power and size, they spared a moment to gawk in rebellious incredulity; then, grumbling, they turned to the incoming Militarum.

Two of the Sisters rose, their armour battered and damaged. Two did not. About her, many orks also did not regain their feet – though several looked like they had been slain by their comrades.

Katherine pointed her bolter at the faceless, eyeless monster. It could not see her, but it bared its remaining fangs.

'You face His wrath,' Katherine said, her voice a paean. 'His shield and His daughters! We do not falter, we do not fall, we do not fail! And we do not fear! Now, in His name, you *will* perish!'

But she did not pull the trigger – there was no need. One of her Sisters cried out over the vox, her voice like a tocsin. And there, streaking down through the sky, came the searing line of His wrath. It plummeted, swift and burning, like a falling star: a streak of molten metal, hissing as it came.

And it was His word and His law.

It hit the ground behind the boss, throwing him forwards onto what was left of his face. Katherine held her shield to defend herself; she was knocked from her feet, but unhurt. Her Sisters, too, had tumbled from the impact, but they scrambled back up, weapons bristling.

The air was full of flame, and ash, and the sudden hot winds of convection. The meteor was an angled corner, though the heat of its re-entry had blurred its metal edges to a molten softness. And it glowed, its glare like an angry eye.

The warboss, fallen forwards like a broken statue, did not move again.

The orks were scrambling around, now, shouting amongst themselves, the grots and gretchin shrieking. Holding her shield high, her voice loud through her vox-caster, she continued to shout, 'Such is the fate of those who defy the Emperor! Such is His strength that we carry, His wrath that we will rain upon your heads. You cannot face us, xenos scum!'

Behind the horde, the tanks opened fire.

The crowd of orks was thinning, now, running in every direction. A few at the front, the bigger creatures, were still snarling and surging forward, but their support was fading fast. They eyed the fallen boss, and then the Sisters.

And the Sisters answered with a full suppression from the heavy bolter, with the roar and flash of the flamer, with the smaller bolters barking rounds into the clouds of overheated ash.

The commander's voice bellowed orders to advance.

Jeering empty threats, the last of the orks fled.

At the end of her tale, Silvana looked around at her Sisters. 'We have heard a tale of rage, tightly controlled, a tale of pain, and what it teaches. Mine is a tale of daring, Sisters, of a bold plan and a bolder execution, and of His blessing that comes with both. Do you understand?'

'I'm beginning to understand,' Avra said, 'that you...' She paused, not sure how boldly she could speak, but went on with her chin lifted. 'That you... test each other.' It wasn't quite what she meant and she searched for the right words. 'That you... that you don't all sing the same tune, or the same notes, but that the hymn you make together is–'

'Harmony,' Arabella told her, smiling.

'Harmony,' Dominica repeated, seeming pleased with her realisation. 'An individual voice can sing His praise. But it takes more than one to raise the full might of a chorus.'

'I understand,' Avra said, again. Dominica gestured at Arabella, who smiled, her expression like the sun coming up.

'I'm glad,' Arabella told her. The youngest of the Sisters reached out her hands, took Avra's in her own. 'I'm glad you are here, my new Sister, and I'm glad to make you welcome. And I'm also quite glad to no longer be the youngest of our march.' A flicker of mischief, and Dominica raised a warning eyebrow. Arabella stiffened, but Avra had the impression that her light humour danced ever below the surface, her own manifestation of faith.

Her own part of the chorus.

'And so,' she said, 'it falls to me to tell you why we are together, united in our march across the galaxy. And why we are Sisters, both of and in Battle.' She shot Silvana a smile.

'It grows late,' Dominica said. 'Speak on.'

THE TALE OF ARABELLA

Kneeling to Silvana's right, Arabella cocked her head sideways and gave that wonderful, shining smile.

'Welcome, Sister,' she said, her voice light and easy. 'I am Sister Arabella of the Sacred Rose. I am negotiator and liberator. It is my task to carry His light, to care for the people and to free humanity from the faithless. Where the devotion of worlds fades, I bring them hope.' Her tone was bright, almost lilting. 'I also have the task to train you in our empathy, and in how we work in both concord and coherence.' She paused, and there was a twinkle of mischief to her green eyes. 'But not tonight. Once we have concluded the Service of Tales, we must pray for the muster.' A hint of amusement. 'And, while my Sisters may not have confessed it, even we must rest.'

Shocked by her almost playful tone, Avra glanced at Dominica, at the faintly disproving rigidity in the older Sister's shoulders.

'Your question, Sister,' she said, almost stern.

'My question,' Arabella said, 'is very simple. I seek to understand your soul. Do you carry hope?'

'I walked upon Sudesh,' Avra answered. She was more confident this time, understanding, now, what was expected. 'And the people had surrendered to despair. Disease was rampant amongst them, and they had lost that which they loved the most – wives and husbands, children and parents. My Sisters Hospitaller were there to succour their ailing flesh, but I carried His light to their hospices, to their valetudinariums, and to those that died on the streets. And thus, He blessed me to bring them hope.'

Lucia nodded. 'A good tale,' she said softly.

'I thought so,' Arabella responded with a sound that might even have been a chuckle. Then she composed herself, and recited more dutifully, 'Join us. In His grace and wisdom, and be welcome. We guard your sides and your back, and we stand together in His name, bringing His faith to all.'

She leaned across the circle to grip Avra's padded shoulder briefly in her hand, then said, 'I'm sure you have studied your histories suitably diligently.' She smiled. 'But the Orders of the Bloody and the Sacred Rose were founded by Deacis VI, some two hundred Solar years after the death of Sebastian Thor. And in Deacis' blessed wisdom, he appointed one to each Convent, the Bloody Rose to the Convent Sanctorum on Ophelia VII, and the Sacred Rose to the Covent Prioris on Holy Terra. My Sister Dominica will tell more of the heartworlds and Segmentum Solar, such is not my task. Instead, I will range widest of all, to bring you a story of both darkness and light.'

Her armour, like that of the others, was black, and scattered about it were the white, pearlescent petals of her Sacred Rose. They suited her, gave her a shine like Silvana's. But where Silvana's was age and dignity – gravitas, Avra thought – Arabella's had a shimmer of youth and idealism that was a wondrous rarity. It pulled like a beacon, like the glow of the sarcophagus itself.

'At the edges of the galaxy,' Arabella said, 'scattered across the Eastern Fringe, there are worlds without number, a million planets forgotten, all untouched by His light. The Great Crusade brought His blessing to many, welcoming them back to the Imperium of Man. But the void is endless, and even He, perhaps, cannot see it all.'

'Enough embellishment, child,' Dominica said, a sharp flex of warning in her tone. 'Tell your tale.'

'My apologies, Sister.' Arabella lowered her eyes, though her shimmer did not fade.

Engines rasped again from the outside; again, the floodlights passed over the chapel, making angles of light flee suddenly across the floor.

'My tale will reach to the void's very edges,' Arabella said, 'to the world of Vassis Morugo, lurking upon the outermost limit of our Sisters' lore and ken. It is a dark world, a world cut off from its star, a world of chem-hell and steam, of corrosion and pollution. Exploited by cruel masters, its menials were bent beneath the demands of savage leadership, as cut off from Him as they were from their cloud-shrouded sun.

'And the enemy,' she said, a vivid thrum to her tone, 'likes nothing more than a vacuum of faith.'

Arabella, it seemed, had a flair for the dramatic. This time, however, Dominica let it pass. The younger Sister picked up one of her petals, turning it to catch the light. Outside, engines growled softly.

'Where He is forgotten,' Arabella continued, 'so the ancient foe crawls, creeping inwards. Where masters become greedy and cruel, so the enemy stirs to glee and wakefulness. And where there is contamination, so there come the powers that revel in it, and in its sheer inevitability.'

A shiver passed across Avra's shoulders. She knew the powers to which Arabella referred, though she would not name them, not aloud and not in her thoughts. To do so was to call them close, and such things were both blasphemous and unwise.

The others were praying, the murmur of their voices soft and melodious, weaving one through another, as if to form a backdrop to Arabella's tale. The younger Sister raised her voice, not to drown them out, but to complement them – the solo at the head of the choral recital.

Avra wondered if Arabella had been a singer. Performance seemed to suit her, and the others had used the word 'harmony' more than once.

But the Sister had begun her tale.

Always, in times past and in times present, the presence of the foe calls out across the void. And so, Katherine arrived upon Morugo with a force of the Fiery Heart at her banner and at her back. Here, she beheld the tragedy of the world, of its lost and faithless people. She looked upon their bent spines and their filthy faces, upon the despair in which they lived their lives, and she resolved to wipe clean this contaminated place. To return it to Him, and to purge the enemy in cleansing and ultimate fire.

Yet she did not.

Outside, engines rasped again. They were becoming louder now, underpinned by shouts. Dust and wind whirled petals along the floor.

'Our Sisters Hospitaller,' Arabella said, 'see Him as an Emperor of Mercy – be that the mercy of ending pain and of releasing souls to His presence, or the mercy of healing, of survival to continue His work. And you have heard, my new Sister, the watchwords of the other Orders. For Mina, it is rage and the discipline to control that rage. For Lucia, pain and the wisdom within that pain. For Silvana, the daring to take us to war's very forefront, and beyond. Yet we are all parts of one whole, petals of one rose. We balance, each to one other.' She smiled. 'You are beginning to understand this, I think.'

Avra nodded. Her eyes were stinging and she was not sure if it was too much soot or the intense emotion of the moment.

'So when I say that our saint was touched by compassion, do not think of it as weakness. It is just another petal, another part of the hymn, another facet of our praise to Him.' She looked round at the others as if she expected a challenge, but no one gainsaid her, and she continued.

Many of Morugo's people were warped beyond redemption, touched by the enemy in mind and heart and flesh. For them, there could be no healing, only the last relief. But among them, there walked those still human, still with courage untouched by the foe, their limbs weary but strong, their thoughts despairing, but clear of rot. And these were not in ones and twos, but in tens and twenties, perhaps in hundreds or even thousands – the tale does not say. But they were enough. And our saint gave the order: the Sisters were not to purge the world entire, not unless they were left without choice.

Instead, Katherine would restore to them their hope. She would lead the fight against the enemy commander, and against his corrupt leadership.

And so, she raised her banner, and her voice, and she began to sing.

At the word, Arabella raised her own voice in song, a Litany that Avra had never heard. The Sister's voice was a clear soprano, as pure as white ice, as holy as a glassaic window. And it carried His praise upwards to the open roof of the little chapel, upwards to the stars that glittered above, turning and turning as the tales wound on. Lifted by its wings, Avra looked up and could see the very first touch of the sunrise, the paling of the sky.

A flicker of vision came to her: the rise of Sol, yellow and perfect, over Holy Terra. Overwhelmed, she found the water in her eyes flowing free, and lifted her hand to wipe it away.

Next to her, Lucia smiled, stretching out to grip her shoulder.

'There is no dishonour in weeping, my new Sister, not in the proper time and place. And here, you may bare your heart without fear, and without shame.'

Avra nodded, blinking, and Arabella reached the end of her hymn, letting the last note fade away. Outside, the engines had stopped. Everything was utterly silent almost as if her voice had stilled the entire camp.

Her tone soft, the Sister picked up her tale once more.

At the touch of Katherine's song, so the people crept forwards. Cautious, fearful, their filthy faces streaked with tears as if the water washed their very sins away. They fell to their knees before her, and they begged her to lead them, to show them to the light of which she sung. She told them to stand, for she was not Him; she told them to take up what weapons they had, and to follow.

And so did her March of Faith begin.

She walked strong, her devotion borne before her like His very blessing, her banner held high. Light shone from her, banishing the darkness, the malice, the seething pollution of this damned world. Where she walked, the rusting metal was made anew, and her boots rang upon clean steel. Where she sang, so the black, swirling clouds were banished, shrinking from her as if in fear of her approach.

And the people heard! They came forth, slowly, warily, more and more of them. Given her courage, they joined her song, lifting their own voices to His praise, and rediscovering Him as they did so. And His blessed presence grew among them like the Sacred Rose itself, its shine growing wider and wider. And the wider it reached, so the more people heard it, and came forth.

Soon, a throng of new faithful followed her, and all of them were singing.

* * *

Arabella paused, the petal still in her fingers. All of the Sisters watched it as if mesmerised, though they had doubtless heard this tale before.

She lifted the petal to the saint's holy light, the very same light that she had carried, so long ago. Letting them all see it, Arabella suddenly closed her fingers with a hard, sharp gesture, crushing it utterly to a glitter of drifting dust. Her voice dropped to a whisper, making them all lean forwards.

But there were others, who also bore witness to that light, and who were not touched by Him. They were aware of His presence – for how could they not be? – but it brought them no joy. Instead, it brought them terror, and anger, and rage. Those among the population who were touched by the foe, already warped and mangled, bursting with heresy and unbelief – they also followed the saint, skulking in the shadows as the light passed them by. And they, too, had a purpose, growing within them like a canker. They had a master, bold and evilly beneficent, generous with his corrupt gifts. And he too issued a call.

A *summons.*

'The light is a lie,' said the enemy. 'A falsehood. It will strip from you the gifts that I have given, slay you without mercy. It will burn and harm you, sear bright into your eyes, cut harsh into your flesh that I have blessed. I – *I!* – am the god of this world, the only god you need. You who bear my gifts, come unto me!'

'Beware, my Sister,' Dominica said softly, her voice a growl. 'You tread a dangerous path with your theatre. Call not the foe, lest the foe comes.'

Arabella paused, nodding soberly, then continued.

Katherine's Sisters, the Order of the Fiery Heart, were deployed to seek the enemy's followers where they could, ranging out across the planet's high and creaking walkways, catching and destroying the misshapen and the tainted. But still, these twisted beings mustered in their hundreds, scuttling and whispering, seething and plotting. They crawled along the pipes; they climbed up the manufactorum walls and ran along their roofs. They lurked within the great and silent machines.

And they did not stop.

Conscious of the threat, but focused upon her mission, Katherine continued forwards, her song still raised aloft. About her, the metalwork echoed to her words, singing in the high wind as if it sang along with her, welcomed her and the deliverance she promised, in His name. Guided by her faith, her heart lifted by her faithful, the saint walked on. And His wisdom guided her, with every note she sang.

She *knew* where the enemy waited.

And, as the knowledge came to her in His touch, so did her song sour to a minor key, eerie and mocking. And her hymn became a dirge.

Arabella sang again, a snatch of weird music, distorted and wrong. A shudder went out through the Sisters.

'Desist.' This time, Dominica was really angry. 'Your drama gets the better of you, my Sister – I have warned you about this already. One does *not* voice such things.'

'I do not voice...' Arabella paused, a flush to her face. 'It is a minor key, no more. Nothing–'

'Get on with your tale,' Dominica barked. 'As we have observed, we are running out of time.'

'Yes, my Sister.' Looking genuinely chastised, Arabella began to speak more swiftly.

And so did Katherine find herself climbing a great spiral of rusting metal steps. They rang at her boot-strikes, notes clashing and loud, but she ascended them without fear, her Sisters at her side, her throng of faithful behind. She bore her shield high and shining, and she crested Morugo's very highest point, a latticed steel platform bearing a host of vox-antennae.

Here, there was wind, though thick and faint. The clouds had thinned and she could see the smallest sliver of the planet's reddening sun. The platform seemed unstable – rust ate at the handrails, chewed its way across the floor. It curled round the antennae like some blotched and living serpent. The height was not safe, but the saint was unworried. He had guided her, and she was in His hands.

She was also not alone. At the platform's centre, surrounded by the antennae as if they were worshippers, the rust had coalesced to a huge symbol, a symbol of terror and blasphemy, a symbol we do not describe. And upon the far side of this symbol, at the edge of the opposite walkway, there stood a being, its arms upraised, the last clouds wreathing about it as if they stroked its very skin.

The Sisters had not surprised it. At their arrival, it lowered its arms and smiled at them, its expression like pure indulgence. Amid the people's poverty, it wore rich pendants, costly robes now stained with blood and fluids. And from it, there came a wave of savage hunger, of *need*. It was as unconstrained as pure sensation, an assault upon their minds and souls.

It sang to them, *'Welcome.'*

The word was but a single note, vibrating from wind and steel. Yet it echoed louder, and louder, as if it was reflected by the whole of Morugo's surface, as if it was sunk into every piece of metal that rusted here upon this world. As if the antennae themselves were some terrible, daemonic instrument. It hummed harsh in the Sisters' ears and armour, seeking to strike at their souls. To bury them in a lushness of sound.

But Katherine and her Sisters raised the Litany in return, a chiming of vocal perfection, and the creature stopped, its mouth spread in a mocking leer.

'You will need more than music,' it told them, 'daughters of conceit.' Its voice was rich with appetite. 'Witness my world,' it said, 'and what it has become. I was governor here, once, lord of a dark and gloomy backwater. But behold! Look upon what I have wrought! I have found rewards beyond imagining, and I will spread them among my people like joy. I will take away their pain, their suffering, their hunger, their loss. And instead, I will gift them this...' He spread his arms wider. 'This celebration!'

Katherine did not respond with words. She raised her bolter and fired, but the air shimmered visibly and the round struck it as if it were armour. The force field rippled, echoed, but stayed firm. Her Sisters raised their weapons but she held up a hand.

'Wait,' she said to them. 'We must study this barrier.'

They spread out to an extended line. Behind them clustered the planet's new faithful, those who had responded to Katherine's clarion call.

The governor looked upon all of them, and sneered. 'Weaklings,' he said, amused and scornful. 'Your petty tunes are of no relevance, not here. Your souls are yet mine to do with as I please. Witness!'

Again, he raised the hum of invasive sound. Defended by their faith and their baffles both, the Sisters did not flinch, but the people of Morugo twisted under the assault, putting their hands over their ears and buckling to their knees. Many bled from their eyes and noses. Incensed, Katherine raised her voice and her vox-caster to bury this attack, but even as she did so, she realised the cunning of the governor's plan.

Beneath them, the trailing group of warped menials had not ascended to the planet's heights. They waited below in gangs, their filthy faces turned upwards, watching the rotted metal above. The platform, already corroded, was quivering under the onslaught of the noise. The toxic power of the governor's hum was pitched to make the metal vibrate.

And then, with a creak, it collapsed.

Outside, a colossal crash accompanied Arabella's last word. All of the Sisters jumped, every one reaching for her weapon, but the noise was not repeated. Instinctively, Avra sent a query out over the vox, but the voice of the Order came back to her.

'Be at ease, Sister. There is no need for you to break your vigil.'

Warily, she looked at the others, but they too were standing down. Their shoulders relaxed and they lowered themselves once more to their mats. She noticed, though, that their weapons were even closer than before.

Shouts were sounding outside, and the voice of the Order's Sister Superior came clearly back through the lightening air.

'Go on,' Dominica said. And Arabella continued.

They fell. Saint and Sister, menial and faithful. With a creak and a screech, the platform tore away from its supports, splitting at the very feet of the foe. And it plummeted, crashing through layer after layer of the rusting metal below – through walkways and gantries, past towers and railings and steps. The Sisters tried to stay upon their feet, but the faithful that followed them were pulled from the platform's edges, ripped from their places by the shattered ends of struts.

And the enemy laughed.

With a final smash, they hit the bottom. The platform shattered, knocking even the Sisters from their feet. Surrounded by the wounded and the broken, they were up again in a moment. Weapons in hands, they looked up. Above them, there were endless gleams of broken metal edges. Bodies hung from many, still struggling. And high above that, the governor still stood, and laughed.

Katherine gave a great cry, a rallying of courage. And those people who were still uninjured, still touched by His new strength – they raised their tools and they threw themselves from the platform's edges, and out upon the waiting faithless.

The battle was bitter, furious, savage. The Sisters shot where they could, where the corrupted menials broke through the lines of the saved. With her shield, Katherine stormed to the forefront of the counter-attack, wading into the slavering surge of twisted bodies and throwing them down, one after another. Above them, the governor laughed on, his voice like thunder, rolling down through twisted spars. Sound wreathed him like power.

But Katherine did not care. Blazing the words of the Litany, she pressed forwards, fighting ever on, striving to gain a secure footing. Yet for every one she slew, there were ten more, for every ten, there were a hundred. The voice of the foe had called them, and while she was truly blessed, she was but one. Beside her, her Sisters were buried by twisted menials, a dozen of them, more, throwing themselves forwards with no thought for their own lives, knocking a Sister over. Furiously, the Sisters fought back, breaking hundreds of the warped figures. But still, more and more came, heeding the call of the governor.

And our saint made a choice.

Below her, a Sister had fallen. A second Sister stood over her, defending her until she could rise.

'Hold!' Katherine called over the vox. 'We will regroup!' And she gave her Order new commands.

All around them, the faithless still pressed inwards, throngs of them seemingly without number. Katherine took a moment to scan, to pick the attackers' weakest point. They would assault that point, and break free.

'Now!' she cried.

In His name, they moved as one, pressing their assault against the foe.

'And *fire!*'

The Order, five of them now remaining, opened fire. Warped and unwarped alike were shredded by a fusillade of bolter rounds, melted by cleansing flame. Bodies ignited, or tumbled. And the Sisters fought to find a stable stairway, and a route back up to the governor.

Arabella paused, and the voice of the Sister Superior came again from the outside. All six Sisters were tense now, very aware of the motion that surrounded their sanctum.

Arabella went on, her voice soft. 'I am sure I do not need to explain our saint's decision. She had been willing to save the uncorrupted, and she had done so. In freeing their minds and their souls, in giving them the light and courage to fight back, to resist the governor's control, so she had allowed them to die with what honour they could muster. And it was enough.'

'We understand,' Dominica said. 'Tell on.'

In the heights, the governor's laughter had stopped. Angered at the failure of his plan, he called louder, called more of his people, called a planet's population ever-thronging to his shout. But the Sisters had slain almost all that had responded swiftly, and the others would not reach him in time. At the height of his world, he stood alone.

Far below him, Katherine looked to left and right, swiftly identifying two surviving stairways and deploying her Sisters to run up this way, and that way, to surround the governor's location. They obeyed without question, and the music of their boots rang again, chiming out through the steel heights of the planet.

And so, they returned to the topmost levels. They closed upon him like pincers, their bolters aimed across the hole he'd made. Far below them, the battles raged on. The last screams of the dying floated up through the clouded air.

Katherine emerged upon the heights, her shield and bolter in hand. She was facing the governor's back, but he turned to confront her, and she saw that his face was florid with luxury, his jowls loose and flapping.

'You cannot face me,' she said. 'I am His daughter, and I do not fail.'

Again, she raised the words of the sacred Litany. Again, her vox-caster sounded her hymn to the sky. Her Sisters, all around, sang with her, their hymnal counterpointed by the fading screams from below. The saint bore her bolter, but it was her hymn she used as a weapon, the pure sound of her faith. And the planet sang, the metal sang, the antennae sang soprano. Ripples shifted through the air, rising to the sun, making the rust withdraw from even the foe's feet. They shivered through the sounds he wove, his unholy defences, and they at last tore them down completely, leaving him helpless.

He curled his lip at them, defiant even in his defeat.

And, with the last words of the hymnal, their power manifest in song, so did his own heights collapse, and drop him down, down, down… to his own shattered symbol, far below.

Arabella stopped. She had picked up another petal and was turning it in her hand; with the other, she reached out and picked up one of Mina's and then lifted them both.

'I do not know the literal truth of such a tale,' she said. 'For I have never seen a foe defeated by song alone. In my heart, though, I believe that it is allegory, representative of what we must be, what we must strive to be. My new Sister,' she said to Avra, 'we must sing together. We must understand one another so well, as family, that no orders need be given. We must work with the harmony of perfect song, with the smooth precision of machine-spirits. We are not only warriors, we are exemplars – we are flags. We *are* Katherine's banner, we *are* her Order, her bearers, her Fiery Heart. And where we walk, so we carry her with us, not only physically, but in our every word, our every prayer, our every deployment and combat manoeuvre.' Her face had taken on a new seriousness, and Avra could see the passion and belief that underlaid her humour, understand why she, too, had been chosen to join this march. 'We *are* the Sisters of San Loer, as close as He has permitted. And where we walk, we don't only bring faith or leadership.

'We bring victory. In His name. And in hers.'

She held out the white petal, watched Avra take it.

'Embrace your new name, my Sister,' she said. 'And let your voice rise with ours, out across the battlefields of the galaxy.'

As she finished, Avra could feel the lift in her heart, could understand why people across the Imperium – and beyond – would follow the call of the Sacred Rose, His call, to the ends of their worlds. Dominica was nodding, a stern approval in the gesture. Mina had schooled her expression to calm; Silvana had a glow that reflected Arabella's, as if the Shroud itself approved.

Chuckling softly, Lucia said, 'It is well that we are all so different, is it not? For in that way, each of us overlaps the limits of the others, and thus, we may understand the human heart in its entirety. And in that way, we can bring our call to all that bear witness to our march, and to the sacred casket we bear. My Sister,' she said, addressing Dominica, 'it falls to you to tell the final tale, a tale of worlds much closer to the heart of the galaxy itself. The battlefield wakens and muster will be upon us before much longer. Will you speak?'

'I will speak,' Dominica said, her voice low. She arced one

graceful eyebrow at Avra. 'For it is my task to… bring this tale of hope down to a solid and wary practicality. To eyes and ears, to careful watchfulness, of even the most faithful.' She stopped, fixing Avra with her dark gaze, the look oddly penetrating. 'For even His Most Holy Church can be touched by the foe.'

THE TALE OF ALICIA DOMINICA

To Arabella's right knelt Alicia Dominica, her armour black as secrets, her cloak as red as shed blood. Her face was lifted to His banner and to the light of the relic saint. In her hands, she bore the Simulacrum of the Ebon Chalice itself, its contents in shadow, and there was a powerful sense of self-assurance to the way she knelt, to the angle of her chin; a certain pride to the set of her pauldrons. She seemed very like Mina, as if she could face down the enemy entire, but her stance felt austere in a way that Mina's had not.

'You are welcome, my new Sister,' she said. Her voice was calm, flat and strong. 'I am Alicia Dominica, foremost of the Adepta Sororitas, founder of the First Order, Matriarch of the Ebon Chalice.' The words were measured, but there was a distance to them, a weight like some merciless responsibility. 'I am the guardian of His word, and of all that it contains. It is my sacred task to scour the foe from the galaxy's heart, to defend the Segmentum Solar, to seek out corruption and heresy at the very core of the Imperium. To castigate even other Sisters, if such becomes necessary.' She turned like a threat, her face lean and lined, her eyes dark. 'And I ask to understand your faith. You must be Sororitas in word and deed, heart and soul, mind and backbone.' The last word was delivered like a blow. 'So I ask you – what do you *fear*?'

The question was unexpected, and Avra almost blinked. She cast her mind back through her two years of missions, but was reluctant to voice what felt like a confession.

Lucia shifted, her armour creaking. Oddly, Avra had the impression that she wanted to say something, but would not.

Collecting her thoughts, Avra answered. 'As Katherine, Sister, I must have no fears. My heart must be filled with fire and I must quail at nothing. Yet I am still Avra in parts of my soul, and I… I fear to fail. To be unable to bear this…' She swallowed. 'This blessing that has been given to me.'

For a moment, Dominica did not move. Her expression stayed cold. Then, slowly, she nodded. 'You are honest, Sister. And I am glad to hear it.' Voices came through the darkness, shouts of early orders. 'But there is no place for faintness of heart. We stand together, and we do not falter. You know this, or you would not be here.'

'Yes, Sister.'

More shouting. It seemed oddly unreal – another life. *Her* other life, her past life.

'You have heard,' Dominica said, 'many tales of the darkness of the Imperium. Tales of battles, tales of invasion, tales of worlds polluted. Tales where our saint has fought at the very vanguard of the God-Emperor's wars.' The dawn light was getting stronger now, a faint blur across the flags. 'Mine is not such a tale. Instead, it falls to me to take our service back to the heartworlds. Not to Holy Terra itself' – shadow flickered, fleeting, across her expression – 'but to Segmentum Solar, and to the shrine world of Elena, a world of the Ecclesiarchy.'

The others were silent, hands resting on their knees, their heads lowered as if in prayer. There was a seriousness to Dominica, a darkness to her eyes, a shadow to the way she knelt that made the lines down her face look almost like knife cuts – harsh and unforgiving. She was of similar years to Silvana, but where Silvana's age gave her a shine of grace and wisdom, in Dominica, they looked more like weight, like the burden of her secret, her great responsibility.

Despite her low voice, its softness almost a growl, she commanded the Sisters' complete and undivided attention, and they did not interrupt her. Conscious of some unspoken expectation, Avra composed herself to listen.

'Before I begin,' Dominica said, 'I need you to comprehend something. The others have all heard this before, yet it is essential that you understand what I am about to tell you.'

Avra looked up, meeting the older Sister's eyes. There was something in them, something... She wanted to look away, but controlled herself.

'You are aware that my Order is based upon Holy Terra itself. When my vision came to me, when I beheld our most sacred Sisters, kneeling upon the stone floor of that world so far away, I was... overcome. I was still young, barely from the schola, and the sheer size of the realisation was too much for me. I denied my calling, pleading that others of the Order were more worthy than I.'

Her tone thrummed with notes of both shame and warning, with a huge tumult of other, tangled emotions that Avra could sense but not hear clearly. Dominica kept speaking, her voice carefully flat, as if to keep a lid on the turmoil beneath.

'The canoness of my Order was wroth with me, with my fear. She took me to the very gates of the Imperial Palace and she bade me–'

'You have seen...?' Avra, her heart in her mouth, her skin afire, could not finish the sentence. She had never been to Holy Terra, had never as much as seen the Convent Prioris upon a floating hololith. And the thought of the Palace itself, the very heart of the Imperium...

She stopped herself, making the sign of the fleur-de-lys, praying for forgiveness for her arrogance, for having the temerity to even contemplate such a thing.

'I did not pass beyond,' Dominica answered, her voice still tightly controlled. 'Such would have been… too much. But I have stood without the Palace itself and heard the words of the Eternal Prayer. Despite my youth, and my fear, I was so blessed…'

She stopped, swallowed. The others said nothing, but Avra could sense their support, the harmony of their Sisterhood.

'Thus, was I shamed from my cowardice.' She smiled, though the expression was oddly sad. 'I took up my role, the mantle of Dominica herself, and all of the secrets borne therein.' Again, that fleeting touch of darkness – yet it was not the darkness of the enemy, nor the darkness of despair. It was the darkness of a flame carried so deep within her soul, a flame that forged the crude ore of a shocked young Sister into the pure, edged might of Dominica's exemplar.

Truly, she was the ultimate Sororitas, and this march was hers to command.

'I hear that prayer, my young Sister, always. It is in my heart, its hymn never-ending. I hear its call, and its demand, for it will never leave me. And it has given me the courage to carry the chalice of my Order, its insight, its bravery and its wisdom. And to face the most insidious foes of all…'

Feet raced past outside. The Sisters did not move.

'Our own corrupted.'

She paused, and still the others said nothing. Avra found that she was holding her breath, that something in her mind and heart was changing under the forging hammer of Dominica's words. It was a new realisation, some wondrous epiphany solidifying to new fact, new faith and understanding. But it was not quite ready, not yet.

Her hands in her lap like the others, she waited.

'And so, to the world of Elena,' Dominica said, and began her tale.

Katherine travelled to Elena. She was there unaccompanied, walking its roadways unescorted by her Sisters, by any presence or voice but His. About her towered cathedrals colossal, their stone clean and carved with prayers, their great glassaic windows rich with colour and with His image, their statues rising vast and heroic to skies of blue and white, to a yellow sun whose touch was a benediction. Paved boulevards were lined with ranks of shining lumens. Wide rivers flowed clear, carrying gifts and offerings, and everywhere there walked His faithful, from the rich robes of the High Deacon himself, all the way to the humble brown of the scribes and students. With them walked scholars, walked our Sisters Dialogus come to study at the librarium, walked pilgrims with their eyes downcast. And all heard His blessing in the words of the never-ceasing sermons, and in the tolling of the great bells of prayer.

But our saint was neither scholar nor pilgrim, and the wisdom she sought was of a different shade. For He had come to her in a vision, showing her a flowering of corrupt flame at the heart of this world's holiness. The High Deacon had been performing 'miracles', conjuring flames and visions, promising to heal the sick and cure the infirm. It was said that he had unseemly cravings of the flesh, and that he practised unholy rites. And he took from his pilgrims wealth – not to offer as alms, nor to raise churches to His grace and glory, but to furnish himself with rich foods and fine wines and glittering gemstones, with lush fabrics and precious metals.

Katherine, her heart afire, was there to decry his corruption.

Yet such things are not as simple as they seem.

Dominica picked up the chalice, lifted it to the saint's soft light as if she presided over a communion. She prayed softly, her lips moving, and the others watched, compelled. Even Arabella was silent, her expression rapt.

Called by Him, our saint carried both anger and authority. She strode down the boulevards, and the pilgrims tumbled from her path; she found the Great Cathedral of the Heart and the Soul, almost as if it burned with its corruption visible. And she threw open the double doors with a slam like a demand, stood framed within their archway with her armour haloed in light.

In the pulpit, midway through the flow of his sermon of sin, the High Deacon knew no shame. Instead, at the sight of her, he raised his arm and roared, the sound ringing through the building's huge vault.

'There!' The word was like an organ-note, brassy and powerful. 'There is the one, come to deny His miracles! There is the ancient enemy, the very foe, daring to bear its likeness here, upon Elena! To wear the face of the Sororitas and to carry it into the very heart of His Holy Church!'

At his cry, lies and blasphemy though it was, the congregation came to their feet. And there were not one or two or ten of them, there were hundreds, caught in the web of his words. The cathedral rustled echoes at their movement, whispered hatred as they turned as one, and every one of them had a face etched in loathing.

'My Sisters.' Dominica paused, still with that odd tension, that sense of the secrets that enveloped her. 'We have all seen the same sacred vision. The holy convent, the terrible duel. And we understand that even Katherine herself was once deceived by lies.' She would not utter the name, but it hung in the air just the same. Avra shuddered.

Vandire.

Petals sighed across the ground: rage and hope. Raising her

gaze to the coffin, the reality of its presence struck her anew: this really *was* Katherine. She was not just a tale, not just a vision, she was verily the saint herself and she was actually *here* – Daughter of the Emperor, Sister of San Loer, Our Martyred Lady. And Avra would carry her shield, her sword, and would walk at the head of her march…

A shiver went through her, her shoulders almost rounding under the full weight of the responsibility. A prayer passed her lips, but Dominica was still telling her tale.

Katherine bore the faithless congregation no mercy. Like their leader, they had fallen and their lives were of no matter to her. She raised her bolter, and aimed it at the deacon himself.

'Repent,' she told him. 'On your knees, sinner. Or I will shed your blood before His altar as a warning to all who profane His name.'

The deacon did not acquiesce. Laughing with a sound both hollow and terrible, he spread his arms to his flock. 'Defend me,' he called to them. 'And you will ascend in glory.'

Without hesitation, Katherine pulled the trigger. The blast was loud, a harsh bellow of fury, but the deacon was already moving, ducking down behind the pulpit's stone. The round struck and detonated, the noise a shock that rang from the building's vaulted ceiling.

'Hold, in His name!' Katherine called her orders at the deacon and his followers both, but they paid her no heed. She walked forwards, striding up the aisle towards the nave, but the congregation flowed outwards into her path, clawing at her armour, clinging to her shield and her weapon, trying to stop her movement. Their profane flesh hissed as they touched her, but they did not stop. Angered at their betrayal, she trampled them where they stood, but there were many of them and her progress was slowed.

She was fighting her way forwards when the real assault came.

* * *

More voices from outside, the bellowing bark of a duty sergeant, the calm tones of the duty Sister Superior in return. The sky was growing lighter by the moment. Avra paused in her prayers, but Dominica was still speaking.

'For the deacon was not only a blasphemer,' she said, 'preaching falsehood to his congregation. And his attack did not come at her physically.'

She turned the chalice, letting it catch the light.

'No,' Dominica said. 'The attack came at her mind, at her faith, and at the courage of her fiery heart.

'The deacon was a witch.'

The word stirred across the floor like the whorls of dust, rose like a ghost to tangle in the saint's light.

Despite herself, Avra shivered, but Dominica had not paused in her tale.

He attacked with temptation. With the lure of great power. Not with pleasures and with false miracles, but with something far more significant. Something personal and martial and soaked in blood and rage and song and glory. Images tumbled within our saint's thoughts: she stood at the head of a great force of warriors, a huge banner in her hand, its heavy cloth flapping against a storm-clouded sky. She bore a great blade, held aloft in fire; she issued a rallying cry that rang from one end of the Imperium to the other. And the faithful, they loved her. They flocked to her in awe and in worship. They fell at her feet and they gave their lives to her, fed her with their souls. And she blazed with the holy light of Sol itself.

Dominica lowered the chalice, and Avra could see that her hands were shaking, but whether that was with the force of the vision, or with the chest-tightening shock of the suggestion that it carried...

'I do not need to emphasise,' she said, 'the sheer sacrilege of the implanted suggestion. Its implication is enough, and I…' Her frown deepened. Placing the chalice to her right, she closed her hands before her, interlinking her fingers to hold them steady.

The call was mighty. Katherine's thoughts were filled with it – she could be the highest child of the Emperor, the greatest vessel of His light and blessing. She could have the weight and power of one of the Adeptus Astartes, as much daughter as His greatest sons. She could stand at His side, her armour towering; she could fly His banner, back and forth, across the entire breadth of the void, and where it passed, so the enemy would quail. They would flee before her, and every xenos would fall to its knees in whimpering terror.

She could wield such might…

In the heart of the deacon's corrupted cathedral, Katherine stopped. The wave of the faithless continued to assail her, but she stood like a statue, unmoving. She paid them no heed; she was frozen, still as death, in the glare of the tempter's image.

Stopping, Dominica made the sign of the aquila, a gesture that might have been penitence or purification or both. She lowered her head in reverence and the saint's light shone from the white threads in her dark hair.

'I say to you, my Sisters – the foes of our own thoughts are perhaps the greatest foes of all. Who among us,' she said, as she looked round at each face, 'has not felt the touch of temptation? Has not celebrated the strength that she bears, her battles and victories? Taken high-hearted joy in her combat and skill?'

Mina was nodding, her dark face intense with recollection. Avra flushed, remembering all too well the blaze of battle-adrenaline, how it surged through her blood, how it shouted from her throat in the words of the sacred hymnal.

'They say,' Dominica said, 'that every Sister must face such enticement. Must vanquish it before she takes her Rites of Ordination. You have heard,' she said, addressing Avra, 'how each of our Orders tests itself, and thus finds triumph over that lure. By discipline, by pain, by daring, by hope. But all of these things, my young Sister, they come from the same place – they come from Him. We may embrace them fully, even exult in them, but we must never forget that they are but His blessing. And that they come only from His touch within each of our souls.' She gave the twitch of a smile. 'This, the witch did not comprehend.'

Lurking behind his deacon's guise, behind the safe stone of the pulpit, he thought to turn the saint's victories inwards, to use her very skills against her. He thought to turn her gaze from Him unto only herself – to her own victories, her own glory.

At first, she defied his temptation. Refusing him, she raised her voice in the Ancient Litany, and her armour blazed with ferocity. Dazzled, the congregation fell back from her, each one seeking cover behind their pew, but where the light touched the sinners' flesh, so it flared to red flame and was gone. Hollow wails of pain and despair became emptiness, mere dust that drifted in the breeze from open doors. Many tried to flee, but they could not escape that light. Others fell to their knees in penitence, but the light took them also, and they, too, were gone in flashes of flame.

Yet the wooden pews, carved with His image, remained untouched.

And Katherine reached the pulpit.

Again, Dominica paused, and the Sisters waited, still silent, for her to continue. Unlike the tales of the others, this one had not been interrupted, and Avra found herself studying Dominica's face, that touch of secrecy and darkness that she still carried about her.

There was a stern distance to her, a severity that was almost a haughtiness. It was deep and subtle, something in her bearing... It seemed neither unholy, nor prideful; more an awareness of who she was, and the role that she carried.

The deacon was still there, his expression sneering, uncaring of the deaths of his followers. He was portly, florid, pompous. As Katherine raised her weapon, he opened his arms as if to greet her like a brother.

'Ah, Sister,' he said. 'So you are come to me at last.'

'You do not address me.' Katherine pointed her bolter at him. 'Traitor!'

'You will not fire,' the deacon told her, smiling. 'Not here, not again.'

In her hand, the bolter was red-hot, her gauntlet was red-hot. Her skin shrieked with pain. Her flesh ignited, melted, even as the flesh of the congregation had done. The agony of it nearly took her to her knees.

But it was illusion... The song of the psyker.

And Katherine would not be defeated by lies, never again. She pulled the trigger, the muzzle of her bolter aimed straight between his eyes. The round went straight through him, detonating upon the pulpit steps. Shards of stone flew.

'That was foolish,' he said. 'The Frateris Militia are on their way.' The image of the man flickered back, standing exactly where he had been. 'I need a leader,' he said. 'A warrior, a demagogue without peer. A voice to raise an army. And now, Sister, you are mine. And you cannot gainsay me.'

He made no gesture, no performance, but the illusions came upon her again, burying her in a landslide of imagery. In the place of His image in the glassaic windows of the Convent, there was a figure in armour, as black as the void itself. Its heart burned upon its chest, a halo of fire that bathed the cathedral in a light blood-red. A great cloak flew behind it. Down the sides of the nave, that image was reflected in the lines of stone statuary, their carven figures standing stern, their grey now flooded with basalt-black, their every heart afire. And in the firelight there massed soldiers – others in night-black ceramite, armed with blade and bolter, the men and women of the Astra Militarum – all on their knees, their heads bowed in terror and worship. With them stood the Mechanicus, their billowing cloaks as red as the flame itself, their augmetics glinting like precious metals.

In the tumble of the witch's vision, she saw them, and their adoration, and she loved it, needed it. Craved it with a hunger she had never known. Acknowledging their veneration, she pulled herself from the window, and the glassaic shattered and she moved, sparkling in slow motion like some halo of dancing lights. She raised her arms and her voice, both larger than the very building, and she sang that Litany so ancient, the words that she and her Sisters had written...

'O Empress, deliver us!'

It was a rush of pure supremacy, lightning in her veins and through her skin, giddying with enticement. It called to her, lifted her, promised her – every victory she could ever have dreamed. Even more than His daughter, she could be...

By the Throne!

No. I will *not.*

The images froze solid at her refusal, shards like pure ice, held fast in their places.

'This is falsehood! This is *beyond* atrocity!'

The black cathedral was a lie. And this was not just mere blasphemy. This was a profanity so utterly extreme that it could not be borne, should be ripped out by its very roots. It sickened her to her belly, even in the pincer-grip of the witch's might: this was not only impossible, this was the worst sin of all, the ultimate in betrayal.

Pride.

And such pride! With her shock came understanding – the Litany she had sung was wrong, an assumption of suffocating arrogance. She could hear the words with her own ears, not through the filters the witch had put upon her, and they rang like empty metal, their music flat. The black cathedral was still about her, its illusion draped like the rich fabrics of the deacon, but its worshippers were silent, and its floating cherubim hung still as death. Their eyelids clicked, cold and steel, the tiny movement echoing on a cold and hollow wind.

She said, again, 'I will not.'

The witch increased his pressure – the cherubim twitched, the worshippers tried to move. Ice-shards fell to the floor and shattered, scattering shining dust.

Embrace it, he told her. *Take up your mantle! Lead the galaxy in war! Soak up the adulation of your forces like the light of Sol itself.*

But she did not, could not, would not. The sacrilege was ultimate, and her faith was iron and steel and ceramite.

In His name, I will never *again be deceived by lies!*

Dragging her mind back, feeling the heat of the flame in her heart, she forced herself to turn and confront the now empty glassaic window. The window where He – and only He – should stand. But it was a hole. A gap. A window onto nothing.

Realising the profoundness of his error, the witch made another attempt. And even as Katherine visualised His image back in the glassaic, the darkness in the window grew. It swelled outwards, swirling; it became a sucking singularity that pulled at her, her thoughts, her faith, her courage. She faced it, her feet planted solid against the wind, and she saw the hanging fragments of the glassaic twitch, then tug free from their lead-lighting. Spinning, shining, they were pulled into the window and were gone. The cherubim turned one about another as the wind took them, then vanished as if they had never been. The organ-pipes, the false statues, the very cathedral itself... they were all lengthening, twisting, spinning into a sickening, turning spiral.

They were sucked down to the darkness, and they were gone. Katherine stood alone in eternity, a silent figure in the very void itself.

'This is what will happen,' the deacon said, his voice like the softest of brushes. 'If you do not take the power I offer. The galaxy will fall, and there will be nothing left. Rise up!' His voice was warmth, comfort; it was the only other thing that existed in the void. 'Rise up, O Empress! Bear your weapons, defy your foes. You can prevent this end, if you will take up this banner!'

But Katherine said, 'No.'

And the word was rock. It was the stone of her faith, the solidity of her shield. It was the fire in her heart, the touch of His presence.

She was a leader of warriors, a winner of wars, but they were not in her own name. That window was empty, not of her image, but of His. Not of her bravery and leadership, but of His authority and presence. She fought only in His name. And He would not leave her, whatever the threat that this witch might conjure.

Her hand still smoked, but her heart burned brighter. Without knowing how she had fallen, she realised she was on her knees. She still could not see, but she came back to her feet, knowing that the witch was close.

She repeated, the tone like some great bell, 'No. I have been deceived once, and the galaxy hung upon the balance of that falsehood. Never again will I, or any Sister of Battle, believe the honeyed words of the heretic. We follow His call, and no other. And you, witch, will *die!*'

The word echoed in the emptiness, loud as a shout. Hearing her own voice gave Katherine stability – there was grey stone under her boots; there was the chiming, acoustic echo of a vaulted ceiling, high over her head. And she began to sing once more, to sing to the void in the window, to sing to the holy cathedral that she still could not see for herself.

And her voice reached out across the darkness, and so did the darkness fall.

Dominica stopped, picking up the chalice once again. Early light was blurring on the floor, now, and there were more noises of movement from outside. The reveille, the call to muster, was almost upon them.

The Sisters rustled in their places, armour clattering. Avra's knees ached from the long service, but she made no complaint, only waited. Pain, as Lucia had already reminded her, told you that you were alive. Fighting.

Very softly, Silvana said, 'Tell on, my Sister. The dawn will catch us very soon.'

'There is little more to tell,' Dominica said. 'Like so many of our saint's tales, this may be truth, or it may be allegory. It may be somewhere between the two – for there is ever truth in fable, and fable in truth. What purpose the corrupt deacon had for our saint's power and command, we know not. Perchance he wished to raise an army, begin some rebellion – the tale does not recall. Nor does it remember his name, or whether the Frateris Militia came to that cathedral, so long ago and so far away, and witnessed the end of our saint's struggle, the celebration of her hymnal, and her return to the light. It does not even tell whether she slew the witch–'

'That is not in question.' Mina's voice was a growl and Dominica permitted herself a chuckle.

'Indeed,' she said. 'That is not in question. But I do know that this story carries the greatest message of all, the one that the Order of the Valorous Heart carries with it across the galaxy.'

She paused, still holding the chalice.

'Faith, my Sisters,' she said. 'The message is faith. Alicia Dominica saw Him, in all His glory. She carried the secret of that audience like a shard in her heart, the first Sisters of her Order likewise. And I have stood at the gates to the Imperial Palace and that...' She frowned. 'That was as much as my own heart could bear.

'And, as Alicia Dominica poured out the Grail of Ages upon the battlefield, and His voice was heard, so in this, the chalice of my Order, do we come together as Sisters in His light. In this vessel, we bear understanding, we bear wisdom. And these bear the indomitable wall that is our belief in Him. For just as Katherine beheld that empty window, and nonetheless raised her hymnal to His name, so we have no need to see Him – because we have faith. Because our faith is complete and untouchable. Because He is with us, and it is everything that we are, and everything that we strive to be.'

She looked round at the others. 'We do not see Him, my Sisters, yet He is always there.'

Her gaze stopped on Avra, who offered her a solemn nod.

'And thus,' Dominica said, 'in this chalice do I bear "faith" as the watchword of not only my Order, but of every Sister of Battle. We will never be deceived again. Not by psyker, or by traitor, or by witch. Not by the enemy, or by any xenos force. For He, and our belief in Him, will always be stronger.'

There was a pause, a murmur of prayer. Dominica let it continue, let it whisper to a close. Outside, orders barked louder; engines were beginning to growl.

'And now, my new Sister,' Dominica said, 'you will offer a tale of your own. Not a tale of our saint, but one from your own life, perhaps one where you have felt her presence – and His – most keenly.' She smiled, her carved face softening briefly. 'And at its end, you shall be Katherine, both within and without, and you must carry that mantle from the moment you leave this building, and you must never, *ever*, let it fall. But just for this last moment, we would know Avra, and understand your heart.'

Avra nodded, let the light from the coffin touch her face. She thought about her family, her father, her brother; thought about the young soldier in the camp – she had never even asked his name. Yet she knew the tale she would tell; it seemed to fit, the last key that would unlock the door in her soul.

And allow her to take up her shield.

THE TALE OF AVRA

Dawn light pooled on the floor, bringing a new and brilliant gleam to His sacred hanging, to His head and blade, and to the still-hovering bodies of the cherubim. They were moving now, almost as if impatient, their wings driving a faint and downward draught.

Under them, the little chapel seemed full of expectation. Like the light, it touched the bright and broken ceramic of the building's walls, making them shine in myriad colours. It shone in the eyes of her Sisters, each one as sharp as a gemstone and Lucia's augmetic sparkling red. It shone from the presence of the sacred artefacts and from the coffin of the saint herself, its black banner flowing down the steps. To Avra, it seemed to spread even further, outwards past the headless walls to the squad of her Order that stood upon holy watch, and further still, to the still-sleeping Militarum, keeping the enemy from their dreams.

At its focus and centre, she faltered. She rallied her thoughts, offered a prayer. Her heart, which had eased at the tales that had surrounded and buoyed her, began to beat again with nervousness – with the sheer, incredulous enormity of all of this.

I cannot be Katherine, I–

Sternly, she silenced her doubts. He had called her. The saint had offered her her name. And had not Dominica herself told her that she belonged?

To this new family?

She offered the Litany of Cleansing, the words as calm as clarity, and her Sisters echoed her, their voices chiming, encouraging.

'While I may walk worlds of darkness and terror, there you shall walk with me. I shall know no doubts, no fears, in your name.'

Thankful for their reassurance, she composed herself, and said, 'You have requested, my Sisters, that I do not tell you a tale of our saint, though I remember them well from my years at the schola. I am yet Avra, and the dawn now rises when I must lay down both my name, and my previous life. And so, I will tell you the tale that brought me to my vision.

'It is the final story of who I was.'

Dominica, to her left, nodded, indicated that she should go on.

'So, this is a tale of my family,' she said. 'Of my father, of my brother Talan, and of the creatures of the enemy that steal silently through our camp.'

She felt their encouragement, though she did not look up; her eyes were now on her knees, and her hands, resting palm down upon them. Lucia's ring shone back at her.

'And of how I came to be wandering the camp alone.'

'Surely, you were under orders?' Mina said, her dark voice soft. 'The Sisters of Our Martyred Lady have been walking the site, bringing His faith and courage to our weary brothers and sisters of the Astra Militarum.'

'That is true,' Avra said, glancing swiftly up. 'However, it is also true that I volunteered for this duty, because...' She frowned. 'Because I had known a moment of fear, earlier in the day. A moment where the foe reached out its claws for my heart.' The words were confession, heavy with significance, yet the release of them immediately lightened her soul. 'I was shamed. And I sought to offer suitable atonement for my lack of faith.'

Atonement, she thought, *and more.*

She did not speak the final thought aloud, though she knew the truth of it. She needed to tell the tale in full, not only so her Sisters would understand, but so that she could understand it herself.

And absolve herself of its weight.

Around her, her Sisters said nothing. The flow of their understanding felt strong, though beneath it, she felt their curiosity sharpen. Avra forced herself to look up further – at Him, at His judgement, at the cold, hard eyes of the cherubim. She should be attending dawn prayers, the celebration of the rise of Sol on far-distant Terra. When she lowered her eyes once more, she caught Arabella smiling at her. The strip across the young Sister's nose was flaking with loose skin, and this touch of her humanity felt like a blessing. A reminder that vulnerability was normal.

It was surrendering to it that was not permitted.

'You are doubtless aware of my Order's commands, and of where we were located for yesterday's operation?'

'We are aware,' Dominica said quietly, not wishing to interrupt.

Avra nodded. 'Under the orders of Major Haro, and of Sister Superior Melina, my squad has been located at the far left flank, and in the vanguard, as is proper. Yesterday, our mission parameters were to accompany a tech-priest of the Adeptus Mechanicus, and a single squad of Militarum, to a great, stone pedestal – the remains of some long-toppled statue – in advance of our own front lines. It lay a distance from us, out across no-man's-land, but its vantage could prove crucial – an ideal platform for a sniper or for heavy weapons, for whichever side managed to secure it. We were to ascend that pedestal, and to purge any lingering foe.'

Silvana nodded. 'We know where you mean.'

The rest of the Sisters said nothing, and she guessed that they would have known about the directive, as they would know about every order given by both the Sisters Superior and by the major.

She took a breath, continued. 'You know that the day was hot, the air thick with a rising shimmer. We departed the front rank of the advancing army and we moved swiftly, our heads down, out across the plain. The augurs of the Sentinels had mapped the ground ahead of us, allowing us to cross minefields and wires safely. We looked always for the foe, but we were not assailed. Successfully, we reached the location.'

She could see it in her mind's eye, like some huge and flat-topped molar tooth, growing larger as they had moved close.

'Without mishap,' she went on, 'we achieved our target and encircled it successfully, finding no enemy. As Sisters, we stood guard to ensure the squad's safety. Yet, despite attempts, they failed to ascend the vantage. The stone was smooth and unfamiliar. It defeated the tools of the soldiers, and they could not gain a foothold.'

She stopped, remembering. The day had been baking, the air wavering with rising heat. Above them, the pedestal had been colossal, a vast memorial to some fallen hero. It had engravings of soldiers, each as big as an armoured Sister, carved into its sides. And despite the relentless beating of Kiros' soot-smeared sun, its shadow had been eerily cold, a dusty, dirt-laden wind whining as it scoured past.

'By His blessing, however,' she said, 'we found that the pedestal was cleft in two, and that a great fissure ran through its heart, sharpening its winds to an edge, all laden with grit. In here, our adept was able to climb.' He had moved up the crack in the rock with a dexterity that had been almost uncanny. 'He drove claws and attachments into the stone, and behind him he left a long steel cable. The ascent would be somewhat ungainly' – she smiled, though the expression was saddened, laden with memory – 'but it would enable us to complete our mission.'

'The Sentinels had declared the location secure?' Silvana checked back on an earlier part of Avra's story.

'Even they make errors,' Arabella said gently.

'And the foe moves with both cunning and swiftness,' Mina agreed. 'As we have already seen. Speak on, my Sister.'

'I cannot speak for the Sentinels' omission,' Avra said. 'But I suspect that the foe had withdrawn deliberately, to lure us into the trap. Unaware of this, but cautious, we followed the path that the Mechanicus adept had made for us, intending to climb up the fissure.

'But the enemy was lying in wait.'

She paused again, recalling the wash of sickness that had taken her as they'd realised their error. It was less the shock of the incoming physical assault, less even the fact that they were caught from all sides, and more the twist of knife-blade knowledge, the sudden, sick understanding that they had been wrong.

Into the trap.

She lowered her eyes back to her knees, and went on.

'We were ambushed,' she said. 'The enemy permitted the tech-priest to attain the top of the plinth, and to complete the unrolling of his cable. I believe that they intended to assail him silently, and then attack us, one at a time, as we reached the top. But the Adeptus Mechanicus are not without combat resources of their own, and he lived long enough to communicate the alarm, a burst of binharic over the vox.'

She remembered it like the strike of a weapon, that familiar, high-pitched whine.

'Leaving two Sisters to guard, we moved. But the foe had already deployed their contingency – in the centre of the crack, a pile of massive rocks was set tumbling down upon our heads and shoulders. They were the remains of the crumbled statue, each as wide as the fissure would permit, and far too heavy to lift. My Sister Superior...' She stopped, closing her eyes. 'Sister Superior Melina, testing the lowered cable, was slain, trapped under a mass of falling stone. Her armour' – she paused again, remembering the horror – 'her armour was compromised, though she yet lived. But we could not lift the rocks from her, even powered as we are. They were simply too heavy. Crushed by impossible weight, she died not in combat, but slowly–'

'She was assailed by the foe,' Dominica said, brooking no argument. 'She perished in combat, and in honour, and her soul stands in His glory, at the feet of the Throne.'

Avra was blinking fiercely. The Sister Superior's defiant, final hymn echoed in her thoughts, a symbol of the courage with which she had faced a horrific death, a death that her squad could do nothing to stop, though they had tried. The Militarum had carried both pitons and entrenching tools and the Sisters had attempted to use these as levers, or shovels. But they were too short, and were snapped clean in two by the colossal weight of the tumbled pieces of statue.

'Unable to climb,' Avra said, 'we fell back and regrouped, attempting to devise a new strategy. There was little shelter from the fissure above and scatters of dust and pebbles fell down upon us. We endeavoured to free our Sister Superior, but despite our efforts, we could do nothing. We could only listen to her sing, defiant to the last.'

She paused, still blinking at the memory. In those first moments, there had been flickers of genuine panic, the entire fissure seemingly filled with noise and menace and shadow. Melina's dying voice had still sounded, her hymnal echoing in the space, but the squad sergeant had been barking orders, and the Sisters had been forced to abandon her, needing to defend both themselves and the soldiers.

'No further rocks came,' she said, 'only hissing trickles of sand. Nothing moved above us, though we knew the foe was there. We sent a message of warning back to the campsite and we moved back to back, the Militarum between us, taking what shelter we could. There was little space to muster a defence, but we expected to be assailed at any moment.

'As you say, however, they are both cunning and terrible.'

More grey light was filtering through the windows, now. The air, which had been chill with Kiros' bitterly cold night, was beginning to warm. It would be hot, and soon.

The expectation surrounding Avra was beginning to swell, a subtle pressure for speed. Telling her story was like pulling a splinter from her heart, a splinter that would let its blood and guilt flow fee. She had yet to confess the full nature of her shame, yet the tale was already cleansing, in its way.

She continued. 'Shadows of the enemy passed across the top of the fissure, phantoms like shapes of fear – more motion came from the edges, silhouetted against the light. There was laughter, rich and mocking, voices taunting us. More stone fell, not great slabs but a rattling of smaller, sharper rocks, and we remained vigilant, defending the soldiers at our centre.' Her hand touched her bolter. 'Several of them were injured, but they made no complaint, facing the enemy fearlessly.'

Her brother's face; her father's. The young soldier she had saved.

'But then...' She stopped and shuddered, before continuing, 'The foe changed their tactics. Knowing that we were all but helpless – Adepta Sororitas as we are! – they dropped... *corrosion* upon us, I know not what else to call it. And we could do *nothing* to fight them.' She paused again, frowning. 'I do not need to tell you the frustration and anger that such a feeling causes. We are Sisters of Battle! We are never helpless! We face the foe, slay it! We do not remain stuck in a *fissure*.' Melina had still been singing, though her words had become agonised, breathless, as her chest was slowly crushed. The squad had prayed for her, joining her in her hymn.

With some vehemence, Avra went on, 'Yet, with our exits blocked and little cover, we were caught. And they loosed some foul, dark ichor, dripping in heavy falls from their vantage. And with it, they laughed, more mockery, boasted words of their "gift" to us. And that laughter was rich, like rot, like the mould that grows upon dead flesh. There was nothing we could do to stop them.

'It was not aimed at us, our armour is sealed. But the soldiers...'

She stopped, again, remembering. The remaining members of the squad had burned where they stood, each one melting like a waxen seal, right down to their dust-covered boots. Some had tried to sing, joining the Sister Superior in her last notes. But the *screaming*...

In the fissure, it had echoed like pure horror.

'We tried to defend them.' She repeated the words like a mantra, her hand on the shield. 'We tried. But we failed, just as we failed to preserve the life of Sister Melina. They just–'

'You have faced the foe.' Dominica spoke for all the Sisters. 'Such is no small matter. The ancient enemy comes in four forms, you know this. But, whichever you face, they will use the same trickery – they play the darkest corners of your own mind against you. Your heart, your fears, your needs.' Her eyes searched Avra's face. 'Your memories.'

She spoke as if she knew about Avra's family, and Avra realised that she probably did. But Avra would have no secrets from her Sisters. Not from her Order, and not here. Secrets, as Dominica already knew, were heavy things to bear.

'Yes, Sister.' She rallied herself, and went on. 'The Militarum did not all perish, though they were terribly injured in both mind and body. There was one of them, younger than I, who had been fully covered by the tangles of the fallen rocks. He was a big man, dark and strong, his shoulders as broad as mine in armour.' Again that sad smile. 'Before our commanding Sister could give orders, or retrieve it herself, he wrested the squad's lascannon from its mounting, and with the weapon in his bare hands, he opened fire at the shadows above.'

Silvana raised an eyebrow. 'Surely, such a weapon cannot be wielded–'

'Anger,' Mina said to her Sister, 'is His blessing. And there are times when He will gift great strength, huge determination, and a focus that is more than human. One does not have to be a Sister of Battle,' she said, the faintest quirk of humour in her tone, 'to feel the blessing of His holy wrath.'

'Truly,' Avra said. 'He was a madman, in the grip of some vision, perhaps. He had the blessed strength of the Adeptus Astartes, gifted surely by His grace. His hands hissed with steam where they touched the corrosion upon the weapon, but he did not care. He had bitten his lip, and blood flowed down his chin. His fire cut into the leering shadows of the foe, blew stone chips from the lip of the fissure. He ascended the pile of rocks, and dust and pebbles fell down upon us, rattling like rain upon our armour. And still, he kept firing until, at last, he could recharge the weapon no more, and he collapsed.

'The enemy waited for his fire to stop. And, as the lascannon fizzled to a halt, they came howling in upon us.'

From outside, its timing as sharp as a slap, came the loud, hard tocsin of the reveille. It cut across the early morning like a peal of shock, yet seemed almost part of the story. A grumble of rising movement followed it; hardy sergeants already up, bellowing at their troops to get moving. It was not yet fully dawn, but the muster was almost upon them.

Avra said, 'We shot with our bolters, and our lines of fire were clear. At first, it seemed that they did not have the force to break our formation. Many of those that assaulted us were merely cultists, lightly armoured and with little in the way of weapons – they fell by the score. From above, more of the corrosion dripped down upon our shoulders, and upon the bodies. Friend and foe alike were simply eaten away, dissolving into fluids and steam. Our attackers died, screaming, just as the Militarum had done, and the tactics of the enemy made no sense to me.'

Feet sounded outside; there was the voice of Sister Superior Aliaah, still on duty. Avra spoke on, conscious of the time and of her new, as yet unknown, duties.

'Soon, their ploy was revealed. Underfoot the stone became treacherous, slick with ichor and with liquefying flesh. Some of the bodies were still moving, even as they sank in their own dissolving gore, their hands half-melted, raised in pleas for help, their bones outstretched like sticks. Defended by our sacred armour, we were immune, but the horror…' She stopped, swallowed. 'Mocking rains of rocks and debris came with it, taunting us with our own slow death, as helpless as our Sister Superior, and crushed in the mulch below.'

Outside, the camp was swiftly coming to motion. Barks of orders cut across the dawn; the air seemed to crackle with sharp, hard bursts of digital communication. Somewhere, more Sentinels were already moving, replacing those that had been deployed overnight.

'"You are trapped," a voice said to us, warm and rich. "Your very armour will be your ending, Corpse-Daughters. I will grant to you your greatest wish, your wish to die. I will fulfil every sick and twisted need you have ever had – you will know your deaths. But not as you imagine. You will know pain, anger, and darkness. You will know what it is to face your fears, and to fail. You will sink slowly, into the gore that we have made. You will be helpless, unable to move. And before we reach you, you will lose your *hope*."'

As Avra spoke, she looked round at the faces of her Sisters, each one in turn, each one an icon.

Dominica, her voice gentle, said, 'Truly, my Sister, it was His will for you to be in that fissure. To face a foe that mocks us, each in her turn.' The others were nodding, their expressions unsmiling; even Arabella seemed serious.

Avra had raised her face to Him, and to the saint; let the holy light break over her, let the tales her Sisters had offered hold her strong against the horrors of her own.

'At the words, there came a great silence. We stood in a quagmire, a quagmire of tumbled rocks and rotting flesh, our boots stained with the remnants of the soldiers' humanity.' Tears were sliding down her face again. She paid them no heed. 'Our Sister commander gave the order – we must still ascend the fissure. In His name, we must achieve the target, and purge the enemy from the pedestal.'

She stopped; the sickness of the memory was too much. Her face still bathed in the light, she broke into a hymn, unaware of the tears that had overflowed and were now trickling down her cheeks. Her Sisters passed no word of judgement, and somewhere, buried in a tiny corner of her heart, she wondered if each of them had faced this, their darkest, deepest fear; that moment of intense, personal crisis that was His greatest test.

'As I moved for the pile of rocks, I saw that the young man was still alive, still gripping the lascannon. Lying in the thick swamp of his fellows, his camo and flak already rotten, his flesh seeping out from under him. I prayed for him, and he opened his eyes and looked at me. But his gaze was not the sacred rage that had sustained him, nor was it the trained reaction of the soldier. It was not even the fear that one would expect – such would have been understandable. With any of these, he would surely have perished in honour, his soul's respite assured. No, in his gaze, there was only the pollution of the foe.

'And I faltered.'

The word was a shudder of admission. In that moment, she had seen the face of her brother Talan, a face that was a million, billion Astra Militarum soldiers, that was all the men and women who had given themselves to slay the enemy... but who had been denied their redemption, and who would never see the Throne.

Her tears poured more thickly, and her voice caught on a sob, her shoulders shaking. The noises of the outside had fallen away, almost as if He Himself had cupped His hands over the story, allowing her to tell its end.

'In that moment,' she said, 'I was bereft. I saw no courage, no honour, no nobility in his death. The enemy spoke to me, personally, and deep in my heart. It told me that there was no sacred martyrdom, no Throne, no redemption. There was only nothingness, the howling void. It told me that the very tenets of my Order, of our saint herself, were a fabrication, woven from both arrogance and folly...'

She stopped again, very conscious of the saint's light in the chapel, of her soft glow. To speak such words in her presence! Again, she began to sing, her words full of penance and regret. Sparkles of tears dripped upon her underarmour, shining briefly before they vanished into the black softness of the padding.

Outside the front of the chapel, Sister Superior Aliaah suddenly barked a command, making Avra start – she still had her vox-channel tuned to that of her Order.

'You are Adepta Sororitas,' Mina said, her voice brooking absolutely no denial. 'A Sister of Battle, a Daughter of the Emperor. You have been chosen as the exemplar of the saint herself, called by Him to bear her sacred coffin, and to bring her courage wherever you stand. You say you were bereft of your very faith?' Mina's voice was dangerous.

'Not of your faith, perhaps,' Lucia said softly, 'but of your focus?'

'I understand,' Arabella said. 'In that moment, you lost your hope.'

Avra's face contorted, she gulped air as the tears came again.

'How many souls,' she said, 'fighting in His name – how many souls have perished? They lined up in my mind, billions upon billions, their ranks stretched back into centuries beyond counting. My father died with honour. My brother died, but it was not in combat. He was no traitor, but he too was denied his salvation – his death meant nothing, and was in vain. His soul will never reach the Throne. And in that moment, as that young man lost his own life, I remembered Talan, remembered the numberless others like him, all lost to His glory – and I likewise lost myself. I paid my orders no mind, and I threw myself upon the pitons that the enginseer had left for us. I desired only to perish – yet that desire was not to lay down my life for Him, or even for my brothers and sisters. It was for myself. To prove to myself that the man's death, that all those soldiers' deaths, the deaths of my brother and of Sister Superior Melina, had been worthy, after all.

'I moved not with courage, but with the denial of my own fears.'

'Avra,' Dominica said. 'Sister Melina died in combat, facing the enemy. The same is true of your brother Talan. You know this, in your heart. The enemy played only upon your fears.'

But Avra went on, reciting as if she could not stop, still pulling that splinter from her heart. 'I failed.' The words came with an admission that was almost ironic; a smile flickered across her face. 'In His wisdom, He did not grant me my martyrdom. Yet, in my madness, I drove the foe back from the edge of the fissure, allowing my Sisters to ascend and our mission to succeed. We secured the location, as ordered.'

'You achieved your mission,' Mina said. It was a statement of approval; of flat, military accomplishment.

Avra nodded. 'A second squad was sent to relieve us, and we returned to the camp. Yet still, my soul was unquiet, and my failure haunted my thoughts. He had refused me, or so I thought, and it gnawed at my heart–'

'Your brother,' Dominica said, stopping her, 'died at the Battle of Belshar.'

'Yes, Sister.' Avra glanced round. 'He was younger than I, barely nineteen. He joined the Militarum as soon as he was of age, wishing to honour our father's memory. I had intended to do likewise, in my earliest youth, but He had other plans for me, and I attended the schola. My father would have been very proud of us both.' She looked up, at Dominica's lean, shadowed face. 'Yes, he died upon Belshar, but it was not in combat. His Salamander crashed, he perished in flames. He disgraced...' She swallowed, hard. 'Disgraced our father's record and memory by not facing the enemy.'

'He died for the God-Emperor,' Dominica said. 'As did Sister Superior Melina. As have done a billion others, every fearless soldier of the Astra Militarum. Talan died in faith, fighting His wars. And he kneels now at the foot of the Golden Throne.'

Avra caught her breath on a sob, scrubbed her hands over her face. But her speech was like a confession and still, she could not stop, not until that splinter was fully, finally free.

'I was relieved of my duty, but I could not rest. Shadows grew upon me, phantoms of my failure. The prayers in my heart twisted in upon themselves, and the enemy's whisperings clouded the corners of my mind. I could see only my brother's death, and my despair grew. I volunteered for the camp duty, but was refused. I had been too close to the foe, and I was told to recite my Litanies until my heart settled, and I could see Him clearly once more.'

'You disobeyed the order?' Mina said, one eyebrow raised.

'I disobeyed the order.' The shame was creeping into her cheeks now, a flush like the colour of Mina's rose. 'I know I should not have done so, but I sought... needed...'

Redemption? Forgiveness? Clarity?

'The enemy never ceases to test us,' Silvana told her. 'It knows our darkest secrets, the tiny cracks in our soul like the fissure in that rock. And it prises its curious talons into those cracks and attempts to wrench them wide.' Her eyes were on Avra's face, making the point. 'It knows you, my Sister. As it knows all of us.'

Dominica was nodding, her face carved in seriousness.

'Yet, in its choice of torment,' Silvana went, 'did the enemy also not serve His design? Did your distress not bring you to us?' There was a smile on her face, crinkling at the corners of her eyes.

Avra shot her a look. 'You are saying that the enemy does His will?'

'Ah, my Sister,' Arabella said. 'There you touch upon a question most complex. He is all-powerful, hence the foe only exists because He permits it–'

'The foe is not of His creation,' Mina said. 'I do not need to remind you–'

'Yet when the foe tears through to our reality, does it not–'

'Enough,' Dominica growled. 'This is not a librarium. We will leave the theoretical arguments to a more suitable time.'

Arabella's lips twitched. Leaning forwards, she said, 'I would say, my Sister, that you walked the camp seeking your lost hope. That your desire to locate an enemy was less a need to throw yourself into martyrdom, and more a need for an answer. A quest for His light. And did you not save the young man's life, even as you sought to lose your own? Whatever the motivations of the enemy, and however we may debate' – with a flash of her earlier humour, she raised an eyebrow at the other Sisters – 'your actions today were in His name, and they have brought you here. You must comprehend – your brother's death was but a part of His design. Had it not been for Talan's sacrifice, for your battle today, He would not have blessed you to defend that soldier. And you would not have come to us. And now, they are *all* your family, all your brothers and sisters, all across the galaxy. And you will ensure that their deaths have meaning.' Her smile was radiant. 'Until the day He calls you to the Throne.'

Dominica nodded, severe but approving. Outside, the camp was alive with the sounds of movement.

Avra's shoulders shook. She thought about the other soldier, the young woman who had been torn clean in half. At the time, she had felt a moment of odd, buried envy, yet she had reached for her weapons and courage instinctively, as her faith and training had taught her.

'Their deaths have meaning,' she repeated. And, raising her face to the light of the saint, to His light, the shine of the embroidered hanging, she felt that splinter of pain work free from her heart at last. Talan's life had not been given in vain. She would stand by her brother, by all her brothers and sisters, in the future.

And her own death would come, when He willed.

'We are out of time, my Sisters,' Dominica said. 'This morning, we push out across the wastelands and assail the foe. There are many emplacements like the one you assaulted,' she told Avra, 'there to defend our advance. And we will stand at the army's centre, be its heart and its courage.' The cherubim were shifting as they flew. The breeze from their wings grew stronger. 'And where we march–'

A scrape of ceramite boots interrupted her. In the chapel's doorway, there were two young Sisters, their armour black, bearing a sacred chest between them.

'Ave Imperator, Sisters Exemplar. We bear our Sister's sacred armour, newly repaired and cleansed.'

Avra's sisters-in-arms – or they had been. They placed the chest down and respectfully backed away.

'Wait,' Avra said. They were the tiniest fragment of her old life, and they were retreating from her. Leaving her with this huge responsibility.

'Permission to speak,' one said.

'You may say your farewells,' Dominica told them. 'But make

them swift. The foe will not wait. Sisters, we must pray, arm and be ready.'

Four of them rose to their feet and smoothly ascended the steps, each kneeling as she reached the top. Arabella stayed, tidying the remains of their meal. Remembering Lucia's tale of the Repentia, and of the saint's oldest friends, Avra moved to thank the Sisters of her Order.

'You do us a great service,' Sister Rene said. She was unhelmed and the saint's light bathed her dark face like a blessing. 'We are proud of you–'

'Pride is a sin,' Juliette commented, her green eyes shining. Both of them seemed to make a conscious effort to not look at the coffin, keeping their gazes averted. 'We know you're not Avra, not any more. But to be Katherine, to walk the galaxy...' Her gaze was lost in wonder, searching Avra's face. 'We are honoured to follow you. Always. Wherever you may lead.'

Unable to speak, she embraced them both, the edges of their armour hard against her padding.

The second tocsin sounded, followed by a clatter that was Dominica, coming back to her feet. Politely, Rene and Juliette backed away.

'Thank you, Sisters. Ave Imperator.'

They returned the salute, and were gone.

Avra opened the chest, began to remove her armour. Dominica gestured, and the others surrounded her, positioning her chestplate and backplate, her pauldrons and vambraces, mag-fastening each in place. A prayer flowed between them and Avra was again reminded of her Ordination, of the very first time she'd donned her armour for real.

'And so,' Dominica said, stepping back, 'the Service of Tales is concluded, and warfare awaits. We have spoken much of ourselves, less of the unit to which we belong – but we do have a military objective. For now, my Sister, your armour is incomplete. Mina, if you would.'

The red-armoured Sister moved to the wall beside the altar, shifted a swathe of dark cloth. From outside, as if the timing had been decreed by His blessing, the voice of Sister Superior Cico broadcast the dawn prayer, her words strong over the vox. Avra could hear the ragged, rougher voices of the Militarum – they must be at full muster.

Awaiting the orders to advance.

Mina turned back, bearing upon her arm the Praesidium Protectiva, a kite-shield almost as tall as she was, its front illustrated with a flare of holy light. In her other hand, she bore the Martyr's Sword, crackling with might and energy. About the artefacts, the chapel itself seemed to quiet, to hold its very breath in awe.

'Take up your shield,' she said, 'your sword and your name. You are Avra no longer. You are Katherine Elysius, Katherine of the Fiery Heart. You are Our Martyred Lady, your anointed sword spills the blood of the foe, and upon your holy shield does the enemy crest and shatter.'

Avra – Katherine – took both as they were handed to her, marvelled at the weight of the relics, at their history and lore. Bearing them, she felt her soul fill with light, and understood, at last, that she could carry shield, and sword, and the name she newly bore.

THE TRIUMPH OF SAINT KATHERINE

Outside the chapel, the camp was in motion.

Katherine had half expected a fully polished parade ground muster, a procession or celebration, but this was not a company on display. The awakened platoons were grim, now; their humour dark, their tents and bivvies gone. The next wave of Sentinels had already left, skirmishing out across the badlands. She caught glimpses of the formed-up soldiers, rifles at their shoulders, listening to the morning's orders. Where the scouts led, the infantry would not be far behind.

A line of guards still stood along the perimeter wall, and with them, the Master of Ordnance stood like an icon, her attitude solid, her augur glinting in the morning sun. The remaining heavy weapons platoons – those not despatched to hold tactical points – awaited her orders. The air felt tight, sharp.

In her heart, prayers rose like adrenaline.

'Walk forth, Katherine.' She had the Sisters' vox-channel, now, and Dominica's voice was a burr of soft warning. 'Show no hesitation.'

Lifting her chin, she walked down the steps.

Her head was bared, and instantly she was conscious of the change, of leaving both service and sanctum behind. The wind was already beginning to climb, sweat-warm, tinged with metal and threat. It stirred the dust at her feet, rattled grit against her armour. She felt the eyes that turned upon her; saw the scattering of still-loose soldiers sinking to their knees. The chains of the cherubim creaked; the coffin's glow seemed to touch her back with both light and expectation. She bore the great shield, her sword in her other hand, her bolt pistol and helm at her hips. To one side, Arabella's censer burned with the promise of battle, to the other, Dominica's chalice flared with a new and castigating flame. And she could feel the presence of the other Sisters' artefacts: Mina's tray, its bloody petals fluttering free, the shine of the Argent Shroud, the Valorous Heart's red glow.

Mina's voice came over the vox. 'Sister Superior Aliaah, you and your squad will walk with us. Sister Superior Cico and Sister Fiann, take your squads to the right and left flanks.'

'Sister.'

Black-armoured figures ran, and Dominica said, 'Katherine, the major.'

And there he was: Owai Haro, the Jaguar himself, named for the dappled burn-scars across his hard, dark cheek. He'd got them as a new recruit, in a fire – and he'd made them his own, building his company and his reputation upon them. For all his rank and his grey hair, pale against his skin, he, too, could have been her brother.

All across the galaxy.

'Ave Imperator,' he said, offering them the sign of the aquila. His voice was deep, and it rolled like tank tracks. 'The honour is ours. I am blessed to stand in the presence of our most holy saint. I regret the lack of ceremony, Sisters, but we do not have time. Our Sentinels confirm – the monster is in motion.'

With him was his banner-bearer, the Jaguar flag at his back, and the enginseer that Katherine had seen the previous night, surrounded by a grinning flotilla of servo-skulls. The tech-priest's semi-human face was unreadable, but the banner-bearer was little more than a lad, a single pip upon his shoulder. He gazed at Katherine, eyes wide, then remembered himself and looked at his boots.

'Major,' Katherine returned, her voice even. She had no formal wording, but the Service of Tales had bolstered her, and her footing was secure. She felt strong, elated, eager to meet the enemy, to hold the heart of the army round her. 'It is our honour to be here, in His name. And our honour and duty both, to face the enemy.' She could almost hear Dominica prompting her. 'Before us, they will falter, and flee.'

Servo-skulls twitched and hovered, tools and jaws clacking. Haro gave a grim, curt nod.

'Sisters, company HQ will muster at defence tower delta, ready to advance. Platoons one, four and six will move out ahead of us. The Sentinels report…' He paused, a frown ghosting his face. 'The enemy numbers are swelling, and they are *hungry*. They are not yet in range of the outposts, but we suspect them within the hour.'

Echoing his words, orders barked from vox-casters and the first three platoons stamped to dismissal, then ran for their muster locations. Katherine knew the drill: they would move, extended file, out across the badlands, until the enemy was engaged.

Mina said, 'The great beast is our target. Do you have its location?'

'It leads the lines of the foe.' Haro's jaw jumped, though his stance was upright. 'The corrupted people of Kiros make up much of its support, and they follow it eagerly.' Ghosts crossed his expression. 'They must be freed from its pollution.'

From behind the coffin, her Shroud now hung at her back and shining with a light of its own, Silvana's soft rasp said, 'You cannot face this beast, major. You will leave it to us.'

'In His name,' Haro returned, 'and with you at our side – we will reclaim Kiros for the Imperium.'

* * *

We will reclaim Kiros…

The previous day, as the squads of the Order of Our Martyred Lady had fought through the broken streets, much of Katherine's vision had been obscured by soot and dust and flame. Now, moving out from the campsite's carefully rebuilt defences, she recalled those shattered walls, the snapped-off feet of the nameless statues, the squads running and dropping and running again – that so-familiar skirmish manoeuvre that she'd learned at the schola.

That she would never use again.

Now, she walked like an emblem, her sacred shield before her, both banner and bastion, her sword borne aloft like a firebrand. Out here, the streets had gone, cleared back to a wasteland of tumbled stone, of craters and wires and lingering menace. The wind was gusty and fierce, buffeting at her sides. Smoke and dust were already rising, obscuring her sight of the platoons ahead, and of the gleaming black armour of Sister Aliaah and her squad. Yet through it, Katherine carried the light; it rose at her shoulders, it rose in her heart, in her being. Its brightness was a beacon: mental, spiritual, physical.

It made of her shield a wall, an unbreakable fortress.

The six Sisters did not speak, though their vox-channel was open. Between them, the ancient hymnal flowed like pure thought, harmonies curling from one Sister to another. This was more than the Litany; it was a node, a kernel.

'A spiritu dominatus.'

The steel-shelled seed of faith from which pure courage grew.

'Domine, libra nos.'

They moved on, attentive and watchful, the dirt and smoke growing thicker. The heat was climbing swiftly now, the wind like coughs from a furnace. As the unseen sun rose higher, sweat tickled the sides of Katherine's face. Occasional barks came from the soldiers' vox-casters; at times, the lights of a Sentinel would flare past them and vanish again.

To her side a hovering servo-skull emerged from the smoke as if checking on them, then sank away once more. The chains of the cherubim creaked.

In the vox, his tone firm beneath the echoing of their hymns, Haro said, *'Lieutenant Natera. Report.'*

'We have contact, emplacement beta.' Natera's tone was cold, brutal.

'Range?' That was Renagi, the ordnance master, back on the wall.

'Four hundred yards, and closing.'

'Then fire.' Haro's snarl was all repressed rage.

Before the Sisters, the smoke changed to storm. There was the crack and boom of heavy weapons, the slash and glare of lascannons. The defiant singing of Sister Aliaah and her squad. Streaks of harsh brilliance came from somewhere ahead, then the colossal billowing booms of impact. Mortars coughed, their shells becoming hollow detonations.

The smoke grew thicker, hot and choking. Katherine blinked grit from her eyes.

'From the lightning and the tempest!'

'Report!' Haro said again.

'Beta, dead ahead.' Natera's voice was harsh; he coughed in the vox. *'Three hundred yards. Advancing* fast!'

Haro's voice was calm as iron across the company vox. *'Lieutenant, maintain the bombardment. Captain Mai, hold your position. Take cover, await orders to advance. Sister Aliaah–'*

'We hold our position, major.'

Katherine did not need to see to understand; the infantry would take the closest concealment, dropping and covering the morass ahead of them, a field of lasrifles poking out across the ruinous flat.

'Our Emperor, deliver us!'

In the vox, Natera's voice: *'Emplacements gamma, beta,* fire!'

Heavy weapons thundered defiance. A moment later, Natera said, *'Warped humans, minor warp spawn. Nothing we can't...'* The voice paused. *'Shit.'*

'Natera.' Haro's voice brooked no compromise. *'Report.'*

And there: the first waves of fear.

Still blinking, Katherine felt them come, growing like convection, curling like a swirl and eddy of sickness. The song of their surrounding Sisters grew louder, challenging the murk and the terror.

'From plague, temptation and war!'

With them, Dominica's voice rose, the hymnal gaining a sudden, furious edge. Above it, Arabella raised her own voice, her pure, cold soprano sharp enough to cut at the air's thick heat. Silvana sang a soft, regular rhythm, almost like poetry, twining through the other two, and the hair rose on Katherine's forearms. There was a real, thunderous power to Dominica's voice, a depth and timbre like some great, bared blade. The red glare of her chalice was still visible through the smoke.

And then, Mina, Lucia – Mina taking Silvana's rhythm and making of it a drumbeat like some merciless, mighty march; Lucia's voice as pure as Arabella's but carrying an aching, poignant note, like impossible pain and the clarity it brought.

Katherine knew the sacred hymnal, but not like this. She'd never heard these harmonics. The ripple of exultation crept up her shoulders, up the back of her neck. *This* was the manifestation of the Service of Tales – this was the Sisters' differences, and it was their unification. It was their ringing celebration of the six Orders Militant, of the Adepta Sororitas entire, of their faith and courage and everything they stood for.

It was the place they overlapped, the centre where they stood together.

'Our Emperor, deliver us!'

The song carried her, too, and she raised her own voice, her softer contralto singing with Dominica. For the faintest moment she saw again the miracle of her vision...

Sisters, kneeling upon a flagstone floor.

But she belonged, now. She had seen that vision for a *reason.*

Your brother's death was a part of His design. Take up your shield, your sword and your name.

The light of the saint seemed to grow, banishing the smoke and the filth. She could hear Haro, muttering a prayer across the vox, could *feel* the heart of the Jaguar as it lifted. She could hear Aliaah, stern and strong. Like a sacrament, light and blessing spread from the coffin; the sheer resonant power of the hymnal rang from the march's vox-casters. It spread out across the battlefield, a rallying cry that was the saint herself, her fiery heart, her Wars of Faith made manifest.

She was *here.* In His name, and in hers, they would not fail.

To Katherine's other side, Arabella drew her bolt pistol. Her sense of mischief had hardened, solidified into a grim, edged courage that promised death to the foes of the light. As if hope, too, could be a weapon.

'Give me range,' Haro barked. *'I need a location.'*

The smoke and dust were parting, now, driven forth by light and sound. Through the retreating billow, the red cloaks of the Order, now soot-stained and torn. A running Sentinel came past them – the pilot bringing it back from the front line. Its gait was erratic and smoke poured from the cockpit. It must have said something, because Haro snapped a command a moment later.

'Emplacements alpha through delta, retire to secondary positions. Captain Mai, listen up. And fire!*'*

Mina said, like a growl, 'Incoming.'

The tension in Katherine's neck grew sharp, cold. Clamping her hands on blade and shield, she sang, still, with Dominica.

'From the scourge of the Kraken!'

Smoke swirled, obscuring her vision. She heard the thunder of bolters; the relentless cracks of heat that were the moving infantry. *Talan!* She could–

A wash of sickness and terror broke over her. *By the Throne!* It was tangible, physical enough to almost knock her to her knees. It came on like a tide, a roar of putrid mockery; it broke over her in a wave of nausea. Despite the hymnal, her belly roiled, cresting like polluted foam. Refusing to acknowledge it, she sang with more volume, more vehemence. More *rage.*

'Our Emperor, deliver us!'

Voices came across the vox, breaking up now. *'The... many... em!'*

Figures staggered through the smoke to their flanks. Petals, red and white, swirled round them; Silvana's Shroud flapped like a trapped thing. Voices screamed, horrific and masculine, a terrible sound that cut–

Silence.

Only the Sisters' hymn, now echoing vast and hollow, out across pure ruin. Katherine had not heard an order to hold fire, but the infantry had stopped shooting. The smoke had retreated further, and she could see Sister Aliaah and the black armour of the Order; they were kneeling in fire positions, but they were still.

The vox crackled and spat. It felt like it was waiting.

She cried a challenge, her voice loud. 'From the blasphemy of the fallen!'

Then, like a lone, staggering ghost, a solitary figure came into full view, a young man in camo and flak armour, his brassard with a single chevron stripe. Vomit stained his chin and chest. His face was acid-burned, and he was gibbering like an insane thing, his laughter climbing higher, even as he staggered and fell. He had no rifle.

Haro snarled, *'Ma... ort!'*

Nothing. The vox echoed with a rich, thick laughter, with humour that swelled like a distended belly. More figures came now, silhouettes in rising dirt, staggering like the first. Mockery rolled from them like heat, like the thick smell of decay.

Merciless, Aliaah snarled an order and Katherine heard the unmistakeable thump and bellow of the squad's heavy bolter, the words of her Sisters as they picked up the Litany once more.

'Our Emperor, deliver us!'

Shambling figures were shredded and fell. Haro repeated his order. A second later, Mai's voice came back.

'There... oo ma...! ...verrun!' The vox bubbled like acid.

'Aliaah!' Mina's snap was hard, spoken aloud. 'Cover their retreat.'

The Sister Superior gestured, and the seven of them ran, their hymnal still broadcasting.

Silvana said, 'We will slay the beast. Break the enemy's hold on this planet.'

'Agreed,' Arabella said. 'Or our hope is lost.'

'Agreed,' Lucia said. 'We will take the pain upon ourselves.'

'Agreed,' Mina said. 'We will move with Aliaah. Offer cover to the troops.'

'It is decided,' Dominica said. 'We are united.' The word sounded like a great clang, like hammer striking anvil. 'Katherine – we march.'

They marched.

Carried by song, the saint borne in faith and light and sound and fury, the smoke parting before them in waves like awe, they marched.

Around them, all was devastation. The heavy weapons had pulled back and the infantry had been overrun with shocking swiftness, unable to react fast enough. Katherine passed a Sentinel, lying on its side, one foot still twitching. Gore and fluid covered its ruined frame. A second line of defence still lay before the campsite, but she understood the Sisters' objective now – there was a great enemy here, and if they did not face it, then the mission would fail.

And Kiros would be lost to the foe.

Cherubim wings beat like determination, stirring at the air currents; the ground was strewn with bodies. Blasted craters shimmered with lingering heat. Great curls of wire stood across their way, but Aliaah and her Sisters were already there, their armour now dented and covered in dirt. They trampled and cut, and made way for the saint to advance.

Returning to the full cry of the hymnal, the Sisters' words rolled forth in clarion challenge. And something finally connected in Katherine's teachings, some touch of His blessing: the words 'Our Emperor, deliver us' were not a plea for Him to manifest, to take their battle, their responsibilities, upon Himself – they were a crystallisation, a forging.

A *catalyst.*

And they allowed the Sisters to wreak His wrath upon the foe.

'From the begetting of daemons!'

And as they marched, so there came His miracle.

First in ones and twos, and then more, and then more, the battered soldiers rallied to their sides. Most were burned, or injured, or scarred by acids; some were fearful, others furious. But they came, their rifles still at their shoulders, and they took up the cry of the hymn, echoing the Sisters' call.

Beside Katherine, there were clean streaks down Arabella's face, though her chin was lifted. To her other shoulder, Dominica's chalice blazed like pure wrath.

More came, and more. And the more of them there were, the more Katherine understood: just like every one of these men and women were her family, so they were also the lessons that her Sisters had taught her. They were pain, they were hope, rallying amidst the wreckage; they were daring, coming forth to face the foe; they were discipline and anger, they were pure and righteous faith. Every one of them that joined the march brought a spike of emotion to her throat, and she found herself walking the battlefield, her voice caught upon hooks of huge feeling…

This – *this!* – was the Triumph of Saint Katherine. Not just her life, her Wars of Faith, her martyrdom, but the glory that she sustained in His name, the lives that *still* rallied to her call. Katherine's throat closed. Unable to sing, she continued to march, head and shield high.

And then, Aliaah's voice said, 'Hold.'

Reacting instinctively, Katherine held up a gauntleted fist and the new force stopped.

And a voice ahead of them said, ***'Welcome, Corpse-Daughters. I've been expecting you.'***

Wreathed in smoke, the thing was huge.

Still a hundred yards away, it was a mountain of blubberous and infected flesh, riddled with maggots, oozing with creatures nameless and terrible. A great wave of stink rolled before it, decay and disease, old food and rotting bodies. It carried a huge, metal flail, chattering skulls upon rusting chains. Yet its face was lit with a smile of pure beneficence, an expression of warmth and generosity, as if they were some long-lost… Some long-lost *family.*

It taunted her, and she knew it.

Lumbering forwards, it shook the ground.

'I see you've brought me a gift. How thoughtful.'

Its words were rich and generous, lush with corruption. The stench rose like green smoke, palpable and vile. The soldiers had stopped singing, many of them paling to ghost-white, or leaning over to retch. Some had curled into a ball; others were clawing at their faces as if the smell ate at their skin. Creatures scrambled from the thing's body, eager to feed. They seethed over the ground.

'Fire!'

Aliaah, her tone pure steel. The squad of Sisters held its ground. They loosed their bolters at the monster but they may as well have been shooting some vast cadaver – the wounds opened, but the monster did not seem to feel it.

'Our Emperor, deliver us!'

Dominica, furious, was still singing, her voice a paean, less harmony and more pure, focused righteousness. Mina's carried rage, as scarlet as las-fire; Silvana's had an edge of audaciousness that glittered like a pure-white knife.

But the thing did not care. It came forwards, shaking the stone, shedding maggots as it moved.

Arabella shouted, loud over the hymn, 'We do not fail, we do not falter! Hold to your hope, soldiers of the Imperium! He is with you! The saint is with you, and she will bring *victory!*'

Shakily, the soldiers began to stand, to reach for their weapons. They tottered, but their discipline was good – as the writhe of creatures came on, they opened fire, the first tiny sparks of the conflagration. Somewhere, an officer was shouting orders.

The thing laughed, a great bass boom that seemed to echo the full length of the battlefield, flattening the last standing walls like dry sand. Shrugging off Aliaah's assault, it came closer, like some huge and mobile groundquake. Her squad kept firing, and the thing laughed louder, rich with humour. Before it, the blasted flat was alive with viciousness, swarming with hunger. Worms and insects writhed and wriggled, squalling, but the las-fire was stronger now. Gore and fluids splashed. Voices cheered, ragged with new courage. Somewhere, someone started a hit total.

'Three! Four!'

The humanity of it was touching, a mote as tiny as a single soldier, yet as vast as the Emperor's Hammer. *My brothers. My sisters. All across the galaxy.*

The monster bellowed; Katherine stood like a statue. She had no fear, only certainty. Light blazed behind her, made of her an icon. Red flame glowed to one side and white petals to the other. Crashing the sword upon the shield, a defiant, metallic ringing, she challenged it.

'I am Katherine! I stand in His light, in the glow of the saint herself, and I say – you will not take this world! You do not belong here, spawn of the Enemy! *Begone!*'

The thing eyed her and stamped forwards. It crushed one black-armoured Sister underfoot, and bared its rotted teeth to snarl at her with thick, yellow spittle. Its breath was enough to crumble her armour; to flay the very skin from her face.

She did not move.

It raised the flail, the thongs rattling like live things, twisting and hissing like serpents.

Still, she did not move.

Her Sisters cried, as one, 'From the curse of the mutant!'

The incoming blow was immense, sending her skidding backwards, but her shield rang with a tone like a great bell, echoing out across the ruin. She heard bolters, her Sisters – both her Sisters Exemplar and the standing Sisters of her Order. She heard las-fire, the snapped orders of the still-upright officer.

The climbing kill-tally of the nameless infantryman.

Dirt billowed back and forth. Across the ground, the slithering masses of creatures were dying in smoke and stench. A flamer barked and they went up like fuel, popping as they burned. Others slumped to molten flesh and pools like acid. The steam that rose was caustic, making the soldiers pull back.

Above the Sisters, cherubim hovered, cold-eyed and lethal. If the monster affected them, they did not show it.

And the *light*...

Where the saint's light touched the beast, so its flesh was

beginning to burn. Curls of greasy smoke rose from its body; its skin crisped and peeled back, revealing more of the putrid organs beneath. And those organs were swelling, exploding, as if roasted by some great heat.

The flail came down again, a crashing impact that rattled Katherine's teeth; its feet crushed another Sister even as she tried for a better shot. Katherine's mind was filling with her vision, with those shifting, dancing boots, with the duel...

With this very shield.

You are Katherine Elysius, Katherine of the Fiery Heart. You are Our Martyred Lady, your anointed sword spills the blood of the foe, and upon your holy shield does the enemy crest and shatter.

With a great shout, she drove her sword at the monster, exactly where the light had struck it.

And the beast *screamed.*

It was a terrible, tearing noise, a noise that rent the sky, that shattered the ground asunder. It bowled the soldiers from their feet, made the Sisters stagger. For an instant, their hymn faltered.

But Dominica cried, 'No! We will see this thing *slain!*'

And the cry was enough. The beast seemed almost to recoil. At its feet, its swathe of maggots and worms was decimated, burning. The smoke was obscuring Katherine's vision as the monster started to falter. She struck at it again, caught another blow on her shield rim.

She cried, 'Our Emperor, deliver us!'

Aliaah echoed her, a split second later. Her squad were still firing.

Above them, the beast staggered at the barrage. Every rifle, every bolter, every voice, every warrior loosed His wrath at the foe. And the light tore deeper into the wounds, deeper into its terrible body. And where it touched, it burned, cauterising and destroying.

The monster bellowed, its outrage immense. It stamped and

roared, lashing about itself with the flail. Bodies broke, flew, but still the assault did not stop.

'Keep firing!' The order came from Mina, her pure rage burning in her words.

Then Arabella's cry: 'In His name!'

The beast shrieked higher. About it, the air began to froth and twist, the smoke eddying in sucking patterns of colour.

'Now!' Dominica roared. *'A morte perpetua!'*

Understanding instantly, Katherine threw her full, armoured weight behind her shield and charged the beast, slamming into its burning belly. She was surely too small to knock it back, but she had the saint's light and blessing, and His very presence, carried with her, and the thing staggered.

Furious, it brought a closed fist down on the top of her head. She had no helm, the blow should surely have shattered her skull; her head rang with impossible pain, her hymnal fell from the air. She could feel – smell – burning flesh. Her own. Blood matted her hair, flooded her eyes, ran into her mouth. But she struck the thing again, driving it backwards, slammed her shield into it bodily, over and over and over and *over*, knocking it back.

It squalled, like some angry child, hammered at her again, but she held her ground, her consciousness swimming. It stamped and roared, thumping the ground to both sides with the huge flail. Around it, bodies broke. Katherine's knees were like water, but she did not fall, she struck it again, again, with shield and sword. Her Sisters opened fire, Sisters of March and Order both; the Militarum soldiers' lasrifles chewed charred holes in its belly.

She heard Dominica's voice, ringing as if from far away. 'That Thou wouldst bring them only *death!*'

At the final word, the beast flickered. Katherine stopped, blinking, struggling to focus. The thing was fading, twisting, turning in on itself like some horrific, dark whirlpool. She felt its pull, dug the base of the shield into the bloody ground. Her cloak flapped like a live thing, as if trying to escape. Soldiers shouted as they were pulled from their feet.

But Dominica, her Sisters, Aliaah – they were still singing.

'That Thou shouldst spare none! That Thou shouldst pardon none!'

Under their onslaught, the daemon shrieked, the sound cutting like broken glass. And Katherine joined her voice to the final line.

'We beseech Thee, *destroy them!*'

With the detonation of a falling citadel, the thing was gone.

Staggered by the sudden lack of resistance, she almost fell. Dominica caught her elbow.

'Stand, Sister.'

Katherine could not see, but stayed on her feet.

Arabella said, in the vox, 'You do not let them see you fall, Sister. No matter the battle, no matter your injury, you remain their icon.'

'Bear the pain,' Lucia said.

'Aliaah!' That was Mina's voice. 'Report!'

'Three of my squad have attained His grace,' the Sister Superior said. 'But the onslaught of creatures is defeated. They cannot be, it seems, without their master.'

'That is well,' Silvana answered. 'We have taken the battle to the beast, and we are victorious, but the force is still lingering, and another commander may yet rise. We should return to the camp, re-form.'

Katherine's knees shook, her head pounded with a pain like she'd never known. Her ears rang, her skin still burned.

'Walk,' Dominica said. 'As the tales have taught you. We are the Triumph of Saint Katherine, and we return with victory.'

Cheering.

Her hair matted with blood and slime and water, her face filthy, her sword and shield and armour covered in the gore of the monster, Katherine returned to the camp. With her, her Sisters, bearing the saint in glory, and her Sisters of the Order, their weariness tangible. With her also, the walking survivors of three infantry platoons, many of them bearing injured comrades.

The vox had cleared, its hissing mockery gone.

'Major Haro,' Dominica had said. 'We have slain the beast. We cannot claim that the battle is over – there is a long fight yet ahead of us, and the Treatise has yet to be retrieved. But we have achieved our objective – the monster is dead. In His name.'

'In His name,' the major had replied.

And the Jaguar was there to meet them, sinking to one knee as they came back to the campsite. Around him were the men and women of his company, still not the parade ground muster that Katherine had half expected, but battered and weary figures, their armour dirty but their camo-streaked faces alight with celebration and new hope. They followed their commander's lead and their voices were raised in song: the hard, marching hymnal of the fighting Militarum.

Among them, she saw the face of the young man from the previous night – how had it only been yesterday? Despite the pain, Katherine caught his eye and gave him the faintest smile. Overcome, he lowered his head, offered her the sign of the aquila.

The major came back to his feet.

'Ave Imperator,' he said.

Her knees like water, the pounding of her skull like some great, hollow drum, Katherine wanted only to rest the weight of the shield on the ground. Her arm pained her where it had taken the blows of the beast, her stomach still churned with its smell.

But she stood upright. Within her gauntlet, the tiny steel pin of Lucia's ring reminded her – *the pain tells you that you yet live, that you fight on.*

Beside her, Dominica said, 'Tend to your wounded, major. But remain vigilant. Though the enemy is headless, it may yet strike back.'

'Truly, Sisters,' Haro said. 'You have brought us great honour.'

'But not yet victory,' Silvana told him. 'Come the darkness, or come the dawn, there will be another battle.'

Katherine was almost tottering. Fluids were still seeping down her face, though her wounds no longer hurt. She could see the beast in her mind's eye, towering and terrible, but it burned, burned at the touch of the light. And that light was tumbling through convent windows, slants of blessing on a flagstone floor.

'There is always,' Haro observed, 'another battle.'

'Truly,' Katherine said. The word came from her, yet it also seemed to sound across years without number. Across centuries, across millennia. Across every tale she'd heard, across Wars of Faith, across a galaxy entire. In the buzz of her concussion, it echoed from convents ancient, from Sisters lost and slain, from memories like soldiers, ranks upon ranks, stretching back into history.

From the figure at their forefront that was Talan, blessed at last.

They do not die in vain.

Their billion voices spoke, flowing through her like a conduit.

'We are His faithful,' she said. 'Wherever the enemy lingers, there we shall be. Wherever xenos rise, we shall put them down. Wherever witch or psyker threatens the Imperium, we shall tear out their corruption by the roots.' She paused, her eyes closed, swaying. In her mind, the image wavered and then refocused: *a flagstone floor, six Sisters kneeling.*

The convent at San Loer.

And it was not overwhelming this time. It felt almost like home.

In the image, one of the figures turned, touched her with a smile.

'And would we,' Saint Katherine said, 'praise Him any other way?'

ABOUT THE AUTHOR

Andy Clark has written the Warhammer 40,000 novels *Steel Tread, Fist of the Imperium, Kingsblade, Knightsblade* and *Shroud of Night,* as well as the Dawn of Fire novel *The Gate of Bones* and the novella *Crusade.* He has also written the novels *Gloomspite, Bad Loon Rising* and *Blacktalon: First Mark* for Warhammer Age of Sigmar, and the Warhammer Quest Silver Tower novella *Labyrinth of the Lost.* He lives in Nottingham, UK.

David Annandale is the author of the Warhammer Age of Sigmar novels *Callis & Toll* and *A Dynasty of Monsters,* and the Neferata titles *Mortarch of Blood* and *The Dominion of Bones*. His work for Warhammer 40,000 includes *Ephrael Stern: The Heretic Saint, Warlord: Fury of the God-Machine,* the Yarrick series, and several stories involving the Grey Knights. His Horus Heresy titles include the novels *Ruinstorm* and *The Damnation of Pythos,* and the Primarchs novels *Roboute Guilliman: Lord of Ultramar, Vulkan: Lord of Drakes* and *Mortarion: The Pale King*. For Warhammer Horror, he has written the novels *The House of Night and Chain* and *The Deacon of Wounds*, as well as the novella *The Faith and the Flesh*. David lectures at a Canadian university, on subjects ranging from English literature to horror films and video games.

Danie Ware is the author of the novels *The Triumph of Saint Katherine* and *The Rose in Darkness*, the novellas *The Bloodied Rose*, *Wreck and Ruin* and *The Rose in Anger*, and several short stories all featuring the Sisters of Battle. She lives in Carshalton, South London, with her son and cat, and has long-held interests in role-playing, re-enactment, vinyl art toys and personal fitness.

An extract from
Pilgrims of Fire
by Justin D Hill

War was already raging on the Obscurus Front the year the pilgrim fleet set off from Ophelia VII. They were to retrace the route of Saint Katherine's first War of Faith, their ramshackle ships chained together in a Gordian knot of piety and hope.

The fate of one would be the fate of all, the pilgrim-chiefs declared, the believers suffering together the travails and privations of their holy expedition.

They were plagued by all the dangers of the galaxy. Millions were lost to sickness and starvation. Attacks by xenos, renegades and pirates took countless others, while those of brittle faith fell by the wayside to lives of penance and prayer.

Empty warp ships were cut free and abandoned to the void. But after a decade, a billion souls yet remained, joined firmly by a tightening bond of belief. Their last ordeal was the desperate crossing, through the Fey Straits to Holy Cion.

This journey had twice repelled Saint Katherine. They all understood the danger, and gave themselves over to days of prayers and sacrifice and self-flagellation. There was an air of mourning as the fleet moved towards the Mandeville point.

The augurs were not good, and the warp was in a state of ecstatic tumult. When, at last, the pilgrim fleet broke into realspace, the tethered craft hung together, too weary and broken and stunned to do anything but offer prayers of gratitude to the God-Emperor, after years of travails, for their safe arrival.

The paean of thanks was heard by the astropaths on the shrine world of Holy Cion. Their tower was set in the upper reaches of the Abbey of Eternal Watch, which sat atop the vast stone outcrop known as the Bolt. A great cylinder of black granite which loomed over the surrounding Pilgrim Plains, the Bolt looked as though it had been fired into the planet's crust from some titanic orbital cannon.

Upon its peak, the Sisters of Our Martyred Lady maintained their guard. A cherub brought the news to the high chamber of Canoness Ysolt, where the venerable warrior was at prayer.

The messenger entered the chamber on fluttering white wings, anti-grav generators humming, the iron skull-face speaking in deep, resonant tones.

'Canoness. Tidings have come. The pilgrim fleet has arrived.'

Cion's output of prayer and faith and devotion was as integral to the Imperium of Mankind as the production of any forge world. But the canoness' mind was concerned with disturbing portents. Shadows seen at night, mad laughter coming from empty rooms, reports of ghosts of sobbing women. And now the population of Cion were approaching a state of starvation. A pilgrim fleet was the last thing they needed, a doubting voice said. But, she reminded herself, faith was like a blade. It was there to be used. The Emperor would provide.

Ysolt steepled her fingers. Her voice was strained. She said a brief prayer of thanks and addressed her cherub. 'Sound the Bell of Ancestral Transgressions,' she said. 'I will take the augurs. The Feast of Landing must take place. We must welcome the faithful upon our holy soil.'

There were five hundred Battle Sisters within the Abbey of Eternal Watch. They exerted a gravity upon the population of Cion like celestial bodies. In better times the festival had been a moment of due solemnity. But the better times were now a distant memory for the serving women who worked in the bowels of the abbey.

The years of gathering privations had ground the working young girls down to a state of hunger and exhaustion, and none were hungrier that evening than Branwen, a maid-of-all-work, scrubbing the abbey stairs. She had scoured all the way from the lower gallery to the Sisters' refectory, and now her knees were sore, her shoulders ached and her stomach was as empty as an ogryn's brain.

'Hurry, girl!' one of the serving women said, as she carried a bundle of dirty sheets down towards the laundry. 'They're serving repast downstairs.'

Branwen nodded, but she saw with horror that the woman had left dirty footprints across the wet floor, and she said a prayer of contrition as she wiped them clean again. The trail led her right across the vaulted space. She paused at the refectory door and looked up. The gothic arch soared into darkness, statues of Sisters towering over her. The heavy oak doors were closed.

'You, girl!' a voice said.

Branwen jumped.

'Come away from there! What are you doing? Are you listening in?'

'No, ma'am!' Branwen said, but she looked as guilty as the hanged.

Tula, the Mistress of Chores, caught her by the ear and slapped her across the scalp. 'Shame on you! Soiling the sanctity of this place with your presence. You're just a bastard foundling. Away from that door!'

Tula tutted to herself as she dragged Branwen away. 'What do they say about cleanliness?'

'It brings us closer to the God-Emperor,' Branwen said.

'Indeed,' Tula said. 'And it seems this corridor is a long way from Him, who sits in majesty upon His Golden Throne.'

Branwen had tears in her eyes as she sponged her way along the flagstone corridor, dunking her brush into the bucket of caustic soap and slapping it down onto the dirty steps.

It was true, of course. She was a foundling. Everyone knew the story. An unwanted babe, spat out of the city and left at the abbey gates with just a swaddling blanket wrapped about her and a few hours of life within her hungry frame.

She would have died but for the charity of maid-of-all-work Kolpitts, who had taken her in and raised her as her own. And Branwen had tried so many times to be worthy of the life of servitude and prayer. But it was so very hard… Especially when she was *so* hungry.

'Careful!' a voice said.

Branwen had not heard the Sister approach. And now she had splashed the Sister's armoured boot with filthy water. She did not dare look up. 'Forgive me, holy Sister!'

The Sister knelt beside her and put her hand out. Branwen flinched as the Sister's hand touched her chin and lifted her face. Through her tears the maid-of-all-work found herself looking directly into the Sister's eyes. Her suit of armour was black as night, with a curling tracery of interwoven stems, acid-etched into the ceramite. Her face was fine as marble, her gaze resolute. Branwen was mortified. It was not just any Sister, but Lizbet of the Sacred Sword, the most sublime of the Battle Sisters in the abbey. Stories filtered down to the scullery maids of her skill with bolt and blade. Of terrible foes cut down in their pride. Heretics purged. Vengeance made real.

'Forgive me!' Branwen whispered and tried to pull away, but

Lizbet held the maid's hands. They were scabbed and raw. Lizbet pressed them between her own and spoke a prayer of spiritual fortitude. At the end she said, 'For your enemies are brought down and broken, and we are risen and victorious.'

Branwen stared like one smitten. Sister Lizbet rose with the gentle whine of servos, her black power armour gleaming with reflected candlelight.

The refectory door opened and Sister Lizbet passed inside. For a brief moment the sound of prayer spilt out. Branwen could not understand a word, but the sound transfixed her. So pure, so transcendent was the song of angels that a wave of raw emotion swelled within her, filled her heart with fierce joy. She could still feel the touch of Lizbet's hands and as she looked at her own, she saw that the raw scabs were gone.

Tears of joy rose through her as she finished her scrubbing and hurried down to the abbey cellars, bucket in one hand, rag in the other. The edificium was a place of wide walkways, heavy with prayer, but the stairs wound down to the servant quarters. They were dark and narrow, the undressed stone marked with simple icons of faith.

Branwen rushed into the slop hall, tipped the dirty water away, hung her bucket onto its hook, dried her hands upon her skirts and hurried through the wide chambers to the scullery.

It was the only warm room, where the maids sat before the fire in the moments when they could draw breath. There was a long trestle table, with plain wooden benches along either side, and a cast iron candelabra hanging from the stone ceiling, the candle flames guttering in the draughty chamber.

Branwen saw the table was empty, the stacked wooden plates picked clean. The day's single meal had been eaten.

Branwen would not cry, she told herself, not when others were out there on the Obscurus Front, dying in their millions. The

God-Emperor suffered for all time upon the Golden Throne, and what was her hunger compared to that?

She lifted her face to the candle flames to stop the tears from falling, and one of the cooks breezed in with a damp cloth and wiped the trestle boards clean.

'What's wrong, girl?' the cook called out. 'Don't you have work to do?'

'Yes,' Branwen said, 'but I have not eaten since yesterday, and I came down and–'

'Then don't be late next time!' the cook snapped.

'But–' Branwen started.

'Throne above! The pilgrim fleet has arrived, girl. We don't have time for your fussing.'

YOUR NEXT READ

DARK IMPERIUM
by Guy Haley

The first phase of the Indomitus Crusade is over, and the conquering primarch, Roboute Guilliman, sets his sights on home. The hordes of his traitorous brother, Mortarion, march on Ultramar, and only Guilliman can hope to thwart their schemes with his Primaris Space Marine armies.

YOUR NEXT READ

MINKA LESK: THE LAST WHITESHIELD
by Justin D Hill

Cadia has stood in grim defiance against the enemies of the Imperium for ten thousand years, an indomitable bulwark against the forces of Chaos… but now, the 13th Black Crusade has come, and there will be no victory. Here, Minka Lesk will be tested in the very fires of a world's destruction.
